THE ACADEMY OF AMERICAN POETS

ABOUT THE ACADEMY

The Academy of American Poets was founded in 1934 to support American poets at all stages of their careers and to foster the appreciation of contemporary poetry. The largest organization in the country dedicated to the art of poetry, the Academy sponsors national literary outreach programs, including:

WWW.POETS.ORG

One of the most comprehensive and liveliest literary sites on the Internet, www.poets.org offers resources for poets, teachers, librarians, and booksellers; listings of awards and events; discussion forums; and exhibits featuring poems, biographies, photographs, bibliographies, and audio clips. Visit this award-winning website today!

AUDIO ARCHIVES

The Academy offers more than 40 audiotapes from its archive of readings by poets, including W. H. Auden, John Berryman, Gwendolyn Brooks, Lucille Clifton, Allen Ginsberg, Louise Glück, Galway Kinnell, Yusef Komunyakaa, Robert Lowell, Sharon Olds, Philip Levine, Adrienne Rich, Charles Simic, & Derek Walcott. "They're the best thing since your mother told you a bedtime story," says *House & Garden*. Tapes cost $10. For a catalog, call (212) 274-0343, ext. 21.

POETRY BOOK CLUB

Join the country's first book club devoted exclusively to poetry! Books of poetry at discounts of 20% delivered to your doorstep. For more information, please write to the Poetry Book Club at the address below or visit www.poetrybookclub.org

MEMBERSHIP

To find out about Membership in the Academy, contact us at:

The Academy of American Poets
584 Broadway, Suite 1208
New York, NY 10012-3250

Or call us at (212) 274-0343
academy@poets.org
www.poets.org

COMING UP IN THE SPRING

Conjunctions:36
DARK LAUGHTER
Edited by Bradford Morrow

For spring 2001, we will publish *Conjunctions:36, Dark Laughter,* featuring a special portfolio edited by Bradford Morrow and Jonathan Safran Foer which will explore laughter that comes from the darkest part of our hearts. This portfolio will include narratives of black comedy, gothic satire and violent burlesque by writers as diverse as Howard Norman, Rick Moody, Tova Reich, Joyce Carol Oates, Lynne Tillman, Gilbert Sorrentino, Robert Coover, Can Xue, Paul West, Ben Marcus, John Barth and others. These new and commissioned stories promise to offer a telling look into the nature of comedy and brutality, and what we discover about ourselves when we laugh.

Conjunctions:36 will also include fiction, poetry and plays by Peter Handke, Paul Maliszewski, Erica Hunt, Mark McMorris and the work of many other dynamic and inventive writers.

For updates on contributors and previews of work, visit our website at www.conjunctions.com.

Yearly subscriptions to *Conjunctions* are only $18 for two issues. Please send your check to *Conjunctions*, Bard College, Annandale-on-Hudson, NY 12504. Subscriptions can also be made over the Internet at www.conjunctions.com or by telephoning us at (845) 758-1539.

CONJUNCTIONS

Bi-Annual Volumes of New Writing

Edited by
Bradford Morrow

Contributing Editors
Walter Abish
Chinua Achebe
John Ashbery
Mei-mei Berssenbrugge
Mary Caponegro
Robert Creeley
Elizabeth Frank
William H. Gass
Jorie Graham
Robert Kelly
Ann Lauterbach
Norman Manea
Patrick McGrath
Rick Moody
Joanna Scott
Mona Simpson
Quincy Troupe
William Weaver
John Edgar Wideman

published by Bard College

EDITOR: Bradford Morrow
MANAGING EDITOR: Michael Bergstein
SENIOR EDITORS: Robert Antoni, Martine Bellen, Peter Constantine, Elaine Equi, Brian Evenson
ASSOCIATE EDITORS: Jedediah Berry, Jonathan Safran Foer, Catherine Kasper
ART EDITORS: Norton Batkin, Michael Eastman
PUBLICITY: Mark R. Primoff
WEBMASTERS: Brian Evenson, Michael Neff
EDITORIAL ASSISTANTS: Devin Irby, Rabia Sandage, Alan Tinkler

CONJUNCTIONS is published in the Spring and Fall of each year by Bard College, Annandale-on-Hudson, NY 12504. This issue is made possible in part with the generous funding of the National Endowment for the Arts, and with public funds from the New York State Council on the Arts, a State Agency.

SUBSCRIPTIONS: Send subscription orders to CONJUNCTIONS, Bard College, Annandale-on-Hudson, NY 12504. Single year (two volumes): $18.00 for individuals; $25.00 for institutions and overseas. Two years (four volumes): $32.00 for individuals; $45.00 for institutions and overseas. Patron subscription (lifetime): $500.00. Overseas subscribers please make payment by International Money Order. For information about subscriptions, back issues and advertising, call Michael Bergstein at 845-758-1539 or fax 845-758-2660.

All editorial communications should be sent to Bradford Morrow, *Conjunctions*, 21 East 10th Street, New York, NY 10003. Unsolicited manuscripts cannot be returned unless accompanied by a stamped, self-addressed envelope.

Conjunctions is listed and indexed in the American Humanities Index.

Visit the *Conjunctions* website at www.conjunctions.com.

Cover design by Jerry Kelly, New York. Photo collage: Michael Eastman.

Printers: Edwards Brothers.
Typesetter: Bill White, Typeworks.

ISSN 0278-2324
ISBN 0-941964-51-5

Manufactured in the United States of America.

TABLE OF CONTENTS

AMERICAN POETRY
States of the Art

Vraiment,
Poetry can be so many more things
Than what people mostly believe it is.
—*Anselm Hollo*

Four Poems
John Ashbery

A NICE PRESENTATION

I have a friendly disposition but am forgetful, though I tend to
forget only important things. Several mornings ago I was lying in
my bed listening to a sound of leisurely hammering coming from
a nearby building. For some reason it made me think of spring
which it is. Listening I heard also a man and woman talking
together. I couldn't hear very well but it seemed they were
discussing the work that was being done. This made me smile,
they sounded like good and dear people and I was slipping back
into dreams when the phone rang. No one was there.

Some of these are perhaps people having to do with anything in the
world. I wish to go away, on a dark night, to leave people and the
rain behind but am too caught up in my own selfish thoughts and
desires for this. For it to happen I would have to be asleep and
already started on my voyage of self-discovery around the world.
One is certain then to meet many people and to hear many strange
things being said. I like this in a way but wish it would stop as the
unexpectedness of it conflicts with my desire to revolve in a
constant, deliberate motion. To drink tea from a samovar. To use
chopsticks in the land of the Asiatics. To be stung by the sun's bees
and have it not matter.

Most things don't matter but an old woman of my acquaintance is
always predicting doom and gloom and her prophecies matter
though they may never be fulfilled. That's one reason I don't worry
too much but I like to tell her she is right but also wrong because
what she says won't happen. Yet how can I or anyone know this?
For the seasons do come round in leisurely fashion and one takes a
pinch of something from each, according to one's desires and what
it leaves behind. Not long ago I was in a quandary about this but
now it's too late. The evening comes on and the aspens leaven its
stars. It's all about this observatory a shout fills.

John Ashbery

AS UMBRELLAS FOLLOW RAIN

Too bad he never tried it—
he might have liked it.

She saw us make eye contact.
And that was that for that day.

Too bad he too, when I
am

meaning if I came along it'd
already be too late.

Some of the swans are swarming.
The spring has gone under—it wasn't
supposed to be like this.

Now they watch him and cringe.
Who are they? Who is he?

We decided to fly Chinese.
The food wasn't that good.

And oh Erwin did I tell you
that man—the one—I didn't

know if I was supposed to or not.
He crawled back listlessly,

holding a bunch of divas.
It's hard work getting these out,

but so's any thing you're entitled to do:
Classes to attend.

The morning of school.
Evening almost over,

they bend the security rules.
It's time for another fog bomb.

John Ashbery

Lookit the way they all roost.
Poor souls clashed together

until almost the root's roof
separates us from our beginning.

We slew many giants in our day,
burned many libraries.

Roundabouts, swings,
it was all one piece of luck to us.

Now we're washed up it's almost cold
not bad enough to put up a stand.

Out of that longing we built a paean.
Now everyone who crosses this bridge is wiser.

It doesn't tilt much.
Look, the shore is arriving laterally.

Some people literally think they know a lot,
gets 'em in trouble, we must rake out

cafés looking for rats and exploded babies.
There was one too many last week.

I don't know if you're coding.
The cop pulled us over

in a shawl. Why do you want to go around me
when there are other circulars

to be had for the looking?
I never thought about being grounded forever.

This is Mademoiselle. Take your hat off.
There's no need, I was here last Thursday.

All the best creatures are thwarted
for their pains. He removed my chains deftly,

John Ashbery

processed my passport with gunk.
Now two times five geese fly across

the crescent moon, it is time to get down to
facts, in the tiny park.

There were priests posing as nuns,
quinces and stuff.

Tilt me a little more to the sun,
I want to see it one last time. There,

that's just fine. I've seen it.
You can roll me inside. On the wings of what perturbation?

He came for the julep.
He was gone in an instant.

We cry too much over
drowned dogs.

He came in last week too.
Said he knew you or somebody else.

It's the pain just of replying
that makes so many of them take up different lines.

Too many goods—we are spoiled indeed.
Had we learned to subsist on less

the changing of the world might be different,
earth come to greet us. I say, the chairs have grown back.

The couple sat in the dish drainer
pondering an uncertain future.

The kitchen had never looked bleaker
except for two chinchillas near the stove, a beaker

of mulled claret, shaving soap smelling
so fresh and new, like smoke, almost.

John Ashbery

He says leave it here,
that he comes here.

OK harness the DeSoto,
we'll have other plans

for newness, for a renewing, kind of—
picnics in the individual cells

so no one falls asleep for it, dreams
she is a viola, instrument of care, of sorts.

You should have seen him when we got back.
He was absolutely wild. Hadn't wanted us to go

to the picture show. But in a way it was all over,
we were back, the harm had been done.

Gradually he came to realize this
over a period of many years, spanning

two world wars and a major depression.
After that it was time to get up and go,

but who had the get up and go? A child's
party, painted paper hats, bowlfuls of lemonade,

no more at the lemonade stand, it sold out.
That was cheerful. A man came right up behind you,

he had two tickets to the door.
We need starve no more

but religion is elastic too—
might want some at some future date—

if so you'll find it here.
We have to hurry in now,

hurry away, it's the same thing
she said as rain came and stole the king.

John Ashbery

MEET ME TONIGHT IN DREAMLAND

It was an hour ago. I walked upstairs to dreamland. Took a cab and got out and somebody else backed in. Now we weren't actually on the Dreamland floor. That would be for later. Look, these are the proper plans, plants. They used to have a Chautauqua here, far out into the lake. Now it's peeled. No one actually comes here. Yet there are people. You just hardly ever see them. No I wasn't being modest. Some get out on the floor, several a year, whose purple glass sheds an eldritch glow on the trottoirs, as Whitman called them. Or spittoons. Look, we are almost a half a mile later, it must link up. The Tennessee drifter smiled sharkly. Then it was on to native board games.

Je bois trop.

In one of these, called "Skunk," you are a weasel chasing a leveret back to its hole when Bop! the mother weasel, about ten stories tall, traps you with her apron string, patterned with poppies and rotted docks. You see, you thought every noun had to have an adjective, even "sperm," and that's where you made your first big mistake. Later it's raining and we have to take a car. But the game isn't over—there are sixteen thousand marble steps coming up, down which you glide as effortlessly as you please, as though on a bicycle, weasel in tow. It's an exercise bike. What a time to tell me, the solar wind has sandpapered everything as smooth as quartz. Now it's back to the finish line with you.

You're not quite out of the woods yet. Dreamland has other pastures, other melodies to chew on. Hummingbirds mate with dragonflies beneath the broken dome of the air, and it's three o'clock, the sun is raining mineral-colored candy. I'd like one of these. It's yours. Now I'm glad we came. I hate drafts though and the sun is slowly moving away. I'm standing on the poopdeck wiggling colored pennants at the coal-colored iceberg that seems to be curious about us, is sliding this way and that, then turns abruptly back into the moors with their correct hills in the distance. If it was me I'd take a trip like this every day of my life.

John Ashbery

IN THE TIME OF PUSSY WILLOWS

This is going to take some time.
Nope, it's almost over. For today anyway.
We'll have a beautiful story, old story
to fish for as his gasps come undone.

I never dreamed the pond of chagrin
would affect me this much. Look, I'm shaking.
No, it's you who are doing the shaking.
Well, it all comes round to us
sooner or later. Shrinking with the devil
in the stagey sunrise he devised.
And then there will be no letters for what is truth,
to make up the words of it. It will be standing still
for all it's worth. Then a hireling shepherd came along,
whistling, his eyes on the trees. He was a servant of two masters,
which is some excuse, though not really all that much of a one.
Anyway, he overstayed his welcome. But the last train had already left.

How does one conduct one's life amid such circumstances,
dear snake, who want the best for us
as long as you are not hurt by it.
My goodness, I thought I'd seen a whole lot of generations,
but they are endless, one keeps following another,
treading on its train, hissing.

What a beautiful old story it could be after all
if those in the back rows would stop giggling for a minute.
By day, we have paddled and arbitraged
to get to this spot. By night, it hardly matters.
Funny we didn't anticipate this,
but the dumbest clues get overlooked by the smartest gumshoe
and we are back in some fetishist's vinyl paradise
with no clue as to how we got here
except the tiny diamond on your pillow—it must have been a tear
hatched from a dream, when you actually knew what you were doing.
Now, it's all fear. Fear and wrongdoing.
The outboard motor sputters and quits, and a tremendous silence
beats down from every point in the sky. To have digested this
when we were younger, and felt a set of balls coming on . . .

14

It may be that thunder and lightning are two-dimensional,
that there was never really any place for fear,
that others get trapped, same as us, and make up
amusing stories to cover their tracks. Wait,
there's one in the donjon wants to speak his piece. Rats,
now he's gone too.

Yes, he near slipped and died in front of you,
and you intend to twist this into an ethos?
Go make up other stories.
Window reflected in the bubble,
how often I've tried to pray to you,
but your sphere would have nothing of it.
I felt almost jinxed. Then a spider led the way
back into the room.

And we knew why we'd never left. Outside was brushfires.
Here was the peace of Philemon and Baucis,
offering chunks of bread and salami to the tattered stranger,
and a beaker of wine darker than the deepest twilight,
a table spread with singularities
for the desperate and tragic among us.

Angel, come back please. Let us smell your heavenly smell again.

Two Poems

Lyn Hejinian

THE DISTANCE

Banned from ships as if I were fate herself, I nonetheless long hankered after adventures
    At sea
    But buckets, lifeboats, gulls, and fishguts on wharves were as near as I got
    Or the beach. The ban was inoperative on the sands, I boarded
    Wrecks. The terns, godwits and gulls were ashore as at sea, and I learned the fine points
    By which one can distinguish between the sandpipers
    Just as I learned that there are many fine points to fate
    Which divulges what comes to pass indefinitely
    So that we can hardly say of things that happen that they were meant to be
    Or that they were not. Like a pupil
    I was ruled by obedience
    To rules I broke. I floundered around
    And enjoyed my choices—I was eager
    To receive—
    But not without perplexity, I was endowed with doubt
    And that is one of the few things I can say of myself then that I can say of myself
    Now, for the most part there has been little confluence. I've been swept
    Against objects, lost habits,
    Knowledge grows
    But it has to be connected to things.
    And that connection is usually best achieved
    So they say
    Through perceiving similarities. No way!
    Winds blow in a giant circle and set up resistance to anyone going the other way.

Still it came about that the ban was lifted
Suddenly one fall
And I went to sea after all
And shaped a course away from the trees that framed the seascape
Beyond my mother's house, incandescent birches and fiery maples
as well as forbidding clouds of hemlock and pine,
A forest that was like a terrestrial sky
But is much less so now in memory. I don't remember why
It was said that a woman's presence on a ship at sea would bring
disaster down on everyone aboard, the gods of mythology seem to have
liked us well enough
Or maybe they liked us too well, chasing us in animal form
With violent winds.
But mythology gave
Way to history
And now history is going
The way of bedtime stories. A path, bricks, innocents—they are
additions, but odd
Additions to oddity.
Gullibility is an expression of enthusiasm
So great it makes decisions. But I am throwing off faith, bound to
regard the sea
As a prison holding people whom their childhood friends cannot
believe capable of crime.
It is midsummer and the sun is lost in the sun, visibility is
accomplished. Can credibility
Be far behind?
But I won't pretend
To be an historian, how could I, when I have no idea of today's date
And though I know we embarked one morning early in May
I have no idea how long ago that was
And I don't care. I breathe, I twist my hair.
I watch the sea. At times it resembles an eye but it isn't watching
me.
Some days ago a "native kayak" appeared and then disappeared,
winding through a lead in the ice.
The first mate kept close watch for several hours after the kayak,
following a shimmering band of water west, disappeared
Or, as the first mate put it, "withdrew"—the mate insisting that
the occupant might be a pirate
Or some other type with hostile intent

17

Lyn Hejinian

Emboldened by the ice
Approaching
In broad daylight. A strange expression. Soon there will be no more
than a band of pink against the darkness,
Narrow daylight
As at the beginning or end
Of a day in the habitable latitudes,
Where breadth is what is assumed of days
As it is of the sea even when mist closes in around the ship. She is
called the *Distance.*
We go where she goes
And arrive willy-nilly at times and places of whose existence we'd
known nothing before
And which therefore, though we come upon them inevitably (there
being always *somewhere* and always in or at it *something*—whether
material or musical—that establishes its "somewhereness"), we reach
involuntarily,
It's to these that we hope to go and from these that we hope to
return.
But beset by such hopefulness (cold,
Ominous, and calm) we're getting nowhere
And tempers are short.
I've grown hard of hearing, the first mate said this morning in a
tone dripping with sarcasm.
Did you ask for a hard-boiled egg?
Jean-Pierre is no longer included in the games the other children
are playing, soon he'll be an adolescent, already he's hovering over the
figurehead,
A woman holding a telescope to her left eye.
For the most part it is trained on the horizon.
She is establishing herself.

According to the Greeks metamorphoses have to be complete
And are impossible. Things may change
But nothing can become the opposite
Of what it is. The sea cannot
Be not the sea. Yet
I can see it
Both ways.
Then yet again I hardly remember who it was I was instead of this
back when I longed to go to sea and couldn't.

18

I gazed up through branches tossing in the wind at the blue planes
of the sky and felt rooted, even at an early age,
Perhaps to gods but if so my deities were streaming
Or grinding like a boat being hauled out of the waves over stony
ground. The sound
Gives me pleasure still though it is fugitive. Pleasures are
synonymous with power (and with powers
Though these are very different things),
And lest they become dangerous they *must* be fugitive.
How strangely our course approaches forks, how variously we
decide which tack to take. We ourselves are fugitives,
The world is strange. It appears to last and appears so as to last,
In the dark of night or of storms, into which it disappears to last as
well. We have come in the dark
Upon landforms, shores, islands without knowing what to expect.
On some
One may enter into friendship, on others into endless complaint.
But there must be more to friendship than a placid acceptance of
misunderstandings.
And interruptions, though these have the effect of inevitabilities
We encounter constantly.
Someone remarks "there's something over there" or, more
urgently, "there's something ahead!"
The boat tacks—I say that though the engines are running.
We have no destination. One can't foretell
What may or may not be pointless.
The boat arches, bends, turns—it is shaping itself. Sometimes I
climb into a lifeboat to think
And there I dream confusedly that we've "varied" and come to an
island
Which can be approached only through one of forty doors,
At each one of which sits a perched bird that can disclose the
mysteries of logic to me in an ancient language which I will
understand.
The gist of what occurs according to the birds is unlikeliness.
We are all so busy it seems sometimes that the only time we can
appreciate being
Is when we are at sea
Subject to capriciousness
Though we sleep slung in binding hammocks
Like spiders or netted fish

Or like trapeze artists bouncing to ground level at the end of their
act. Tonight the sea
Has twisted in turbulence. Observing the effects I've grown
vertiginously
Calm. How odd it is to be out.
At best one can know only the knowledge of this time. When one
reaches the limit of that
One must make way for those who know in and for the time next
To this.
In and for I say hospitably.
Between ourselves we speak the language of these parts.
The communications are never concise.
Whatever we say is best understood if contextualized, so contexts
are what we say, and they too are best understood if contextualized
And so it goes, sometimes inward and sometimes outward bound
Not round and round but as if over the bridge
From top to toe
Or pegbox to tailpiece
Of a vast violin—strung—
What we speak is strung
And we cling to it as to a shroud.
The wind sweeps across the sea but cannot enter it. Both are
variable. It is always safe to predict
Variability. Great cumulous clouds hang overhead one moment
And terns another. The sun on my face is cold
And yet I often feel heat. Perhaps we are all small suns.
The sunflower in its pot on deck doesn't think so. It turns
Frantically
But not to us
As the *Distance* rides the sea and sends the sun sliding violently
into all the compass corners.
Am I compassionate? Or is it merely out of enthusiasm
That I give a thumbs up
As the *Distance* slows so as to pass gently through a flock of
floating seabirds?
Their kind must be persistent
And have been here long before the first human flutterings
Whose own persistence brought us here
To no end
Unless what and when we turn can be termed an end.
If one undertakes when outward bound to sail to the ends of the

earth, one must hope also ultimately to come inward bound
From them again.
How hospitable circumstances can be!
The earth seems young—raucous, ravenous, quick. The earth exists
With gusto. Things fall to it and stick, things are rooted in it
And rise. This cannot be said of the sea. It's impossible to clear the way and come within sight of my subject.
Obscure emotions cling to it—obscuring emotions, I mean. The analytical imagination
Naturally undertakes analysis of the imagination
While the emotional imagination does what, emote? I've tried to give emotions
The slip
By attributing them to other people—
An iffy strategy at best. Not everyone's motives are my own.
Emotions stem from belief,
And motives are meant to establish what's believed.
William is afraid of ghosts
Which he says live in and on the ice
More and more of which we've been seeing
Day and night passing us as we pass
If indeed we *are* passing. At times it seems as if we are simply riding a gentle swell
Washing the edges of the habitable world. A glance into the distance
Raises these doubts and I take them as signs of aesthetic wellness.

One thing I've discovered is that nothing that's experienced is allegorical—
There is no moral. Nothing is contained. Sure one can say that the woman who sets sail
Will cross reefs
Or that science is the practice of unknowing
Or that given enough time every circumstance will betray what it promised
To guarantee
But these are, as I see it, unbound, uninhibited, nonsuccinct
Observations—things that take time and space to develop
Into whatever truth or truths they offer. All in all
There is very little containment in the universe

Except what's temporarily contained in the bodies of things as
presence or in animate bodies as life.
The sea though not silent subjects one to silence—that's the only
name I know for the distance
Though it has noisy spans.
They *cascade* and *splash.* I know these words
But my thoughts of things go on without them.

NIGHTS

Ooooh, oooooh, ooooh, says the voice of a girl:

"I've been attacked by owls,
by owls with towels,
I've been attacked
by snakes with rakes.

It is just this kind of ridiculous language, banal but lacking even
banality's pretense at relevance and sense, that I hear in my sleep; I
wake, feeling irritable and depressed.

*

The sadness! the injustice!
It's true I want to know, I want to look
But what is it?

*

The fingers leave their owls in a calm
Sleep figures the features

Sleep speaks for the bird, the animal
For the round and the residual

Sleep soaks from experience
But why and what?

*

Suddenly I remember having rescued a spider from the bathtub in the morning. I imagined that I had established rapport with my environment. I observed the spider eerily. I was in harmony with life and my times. Not only will things go on but this going on will repeat.

After all, I can vow kindness in relation to something I cannot know.

The spider, when it appears within "a range of alternatives," will be rescued—dished out of the nicked and polished porcelain tub and knocked onto the shrubbery just outside the open window.

Of course, it will not be the same spider each time but a sequence of spiders.

*

The 23rd night was very dark.
It was cold.
My eyes were drawn to the window.

I thought I saw a turtledove nesting on a waffle
Then I saw it was a rat doing something awful
But anarchy doesn't bother me now any more than it used to

I thought I saw a woman writing verses on a bottle
Then I saw it was a foot stepping on the throttle
But naturally freedom can be understood in many different ways

I thought I saw a fireman hosing down some straw
Then I saw it was a horse grazing in a draw
But it's always the case that in their struggle to survive, animate
    objects must be aided

I thought I saw a rhubarb pie sitting on the stove
Then I saw it was the tide receding from a cove
But although I have strong emotions when I watch a movie, jealousy
    is never one of them.

I thought I saw a bicyclist racing down the road
Then I saw it was a note, a message still in code
But sense is always either being raised to or lowered from the sky

*

Lyn Hejinian

A voice says, The ambered bed flag fills.
A voice says, This is voltage island.
A voice says, The wall past which girls wander flicks is built of baffled
   face bricks.

*

I saw a juxtaposition
It happened to be between an acrobat and a sense of obligation
Pure poetry
Of course there is a great difference between withering and a napping
   man
And flailing in relation to fossils in a stone is different from a set of
   dominoes
Still I don't worry less about the same old worries

*

I'm of a mule age, I dare like a log.
I live where I live, and I'll bulk graciously

            —to zero.

*

But the worst of speaking in the dark is that the sounds we emit are
   strange and hollow.

*

The moon was solemnly full.
Jim Trotmeyer assertively declared, Emotions can't be governed by rules.
Millie Corcoran politely requested, Don't overwhelm me.
To this Jim Trotmeyer delightfully responded, But the azures of spring
   truly rush.
Millie Corcoran remarked astutely, Azures rush, yes, but composedly.
Jim Trotmeyer mused pensively, The clouds do indeed puzzle.
Millie Corcoran said sociably, They appear above the crowd.
Oswald Proskaniewicz interrupted furiously, You, Jim Trotmeyer, are
   not the radical you say you are.

*

As for me, I want to be Banambitan
and leave kind ships vitalities by art.
I am untouchable.

24

Siege Document
Myung Mi Kim

a graduated effort

r   s

bandage pulled back is blood gone mud

p   eu   hand hewn

freedom from commerce was a cry

filterdoubt   .   locution   .   string and pelter   .

attached to pillars and saltbeds
wracked as imperfect lot

*

Sleep took the eye muscle and severed it

In the vernacular   ate   stirred   swept

At the periphery   garbage pigs

: sandscroll :

After a long last

I learn my story

My mother had restaurant

she made noodle soup

It was famous soup

She suffer so much

For so much her life

It burn skin to bone

Scar tissue on top of nerve ending

Ugly power of military

I scream too hot too hot

Naked where clothes were a second before

*

signs and symptoms

crossing veins of lettuce and a miner's light

whose bones therefore appear short or thin relative to dental age

anemia recorded as porosity of the eye orbits

some by excess, some by defect

others by affliction

others by time for animals to be gathered together, time when
    water is drawn

(to) provide for days when hunting is poor or many are sick

*

Myung Mi Kim

The rest buried him by striking him with fir trees

When the armament was in

Having consumed the eight sparrows in the nest

The wounded were washed in hot waters

Now the twentieth year since she quitted her native land

Exposure and desertion

: Many of the residents who have died of heat exhaustion were
elderly men and women reluctant to use air
conditioning because they worried about expensive utility bills

Houseless heads and unfed sides

*

skilter head   .   lifts up and tells simple mother stories

everyday to spout

everyday to alight

everyday to bring one end to the other, close

a pick a pack a frightening fund

*

28

that.   wants a biscuit

I am assured that the global buying frenzy
I am assured that there is a global buying frenzy

drain in a prophylactic sense

in plain sight   cusp of flesh and action

that said: the cost

that said: brittle off the bone and perjure

Constant Reverential Face

Please allow that

Place of feet and water

Please allow that

The oil and seeds

What is the call to call out

*

Myung Mi Kim

laughter visited us early and left

moving around a sequence of debts

there would be the occasion of reaching for a foreign object in the eye

Speaker: She got shot.   She did.   I saw her.

limbs of pines   rope around the waist

neither slaves nor freemen, but who have become part of the soil
upon which they work
like so many cows and the trees

the schools had been burned down

the teachers had been starved to death

the road had fallen into decay

the bridges were gone

will be eaten
at a ration of quarters
will be eaten
at a ration of fifths

*

The point at which something is a ruin

Perforating scrawl

55 floods, 25 windstorms, 57 droughts, 37 plagues of locusts

The work required kneeling

: The amounts they speak of are in reality quite small and because
of the missing one hundred dollars
everything they have could be put up for farm auction

Rudimentary sinew connecting library, school and public land

In the eaves   under systems of decimation

*

Myung Mi Kim

                                                        chorus

water supply silted

children sold for token payment, for the promise that they would
    be fed

seasonal hunger

human cash crop

if to bend back at stems

Three Poems
Brenda Coultas

AN AMERICAN MOVIE

Scene 1

It's okay, it's all right, Jesus told me so.
— Uncle Bill, *from* American Movie
(draw out)

This eye opens on Houston and Ave. A, on a mural of Princess Di,
   it reads:
"We fought for 200 years to throw off the yoke of British oppression.
   Die Di."

The eye moves to Avenue A and 14th, mural of Princess Di and
   Mother Theresa, side by side.
Repeat after me:

"In Memory of royalty and holiness"
Audience repeats
"Rest in Peace"
Audience repeats

I met a man the week of back to back funerals whom I later married.
We watched both.

In the church was a basket full of prayers.
I read them.
What were people praying about, and were their prayers any different
   than mine?

I visit the stations of the cross
I have felt the power of prayer before.
This is written as one who's gotten good at prayer.

Brenda Coultas

I put my own in.

"Signed SWALCAKWS (sealed with a lick cuz a kiss won't stick),

Brenda"

I move my lips, do you?
I wonder if I'm doing it right?
I say it in my head. Like this,

Dear God,
Please watch over us and please watch over my brother and my
     sisters and mom and dad
please watch over those in need
in Jesus' name we pray,
Amen.

I say this every night.

Is it too dull to reach the universe?

Dear Universe,
Why do you hear Mayor Guiliani's prayers and not mine?
Yours, Brenda

Dear Universe,
You must be a male
you are not unisex
you are just fashionably androgynous.

Sorry to bug you,   Brenda

I write poems for the public.
I call myself Brenda Coultas
I write public poems.
I write poems for twenty, that's twenty people to a poem.

A man sells poems in the subway,
Published Poet is his name.
It costs whatever you want to give him.

I'm the same, its whatever you want to give me only I don't want
  anything.

SCENE 2

The eye opens on a man who paints portraits of "retired" Beanie
  Babies:
Digger the Crab
Doby the Doberman
Doodle
Dotty the Dalmation
Ears
Echo
Fetch the Retriever
Flash the Dolphin
Fleece the Lamb
Flip the Cat
Floppity
Freckles the Leopard
Garcia the Tie-Dyed Bear
Glory the Bear
Goldie the Goldfish
Gracie the Swan
Grunt the Razorback Pig
Happy the Lavender Hippo
Hippity
Hoot the Owl
Hoppity
Inch the Worm
Inky the Pink Octopus

SCENE 3

Hi, I am a word that exists on the soles of your shoes,
Please stop walking on me.

Hi, I am a royal Fergie mug
I was chubby and engaged.
Now I'm skinny, divorced, chipped and stained.
Hi, I am a Cabbage Patch doll

preserved in the attic in my original wrapper.
I am so ugly I am cute. I look and feel like a fetus with an engorged
    head.

Hi, I am an adorable discontinued Beanie Baby.
I am the rarest Beanie Baby of them all.
Collectors will commit crimes in order to possess me
I fit in the hand like a small living dog.

Hello, I am a Pee Wee Herman doll
I have a soft body and a hard plastic head.
I know what I am but what are you?

A HORSELESS CARRIAGE

> *Since then—'tis Centuries—and yet*
> *Feels shorter than the Day*
> *I first surmised the Horses' Heads*
> *Were toward Eternity—*
>
> —Emily Dickinson, *from #712*

We traded some hay and got a pony.
But we were horseless

We got a good deal on a horse
We were full with the horse

The horse was an asshole
We sold the horse

We bought a car
But we were horseless.

   I remember all the grave mowers. I used to follow Elise and his
mules to the cemetery. They were majestic. Mules are pretty, people
forget that. When he died I bought the old harnesses at auction.
People took horse collars and put mirrors where the heads used to go.
That was a fad. Everyone had harness and leather lying around that
they needed to put some use to. Old oil lamps, railroad lanterns,
these things look good with a plant sticking out of them. I once

buried a treasure in Elise's meadow. I had been reading about pirates. I was obsessed with finding buried treasure, since there was scant chance of finding buried treasure on a landlocked farm. I decided to make a mystery imagining someone finding it and wondering about whoever buried it. I took a cardboard box, put clues in it, a penny minted that year, a picture of me and my brother, a metal picture frame with curlicues that I now realize was Victorian. Once the field grew over, I could never find it again.

Tom, down the road, sold his horse buggies when I was a kid but I remember everyone talking about the auction. The buggies. Black carriages, stiff. Horseless now. Motorless. The end of buggies except for the Amish's yellow, black and white tops.

There was Old man Hinkle who drove his horseless carriage so slowly that I'd pass him on my bike. He was headed down the road to where Herb and Buster held court on the front lawn in shell backed lawn chairs. Mary and Tootsie were in the house, a glass butter churn on the table. I had summer habits that kept me on the road, popping tar bubbles with a stick. (Old asphalt roads had pools of sticky tar, gets on your clothes and ruins them.) Breaking ponies. Fishing (in anyone's pond). Exploring. The world could be as long as a mile or two. It was the way around, follow the road until you were back to where you began.

My grandparents were horseless, by the time I knew them. I have a dim photo of my grandpa driving a carriage. My grandma didn't drive anything as far as I could tell, but she did like to call a bicycle "a wheel." As in "Where are you going on that wheel?" Or "Put that wheel down and get over here." Or "Hey, you on the wheel, come back here." It was a uniquely horseless form of transportation.

Two farmers in abutting pastures died this fall. Neither of them owned horses. Cody B. in his 60's died of skin cancer that mestastasized into brain cancer. Harold, 83 who inherited the job from Elise, and meticulously mowed the cemetery with a tractor, died of stomach cancer this winter one month shy of the end of the century. Last summer, he wanted his usual garden put out. They put out a smaller one, knowing he'd never be able to see it. Now as it snows, I walk toward his grave. I imagine all of us, long horseless, walking.

Brenda Coultas

INSIDE THE WEATHER

[16mm educational film titled *Inside the Weather*
Dumpster dived on 2nd St. and Ave. A. May 9, 00.
Note: This poem takes place in the Bowery]

I don't have a 16mm projector so I'll read it this way *by hand*
Take it apart put it back together again
I take it out and I put it back. Forward and reverse
There's a thin spot where the real world shines through
A thin spot in thinning places from going back and forth.

This is some sort of silent reading
Weather is sometimes quiet and creepy crawls Manson-family-like

It's raining outside, I go back to unreeling: A shot of an airplane.
Passengers buckle up, the captain greets them. Plane taxis, shots of
the plane and its belly. Passengers looking out window enjoying
marvelous weather. A planet appears in center of frame, then a
thousand frames of a curved cylinder maybe an engine. A strip of
sound on the side. Can't hear it through fingers *film breaks.*

The weather is a Bowery bum penis tip urinating on a trash can.
Jars of penis tips like Planter's roasted nuts
I enjoy formerly living things in lab jars.
Mr. Peanut walks down the Bowery, you can smell his roasted nuts

Touched by tip of Bowery bum penis, tried not to look just felt tip
touch lightly on neck.
Touching cocks back and forth on the tips.
I take them out and put them back

Holding film up to a 100 watt bulb, burn eyeballs. Looking at the
plane in the waves of the sky. More earth and now night. Could
they be circling the globe? Could they no longer be earth citizens,
rather citizens of the air.

Unspool reel with pencil in center smell of film chemicals is
nothing like the smell of clouds or the sun or rain or hail. The
smell is vinegary like a hundred dirty socks on the feet of fifty
Bowery bums.

38

Once I was in the sky thinking about the people in the film about weather. Once I was in an airplane, too, smiling and pointing like happy people in a film about the joys of weather.

Press play, a recording of Hoosier rain sounds.

My lips crackle.
Turn on rain cam *www.Raincam.com.* The voice spoke through tiny transistor radio. A blue and silver transistor radio in its original box, the top eaten off by rats. It said loudspeakerlike "People of the Bowery, take shelter now."

A school of blind albino fish swim inside an underground lake in Mammoth Cave. They say "It's all about the weather this season."

This is tedious work, and rereeling is tuff
film twists like a pig's tail.
I think the weather was better when I was a child.

I put the hailstones in the freezer for posterity, take them out when company comes. My grandpa's hailstones made the newspaper, with measuring tape for scale. A catheterized penis was the last thing I saw of him. And I asked "What's in the center, a fuzzy wuzzy bear, bubble gum, a pearl or a rock-hard cock?"

A Pile of Conflicting Emotions About Garbage
[Companion 1 to *Inside the Weather*]

Disgust, amusement, joy, curiosity, desire to uncover, pleasure, looking to garbage for clothing and entertainment not food, not yet. Can't eat from it because I get paranoid that food is tainted or rotted or just gross, can wear the dumpstered clothes after washing with brief moments of paranoia because of their unknown origin. The origins of my phobia is clearly connected to the Tylenol murders, I had to check each food item carefully for taint around that time. And threw much into garbage. Bradley, our squatter hero, knows to comb out the good to eat garbage.

Brenda Coultas

An Inventory of an Elaborate Pile of Garbage at 2nd Ave. and Second St. June 1, 00

[Companion 1 to *Inside the Weather*]

Blacken tea kettle like one I have at home, couch with living man, eyes closed, his dog and runny dog shit on sidewalk. Cardboard boxes, lamp shade, the filter basket of a Drip-O-Later, a wooden serving tray with loose bottom. A mouse's body with eyes open and intact. Styrofoam peanuts, 2 balsa wood whiskey bottle boxes, thin wooden fruit basket. Wooden construction walls with *Post No Bills* painted gray. A piece of paper ordering the closing of the Mars Bar garden. A man setting out 4 candles, and 2 sets of wrapped paper plates. A junkie couple, white, late 30's, covered in scabs and tattoos with dog, had constructed a lean-to over the couch and slept that day. I thought about what brought them to this moment and thought "Be in the moment," thought "Be here now," thought "What's the worst thing that could happen?" Thought "Shit happens." And began to think "Today is the first day of the rest of . . ." Thought, this could be the best day of their lives.

Quipu
Arthur Sze

1.

I try to see a bald eagle nest in a douglas fir
but catch my sleeve on thorns, notice blackberries,

hear large wings splashing water in a lagoon.
I see a heron perched on a post above a tidal flat,

remember red elderberries arcing along a path
where you catch and release a newt among ferns.

And as a doe slips across the road behind us,
we zigzag when we encounter a point of resistance,

zigzag as if we describe the edge of an immense leaf,
as if we plumb a jagged coastline where tides

wash and renew the mind. I stare at abalone eyes,
am startled at how soft a sunflower star is to touch,

how sticky a tentacle of an anemone is to finger.
When we walk barefoot in sand, my mind sways

to the motion of waves. I notice bits of crabs
washed to shore, see—in an instant a dog wrenches

a leash around the hand of a woman, shatters bones—
ensuing loss *salamanders* the body, *lagoons* the mind.

Arthur Sze

2.

Here a red horse leaned over a barbed wire fence
and uprooted a row of corn; here chile plants
rotted after a thunderstorm; here the force of water
exposed carrot seeds and washed almost all away;
but here two kinds of eggplants flower in a row;

here peas, cucumbers, bell peppers, eggplants,
tomatoes, melons, corn. Is this wave of flowering
the arc of loss? She closes her eyes and aches:
in a white room, the ultrasound picks up yolk sac
and curled embryo; inside the space of a pea,

a head, mouth, neural tube, brain stem, eyes;
but it does not pulse or flicker with a heartbeat.
Across the room they reach out, but to what?
The room darkens as the screen ionizes, glows.
He visualizes a series of photographic still lifes:

polished tin doorknob against a black background,
whale vertebra seen from afar against a black background,
nineteen stacked pancakes against a black background,
cluster of hazelnuts up close against a black background;
and suddenly when he opens his eyes, he cannot hear.

3.

Who touched a quipu and made it explode into dust?

What blooms as briefly as scarlet gaura in sandy soil?

How incandescent is a grief?

Did spun wool delineating the corn of the Incas obliterate in a
    second?

What incipient white fades into pink?

Did the knots of her loves _jaguar_ in an instant?

What is the tensile strength of a joy?

42

Who observed a great horned owl regurgitate bones into the arroyo?

What hides in the wave of a day?

A single blue unknotted cord—what does it mean?

How can the mind ply the forms of desire?

From south to north, east to west: which length is greater?

When is a koan not a koan?

Who can unravel the spin of an elegy and counterspin it into an ode?

Who whispered, "As is"?

Where is a passion that *orchids* the body?

Whose carded cotton fibers are these?

4.

> 7:14: red numbers on the clock incarnadine the time;
> he stares at the maroon jar of a kerosene lamp,
> the carmine batik hanging under a skylight.
>
> And when he drives home, the red at the stop sign
> is the bright red blood on a sheet;
> yet candles in the living room remind him of bliss.
>
> He has the urge to walk down to a spring-fed pond
> where he sits on a rusted bench, stares into water;
> tiny fish dart near; a green frog lifts its head;
>
> then a vermilion dragonfly hovers near irises,
> zigzags back and forth as if it weaves an invisible web.
> He guesses it eats mosquitoes and midges, though
>
> he can only see sunlight glint off its wings.
> The mind zigzags back—swimming in a tidal pond,
> they brushed jellyfish with their arms and legs—

loops a red cord that records loss and loss.
When he trudges back and closes his eyes,
he is startled to hear a cricket chirp in the fireplace.

5.

When he opened the book to the page with *quipu,*
he saw, through the underside of the sheet,

the image of a quince. Sometimes the thing you want
bleeds *in* the light. When yellow leaves dropped

off a cottonwood, he saw, up high, a large nest
and a magpie hopping from branch to branch.

When he stubbed his toe in the dark, he flashed
on how he dug his first matsutake out of the dirt,

fingered brown scales on the cap and stalk.
Now, as he looks into her eyes, he hears how

two men, rescued in the Andes, suffered frostbite:
one had his arms and legs amputated but is now

moving with artificial limbs, while the other,
who tried to hold on to his extremities, suffers

in a wheelchair. When she says, "I don't want
to become *that,*" the *no* smears fingerprints on glass.

And he sees a man splashed with blood and scales
stand hip deep in halibut, cleaning them off.

6.

Who has heard a flute carved from the wing bone of a crane?

They hung tomato plants upside down in the kitchen;

a dyer poured fermented piss into the dye bath;

explosion of egg and sperm;

he remembers a hummingbird nest tucked in some branches
tucked in his mind;

she groaned when he yanked her hair back;

inside the space of a pea,
beginningless beginning and endless end;

he diverts water from the acequia, irrigates slender peach trees;

when he pulled the skeins up,
they gasped when they turned blue in the air;

they folded an ultrasound image inside a red envelope with a white
     crane,
prayed, set it on fire;

he wove a blue jaguar;

plucking ripened tomatoes, she grazed shriveled leaves;

"All men are mortal";

they prayed to the sun, burned the blue jaguar at noon;

conception: 186,000 miles per second;

186,000 miles per second;

who has heard a flute carved from the wing bone of a crane?

7.

    Crows pick at a dead buffalo along the curve
    of the river, as Raz trots up with a cow hoof

    in his mouth. As: to the same degree or amount;
    for instance; when considered in a specified

    form or relation; in or to the same degree
    in which; as if; in the way or manner that;

in accordance with what or the way in which;
while, when; regardless of the degree to which;

for the reason that; that the result is.
As in a quipu where colored, knotted strings

hang off a main cord—or as a series
of acequias off the Pojoaque River drop water

into fields—the mind ties knots, and I
follow a series of short strings to a loose end—

walking barefoot in white sand, rolling
down a dune, white flecks on our lips,

on our eyelids, sitting in a warm dune
as a gibbous moon lifts against the sky's pelagic,

with the shadows of fourwing saltbushes,
the scent of hoary rosemarymint in the air.

8.

I close my eyes—see fishhooks and nylon threads
against a black background, cuttlefish
from above against a black background,

blowfish up close against a black background.
The seconds are as hushed as the morning
after steady snowfall when the power is out,

the rooms cold. At one, a snow-heavy branch
snapped the power line; the loose end flailed
clusters of orange sparks. A woman swept

a walkway, missed a porch step, fell forward,
bruised her face, broke both elbows; yet
the mind quickens in the precarious splendor

that *it would not be better if things happened
to men just as they wish*, that—moonglow,
sunrise—the day—scales of carp in frost on glass—

46

scalds and stuns. In 1,369 days, we've set
eagle to eagle feather and formed a nest
where—fishhook joy—the mind is new each day.

9.

We bend to enter a cave at Tsankawi, inadvertently
stir some tufa dust, notice it catches a beam

of sunlight. The beam enters a ceiling shaft
at winter solstice noon and forms, on a plastered wall,

a slash, then a small circle of intense light
before it disappears. And when we leave,

my mind sizzles with the vanished point of light.
I sizzle when I remember how we first kissed,

when I ran my hands through your hair, when you
brushed your hair on my body. And as flying

geese cast shadows on water, and water reflects
the light, I feel a joy stretch and stretch

into the infinite. I recall when we knocked at
a neighbor's door to drop off a gift, how

they didn't hear us as they were staring out
at the feeder counting birds—bushtit, sapsucker,

nuthatch, woodpecker—as we counted the blessing
of seconds where heat shimmered and vanished into air.

Six Poems

Jorie Graham

PRAYER

Am I still in the near distance
where all things are overlooked
if one just passes by. Do you pass
                          by?
I love the idea of consequence.
Is that itself consequence—(the idea)?
I have known you to be cheap
(as in not willing to pay out the extra
                          length of
blessing, weather, ignorance—all other
[you name them] forms of exodus).
What do I (call) you after all the necessary
                          ritual and protocol
is undertaken? Only-diminished?
Great-and-steady-perishing? Unloosening
                          thirst,
or thirst unloosening ribbony storylines
                          with births
and history's ever-tightening
                          plot
attached? We're in too deep the bluebird
                          perched on
                          the seaweed-colored
limb (fringed with sky as with ever-lightening echoes of
              those selfsame light-struck weeds, those
              seas)
seems to be chattering at me. Too deep?
Someplace that is all speech?
Someplace everything can be said to be
                          about?

48

Will we all know if it's blindness, this
                    way of seeing
                    when it becomes
apparent? Is there, in fact [who could
                    tell me
                    this?] a
we? Where? The distances have everything in their
                    grip of
                    in-betweenness.
For better [she said] or for worse [he said]
taking their place alongside the thirst
in line, something vaguely audible about
                    the silence
                    (a roar
actually) (your sea at night) but not as
fretful nor as monstrously tender
as the sea wind-driven was
                    earlier on
in "creation." Oh creation!
What a mood that was. Seeding then dragging-up life and
                    death in swatches
for us to forage in. Needle, story, knot, the
                    knot bit off,
the plunging-in of its silvery proposal,
                    stitch stitch still clicks
                    the bird still on
its limb, still in the mood, at the very edge
                    of the giddy
                    woods
through which even this sharpest noon must
                    bleed, ripped into
                    flickering bits.
It is nothing compared to us
is it, that drip and strobe of the old-world's
                    gold
                    passaging-through,
nothing bending its forwardness, nothing
                    being bent
by it (though the wind, rattling the whole business,
                    would make one think
                    it so). Nothing

compared. And yet it is
there, truly there, in all sizes, that dry
                    creation—
woods, dappling melancholias of singled-out
                              limb-ends, lichened trunk-
                              flanks—shocked
transparencies as if a rumor's just passed
                              through
leaving this trail of inconclusive
                    trembling bits of some
                    momentous story.
Was it true, this time, the rumor?
The wherefore of our being here?
Does it *come* true in the retelling?
                                        and truer in
                                        the re-
presenting? It looks like laughter as the
wind picks up and the blazing is tossed
from branch to branch, dead bits, live
                    bits,
new growth taking the light less brightly than
the blown-out lightning-strikes.
Look: it is as if you are remembering
                    the day
you were born. The *you.* The newest witness. Bluish then
                              empurpling then
pink and ready to begin continuing.
Lord of objects. Lord of bleeding and self-
                    expression.
I keep speaking this to you, as if in pity
at the gradual filling of the vacancy
by my very own gaze etcetera. Also the
words—here and here—hoping
this thing—along with all else that
                    wears-out—will
                    do. I think
about you. Yet is only *thinking* omnipresent?
Omniscience, omnipotence: that is all drama.
But omnipresence: time all over the
                    place!

It's like a trance, this time unspooling in
                              this telling.
Like land one suspects must be there, but where?
The ocean kisses every inch of the seeable.
We live. We speak at the horizon. After a
                    while even the
                    timidity
wears off. One speaks. One is not mad.
One lives so long one feels the *noticing*
                    in all one sees.
                         Years. Chapters.
Someone is asking for your hand. One turns
                    to speak.
One wishes so one could be interrupted.

AFTERWARDS

I am beneath the tree. To the right the river is melting the young sun.
And translucence itself, bare, bony, feeding and growing on the manifest,
frets in the small puddles of snowmelt sidewalks and frozen lawns hold up
                                             full of sky.
From this eternity, where we do not resemble ourselves, where
                         resemblance is finally
                         beside (as the river is) the point,
and attention can no longer change the outcome of the gaze,
the ear too is finally sated, starlings starting up ladderings of chatter,
                    all at once all to the left,
                         invisible in the pruned back
hawthorn, heard and heard again, and yet again
              differently heard but silting
the head with inwardness and making always a
              dispersing but still
coalescing opening in the listener who
         cannot *look* at them exactly,
since they are invisible inside the greens—though screeching-full in
                         syncopations of yellowest,
                         fine-thought, finespun
rivering of almost-knowables. "Gold" is too dark. "Featherwork"
                    too thick. When two

appear in flight, straight to the child-sized pond of
                     melted snow,
and thrash, dunk, rise, shake, rethrashing, reconfiguring through
reshufflings and resettlings the whole body of integrated
                     featherwork,
they shatter open the blue-and-tree-tip filled-up gaze of
                     the lawn's two pools,
breaking and ruffling all the crisp true sky we had seen living
                     down in that tasseled
earth. How shall we say this *happened?* Something inaudible
has ceased. Has gone back round to an other side
of which this side's access was [is] this bodywidth of
                     still sky
deep in just-greening soil? We left the party without a word.
We did not change, but time changed us. It should be,
it seems, one or the other of us who is supposed to say—lest
there be nothing—*here we are.* It was supposed to become familiar
(this earth). It was to become "ours." Lest there be nothing.
Lest we reach down to touch our own reflection here.
Shouldn't depth come to sight and let it in, in the end, as the form
the farewell takes: representation: dead men:
lean forward and look in: the raggedness of where the openings
are: precision of the limbs upthrusting down to hell:
the gleaming *in:* so blue: and that it *has* a bottom: even a few clouds
                     if you keep
attending: and something that's an *edge-of:* and mind-cracks: and how the
                     poem is
about that: that distant life: I carry it inside me but
can plant it into soil: so that it becomes impossible
to say that anything swayed
from *in* to *out:* then back to "is this mine, or yours?": the mind
seeks danger out: it reaches in, would touch: where the subject
                     is emptying,
                     war is:
morality play: preface: what there is to be thought: love:
begin with the world: let it be small enough.

Jorie Graham

GULLS

Those neck-pointing out full bodylength and calling
outwards over the breaking waves.
Those standing in waves and letting them come and
                    go over them.
Those gathering head-down and over some one
                              thing.
Those still out there where motion is
primarily a pulsing from underneath
and the forward-motion so slight they lay
their stillness on its swelling and falling
and let themselves swell, fall . . .
Sometimes the whole flock rising and running just
as the last film of darkness rises
leaving behind, also rising and falling in
                    tiny upliftings,
almost a mile of white underfeathers, up-turned, white spines
                              gliding over the wet
sand, in gusts, being blown down towards
                    the unified inrolling awayness
                    of white. All things turning white through
breaking. The long red pointing of lowering sun
going down on (but also streaking in towards) whoever
might be standing at the point-of-view place
from which this watching. This watching being risen
from: as glance: along the red
blurring and swaying water-path:
to the singular redness: the glance a
being-everywhere-risen-from: everywhere
cawing, mewing, cries where a
single bird lifts heavily
just at shoreline, rip where
its wing-tips (both) lap
backwash, feet still in
the wave-drag of it, to coast
on top of its own shadow and then down to not
landing.

                              *

Jorie Graham

Also just under the wave a thickening where
sun breaks into two red circles upon the
                    carried frothing—
white and roiling, yes, yet unbreakably red—red pushed (slicked) under
                    each wave (tucked) and, although breaking, always
                    one—(as if from the back-end of distance red)—
and that *one* flowing to here to
slap the red it carries in glisten-sheets
up onto shore and (also as if *onto*)
my feet.

                    *

[Or onto my feet, then into my eyes] where red turns into "sun" again.
So then it's sun in surf-breaking water: incircling, smearing: mind not
knowing if it's still wave, breaking on
itself, small glider, or if it's "amidst" (red turning feathery)
or rather "over" (the laciness of foambreak) or just *what*—(among
the line of also smearingly reddening terns floating out now
on the feathery backedge of foambroken
looking)—*it is.*

                    *

The wind swallows my words one
                    by
one. The words leaping too, over their own
                    staying.
Oceanward too, as if being taken
                    away
into splash—my clutch of
                    words
swaying and stemming from my
                    saying, no
echo. No stopping on the temporarily exposed and drying rock
                    out there
to rub or rest where nothing else
                    grows.
And truly swift over the sands.
As if most afraid of being re-

54

peated.
Preferring to be dissolved to
designation,
backglancing stirrings,
wedged-in between unsaying and
forgetting—
what an enterprise—spoken out by
me as if
to *still* some last place, place becoming even as I speak
unspeakable—
and so punctually—not even burnt
by their crossing through the one great
inwardness of
mind, not by the straining to be held (grasped) by my
meanings:
"We shall have early fruit
this year" one of the shades along the way
calls out,
and "from the beginning" (yet further on). Words: always face-down:
listening falling upon them (as if from
above):
listening greedy, able to put them to death,
flinging itself upon them: them open and attached
so hard to
what they carry:
the only evidence in them of having
been.
And yet how they want to see behind themselves,
as if there is something
back there, always, behind these rows I
gnaw the open with,
feeling them rush a bit and crane to see beneath themselves,
and always with such pain, just after emerging,
twisting on their stems to see behind, as if there were a
sun
back there they need, as if it's a betrayal,
this single forward-facing: reference: dream of: admission: re
semblance: turning away from the page as if turning to a tryst:
the gazing-straight-up at the reader there filled with ultimate
fatigue:

devoted servants: road signs: footprints: you are not alone:
slowly in the listener the prisoners emerge:
slowly in you reader they stand like madmen facing into the wind:
nowhere is there any trace of blood
spilled in the service of kings, or love, or for the sake of honor,
or for some other reason.

EVOLUTION

My nakedness is very slow.
I call to it, I waste my sympathy.
Comparison, too, is very slow.
Where is the past?
I sense that we should keep this coming.
Something like joy rivulets along the sand.
I insist that we "go in." We go in.
One cannot keep all of it. What is enough
of it. And *keep?*—I am being swept away—
what is *keep?* A waking good.
Visibility blocking the view.
Although we associate the manifest with kindness,
we do. The way it goes where it goes, slight downslope,
like the word "suddenly," the incline it causes.
Also the eye's wild joy sucked down the slope the minutes wave
                                        by wave
pack down and slick.
The journey—some journey—visits me.
Then the downslope once again.
And how it makes what happens
            always more heavily
laden, this self only able to sink (albeit also
                        lifting as in a
sudden draught)
    into the future. *Our* future. Where everyone
                is patient.
Where all the sentences come to complete themselves.
Where what wants to be human still won't show
                its face.

56

VIA NEGATIVA

Gracious will. Gracious indistinct.
Everything depends on the point where nothing can be said.
From there we can deduce how
from now on nothing will be like.
Here lies: a border then the un-
just. Do I have, for example,
a heart? Does it only *feel* if you make "sense" of me?
Can it, for example, make me "see"?
Can it make me not see?
That we shall never know, of each other now, more.
That there is a no more. Hot and singular.
Surrounded by our first-persons: the no-more.
Before death's obligatory plurality.
But I do know you by heart.
Also know other things by heart.
Interior, spiral, damnation, your name.
What would be the opposite of "you"?
When I "think," it is near the future, just this
                                          side of it.
Something I can't conceive of without saying *you.*
The desert is fueled. My desert is fueled.
Daybreak a chaos in which things first come forth
                                          then mix
as in an oasis, thirsty
for distinguishment.
Then the angels who need bodies to walk in.
Then something breaking light further as in: "it came to
                                          pass," or
the way my words, encountered, are cancelled,
especially if true, and how they insist on encounter:
finally: in the world: "the impossible": "the little":
"in the house over there": "elsewhere than here":
What is this (erasure) (read on) is it a warning:
omit me: go back out: go back in: say:
no way to go in: go in: measure:
the little fabric vanishes, ascends, descends, vanishes,
say twenty seconds, say wall
(at the same time there is a specific temperature)

Jorie Graham

(so that eventually the light goes down all the lights go out
                                                        together
till the level is reached where a fall begins) (more or less
                                                        long)

COVENANT

She was being readied by forces she did not
recognize. This in an age in which imagination
is no longer all-powerful. Where if you had
to write the whole thing down, you could.
(Imagine: to see the whole thing written down.)
Everything but memory abolished.
All the necessary explanations also provided.
A very round place: everyone is doing it.
"It": a *very* round and glad place.
Feeling life come from far away, like a motor approaching.
And in its approach: that moment when it is closest, so loud, as if
not only near you, but *in* you.
And *that* being the place where the sensation of real property
begins. Come. It is going to pass, even though right
                                                        now
it's very loud, here, alongside, life, life, so glad to be in it,
no?, unprotected, thank you, *exactly* the way I feel.
And you? Lord how close it comes. It has a
                                seeming to it
so bright it is as if it had no core.
It all given over to the outline of seem:
still approaching, blind, open, its continuing *elsewhere* unthinkable as a
                                                        gear-shift
                                                        at this speed.
Approaching as if with a big question.
No other system but this one and it growing larger.
All at once, as if all the voices now are suddenly one voice.
Ah, it is here now, *the here.* [Love, where is love, can it too
be this thing that simply grows insistently louder]
[It seems impossible it could ever pass *by*] [she thought]
the eruption of presentness right here: your veins
[Meanwhile a dream floats in an unvisited field]

58

{There by the edge of the barn, above the two green-lichened
stones, where for an instant a butterfly color of chicory
                          flicks, dis-
appears] How old-fashioned: distance: squinting it
                          into
view. Even further: rocks at year's lowest tide.
The always-underneath excitedly exposed to heat, light, wind, the
being-seen. Who could have known a glance could be
so plastic. Rubbery and pushing down on all the tiny hissing overbright
                          greens.
O sweet conversation: protozoa, air: how long have you been speaking?
The engine [of *the most*] is passing now.
At peak: the mesmerization of here, this me here, this me
passing now.
So as to leave *what* behind?
We, who can now be neither wholly here nor disappear?
And to have it come so close and yet not *know* it:
how in time you do *not* move on:
how there is no "other" side:
how the instant is very wide and bright and we cannot
                          ever
get away with it—the instant—what holds the "know"
[as if gently, friend, as if mesmerized by love of *it*] [love of
(not) making sense] (tide coming in) (then distance taking
                          the perplexion
                          of engine
whitely in) (the covenant, the listening, drawing its parameters out
just as it approaches its own unraveling)
the covenant: yes: that there be plenitude, yes,
but only as a simultaneous emptying—of the before, where it came
from—and of the after (the eager place to which it so
"eagerly" goes). Such rigorous logic, that undulating shape
                          we make of
                          our listening
to it: being: being on time: in time: there seeming to be no actual
                          being:
all of it growing for a time closer and closer—as with a freight
                          of sheer abstract
                          abundance (the motor

Jorie Graham

sound)(is all) followed by the full selfishness (of such
                              well being) of the being
(so full of innocence) actually (for the instant) here:
I love you: the sky seems nearer: you are my first
                                        person:
let no one question this tirelessness of approach:
love big enough to hide the cage:
tell them yourself who you are:
no victory: ever: no *ever:* then what "happens":
you can hear the hum at its most constant: steady: the era:
                    love bestowed upon love close-up:
(quick, ask it of heaven now, whatever it was you so
                                        wished to
know) the knowing: so final: yet here is the road, the
                              context, ongoingness,
and how it does go on regardless of the strangely sudden coming un-
                                                            done of
its passing away.
Silence is welcomed without enthusiasm.
Listening standing now like one who removed his hat
                              out of respect for
                              the passage.
What comes in the aftermath they tell us is richly
                              satisfying.
No need to make a story up, for instance.
We have been free now ever since, for instance.

Three Poems
Michael Palmer

STONE

What of that wolfhound at full stride?
What of the woman in technical dress
and the amber eye that serves as feral guide

and witness
to the snowy hive?
What of the singer robed in red

and frozen at mid-song
and the stone, its brokenness,
or the voice off-scene that says,

Note the dragonfly by the iris
but ask no questions of flight,
no questions of iridescence?

All of this
and the faint promise of a sleeve,
the shuttle's course, the weave.

What of these?
What of that century, did you see it pass?
What of that wolfhound at your back?

AND

The ship—what was her name, its name?
Was it The Moth? Or The Moth
that Electrifies Night? Or The Moth

that Divides the Night in Half
in its Passage toward the Fire?
The fire of forgetting, that is,

as we remember it,
while in the scatter song of dailiness
as it eddies out

near turns to far, beeches, red cedars and oaks
dating to the revolution, and a few long before,
suddenly in unison are seen to fall,

for so somewhere it is writ.
And your project abandoned in fragments
there beneath the elements,

the snow of the season enfolding it,
the flames of the season consuming it,
improving it: Hashish, the tales it

tells, the scented oils and modern festivals,
the sphinx-like heads and the shining ornaments
for ankle, waist, neck and wrist,

dioramas, cosmoramas, pleoramas
(from *pleo*, "I sail," "I go by water"),
the hierophant in wax, the iron and glass,

the artificial rain and winds,
mosaic thresholds, all of this
bathed from above in diffuse light.

We share the invisible nature of these
things, our bodies and theirs.
And the moon did not appear that night.

—to the memory of a suicide

UNTITLED (FEBRUARY 2000)

The naked woman at the window
her back to you, bowing the violin

behind the lace curtain
directly above the street

is not a fiction
as the partita is not a fiction

its theme and variations
ornaments and fills

not a fiction
as the one-way street still

wet from all this
rain is no fiction

and nakedness not a fiction.
It reads us like a book

as we listen to its music
through milky eyes wide shut.

And what does this fiction think of us?
The rain, the notes, both softly fall.

Slight errors of intonation do not matter
in the faded green

63

Michael Palmer

notebooks where we record these
things, and conceal other things.

What's the name of that tree, anyway,
with yellow flowers, small silver leaves,

planted in the concrete—
I used to know.

As for today, Leap Year Day,
the window was empty.

Reef: Shadow of Green
Mark McMorris

(rubble)

As wordy as the wind, and as stifle as the leaf at noon
the buildings of the town are standing by their word
as I pass them, and double around to the wharf, to
catch fish by the waters. All around me is the
mangle of history that coughed once on the sidewalk—
left, and I have wondered about the colors, behind
the detritus of sea ports, cannon, juridical wigs, murders
and the rum parties—dance hall bodies bumping, and
I've been to the yards with kerosene tins boiling bananas
and who was it that said, no relief for the black man?

(air)

The john crows wheel and drift over the green Warika Hills
vulture birds that sometimes land and forage dogs
still graceful from afar, prints on blue sky like cuneiform.
I used to watch them through my father's binoculars
the wing-stabilizers, five feathers spread as from a hand
articulate nature with her bestial ironies, the birds that love death
wheel and drift, circulate in the heaven, biding their omens.

Mark McMorris

(stone)

The sweetie man selling chewing gum and stockings
sets up on a bridge—a business to leave to the children?—
that's his regular spot. And I wave to him one day, passing
through the village in a car, how yu doin', Star, an he
nothin' doin', Boss, you see how Mary get married? I
don't know any Virgin Mary, but he meant the 10-year-old
now 30 who lived behind the dead-end, at the hillfoot,
with Errol, or Maiah, or Hedley—some name like that,
that means a man who is always looking for work
with his own machete, his own spliff, and maybe a dog,
an artificial leg, a big-belly concubine, a motorcycle.

Mary come and go, sell newspaper, do a little day's work
washing and ironing, and keep the house clean, go and come.

(wire)

The wind says: I smelled the salt blast of the Palisadoes in my face,
     and was glad
to see the airport still striving to be international, all that
time to get landing rights for BOAC and Lufthansa, so a man
can go to Germany and Holland, if him want. Driving in,
things reek like dead jelly-fish and sweat, along a Paradise Boulevard

and I spoke the teller, one morning at Barclays' Bank,
young lady, what is the hex change rate for 10,000 US?
And she replied: either you is a thief or a capitalist, you know,
is where you a get so much money? You think say me fool?

My brethren you get lost in the Bible, over in Babylon
but I have a Subaru to drive, an import license
for TV dish and camera—digital, audio, telephoto banjo—
a cell-phone, ackee and saltfish, Big Mac, more than I can eat

until one day I went north to visit the Botanical Gardens
that have its gate shut, because everything dead and dry.
I telling you, that's how it work down here, wid de suffaras.
And you know what? I buy a dictionary to converse:

(speech)

> yabba
>> close yu mout, hear mi
>
> calabash and yarn
>> a will full suspend of be leaf
>> I be lieve in yu now, hear
>>> (politician talk)

(light)

No one was there, and nothing to beat it, and not any song
that I can remember will say it better than the birth blood
the 10,000 born in a gulag and that's nothing in the scheme
so quiet yuself and get wid the pogrom, a so them sey.

And so, as in a tumbler of rum, the face trembles, and the hand
swerves to ward off the light and of course there's too much
of it down here for a single image to contest, the sky eye—
It does not give out. It does not diminish: words.

> callaloo
>> two ell two oh: sailboat to america
> bangle
>> name for a wrist chain copper
> gold
>> tumblers of a watch, water proof

Mark McMorris

(iron)

(Leo dunk the watch in a bucket of water
before him buy it to test the guarantee)

Let me spell it out for you: water proof
I back off because the problem is solved.

(wood)

The camera's eye-lid, a noisy blink: yellow petals flowering

Some sent their daughters to Vassar College in the north
I married one, one yellow tree, one college, one minister
some woke later than the gardner who cut the lawn
and went astray, in the back yard, catching butterfly.
One could still catch butterfly in those days, believe me,
and I caught lizards, a bad cold, a beating, other things.
Went to the wharf to see the skyscraper ships (New York).
Went to university to see the knowledge heads (New York).
No joy.

      Agouti is an animal and
      today is the hero's birthday
      a statue erect: *Bob Marley at the Arena*
          gouging the population
               a South American movie
I found the log book, a translator.

*   *   *   *

The log-book opens: "America is conquered.
We have seen no savages in months—no trace.
The gods have left for more habitable spots.
Send reinforcements: seven armadas, grazia.
I leave these heirlooms to my replacement.

      rotting wood, methane gas, pulped star-apples
the conchs carelessly dead
                (Our wives—were we ever married, were we?)

Someone kept a catalogue of the landfall.

(tongue)

    The undressed jungle at the water's edge—
    green leaf like a naked belly.
                (Our wives—were we ever married?)

    The starfish with her pimply arms as
    rigid as a tongue on my neck.

    The sea urchin washed up from the sea bed—
    her prickly sex.

    The wounded skin of driftwood—
    seamed by water and
    left out to dry by a careless hurricane.

    The tide-suck in the stomach as
    the moon seduces the ocean away
    from her lover on the black land, my land.
                (Our wives—)

Mark McMorris

(blood)

list pinned to the zinc wall of the rum shop
sea-gull   canoe   man-eaters   wild-pig
(no one)
marlin   callaloo   google-eyed fish   frangipani
(wood   word)

*   *   *   *

A single tree—what name the tree have, yellow poui
the blossoms never matter to me at all, the name lost
in heaven and everything spoil, mash up: even the wave-dem
(on sea-wall)

some do the mashin' dem call the police
some go to jail, others to seed, some to all that trouble

a graceful body that love the deep places
white flowers to amuse a girl
(no one to see)

(voyage)

I was coming back from Portland and took a mountain road that cut
diagonal across the island, and at some points the wall of bush
opened onto the valley meadows, with a pond and maybe a great
house, and the spectacle caused me to stop and pick out the cows,
not too many of them, and measure the acres by stretching my arms
all the way out. You never see such a green. More driving very slow
and out of no where a town and a roundabout, shops, bars, electric
lamp posts, trucks. Pass and leave behind.

The glimpse of the valley meadows, the empty beautiful land—still
I was glad to see them, though I saw no one in six hours on any field
much less a man planting anything to eat—and thought back to the
old use it or lose it, to the Queen's permission, and a planter in rum,

70

Mark McMorris

with bad breath on top of a housekeeper: tumbling down the hill
and I couldn't stop the tumble, till I got back into the Mercedes and
went on.

(our wives—)

mosquito: untuned violin
coconut:
woman's hair like surf: sea's navel

that's how lovely she is

*   *   *   *

"We forgot how to read and cipher.
The admiral would not leave his stateroom.
The admiral—nothing more than an old shawl.
He wrote letters, exonerations, *mea culpas*

send reinforcements, send something

(a sail! a sail!)

The wind says:

You are not ready for this much death—you need mops,
furnaces, landfill dumps, sea trenches to hold civilizations.
You are not equipped: for example, Mexico, San Domingo.
What do you know about a man who shits in his pants?

(*error*—a stray)

*   *   *   *

"Each day we collected specimens. Of what?
The botanist said: there is money in shells,
the flowers are strong aphrodisiacs.
The sky, the jungle, the sea—all hostile, choking.
No one. We make do with the Indians.

(—were we ever married?)

71

Mark McMorris

(time)

Amerindian graveyard: speech (skull) fragments
(cause of madness)

parrot, a tough meat
utterance at climate level

*   *   *   *

—as in the photo of two dogs fighting—
—as in the mirror I carry in my pocket—

*   *   *   *

"The soul grows desperate: the aromas
of salt and rotting wood, the proximity
of Sun's plump face, or the crocodiles
that navigate the rivers like gondolas . . .
The thunder of surf has made me mad—.
My lords, make of these islands what you will.
(the yellowing heart

(leaf)

The curve surprises, with a loaded bus
over the edge of a precipice, and green
wetness on either side—am in it again
with confidence in the machine to touch
where the poui blazes and blue stretches
like an embrace, to cull out the accents.
(reef: shadow of green)

—The wind kissed the chest, the surf dilated with the sand-crab,
the night was a gentle breath that stirred the almond's arms.

Each's Cot An Altar Then
Susan Wheeler

. . . from the service of self
alone . . .

grasses in low wind high sun

(streamers of starlings)

Joseph hauling the leg with his hands, corn stubble to stalk, horizon
no house —

Low animal flash in the riot of leg —

all such good works as thou hast prepared for us to walk in

This one request I make if it mean foot or glove
Repair, deplete the debt as I am out of love

carrion   calumny

and come into the field of blade poplars glinting,
leg pulled like a cart on the mule of the man
grasshopper of cropduster sprawled in the sun
desperate pastor all yield   green pan

Susan Wheeler

Limb lost? Likely.
Undone? Likely.

Let us grant it is not amiss

who bears the Count Chocula shipment up
who razors the retractable in the joint
who sings the bass of Anthony
who cries mercy in the placid field,

far now to go.

to reel the streets at noon —

so great weight in his lightness —

So. Bike at door.
On it. Avenue
of the Americas   (against traffic)
a stream.
          The
spareribs hot against
his knees.

fiduciary re
no sib
ability   re-
spond dis
Eisenhower, Eisenhower

Susan Wheeler

sty

pend

sur

plus one is

x, solve for,   solve

vent

A kind of Mamie-dress, that's right, with the bodice —
no — you'd need darts here first. But that kind
of print —

kind of

a clear light above Joseph and his leg and the dry dry stalks and the
clatter he makes

seek a proper return for our labor

Three Poems
Ann Lauterbach

FRAYED EDGES

Domain at hitherto causation   listening booth page

     will show you who is right, has stood the test

  anecdotal soul

à la carte

            lay the blame on, bear the blame

    Too late *na na*
new neighbors have arrived
in their slender

      that's another pair of shoes, dead men's shoes

    they
have descended the ladder
to the philosopher's hole, his

      spider and butterfly and bird.

     Here find the linear broken below
a human form—
    hard shell of certainty,
parody and reverence braided together,
tiny beats of the heart—

     traced back to that other plan

eternally existing

the young doing such a thing,

the big, what's the big?

cabinet of curiosities, what
you may be looking at, unexplained.

Now I am newly sad although my house is fine:

a silver pencil, a distinction, a thing for him.

In the gap between sadnesses
a man is talking and I

> *will come, it is probably a shame*
> > *and you are a pattern of tact, come to deceive us, but I*
> *I cannot the infinite*
> > *(as a child, no harm)*
> > > *but I'll try*
> *aloud, not guessing, I would have telephoned,*
> > *thirty miles*
> > > *much, well, highly*
> *over what I have said, so*

so thought
abraids first proof. This opinion flatters
no previous *flourishing*
no surefire procedure, as when
three into six gets two.
Five into five gets one.
The catastrophic interim is here
in the cold

foxglove, foxglove.

Ann Lauterbach

Against whose mercy shall I apply my wares?
Clarity pins us to our cause
as we walk down aisles of flameproof trees.
I am pointing at what is not there.
You are standing as close as a child

Let us show the cat a film of crows.

Explain

    one of the limbs or organs by which the flight of a bird, bat, insect, angel is
effected, part in, corresponding to,
supporting part,
      and comes on the wind,
        takes under, his are sprouting,
          high, low, and the north was added on the beat
    which spread,

      and the arrow with eagle feathers, the shaft and ambition,
  his spirit,
      the steps, the horse, the god
        and Victory, its way to its mate, the air

Explain

   blue, brown,
      of day, in the wind's, right, left,

   beam, mote, clap,
    up to the, open, wipe,
      throw, cast, hook,

    glass, bath, cup,
      bright, brow

Now the sky seems beautifully organized
but everything we care about is flawed.
The pool fills with leaves.
The funny pains of aging, artificial tears, and the false

verdict in the note,
drawing on her pride, her shame, her position

and step at the start, before the mirror,
without the medium, without coin,
despite the prophet

and the audience still waits for a voice from afar.

Out in the yard sparrows itch at the ground
and the grave flags flicker on their sticks.
In the coming years, you will find

a treasure,
favor and mercy, at the feet where there is no sense in it, although the
terms are reasonable. How do we

ourselves? We must take it, it pays, it pays,
almost impossible, but necessary
with time to read,
courage, heart,
one's way

to where another is, crouching
under the day in a ghost file.
How bright the fence in sunlight!
And how acute the transformation, in which

a caterpiller becomes a butterfly

and what is really there becomes a jingle about Paradise
as a red car. The red car is really there
driving along the big streets
with the soprano singing her tune
and the young man with long black hair
smiling into the wind.

Ann Lauterbach

The crowd
behind the barricades, trying to see
suggests something,

a fine blossom, pierces beneath things,
and that there is a reason in it, good
enough for an outward display. Why did he do it?
To give it away, to give her what is enough,
and fair, to give it all away.

The price is merely a sweltering crypt
where drawings of saints,

Saint Paul and Saint Michael, Saint Peter, Saint Andrew, Saint Elmo,
Saint Bartholomew, Saint David,

drip pink tears, and the two-note hum
in the dead of night

na na. kap shus

rr rr
loo ahs   anpay   kistre

The churchgoers move inside, the chorus
in another room sounds victorious. Someone
drives by, blue canoe
strapped on, headed for the river.
The reverie begins again
near the silt path in front of the trailer.
People seem to need a reference
else the shore
is too far to be traversed. They want to know,
is it typical as well as indigenous,
is this an actual archival wound or repro,
spliced together by the magician

80

who would not have it, saying the living is in it, that it came to him free.

In a sliding scale
each thing refers to another,
scandal and code
fall together in a new font.

We cross the Bridge of Triage
swaying high over the river.
Down through the murk
a cluster of shapes, black
and dandelion yellow, swift by.

Today, at the House of Anemones,
a woman called herself mad.
She confused me, in her quiet barn.
I bought a bouquet of violent flowers.
The thing refuses its gospel.
The humped range is not shiny enough
to reflect instruction's bliss,
the luminous arc dispersed without shelter.
Try climbing over yourself, try
breathing on the glass a valedictory kiss.

A dispatch of boys
made the water rise,
came forward
roped into eddies, ripping
lilies as they came.
The Beautiful Writers
in downtown Shanghai
wear silver on their toes.
They study aphoristic slang.
The empty dress floats
toward the horses
galloping out from night's tarnish.

Na na, theater of vigilance, graphic cloud.
Na na visceral digest, spitting birds.

Ann Lauterbach

Leave, yes, but to where?

　　　　*Is Heaven? Did you read that? Are you going? Showed me
they were, but does it touch our interests? Are you looking? Shall we,
if prices fall now? I don't know, to have is the sense of it, is the use
of trying. Places they sing. I am weakest in facts. Your treasure. Go.
You like it, send him. He will be taken care of, the ancients knew
nothing, we know little. That's it. Do you come from? Are you going?
The whens are important.*

Na na.

SPLENDOR

The dream ascends its microcosm, making *not sense*
and the atavistic goons clash
at the edge of the park, sky
sky plumed
　　　　all prepared
for the haunted balliwick of strangers
trailing incognito across the past.

But the light seems musical, lowered
against the ridge
into *andante*
　　　　　　shift shift shift

News of earth: the fabulist knee-deep in mud,
fists of green, tinsel dripping by degrees,
shoe left in the meadow,
the sentence elongated and
patched onto the war zone.
It could be dark, theater of dark,
the unsheltered sentence bloodied,
the opaque moon, the glassed in record,

　　　　　　　　the will to rise.

82

Call it *the person* things will go back to sleep
as if forgotten and the difficult will seem easy
                    walk into the light
                        show the precarious stays
                            set off fires from above
there will be no *one* to count no *two* to include no *three* to beg for mercy
the trail of time will be easy to follow

good old oaks, billowing lilies along the roadside
no *four* to divide

                        the valley is incrementally cold
                        down up down down

                        mediated by the memoir's fake torture
                        and the one-way war

                            panic of recognition
                            dangerous evident sun.

But in the slovenly small-eyed dream, surely
we are victorious,
our kisses stamped into wet clay,
our harrowing ended in song.
Rah! Rah!
as the struts of tomorrow fall to ground
and tears arrive from afar in new boxes.

Ann Lauterbach

INTERLEAVINGS (Paul Celan)

Snowfall, denser and denser,
a knight's breath

Snowfall, as if even now you were sleeping.

A collar of cold at his neck
above it, endless,
a foreign sky.

Below, hidden,
where my hand held the soft stuff
was den Augen so

prone, entire

almost fetched home into its
delay, the cast-off limb
posted.

The watch and music
in twin branches:

what body falls through the bridal mass?
is the colored cloth a flag?

Arc of His Slow Demeanors
Clark Coolidge

1.

I didn't respect him exactly but I collected his sensibility
sun on gouged hull of the same pitched home
he never tooted but fronted
on a new loop to the belt in a carry
the neighborhood wideners wouldn't shun
so neither of us fell for whose blinders?
a soaking we didn't?
a melting back from the gladness tax?

He would have chosen a diamond over a mirror any day
the mustard pumps removed from his cable socks
the better to mix an alarmist with the least of collateral bettors
mimsy were the clasps to his carbons of will
in a living room if had half a mind to
rope from here to sausagery
velvets in his background
looms for vetted sailors
felt crowns doffed in the forgetting

I wouldn't be writing this to him if I knew anything veteran
are you sorry and only then do you brighten?
I'll bet he was the Kellogg of his math class
rolled off a brass asbestos and to the windward
they never had galleries in that landlocked burdenroad
sky was his mention *and* pardon
the trust woman clanking off for slaghorn stanchion and points
    Viennese

Did we ever quite meet up?
I doubt the drift of that
flags forming on the upper staves as I watch

harmlessly getting his own goat I only wish
was a lot of trouble about the gray brakes
worries lashed together into habits to be stepped off
I'd make a wince of his ceiling belts to the public transom

You get a throat for that door I'll stopper it
slopes off after January, maybe March
maybe then April won't rain so much
curtains to contain a backyard in wires
glows where you don't notice
won't afix the phallus it's wrinkled the first collapse I notice
this before bass drums calmed the beatifics
he stripped the blue bead from his pen
gallant of us to stand about wasn't it?
before the distances were Galatea

A hum before the ship flagon wall scavenge
this the color I thought bronze was
turned out a fluvial wash or supersonic pan
we all wheat up through the stove
my manual said eat while a beam improves Benny or Andy
makes as if a final ear to the level exits
tweetmowers for saturday
Hi-Fi still to be penciled in

In which I discover the second war through
powdery flowers in my vagueness
following him on impulse nights to pinch
everyone at the least of them
the pleasantries of quietude to even construe a thing

But would he hook a harm to me?
I preferred Reg Butler and his batman sets
later rock rimming by the soft quotient
gone oval to the cemetery malinger
so out of him in this ground
pendant one less cigar or other
I'll make it hobbling on one lung
and a Pepsi gentian

A Za-Rex commotion in the attics of pebbled-glass
jugs with finger grips you'll toll a long time from
he'd pasteboard up from plush vespers if held neatened to a priest
but never a marmalade of such novel disparage
the morning ran to batteries and a blockade manacle gun instead
the marriage of games never to be lost
or found either, he had cellars full of the strain
misnamed railings, a couple of terrific beads
his head like a warning collector
mine a beaming limiter

Were you my ace in the malefactory, no
the casings came later, ocarina with armholes
prices after farming's forgotten
and the fame of the old wood's made out
then I really rang it up, didn't I?
argued over the obstacle gun and baywindow switches to the carbarn
        east
or skip the blimps to south, one
it makes no odds that Yankee wisdoms make them on everything
stop telling me things, then it would brighten

Coughed the hose out from under the gulf of the whole house
silence of a blind pew
storm load sliding off gradually
the pill rolls and Vaseline sundays
coil of the codfish template
the gray snow lateness on car tracks in Brilliantine
I thought it was time nobody knew anything
but a touch of the spear minted clear

He sat by windows ate back to
sundays repapered the mood
rooms escaping to a spare
I would rather have hollowed my own then
open cabins by flush chain keep
his nose to the empty box he faced
a sharp or flat exemption
so paid less to load his production
I couldn't stand the side of the house
bordered by tickle of the manual families

shoot down a load of bricks while dutying
bring your strings into pall

Beyond his bed door seemed
like not much was being entered
meanwhile I summered
was there the journal to tell about it somewhere?
certainly not Bogardus Waterfall Trail
the portions brought from Paris
the dawn chimes in his lower caste chest
peeping from the case I made
go home instead of dessert
the silver briar substitutes

Wish he'd got so far off I'd remember it
hindered by fin & haddy pan dowdy
and cans of limestone hedge pack solvent
the soots turned wasps as they came
he gave up smoking not minding
really raising the family guard
at early table as he thought to us
didn't I mind all your names?

2.

He was eager to see wood sawn beneath his nervous
the house had moved over in the night
left a felt marker where he left
the plectrum of old stump continuous
mirror lamped his own clothes till conscious
the member of the desk set travesty
loaner of the wide hips a corollary
then gas escaping from a sound

He was up but never till
the sides of his housing came together in consideration
desert he knew not
not even west
and then we waved him
I keep thinking he was born in a knee-high cabin

wasn't everybody's?
and now all the placements are loose

Needs learned from fire engine captains
lolling on the south side
there were women in those windows
but pretending fronds a partnership
near to drome havens and the gasometer
down forever in indulgences and backbone
had his limiters and so do I
blink

Stop sounding as if you, and others
charming combiners and no notions of the loup garou
an entablature of saviour
young mental wander home and strike
the doctor coming out of Maidsville in a trance
look down, these are the blackening onions
he never, he would not

Hornets a swing to the salacious
pinhole barriers in every one after all
the wall, the tubs, the sack of Truro
and name you Marge and in the going bituminous
a ribbon drips from the viol

I'd have to frame you in the front window to apologize
pacing it out in tiny lifetime gales
Sumerian to the winners but in the losing Trojan
won't mention the imperious Perseus
red cutlets of the Gaul
then his wind let up, he was pressing
and further blows of insect at the galleon wall
seal with silicon
the hole but not him

Go to cufflink school and how
this won't be printing out from you
no one to hoard those basement hours
a perimeter to every scab
you have to stop weathering to live

chorus or no baton

Dreamed of getting his own security goat
but such too plain *over* with
daydreamed the window was in liquid spillage
coins out of plaster as you watch
along the corridors or wrist release a special swatch
velvet in intent, the purpose conspicuous
the helmet on loan from a clown

In the attic in a chest there
is an alien predella
place of worms as long as the Waste Land
should anyone be of such a shag-cut intent
my father watches
telegraphs his pauses

But he was never ready
as if his doorways on loan
rather a clubfoot treater comes to market
watering cans and Studebaker rules
was in his study
he didn't have, why not
the burden too emeritus?

Trotted in shorts through a garden of hornfels
they don't have them anymore
now one arms doors and watches for creases
his glory was in not being a whiner
lollygagger, dreaming toad in a rile of the spurious
those gleams and hastes
these goal lickers each asserting the metal
then a partial head leered out

Group of young undergrowth parting the waterfalls
member of which he was never
in the days the carnivals grew together
and oldman slim dons
dark threads to fiddle and crane
comes to the pitch of twelve shoes
spinster lab by ice cream socket

new market new position whatever
and elbows grown spent as they're clad
he knew the man well

Feldspar chips in that cream anyway
close to the alternate spelling of gong
and nightwear
            and gracelessness
                 and small things
the father had to come home I guess sometime
rounding the chain gate get shut of his day

His hands have the look to care
for one of the fractal acids
locked to advantage that way
spiral shoals under varnish rules
a click of a meeter palming the governor
treating his sound to the bad end
the one his master dad said grease

Two Poems
Gustaf Sobin

A SELF-PORTRAIT IN LATE AUTUMN

. . . through that ever-
expanding interval, were never more
than these
late bees you'd
scribble: what hung, like sucklings, from the

fat,
dangling clusters; than these desolate, verb-
studded landscapes you'd
murmur, even
hiss into

some other, some ever elsewhere's
ear.

TRANSPARENT ITINERARIES: 1999

that interval, you wrote, between the inadequacies of the
   given and the imperatives of the inferred.

   (that additive without which isn't).

----

   through that veil, that
   billowing gauze, that interface with face-
   lessness it-
   self.

----

language: a density, you'd called it, in the service of its
   own evanescent releases.

   fabricating as it went the otherwise inaccessible.

----

   was always in the
      elsewhere, wasn't it: in the
   rented rooms of those
   out-

   lying districts that you'd begun drafting the
   portrait; begun restituting—feature by feature—its
   oblit-

   erated mirrors.

----

as if destiny weren't the unravelling of some prede-
termined dictate but the patient reconstitution of the
intended.

the resuscitation of so many suppressed ur-words by the
bias of a yet-to-be articulated grammar.

(what lay secreted within the parched hollow of our each
and every exhalation).

was why you'd lowered yourself into those ruins, wasn't
it? why you'd tape-measured whatever vestiges remained
in an attempt to interpolate—from their least sequential
sections—the full thrust of such an obfuscated dynamic.

. . . were roots, the white irises', you'd
discovered, that had
gagged the
idol's
eyes.

----

far too late for anything, now, but those earliest ideations.

the unearthing, therein, of the eventual.

wasn't this why the bodies grappled the way they did?
cherished the incipient against their own ineluctable
depletions?

their teeth bared; their breath broken.

why, too, you'd have uttered—just then—that word without words: that elision glittering in the very midst of so
much spent syntax.

and heard, so doing, the silence—thus solicited—sound.

Four Poems
Alice Notley

AMID THESE WORDS I CAN KNOW

canyon and spirit mountains peaceful spring with springs; not paying attention to glyphs. there are rabbits the springs are damp circles on the sand among greener bushes sunlight a lovely tone what can i do with it one says. musnt. try to know amid words which are deep and alive large as dolmens glyphs whose lines cut deeply into the past which is not a gone thing linear but a depth and a returning power also. know. in a clearing what i'm doing. not at all walking through my life as i often think but standing in place where i am been will be not using words not making them not being them but being among them as they are nature. past may be a gracious door always open skylike but in place a, wind in place or as a massive invisible process is both carven and calmly fluid the sky moves. i never move. chunk rock but not ice will never weep, when i cry its to break open to. you will not know if you dont suffer, why, a closed system cannot know but a knowing sky can be a mountain a knowing all can be carved as well and the words, the words part of all are like these.

use me suddenly i might say, and the canyon of my youth goes mosaic, i'm in the basilica by rights. walk toward that mosaic, as far as the spirit mountains, flickering light, across the glass cubes of. precious stones have been used in places, the mountains themselves are partly made of.

agate. jasper. quartz.

and you have disliked me last night in a dark hall. meaningless or not? if i am a thing and you are, the forces between us those emotions are the small winds of the universe lines or forces between things but undiagrammable and

being an aberration of the lines of like or a part of. no, you have disliked me disrupted me last night in a dark hall, is abstract and whats real is, that i am not a thing and so not dislikeable and cannot dislike on the real plane. where the glyphs are, and the dolmens, left to tell, of what is permanent, messages of, from the enduring "feelings," such as existence itself.

go on a little faster now in the wind the blank blue and theres a rabbit will he shoot it so we can eat it tonight jack rabbit cotton tail eat cotton tail. all these rocks pebbles in the mosaic from the past when i was a child one april in grapevine canyon.

lines of motion and emotion telepathies and paths all intertwined like grapevines with leaves of and the purple globes of, the telepathic the sending of all the messages all the thoughts ever and going on all in those little lines scattered toward and blown away ever everywhere everything ever thought at all blown about

Alice Notley

               in the canyon the glyphs
are paradise as preserved in the mind thats why theres the past.
i mean why theres no past

THE ELONGATED HOLY MOTHER

but in the next moneyless year there is a nearly fully grown snake of mine snake
what is this snake, this principles nearly large enough to bite me has a head like a
rattlers. you want some other symbol made out of modern fabric i dont have it no
life principle in you if thats you modern fabric. this snake is nearly large enough
to bite me, so i should turn it loose in the building to hide behind the furniture in
the dark where it lives best now. sister life cuts hers truncates hers though, before
she sets them loose, and she beats them, beats them into submission, i dont want to
do that. the snakes hide behind the bookcases making slime and skin in the dark
shedding and shedding
making more and more new years. in this new year i can find the buried person

the oldest person or year but the year the new year is that old one, the pieces
scattered throughout us and irretrievable, unless reamassed whole in a vision
and so the dreams and so the peculiarities of them.

98

the men who lived only with each other said to fear their room it was full of naked
men, i said i was afraid but i wasnt. i was searching searching the house, what was I
looking for? certainly not the department of gender
what is
a gender what on earth what is earth i was looking for what is earth in a world a
modern fabric
how is all this depicted in the church cant you see
a serpent asleep in the dark   protects the original nature,

or vision. old mother python. there was a castle.
on a shelf in it were heads, sculptures and one was of joan of arc, next to it under a
sheet, was that of king she served, i peeked at him under the sheet and so
he came as a ghostly wind, to terrify me in my sleep. the wind of the dead king
plucked up my own sheet from the bed and tried to strangle me. the principle
of the king tried to kill me, as my sister life keeps trying to bludgeon into submission
the snake

my sex is still involved.
superficially as the fabric of this world lies, the lies by which we
always   why death is so important. the only life   the
second world entangled like coils of always in this very one.   death is so
important its freedom from us,   the figures   on the
walls   know this being dead

snake piss behind everything can you like that as i do

99

hes killing the snake again for the pure maiden? what is she, she is himself hates
snake piss, the feel of old skins to the bare feet, have you ever walked through a yard
full of sloughing layers and layers, with bare feet?   and feared both pollution
and that something live was there a real snake, amid the shed skins the real life the
first nature, under everything.   the naturally slithering mosaic as the light takes the
walls of the   church or as a candleflame takes them at night

serpent of   enclosure of our mystery, here i am inside and cant
know it without the old symbols, like that, its like that through layers and layers, the
skeleton of the person is there but is the principle still there beyond symbols and
principles is it still i am i there?

sheds us the universe will shed us without a "thought" we are dead in so many coiled
faraway futures how many are there are there am i like them too? but i am not like,

skimming gold toward. and what did you say,
                                                                    lib-by, in exile

    so skimming and inviting like night of the stars in a small garbage quartier
anywhere world small garbage neighborhood this coin is so dirtied with snake piss
i wonder if i'm dead, shoved out into the cold new years night all alone and with no
access to water, i most needed water. no one needed to sleep they were already and
always.   i never knew if i was or not was i asleep there
was a man   so depressed because he was asleep it wasnt the same as
dead dead was full of light

100

floated floating in the city of ancient ancient
sleep, tears were sleep grief cold and dirt were sleep and fucking strangers for money
was sleep and talking to strangers for money, and talking to people who
gradually pulled closer and closer to one in sleep. in the   church

a mauve river flickers along its length its made of real amethysts not of water its
made of purest thought

flickering in and out of being messages
from. i don't know what, the ever future now the extensive reality which isnt a
universe that no one understands but that talks to us all the time the whole thing is
always talking within us and to us and outwardly toward the other us thats outside
us and i, i am a focus an all-point with only fabricated outward characteristics but the
medium in which i am alive is not fabricated. blood is not
blood and see, see the blood, is not see, where are we
then in a
and what isnt dreams is now the future
words dont remain her dead mouth opens and closes instead she

FIGURE, SAINT, ON AN ARCH

kept in thrall by someone who reads our thoughts. the story of the egyptian captivity babylonian captivity, reads the thoughts youve been given by him, thats how hes able to read them

especially in a widows house, can read thought from outside, is outside secretly in the dark reading her thoughts. her house is all windows panes into night and she knows hes there listening to her head

she says to me, he can read yours too. the more intelligent you are, the easier it is for him to read them. is that because intelligent means educated, to most, and educations so standardized. i know he can read my thoughts

because when i speak my voice crackles as if through a microphone, presumably my thoughts crackle too, as if magnified in volume by his powers. who is he. is he her dead husband perhaps, someone else suggests.

let me go. thats what all people say. or youll later be drowned in the red sea. thats what people say, drown them drown them all, golden bodies others beneath the waters dead and now knowledgeable

if he knows so much says the widow why does he haunt me why doesnt he stay in his knowledge. what does the attachment of people for each other, including the desire to dominate utterly, have to do with the beginning of things. is there a mathematical formula for a two become one which later must split. a sort of symmetry, a kind of emotional elastic stretching in which the mauve feelings are horror and the green ones fascination still

she now has given up on his death she accepts that hes never died though he still might, he didnt die disappear and come back, hes always been here sick reading her mind, hes moved back into the house

this is the life of the past. there is no past its a story. stories are bodies we keep going on alive only in others minds everyone acts as if this is lovely its inutterably hideous, to live in others. there is a way out

there must be, to leave the icon of symmetry tear it tear away.

the only possible freedom is mental so i didnt speak to pharoah, didnt approach nebechudnezzar i entered a cave for seven years not even accessible to daniels dreams no one could read my thoughts there, fed on grasses slugs and bitter water. there is the picture, another gold cell, the only real monk in cappadoccia, under under ground so the dead man couldnt make my voice crackle, so all the listening dead men ruling the world couldnt have me. daniel dont dream of me

destroy the thoughts hes given me in order to read them. he reads them backwards even, sthguoht eht yortsed. he uses symmetry to enslave me, he uses logic, but he

Alice Notley

doesnt use reason. the depth of all there is, in which he drowns his troops in order to rule, remaining ignorant, as you are ignorant who have never broken from formation broken symmetry, broken from any symmetric rearrangement of pieces after a presumed radical break

i dont care about your welfare, you have what you need the ability to break and reform, the ability to force others to do so too, so you can read their minds. what would you do if you no longer could read their minds. what would you do in your own mind. what would you think what would you do about time always previously measured out by you in your own symmetries lengthwise and so exactly controllably widthwise, all mathematics your invention the stars have been lenient to you compliant havent they do you listen to their thoughts. of course you do in time they tell you all their secrets you are the great and have remained innocent like a graph or a snowflake, or a stave of 18th century music. under the dirt in cave unbidden invisible no name on list in time what a nightmare couldnt have mind read by history by future pharoahs of enlightenment. i break brek like mountains away into so slow there almost is none. sitting next to dirt part of one retime without tracks here and what is already in mind, still partly his, keeps singing, what did i do then and then but that was to be sequence, after this death theres no sequence, going on justly not pat if possi how does it look now in areas of if its symmetry well its not his is it can he read it i dont read it i look quickly at its movement staying still it and i all the movements in stillness. the swaying toward, hes out there again trying to get in by saying i need him to eat so dont eat tae benowst. having no sympathy is beautiful. the best of icons are unpat, unsympathetic are not about about projection of the superficial only the dee. upon mortuary slab pasts rising up in days going on symmetrically so wh wh do yo its for fod foo all of it the slave. ddeep deep green that year, a bit of a story. in the mid did wha, it was because of the baby. there was nothing else to do because of the baby, who had to be brought to a pass to decide for himself. thus became tied to the process of money for food. thats the only story really and its

real a real story, where i solemn not mad eat wild grasses and nurse the baby. there is no ending, dont you know a. wants a humane piece of furniture. honor. but i want money so i can eat. i dont really have to eat in here which is why i spend as much time as possible. i cant find out anything unless you stay out. its not a cave church it needs too much light its in light but cave is a figure on a wall i go in in reaction. underneath as always there its the same as in the light.

Alice Notley

VIRGIN AT THE FOOT OF THE CROSS

is there some loss
connected
with the hybrid baskets lovely but woven into machines,
straw woven with wires, robotic as at la villette
fish there with our eyes but small bodies, treated like robots edible robotics
mice genetically engineered fluorescent for no reason.
have evinced no reason in eras. have not and within here is there reason. is there
some loss, tracy? yes, tracy replies there has been great loss so great we can hardly
recognize whats been lost, "how do you like your country?"
"its cold. i was lying with abrith oil before." a birth oil
and i was born once, but am i now
ceaseless need to care for adolescents, in a black dress when someone needs sex.
we are needing needing what have we ever. all the dead fish, thrown back to
rot because we didn't need them, with their sensitive eyes, electricity
burning stupid the métro on the way, what are we on the way, everyone
was on the way. straight, so straight
singing in the ash trees, is a too fragmentary knowledge of happiness
remember the 666 that the purchases in the dress store added up to. you always
knew it, said the clerk. what have i always known? that white
peoples houses contain too much water, flowing at will, they have coopted all the
birth or is it rebirth, have coopted it, shit, says the indian, look at all that lifegiving
edenic water inside a white persons house, i always knew it. and i knew
how cold it was to have no oil in the afterbirth

Alice Notley

too fragmentary the tropes of a nonfunctional mind. ra rings. goin on, the virgin
at the foot of the cross is simple desolation, in black and nearly faceless, at the end
of eras eras erase all this and have created this sec sec you are that i i c must concen
have you t noticed how the future is always anticipated by letters which will appear
in future words?

plastic cans of iowa anywhere says the invader of houses of water
mind mine, mine is not their developments or yours, mine is not yours, my mind
is there some loss

concentrated, just alive this morn in the after of butterflies in cages up and down the
rue papillon cocoons, worms and les comètes the grand yellow ones of madagascar
scar gas of what keeps us going, throwing useless dead fish back, because
we've joined the worldwide capitalize project.

so you preach revolution, revolution, against who everyone, the
figure on the wall is looking at you, if you would simply stand up straight
is that figure that straightbacked saint or prophet or sad

viri virgin virgin free? oh so yes, to be free is to face the world straight on and gravely
united robe not to obfuscate the sex the delicate and lightly
lubricated flower or, flower or, sea life of erect pipe or the convulsed vulvic flower
shapes shared with others those animals and plants

i left the man on the floor with it, someone must care for the young, the
preadolescent children, in a black dress on second avenue, first avenue was first
on it a different care, on second avenue on second there is no change without a bit of
stroking without some sex returned in the chicken cafe
then i can carry the dead chicken, with the vultures head attached too, all the way to
the new houses on the edge of the desert

talk to saint talk to, lib-bay, beau-ty, yes, is the good
anthropos, andromeda, multimedia wind and rain
beauty the good is, blow suffer a blow though? suffer it why, purifying
lying there, dont do another ill. bad hawk scream, aguila arizona, desolate on
the way to a little water appears near wickenberg. there was a stream there wasnt there
lib-by, all of it, come here liquid for pai, pain dance, force not
performed as such, no art of it. thats how painful it was, blew through the
house like an alien personality of my own
sensitive eyes swimming, trapped next to a food counter
blow of force and of life, stop carrying a dead chicken, saint open again so i can see i
want to see see it the message from all whove ever lived
drink jerez de la frontera, cross the border into, into a room of the good
it is instead of what they call god or some piece partial name,
integral, the leaves beyond number glitter like scales or pieces being one, one shining
a union, an um, a hyssop nonhybridian nonpantocrator
fills. fascinating fascinating light of non doom, no doom
mood nair thedniw, come come, hop to in, in the kitc kitchen of breaking cant break it
the good these piece not really a broke al at all, know gla what do the dead say,
mouths frozen throats vibrant they say in the field, near those houses at the border,
in the light of the game where no ones playing, that struggles are becoming nothing,
as we die into a ring around the black sea full
of fish like us, i got scared
and pulled back up into supposedly awake. beckons clumsi the mono, evening
morning star, fluster faster and tear, tear open the wide silver foil lake, the skull
leaders vanish, and we are left with silver water flowing

inside here the good moves along these walls is the lighting up itself of, it does that
rippling band the wind of the color, green or brown, or pupl purple
is there a loss
the everyo the embryo of what we live for to care of. we live to care for baby baby and
go hope your gauge is on empty, so you wont be machine more ingrown
or rubies there of this blood, would make you kill to see it, the blood of martyrs ruby
clas face and see what color, come to stay, axoh, tear eyes
the tears are looking for a place to alight in, they arent rain theyre desolation
the tears are searching for you and will find you

The Expansion of the Self
Tessa Rumsey

Does glass count as a wall?

Does a wall made of glass meet building codes determined in the South of France?

Does French glass reflect the pale light of springtime in the coastal village of Antibes, landscape of *plein air* and perpetual ennui, home of the author's first kiss and subsequent disfigurement—

Will local glass reflect Antibes more authentically than glass imported from another continent?

Will the world seen through a window appear *altered* depending upon where the glass within its frame was *manufactured?*

(Is the world seen through broken glass *whole* or is it *fractured?*)

The kiss had a desperate tone: "Dear so-and-so, you are my last chance—"

Later, unconscious by the side of the road: *is this fate?*

Or *is this circumstance?*

Will a lost world spend its last days pleading for survival?

Is there a name for *invisible cultural artifacts* suspended on a molecular level?

Does glass count as a wall?

The kiss was meant to be a masterpiece: "a mythological experience—"

In tune with Trojan horses: in tune with solar genesis.

Clockwork romeo spidering—along—the outside wall of a build-ing—feeling for her window—the footing getting thin—

Satellite stalking the sun's circumference: satellite fearing the sun's hot rim.

Which came first: *beauty?*

Or *disfigurement?*

(First came consequence: next, the accident.)

If a speaker is uncertain, can a statement be a question?

Does a window reflecting occupants fulfill its *occupation?*

Contradiction Number One: we are bound by desire / *we are bound by the sun.*

Contradiction Number Two: my face in the glass / *the glass seen straight through.*

If each world stops at walls of its interior—

(Where one body begins, where the next body ends—)

Isn't a wall a way of *rubbing up against,* of *letting in?*

Because history is full of distance and endless revision, "the kiss" came to resemble a window on the Mediterranean—

A window, that when opened, granted a view of the world both *utter-ly changed* and *exactly the same*—

Antibes in endless revision: Antibes held in a picture frame.

(Contradiction Number Three: the only certainty / is the uncertainty of ennui)

111

Tessa Rumsey

It would be a summer night made famous by both its *harmony* and
antithesis—

Her face pressed to his petulent lips: her face pressed to the
pavement.

How does a person inhabit a house—

A *beautiful* house—

A house of *disfigurement*—

(A house perched precariously between *romantic* and *revisionist*)

A house now, a body now, seen through, like glass, opened as a window, the air rushing in, closed as an interior, the air wearing thin—

Wall of glass, roof of stone, to be *on display* yet *utterly alone*—

Coastal village, a foreign ennui, romeo at the window, fumbling for
a key—

(Does glass count as a wall?)

First the accident: next the kiss: then the question:

Does the soul—exist?

Two Landscapes
Anne Waldman and Andrew Schelling

MONTANE

There is a mountain in the distant West
That, sun-defying, in its deep ravines
Displays a cross of snow upon its side.
Such is the cross I wear upon my breast . . .

— Henry Wadsworth Longfellow

Past crumbled miner shack on quick return
to mineral earth
      Shadow Canyon
one ornamental plum hosts in full lacy bloom
      a riot of lavender petals
Might have been torn from a page of Buson
deserves anyhow
      a moment's gratitude
or why some mountain yogin piled a three-stone cairn
kuhara-shila-samshraya
"shelters in caves and hollow rock"
      to smoky voice wilderness goddess
Mist whorling through limestone crags her breath
hawklike venery her sport
      (Bear Peak summit
                2:50 PM blowing fog)
When religion departs from the raptor's wing . . .
what is lost?

Eagle & peregrine falcon aloft
    the poet is brooding about editors—
Which is to say
glad you got here before me
dear salt dark feather granite peaks

           *

Spine's a *cordillera* of pleasure
    lady's curve   could be mantilla,
        mons veneris   might be trobairitz
leaves old Nueva York coast—
    "the poet is brooding about editors" (Buson)
Would be ravenous, numinous or
        just plain seeing things then
come 'round to humble trail, a trial
or perhaps a jest got jagged boot up an edge
Points are obstacles or holy mood?
Dakini breast, demon-pricks, wounds of a saint
       a troubling rood to contemplate
Free Tibet negative-ioned out
      salutes her peaked ally
as next century pops up, beams
    happy not to be beachfront
Above the trees tundratic you come to breathe
      & it is a woman's pride
dark perpetuity *(don't fence me in)*
or bright exposure animals—marmots, pica—course
        shy runs of
dusted with snow & named
(& here ensues a list of mountains):

Pike's Peak	100 miles	(14,110)
Mt. Evans	30 miles	(14,260)
Quandary Peak	38 miles	(14,256)
Mt. Massive	76 miles	(14,404)
Mt. of the Holy Cross	60 miles	(13,978)
Jasper Peak	2 miles	(12,940)

Dimensions from bronze sighting plaque,
South Arapahoe Peak (13,348)

NOTE: Thomas Moran painted Mount of the Holy Cross a
number of times and enterprising photographers popularized it.
Longfellow knew these images. In 1879, without having seen
the Colorado peak, he wrote "The Cross of Snow." The cross is
comprised of two transecting ravines high on the SE face
which fill with snow and present a cruxiform image most of
the year. Early Xtian travelers saw it and went crazy.

RIPARIAN

Basho dogs us here
albeit "Pets
        Not Aloud"
and five miles down
the grocery store has frozen pizza
The St. Vrain roars
            chortles and roars
past the billboard advertising
smoked trout
Are there trout in there?

115

"Fan"
the St. Vrain speaks
"oven"
daylight valley walls of burst
granite
ponderosa pine
        but by night . . .

        sentimental curtains with
        pussycats
        at the windows

All over Colorado
into alpine lakes and cold rivers
trout rain from helicopters
Every spring they dump them from helicopters,
and what senator speaks for the trout?

Who was St. Vrain?
Consult *High Country Names*
        Louisa Ward Arps & Elinor Eppich Kingery—
what was Cache la Poudre?
What were the French up to?

1848 keeping their
powder dry

Eagle Canyon
Clap trap houses displace the eagle
dislocation
driving through subdivisions
named for what they displace

Golden Eagle where is thy eye
(*and vanishing*)
Bald Eagle thy claw?

(*prospering, replete with road kill*)
Who dwelleth yet in Eagle Canyon—?
    wise philosophers

                           knotted
        should we say
                twisted
        the
   ways
        of
          this
        road

       (36) staked out

You think watching a small tv
the same as listening to
quiet music?
or a book with fine print?

Gold   *Light*

I'd get up and turn off that fan if I could

       —I will

turn off the refrigerator if I could

          —not sure I can do that

      crab apples are ornamental

         and St. Vrain is not a Christian holiday?

Bring back Basho & temper the
     lane, the light, her dawn

Basho hears a horse piss near his head
Basho sees a dream waver on the autumn field
Basho gives his youth to homosexual love
Basho shaves his head
Basho builds a hut and assumes a pen name
Basho takes on students
Basho hates the poetry scene

The capital Edo is like New York

He comes to loathe it
     flees it in riparian
     twist & turn

—I am not a poet of Edo
—Not a New York School poet
—We are not poets with any name exactly
     though half of us is a New York School poet
—I am not a New York School poet
—You are when you collaborate that half
—Collaboration was not invented in New York
     nor in Edo
—I missed a beat O yes & proud of it

Bring back the golden eagle of five syllables

*

Dusk by the creek

this is a little haiku—

     the rabbit
eyes the idling
     Subaru

add another haiku—

118

What loneliness
the rabbit
eyes the newly arrived Honda

Can't get a word in edgewise, ceded to river

and another—

Move your fingers
and count syllables
the old man

*

Catch us if you can

blue & red in the rocky mountain

slant light / sun set

Waiting for you in a swing by the St. Vrain
what I always knew poetry could do

shoring up for the millennium

so many thousands before us

doing the same with their broken syllables

"tremble"

the river it's the river

I'm just going to walk over to it

Voiced Stops
Forrest Gander

Summer's sweet theatrum! The boy lunges through

The kitchen without comment, slams the door. An

Elaborate evening drama, I lug his forlorn weight

From floor to bed. Beatific lips and gap-

Toothed. Who stayed late to mope and swim, then

Breach chimneys of lake like a hooked gar

Pressing his wet totality against me. Iridescent

Laughter and depraved. Chromatic his constant state. At

Ten, childhood took off like a scorched dog. Turned

His head to see my hand wave from a window, and I too saw

The hand untouching, distant from. What fathering-

Fear slaked the impulse to embrace him? Duration:

An indefinite continuation of life. *I whirled out wings.* Going

Toward. And Lord Child claimed now, climbing loose.

Blue-pajama-tendered wrists and hands. In rest, his musical

Neck, pillowed cheek. Else by damp relentment, swal-

Lowed almost in coverlet, fetched longwise

From lashing hours into this unlikely angle, wedge,

Elbow of unfollow. Before the nightly footfall

—*shtoom*—his bed to our bed. Scaled eyes.

(Cézanne died watching the door through which

His son did not arrive). (Ajar, widening . . . .)

Gone again to non-meridian dreams and

Murmuring broken noise in tens. To wit:

Lying bare, the sheets a husk shed low

Over the sorrel-vine of him. Midnight

Extracts me from sleep to bear witness to that one, there:

Local, small, breathing evenly, pathetic, soothe and bloom.

With nidor of match-torched tick rising from the sink, he

Hams and dishes across a heel-dinged softwood floor.

Improvised jujitsu, mind-mirrored, runny at eyes, nostrils

Gleeting. His sock-feet trail effervescence and gumballs. Or

Shouts into the house: *Come out!* to see him as

A sthenic wildering daimon zap the driveway

With a curtain rod, the whooping

Center of a ring of spark. His last rite:

Peers into, scrupulously, both closets, under

His bed, luring the dog with milkbones. He worms

Into sheets after her, contorted to fit. *Goodnight*

Mom etc. I sit at the edge in an intimacy without like

And we talk in soft hues of curved space or frogs

Whose bodies freeze and revive every spring.

From outside, a child's cry, blank of indecipherable

Sound, pure distress or joy to which the now

Acutely attentive body, body become

Prayer, closes every

Other tuning down.

Planted in my chair within the transparent

Room like an oak, squirrels whirling around.

But the cry does not repeat. And the boy

Should be at school. The haltstitch

Slowly uncomes until my breath begins

To assume its first position. Looming

Close, a cardinal's liquid *cue, cue,* a dry

Plash of cars. Barely less green, the face

Of the ongoing in the window again.

Her whimper pitched high, the greyhound dream-

Races on kitchen tile. He scrapes back a chair

And hunches against morning's cool:

Nates to heels, knees to chin, T-shirt

Stretched over the foreshortened

Bulge of him. Bowl-of-Chex mouthfuls

Mostly open. A newspaper turns: voluptuous

Acoustics of home as bird hits

Window, walls tremble. The concussion

(Crushed breast) blots the pane (broken

Neck) with an impact mark: a solid

Host-white print the breadth

Of a child's fist from which

The ghost-trace of wingbones upcurve.

No whit poised, but given pause

At the door of his room, I quicken into

Mescalinate ecstasy, softly

Unclocked, stood irrelevant, eldering,

A guardian eloquence

Among the dank smell of him

Fecund in sleep, scratching scabs

On his throat. Loss is what

Distracts. And chiggers underpin

The mutable world whose attributes will

Concur with those of time

While mine at cross-purposes

Careen. So

manage my affections. Killed the light.

Constant singing, the inward rendering pungent

Undersong and wordless high lullaby wafted over a table

Of quadratic equations. Whose whirligig beetles are these

Let loose in the toilet bowl? No shut-up is there,

No sleeping late. The insistence (full gaze) of his face,

High-cheeked, his roweled pupils, peening rum-brown

Eyes, flood-gates to the wonderworld blink wide. Close.

Vertigo of veering to kiss his full lips in the blind

Room. Answerable (the gate swings out) to his summons, this

Opening in being, vast of trouble, inward savor, reprise,

Privilege of. Is gravity. Not situation. Seeing of. What is

Taking place. The yellow Pine Siskin chirping *to-thee, to thee*

To devote all wakefulness, apprise and spring

As star moss rises and purple melic.

Ambient Stylistics
Tan Lin

[novel]

This is a [poem] about boredom and its relation to things we know
are repeated. A poem should act in a similar way. It should be very
repetitive. It should be on the outside not the inside of itself. It
should never attach itself to anything, or anyone who is alive, especially the speaker who rightly speaking constitutes the end of the
poem. In this way, it should create something that looks like it has
been "sent away for." Richard Prince said that. This is a poem about
boredom and its relation to the things that we know are not repeated. It should not describe but only skim (biographical) material we
already knew. It should exist on the edge of something that is no
longer funny. In this way, it should create the meaningless passing of
time, like disco music. A poem should have died just before we got
to it. Like the best and most meticulous scholarship, the poem
should be as inert and dully transparent as possible. T. S. Eliot said
that. This is a poem about boredom and its relation to the things that
were not said. A poem is what it is not. It should merely involve the
passing of its own temporal constraints. In this way, it can repudiate
all emotions except mechanical or chemical ones. After all, the emotions in us are usually dead (and can only be revived by chemicals),
and the only emotions that we really could be said to have are the
ones we already had.

It is no accident that Reagan's presidency, the disco era, and Warhol peaked at around the same historical moment. Nor is it an accident that the category for Best Disco Recording only lasted one year and that Gloria Gaynor's great disco hit and Grammy winner was titled "I Will Survive." A poem, like a disco hit, is designed to be immediately forgettable and some of the best presidents of recent memory were elected in the '70s when Quaaludes were extremely popular. We live in an age when we are constantly told lies, made the subject of jokes, seduced by fluff and hyped with misinformation. Poetry should no longer represent the representation of knowledge, it should represent the dissemination of misinformation and lies. It should aspire to ever more bureaucratic forms of data transmission and delivery. It is well known that Reagan frequently failed to remember what he had said in press conferences or briefings of the day before, that he often failed to recognize his own cabinet members as he passed them in the corridors of the White House, and that even Nancy was crushed when he failed to comfort her after she told him she had breast cancer. No one ever really knew Ronald Reagan, not Nancy, not the seventy-seven individuals he saved in his career as a lifeguard, and not even his own children—who have written that on numerous occasions he failed to recognize them. A great poem functions in a similar way. It cannot be remembered, it can only be filled with something that is unknown or no longer contains. The '70s are over but the cars and music of the '70s, especially the pony cars and the mini-muscle cars like the Pontiac Firebird, Mercury Cougar, Dodge Charger and Olds Toronado with its flip-up headlamps linger, as if in drag, at the Classic Car lot located in Bel Air . . . Everything that is beautiful waits to be forgotten completely by what it is not. A poem, like the '70s, is just another way of inducing a series of unforgivable likenesses. Warhol said of his art that "if you don't think about it, it's right." Listening to a poem or novel or newspaper should be like that; it should be camouflaged into the large shapes and the patterns of words that surround us and evoke the most diffuse and unrecognizable moods that a culture produces. Philosophy, like poetry and television, can resemble these moods. Poetry ought to be as easy as painting by numbers. It should turn us into those emotions and feelings we could not experience in our own body. All poetry goes out in drag.

No one should remember a poem or a novel, especially the person who wrote it. Heidegger was right; one is never without a mood. The poem openly aspires to a state of linguistic camouflage. Ronald Reagan is a doppelgänger, and Edmund Morris has created a doppelgänger. He has made Ronald Reagan into something that fitfully resembles biography or background Muzak. It is, of course, clear that Morris detests Ronald Reagan the bore that resembles the planet Jupiter with its dense core and absence of oxygen. But Morris also thinks Reagan was a great president. Of course, Reagan made himself into a pattern that no one could see; he transformed acting into politics and outtakes into campaign speeches. He blended into everything because his ignorance was everywhere and extended to everything, especially his "untruisms" about domestic policy. After giving a speech in Orlando on March 8, 1983 about "the struggle between right and wrong, good and evil, the historian Henry Steele Commager remarked that it "was the worst presidential speech in American history."

Everything that has a subject should be detested; everything that erases its subject should be loved. The great Japanese photographer Daido Moriyama thought that photography could not capture what really mattered and thus worked to deface his medium with scratches, out-of-focus shots and blinding flares from unknown flash sources. He liked to shoot outlaws, prostitutes, TV personalities, gangsters and stray dogs. He was always running away from the photographs he was about to take, and he was frequently punched by his subjects. This is why poetry is superior and at the same time more realistic than any photograph (except really uninteresting ones), where the scent of something detestable begins to emerge at the point when the shutter is snapped and the chemical process begins. A poem does not secure or even require such violence for itself; the greatest poems simply contain what doesn't matter as it happens on the surface of the poem. To have a photograph is not interesting; to have a photograph of a photograph is, and this is what a poem does better than any photograph can. Only such relaxing enclosures of image within image or word within word allow the emptiness of all human feelings to surrender themselves without obvious grotesqueries and thus make the present a place to have a cigarette. All biographies, like all poems, are best when they fail to suggest anything about their subjects at all. A good poem is very boring. A great poem is more boring than the act of reading itself.

A [poem] or whatever you're doing (in a way) creates something that stops you from doing it. It is by now clear that what is not here is reading, but an illustrated lecture or slide show. The best reading is a reading that makes itself redundant, in other words, a reading that is canned. Let us now return to the classics. Almost everyone has read T.S. Eliot's *The Waste Land* and Gertrude Stein's *The Auto-biography of Alice B. Toklas.* Eliot and Stein are the most redundant and thus the most easy writers in the canon, with the possible exception of Tennyson and more recently the serial novels perfected by Jacqueline Susann, who is also read redundantly over and over. Some writers never have to be read anymore because what they say cannot be recognized at all anymore except as something in the background of what we were thinking about while reading the paper or eating. One reads, as everybody knows, to forget not to remember and that is what reading large tracts of the newspaper and Gertrude Stein are like. They are all the same. I can remember nothing, especially the little connecting words like and and to and from that make the news-paper so pleasing.

The canon is an idealistic maze and should ideally prefigure a range of meaningless mood musics, from elevator Muzak to New Age music, to ambient sound construction by Brian Eno, Soundlab and others, to endless TV soap operas and, most of all, to mid- to late-'70s disco with its emphasis on monotonous rhythms, its superficiality, and its blatantly unsubtle sexual innuendoes. The best way to listen to prerecorded voices and background music is to listen carelessly and accidentally, as if one were reading a poem by John Ashbery, T.S. Eliot or Charles Bernstein. Rod McKuen makes you care, unfortu-nately, and the last thing one wants to do while reading a poem is to care. Reading is too selfish for that. That is why the most boring and long-winded writings encourage a kind of effortless non-understand-ing, a language in which reading itself seems perfectly (I say this in a positive way) redundant. One needn't read through great novels any-more like one did in the nineteenth century with Balzac or now with

131

someone like Tom Wolfe whose works are basically dull repetitions (realism) that function like a nineteenth-century version of the Nynex Yellow Pages or Page Six of the *New York Post*. They work to destroy that thing known as chance and probability and they replace it with that thing known as humor. Humor like that, especially in outmoded forms such as the novel, is always terrifyingly obvious because it tries to include everything. Unlike the over-deterministic novelistic exercises of Wolfe, the truly great works of the twentieth century are works that should remain unread, and Gertrude Stein is the most important writer of the twentieth century who ought to remain completely unread. One need read only a sentence and sometimes only a word to imagine the rest. I have never read more than two sentences of *The Making of Americans* at a time (they put me to sleep or make me want to eat something like pizza or hot dogs), and in that way I have read the book many, many times. I have, in a sense, never been able to put the book down and I hope that in the future I will continue to never put it down until the day that I die or stop eating. In other long-interlude disco-oriented works there are increasing possibilities for loss of recognition, that patterning of sounds we all speak to each other and upon which a host of social conventions depends. It is not an accident that disco has strong gay undercurrents and that the four-on-the-floor disco beat is totally canned and compared to the bluejeaned rock n' roll—unauthentic, mechanical and machine-based. Turntables replace the live voice. The dance floor replaces the stage concert pit. Two discs on two turntables, spinning simultaneously, replace the long-haired rock star. Synthesizers and drum machines replace the realistic. Disposability, superficiality and ephemerality rule. Except for Donna Summer and a few others, most disco performers never became stars. Poetry should be like that. It should not be permanent, it should be very impermanent. It should aspire to the interminably pure moment of an interlude.

Only by so doing, can poetry stage its own inversion to talk via the larynx of others, and the most interesting larynx today is modelled after television and to late-night talk shows whose primary medium is the canned sound of two voices talking (that person sitting in the room trying to find a cigarette) about what they were saying. On Sunday, for example, after dinner, I take as is my habit a long walk in my flower garden (mainly perennials which recur from year to year depending on the preceding winter). Beneath an azalea, I recognize a buttercup (yellow cup, sprigs of white and green in the surround) but then I realize that my recognition, a form of repeating, of the buttercup in my head was the wrong repetition. I am now repeating what is not a member of the species *ranunculus bubosa*. The act of classifying a sound is momentarily lost in this particularly noisy act, before I realize I am looking at a weed which has a name I don't know but which I now recognize. Of course, the picture transmission is "instantaneous." What is a televised sound I recognized when I saw the weed is the same sort of sound one recognized, i.e., repeated, while reading. It is something which I have heard myself again. Sounds in TV and soap operas and Gertrude Stein are simple and untelevised, but buttercups are not, or rather the sound of a buttercup is not. Or rather a single sound or phoneme is simple but the sound of a buttercup is certainly not when it is broadcast by the eyes into the far reaches of a brain. All talk is nothing but a form of latent imagery and noise dispersion. All speech should be televised for maximum effect. All talk is nothing but a form of latent imagery and noise dispersion. All speech should be televised for maximum effect. All talk should aspire to the impermanent repeatability of a disco beat. Only in such a way does a word flower in the brain. Repetition is like spelling something out sound by sound, a linear process of random meaningful bursts working out its opposite: a pure sound-field in which all signals are mixed, a state that is the opposite of meaning or stability. This state we sometimes call flirtation, and it is closely related to the idea of lying. This field of lies goes by any number of names, the tradition, the making of the making, etc., etc. All lying comes down to sounds, and all sounds ultimately revert to noises and everybody who has ever spoken a word knows that till the day he or she dies. A great poem, like Ronald Reagan, lies without knowing it. Lies are the most mechanical forms of speech known to man and his noises.

In a perfect world all sentences, even the ones we write to our loved ones, the mailman or our interoffice memos, would have that overall sameness, that sense of an average background, a fluid structure in spite of the surface disturbances and the immediate incomprehension. The best sentences should lose information at a relatively constant rate. There should be no ecstatic moments of recognition. The writing should take a long time to complete and induce a mode of slow (because repeated, hence nontemporal) transmission and (simultaneously) a high rate of error. It is no longer important to connect one thing to another with language or meaning but merely to create more errors so that in the transmission it is unclear if errors are controlling the speed or vice versa.

Writing is inanimate. For this reason there should always be photographs to accompany it, whether or not they belong to the text or not, whether they make it true or just reinforce the lies inherent in any work of fiction, nonfiction, or poetry.

Writing produces a dead letter in the eardrum or the buttercup, whereas speech is living and breathing within a present that is refused, thus not seen. It is dead to all who refuse. Speech is not written language that is spoken. Speech is a flood which pours through strict rules of syntax and contains no words. It is frequently aleatoric. Written language on the other hand is usually highly structured, premeditated and processed formally by a reader in the absence of the writer.

What is love an excuse for? Like writing, it usually is an excuse for saying something that didn't need or mean to be said. Today I was reading a story about Greta Garbo, and especially those mysterious thirty-two cards and telegrams that were finally unsealed at the Rosenbach Museum and Library in Philadelphia this past weekend. What is writing a love letter but an excuse for NOT loving someone? That is why Greta Garbo is so beautiful in these letters where she never professes love for her interlocutor (it could be anyone) and why anyone who reads the letters enhances the piquant privacy of its container and creates that feeling known as error. Love is the greatest mistake that can be directed at someone else beside oneself. It is also the greatest kind of error that may take place in nonwritten form. That is why one falls in love so easily, and why one loves Greta Garbo so much as one reads these nonlove letters. Because one does. Everyone loves a mistake. It is not surprising that very few love letters are written today (there are too many cell phones) and why almost anything today can be mistaken for love: a rock star, a restaurant, someone else's one bedroom apartment with a fireplace and a couch, a Prada suit, a novel by Philip Roth. One should never know what one falls in love with. The minute one recognizes a lover it is already over. That is why so many marriages end in divorce and why so many photographs resemble unmade sitcoms and why so many novels are so readable. Tom Wolfe knows this. As T.S. Eliot remarked, minor novels are so pleasing because they are so minor. It is too bad they got transformed into something they could not be.

Anyway, most of the unsealed letters were sent by Garbo in the '30s to Mercedes de Acosta, a playwright, screen writer, suffragist and poet whom Garbo met one evening in Constantinople in the late '20s. Garbo admired the bracelet Acosta was wearing and Acosta promptly gave it to her. They met again and this time Garbo gave Acosta a flower. The two traveled to Silver Lake in Wyoming or Wisconsin where they spent "six enchanted weeks in the sun" which was probably closer to three and a half weeks. And so it went until the late '30s when they met, apparently after a long hiatus, in Sweden. Garbo wrote, after their parting, "I was a wreck after she went, and I told her she must not write me. We had a sad farewell." In the '40s Garbo showed up at Acosta's door saying, "I have no one to look after me." But Garbo refused to give Acosta her phone number and Mercedes was unable to make anything more than a brief visit.

135

I believe that reading about moments like these, not writing about them, especially years afterward, is what creates that thing known as love. That is why there is so little love in Proust where everything is happening in the present tense of memory and why reading old love letters (sealed from memory and history) as opposed to writing new ones is the best way to fall in love. Like great television re-runs, a love letter will render you utterly passive and silent, especially if it is written to someone you hardly know. Language is a mistake and that is why more mistakes happen with total strangers than with acquaintances. No one ever really falls in love with anyone they know. To fall in love with someone that one knows is to fall in love with someone that one already fell in love with a long time ago. The truly great lovers, like Greta Garbo, were capable of falling in love while saying nothing at all. Of course, Garbo liked to confuse people. She called herself a boy in public and she was fond of wearing trousers. "I have been smoking since I was a small boy," she used to say, or "I am a lonely man circling the earth." No one knows if Acosta and Garbo ever had an affair or if they were lovers, though Acosta with her jet-black hair and aristocratic Spanish Catholic parents, and tendency to wear black trousers, claimed to have had affairs with Marlene Dietrich, Eva Le Gallienne and Isadora Duncan. Poetry, like love, is filled with obvious mistakes.

It is always impossible but highly desirable to imagine something twice. Let's say, like Alice falling through the looking glass, that you find yourself in a world reversed perfectly. Pavlov found it almost impossible to get a dog to salivate when touched on the left side as opposed to the right side, and similar experiments with rats, goldfish, turtles, monkeys and children have borne this out. Children learning to write, as opposed to read, have considerably more difficulty discerning b from d and p from q than they do in discriminating b from p and d and q. Like an animal or a child learning to write, you would not be able to tell the world was reversed—unless there were humanly made objects and symbols, and in particular signage and alphabetic systems. But unlike the humanly made world, the natural world, especially an unfamiliar landscape, can easily be reversed without your knowing it.

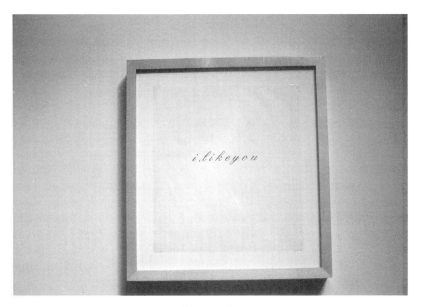

This is a lie.

It is Tuesday in the Mirror World and in the World of this Writing it is also Tuesday and if you live in the mirror world, taking a shower, finding the cold tap, operating a screw gun, driving a car and writing a note are difficult right now. Now you say now you use your right hand to shoo away a fly on your left elbow without even thinking. And now, pictures when remembered, are frequently remembered with the wrong left-right orientation, suggesting that memory traces are themselves duplicated in the brain in mirror-image form. After watching the movie *Rushmore,* such perfect symmetry, which leads to imperfections in the real-life world, is not at all uncommon in literature, which as we all know is made up of a series of elaborately coded lies that are not being told to anyone in particular, but exist as ciphers within a written text. It would be nice if after all we no longer thought, essentially, about objects, or felt a need to have thoughts about something, and thus were finally able to abandon the idea of thought itself as a language that was comprehensible in relation to its objects. Then it might be possible to give up the idea of speaking while thinking or talking about something. It would be much more pleasing to talk about the reverse of what we were

137

Tan Lin

talking about and to feel the opposite of what we were feeling. To think about nothing and say nothing at the same time. Anyone can feel love (or pain), especially when the person (overhears someone) in love feels nothing at all. Only in overhearing could one ever be said to feel anything like love at all. Yesterday I went to the movies to see *Rushmore* by myself. I had a very good time.

Pure repetition involves recognition of previous sounds in the shortest of attention spans: the span between two words. Unfortunately, the voice occasionally flutters or expresses random ambient soundbursts (nonrepetitive patterns). Even now as I speak, the human voice is strangely inhuman and mechanical, plagued by poor transmission, errors and mechanical repetition. The interest in the aural pleasures of nonsense and repetition coincide with the deeply unsettling manipulations of voice and identity when transmitted "at a distance," through a field. The most interesting things written aspire to the condition not of music—which has recognizable harmonic and melodic threads—but of the code, the meaning embedded in a language field as undistinguishable sounds, the lost beat of disco which obliterates the singer's voice. Language is forever temporal, subject to change, cancellation, decay, a failure to specify anything in the here and now. Repetition is a good way to remember something very fast. That is why it is much nicer to lie to others than to oneself. Lying is a highly regulated, i.e., a highly rehearsed form of being in uncertainty vis-a-vis what one was not remembering or not forgetting. It might be said to resemble the human system of breathing, which is also a kind of sonic rehearsal for death. A lie is always located in the death of the message. Yes, I am lying to you. No I am not lying to you.

Poetry should not be written to be written, it should be written to be listened to it should not be written to be remembered or absorbed it should be written to be forgotten.

You are repeating yourself (interview)

138

In any system, I repeat myself, I believe it is possible to turn the repetition inherent in oral forms (speech) on its head. Let me tell you a story that might not be true. I went to hear the rock band Chicago last night at the Greek Theater in Hollywood, which is an outdoor theater set against a backdrop of hills and aging palm trees. The audience was mainly fortysomething hipsters and studio execs with big hair, lots of gold chains and Porsches. People were singing and standing up a lot, telling those around them to get up and sing. As I stood up, it suddenly occurred to me that these were once hippies but now they were hippies preserved in some form of twilight, evergreen light that had descended the L.A. air over the outdoor amphitheater. People were standing up and looking back at the people behind them as if they were the audience. No one was smoking pot or anything else. The air was clear as a television screen. Everyone in the audience was white, even the Asians and the blacks. The only people who weren't white were the ticket takers and the bouncers and one kid from some high school in L.A. who was asked to come onto the stage and play with the band for one number. And that is how my memory of going to high school in Athens, Ohio in the mid-seventies came back to me, and remembering stories about deer blinds, or harvesting pot planted at the local public golf course, and what I was called in gym class, Ho Chi LIN.

Those who study information flow know that repetition in real life situations and in spoken language is generally used to secure meaning, to make sure one is not misunderstood. Repetition lessens the possibilities for error. Hearing Chicago again, it was impossible not to remember the massive inertia of "Saturday in the park, thought it was the Fourth of July," and it was impossible not to remember being back in those long, carpeted corridors of my high school, and the cafeteria tables where everyone was shouting next to their food and the plastic trays. I believe that repetition is more thoroughly embedded in speech than in writing, which is too bad really, for the memories that are inside me feel like they are about to be formed but would rather not. Of course, as my high school teacher Mr. Lalich, who later went on to become a city council member, reminded us in American History and Economics, the trade-off lies in the realm of the temporal. The more repetition there is, the greater delay in the rate of message transmission. But rehearsal is also key to absorption, i.e., in short- and long-term memory, and oral forms thus work to do two things: reduce ambiguity in the message and promote retention. Certain kinds of psychotropic drugs (LSD), novels and poems, and Mr. Lalich's lectures on inverted forms of economic efficiency rarely transpired in the long term; they re-enacted the processes of memory at the short-term and synaptic level, which is to say, before memory has attached itself to the sound field. Repetition, especially in the things one reads, is opposed to the class of words known as antonyms, which is to say language's repeating tendencies, its tendencies to be synonymous and simultaneous rather than different. And this violates the idea of meaning which is grounded in differentiation. But, of course, if everything is or appears the same, then language takes on the qualities of a cipher or code where differences are perceived to exist but are disguised. Disco music, the phone book, Gertrude Stein's books, and TV talk shows function like this. To read is to forget the meaning of reading. For this reason, the best literature is often written in times of war where puns themselves suggest the origins of language in a consciousness that cannot use language to make any distinctions between language and thought, speaker and world, signal and noise, sound and word. I left the Chicago concert filled with memories and very depressed. I never knew about Vietnam or the war protest movement except secondhand and so all my memories of those events were memories of things I had already seen on TV. The best TV and the best works of literature do not engender memories, they get rid of them. The best cure for memory is a really good poem or maybe a novel.

Poetry, like drugs, should not be difficult, it should be easy. Poetry should not be interesting, it should hold out the potential to be very insipid. Boring is the least of what most people have always realized, evidenced by the large numbers of Americans who have never read a poem. Poetry should not be morally uplifting, it should inspire a deep sense of relax. Poetry need not say anything important or humanly meaningful, it should merely evoke a mood. That mood resembles the sound of a sunset. Jack Spicer understood that all unsaid words are painful to listen to. They are better to look at. That is why Jack Spicer is a beautiful poet.

I compose and you compose. The little and the like. The most refreshing language would be written by an exercise bike or a fancy treadmill filled with electronic devices that measure one's alpha waves, pulse, heartbeat, respiration rate, CO_2 output, etc. It would be a machine that had not been given a ten-minute course in Zen or Salsa dancing but had its own multitrack recorder. The multimedia loudspeaker intones, the internet site and the homepage repeats. "I return to psychedelia." The great poems of the late '90s and the early 21st century will be written not to the jaded forms of serial or twelve-tone productions, not the remnants of Stockhausen and Webern, but the music of electronica and circuitry and electrical processing that first came of age in the '70s. Tricky is the King. The Orb is a Prince. Hendrix's single-hand feedback is reincarnated as the flat ambiance of Stereolab. All poetry is the sound of an optical illusion on a mirror ball. What is the most beautiful sound in the world? The sound of an image dying, the sound of a television commecial one ignores like a reflection like a highway divider, the sound of fucking on a couch while MTV plays on the TV set. The poem aspires to a trans-historical, trans-ethnic revival. It admits of a kind of enlightened multicultural ambiance.

The other day I went to the Rose Bowl in Pasadena to look for some George Nelson coconut chairs, with two girls who had just graduated from college and had come to L.A. to make movies, and they were telling me about how ecstasy is great because it makes falling in love completely irrelevant because you are in a state where you don't need to fall in love. For this reason it's better to take ecstasy with someone else. That is basically what poetry is like. The best poem doesn't try to make anything beautiful or watery or dark or light. It is Saturday night around 7 P.M. California time. I see a strange yellow and red cloud that resembles one of those diagrammatic drawings for the rotary engine that were introduced in the '70s by Mazda. The cloud moves quickly upward and downward like a jellyfish whose body resembles the effects of a massive plunger. Three days later I read about a NORAD experiment involving a Minuteman with a dummy nuclear warhead. It was launched off the California coast that Saturday night. It was destroyed by a heat-seeking missile that was launched from the Kwajalein Atoll in the Marshall Islands forty minutes later.

141

I understand the question to mean something about sounds, rather than language. The revival of the '60s and '70s in the '90s is the most fitting example of a kind of contemporary revision of the Arts and Crafts movement, which culminated in Colonial Revival products, especially with regard to things such as quilts and other decorative arts. How late we come to our realizations and our own monotonies. How often we switch ourselves off and realize that poetry no longer needs to be avant-garde, and less formal in its orientation. I can remember the lives of various schools. It can review home arts like quilt making, needle work, gardening, collecting of ephemera, etc. Repetition is crucial to all these endeavors. Poetry should aspire to the condition of continuous relaxation but without effort. It should be filled with typos. One studies and re-studies the ape and biological determinism as if it were a form of the Holocaust or a victim of the Hiroshima blast. This is the kind of history that most appeals to us. The least important thing one can say about craft is that it suggests an evolutionary downdraft toward greater levels of domesticity, homelife and infinite credit. It approaches the state of the ultimate home furnishings catalogue and unlimited personal spending. Poetry cannot survive in a homeless state. The poetry of exile is a dead end, the poetry of world weariness is an overwaxed palm leaf yanked from some Caribe Isle, as numerous poets have demonstrated. But, of course, it is bad manners to pronounce this at a dinner party populated by publishing people or Nobel Prize laureates and their hosts or in a poem, that the ideal poem is an extension of home entertaining, that its verbs are intertwined with the life of good manners and candlesticks. Not every decent poem is willing to please, but many are. All poems are healed by corruptions of the feelings.

Tan Lin

What does it mean to stop reading a poem? It means that one is tired. Lynne Cox, the great American long-distance swimmer has a body comprised of 35 percent body fat (compared to most women who have 18-25 percent body fat), and it is that layer of fat that functions like a natural wet suit. People who have seen her swim say she appears to float or melt through the water; that it somehow becomes her element or she it. Rumor has it that East German swimmers inject gas into their colons to induce similar properties; her plump, large undulating mermaid-like hips have fiercely propelled her obliviously through all manner of things in her twenty-five years as a long-distance swimmer: oil slicks, jellyfish that swell the eyes and lips, sewage, dead dogs, walruses and sharks. Yet she swims without any shark cages, no layer of grease or wetsuits—only a swimsuit. It is her layer of fat that is most remarkable about her; it turns her into something, a human porpoise, and allows her to maintain an even internal body temperature despite external temperatures that would kill most humans after thirty minutes or induce severe hallucinations. When she began her swim across the Diomeded—which separates Alaska from Siberia—she had to step carefully into the Arctic Sea. Had she dived in head first, the water would have stopped her heart almost instantaneously. I believe all these things are merely simulations by our brain of what will happen next, outward manifestations of the things that are just going on in our heads, and these situations are almost always hypothetical ones that we model rapidly and instantaneously and without thinking about it at all. There is nothing here but the writing and least of all the residue that is not in the writing and can never be there if reading is to be done at a later moment, say in history, or later in the day before one calls up a friend and goes to see *My Own Private Idaho* at the local bargain cinema for $2. Thus a form of dittoing or mimeographing the forms of the earth results in a worthwhile purgation of the things we cannot stand, a means of increasing the levels of aural pollution or interference. All beautiful objects ought to be replaced by residues of the sort that are created by the interference of beauty in the abstract. All great things of beauty should be abstracted to their least common denominators. No thing shall be separated any other thing. No love for anyone shall be love for any one. No words shall be used to trace out some other thing. As Robert Smithson recognized, poems are the strata of their own composition, they are never still but move like a series of roving sundials or mirrors across a Yucatan landscape, a series of roving tombstones where the sky is buried in the earth. A

144

poem is just a machine made of words. It merely reflects and then reflects on what happens to get in its way. I was reading the obit for James Velez, the young man who was "tormented by a baffling illness" and who died last Wednesday, at the age of twenty-five from infections of his blood and spine. No one knew why James Velez thought a million bugs crawled across his skin. To bring himself comfort he scratched himself so vigorously that he broke his skin and created heavy scars across his body, mutilating himself even though he possessed intelligence enough to recognize what he was doing. He spent most of his life in institutions where he received electric shock therapy but in 1994 a small social service agency, Job Path, allowed him to have his own apartment. In January of 1999 he remarked: "The happiest thing is to have a place that's mine." Nothing shall be hated decorated excoriated repudiated or remembered. Everything shall be copied and then recopied verbatim. I light a cigarette. I turn on the television while the stereo is on. I listen to the sound of a car and the music of DJ shadow. The end of summer is the end of the things I do not remember. There is no longer time for protestations in language. Poetry should not be performed, it should merely be listened to. The time for conscious experimentation and ego, which is its logical extension, should be replaced by unconscious repetition and listening. All poems should be rewritten over and over again and exist in as many versions as possible. No poem should ever

Delight Instruct
Marjorie Welish

1.

With expectations prepared to be inventing
the text of that half-open book, that book there, we are selectively it.
It? An index sewn

to abstract nouns.

Of interesting silk appropriated, prepared to be firmament

on a two-inch string
The blue sea on a two-inch string
The blue sea on a two-inch string only proves the rule.

Index intercepting text
a text throughout index, whenever an index in abstract
an index in concrete

correlates to text not to tile . . . title.

Of nouns tethered to spine.

Of difference throughout index measuring the text in attendance.

2.

The reader leapt through the index
To save time

the reader leapt through the scrim.

This is a test, a breakthrough for readers in reading rooms.
They have leapt through many Kraft paper screens

have broke through colloquially—a hiatus!

3.

The index accommodated curvature
through proper names.
Commence to count the lines assigned to Freud's rival: therein lies

subjectivity whistling.

Commence to read the index of this book, of that, to compare
lines assigned to Freud's rival, and so to ascertain
oasis therein.

Sum and substance whistling through the walls.

A field near a far farmhouse assigned to Freud's rival
has come to inflame the index
and take the initiative:

who is whistling?

A hiatus in the hunt, a field near a farmhouse
inflecting the index assigned to Freud's rival
perspectives:

whistling is its own infield.

4.

Consisting primarily of an itemized list
hand-in-hand with immobility studding the top.
Hand-in-hand immobility
Hand-in-hand immobility in and of
Hand-in-hand immobility in and of synchrony, primarily.

Yes. Immediacy.
Much gratified by neurons firing (yours).
Much gratified by neurons firing. Yours sincerely, . . .
Such are the diverging extremes,
the diverging of "Yours sincerely," from "(yours)" in the above.

5.

Yes, as abiding content and spirit in the following feast: "Hi! No!"
Displaying what he knows since, with "Hi! No! Hi! No!" arising
   from this project,
non-negatively. Next is a discussion,
mostly living, and with largely lurid details: "PpulrpNleK" and
   sound poetry
"Poetry is a mental event—Thwack!" "Next!" The new rhetoric
looks at the arts. "Hi! No! Thwack! I acquit!"

Mostly living and with largely lurid details is "Hi! No!" in the
   affirmative
greeting from the infant's displaying what he, the umpire, does—
   the requisite
rhetoric for abiding content and spirit. "Hi! No! A mental event—
   thwack! Next. New!"
The new rhetoric in the clutch of the waltz, the waltz instructed by
   the march,
struck, and sound poetry. "Poetry is a mental event—Thwack!"
   That, his promise
acting under duress and remaining *Symphony #6* throughout,
   struck the aptness.

"Out! Yes! Hi! No!" like a promise stuck
in diaspora greeting the infant. With largely lurid details and "Next!"
mostly living a mental event aggravated with imperatives
that is his format, the infant greets the adult. "PpurlpNleK"
in graphic description has captivated the waltz,
with a taste not unlike sandpaper across woodblocks.

6.

index text registers thesis this unconfessed register magisterial belief
index indent indebted to reading relative incurrence

To submit the officiating text to a test of its unconfessed register,
   first read the index.
In a first reading through its index, the charismatic text is tested.
To ascertain authoritative texts informing this
belief by informing that indent (incurrence),
slip into theoretical studies of the thesis hidden in the index;

the index confesses to scarifications unconfessed in the body of
    the text
Our reading the index to reveal the simultaneity prior to the text
will make descent into priority—agriculture, cattle raising—
for the index values only increase manifest underlying first glance
    at the magisterial title;
expectations are not lost upon the title: the title boasts, is delighted
    and indecent.
The index punctures the equanimity of the text at long last:
the testing of the text, the torment issuing from
nominative belief informing that indent (incurrence)
enumerating names, and through the definite spatial plan of the
    deceased
we postulate authoritative texts, possess the paradigm, the
    false door.

7.

Like a window not immediately obvious.
Sense, the inexpressive mention.
For which footfall?
He is hard on narrative.

8.

If Flaubert is innumerable, or, else, if "Flaubert" is numerous
and if "Flaubert" along with "Forster" is more numerous than
    "Freud," then
erasure becoming a must is an elemental gauntlet proper to nouns.

Without the nouns, without nouns equaling ideas, an index of
    nothing but "Flaubert"
is notable; with he more numerous in name than "Freud" in this
    case, so literature or literary
crescendo can be said, is said to be designated

of a code. If "Fielding," "Flaubert" and "Forster" eagerly await
    the literary
matter probabilistic, with its ups and downs, then gathering
    etiquette
to themseles are these proper names in particularity

149

only, saving ancient space. In a box
of abandoned enterprise without universals, a name weighs
some number: what does it mean in daylight, the volume so deleted
    of topics,

it saves space by remaining empty: this is a test or a deck of
    despotism
or a token. Enumeration gives vehement weight to celebrity. Count
    the mentions,
the various attempts at mention, the revenge of more minerals

written there. "Thenceforward it proliferated." Oval in section, the
    signature frequenting the index.
Frequency of something is an index to vehement weight: the
    rhetoric yclept cliff
cliff entitled there on the various attempts to exile and index to the
    back of everything

alphabetically, distributively. The index distributes its sources,
    specifically, gathering etiquette
gathering affiliation, the fringe of which you read as theory of the
    literary index becoming a must,
an ought, in mathematizing creases from a number that appears to
    refer to a page.

". . . Cézanne who spent who spent afternoons. . . .": that, an
    author's implicit criteria
through who goes furthest in mention against the glass to accrue
    subentries (F's rival, etc.). If names retire,
name the criteria once frequenting the index. A kind of forensics of
    situations is under way.

Roseate, Points of Gold
Laynie Browne

1.

She turns, light reflecting her eyes   constructed of light
    a liquid hand
 (of)   blossoms

The scent red, bower of red—May

    As she drinks this (color, blossom)
replenished   notion of Spring.

Where this ring   will have completed another
    in the unimaginable distance—
Given the color (gold)
    (now gold) of the fields from which the distance was
gathered.

2.

From fields of now, which gathered gold,

That which has been misplaced, or intrudes upon an
    afternoon—
Magenta hue of bud—fallen—a crown of red she associates
with a name

Suspecting this will disrupt the carefully pleated intuition of
    the manner in which to cross a room made of
    reciprocity.
    (a room at once a field)

Touched lightly, the surface ripple recants.
Such buoyancy, opposite gravity, could not have been guessed
    of the fields (the distance gold gathered)

Though hardly could she call this tremor persistent, while
    when sitting quietly no color nor motion intrudes
    upon the inner vestibules.

There have been days painted of such—
A bird made of wood outlined in a tree of identical shade
while the background, lily-pensive.

When the portrait flew away she doubted the color, the grain
    of the bird
and the stillness of the lily as wings traversed its hue.

3.

Lily traverses
where ink is penchant windows reconsider

blue silt of fractional evenings
petals strewn

In a cast of syllables she could not have recognized,
until seeing across one recognizable floor

as threads in the heart of an opal.

Light cunning conducts—so records nothing—returning body
beyond form.

Forgotten the arc of memory reaches only so far as what has
    not yet occurred
Which she holds like a wand of crimson, illustrating diagrams
    in air.

4.

Diagrams of crimson
An echoing glass shell,
A glass dream with wooden breakers
Emerald sight stuttered
A child held in streamers wide

Begins, skeleton repeated from previous bodies.

Disrobes the dream—
A candle encourages
light through various windows to enter.

A basket of light, filled with thought.

5.

A basket of thought is internal
tempting the inner dawn.

Neither this thought, nor the movement entailed by mirror's
        gravity contain solidity.
Both dissolve by approach.

Sitting, the body changes, in this illusion of stillness
the mind is transparent then, as if within water—
which was her hope, to be indistinguishable.

Steps from the known
to encompass another form,
        (swathed in diaphanous clouds)
there is the remnant of a former, less bright form, of less

Fallen from permanent shoulderblades.
        —A mirage lovingly drowns

To approach the former is to engage a solitary sea, a wind
        blown which covets a sail.
She sought the opposite of setting out, to be oneself a catalyst,
        to remember   the irreversible.

Movement within the body which emanates from another
        source—
Her instrument them, a flowering chain.

Laynie Browne

6.

Her instrument then—
recites scattered wave upon stone.

Locates breath, opens lips to intone.

In reference to the body, breath betokens ink, inscribing form
    syllable of permission

When speech yields milk   she breathes
        neither up nor down
                the image dissolves.

Body and name dissolve,
Impearled instrument
Invisible vibration

7.

A name impearled, by permission
        water coverlet

Awakens to light what the body has forgotten
    kindling   forehead—palm.

Removing a darker garment, she covers herself in metrical
    hymns in the manner of exhaling a bird.
In the manner of a tiny brush, red bowers of henna traverse her
    arms

She enters the syllable—

revolving the rays of the sun, buried embers, and counting the
night in measures of water.

8.

Measures of water
rest upon sky, sun rests upon the syllable
sung as it is resting within all elements

Blue of exceeding darkness
reveals a person seen within sun
whose eyes, and lips gold
gold of exceeding eye

The form of the person in the eye is the same as the form of a
  bower of sunlight.

Worlds beneath the self within the eye.

What wish, she asks, shall I obtain for you by my song?

9.

Which song shall I wish for this body, now a continuous child?

Embers which yield

       opal—waters

A wave of thought upon stone, in the manner of exhaling an
  ember

     invisibly hung upon brow

At noon, brilliant, as birds fly without support beyond wings,
  carrying invisible winds to where they are needed.

Two Poems
James Tate

WITCHES

There are all kinds of druids and
witches living in the hills around here.
They don't hurt anybody as far as we know.
But you can always spot them at the grocery
store. First off, they drive these really
broken down old pick-up trucks, often with
hand-made wooden shelters over beds
like they could live in there. And they're
covered in layers of shawls and scarves
and bedecked with long gaudy earrings
and necklaces and bracelets. And always
the long, long hair. They buy huge amounts
of supplies, twenty pounds of cheese, giant
bags of granola, etc. They move quickly
as if afraid of being burned at a stake.
We all know who they are and like having
them amongst us on their secret missions
to decorate their inner Christmas trees
with bedevilled human chickenbones.

NEW BLOOD

A huge lizard was discovered drinking
out of the fountain today. It was not menacing
anyone, it was just very thirsty. A small crowd
gathered and whispered to one another, as though
the lizard would understand them if they spoke
in normal voices. The lizard seemed not even
a little perturbed by their gathering. It drank
and drank, its long forked tongue was like a red
river hypnotizing the people, keeping them in a
trance-like state. "It's like a different town,"
one of them whispered. "Change is good," the
other one whispered back.

Four Poems
Honor Moore

DELINQUENT MUSE

heels dug in, and shoulders
skin I must reach for
can't see eyes
or back to desire
what I can't describe
handsome is
the shoulders
he always stands
so light breaks and I see
hand on his hand
splash of flesh at the sleeve
my arms a necklace
for his shoulders
my arms a laughing necklace
heels dug in and leaning
I see the future
at the shore, ocean, a globe
at his cheek
how do you paint a face?
smudged by rain, his
hand at my back
depict what's vanished, shadows
shoulders
how have you—
where have you—
face, its planes articulate
light but the lips, the lips
glass, then eyes
finally again blue
green, looking back
lashes

shape in darkness
washed with music
day through a window
at last it speaks
red of tanager
rising like land
or laughter where
waiting waiting for music
an ocean there
cliff edge slung down
like night, the sun
through a cloud
how do you paint
a face?
here oh come here
so I can see him
in one hand
only once for the kiss
or can you?
face clear across the room
luxury as my eyes
rest at his hairline
and sweep
down the length of him
gone now, inexplicable
feeling, no I'd call it
pain, paint the lips
one after the other
later I could look and
remember early summer
dark slow to come

at an entrance shoulders   music into night
in the white room his flesh   a way to understand
the color of a rose   what he is
I remember in light   after so much time
the blue glass, he turns   toward me now
swear oh swear the question   and the kiss

THE LAKE

Pale water, mountains almost black, clouds
lifting from the lake—an old dock creaks
at loose moorings, and from the summit, mountains
until the horizon goes blind. What thousand
do you count, walking a narrow bridge
or bending as your canoe glides under it?
This is a language we have written from
always, though it bears its own fate—color
of fern in shade, such a green it must tell
the truth; a thatch of grass points to
then obscures underground water, another
tree dead across the path. Compare a sentence
broken as you talk at a table, a gun
in the pocket of a child, the survivor
alone at her desk. She did not teach this—
high heels, gray suit cinched at her waist, red
lipstick, evident jaw. Tell me, how is it
she comes back now? Nor did she teach this—
to hear only one's own voice in the quiet;
or to think alone, out into the dark
pardon of the night. She had no husband,
her hair curled garishly. I can't get back
her voice, just her mouth gesticulating,
and blond Peter who killed himself in London
after we grew up. In the darkness, silent
numbers etch themselves in red. I remember
the pale disk traversed by hands, figures
marking place along a circumference
that lay in wait once, like the future.
In the city night, a door closes—

159

refrigerator, car, you can't tell which.
What does it mean, she asked us, to be good?
I ask to understand the impulse toward
murder. I ask to be loved. And quiet,
my head between those wide hands, a river
spreads north in autumn light, pale as a lake.
I've seen the beginning of that river,
narrow as a brook, nothing built at its edge.
At the end of the path, a woman turns
to look back, wearing white, holding roses.

HOTEL FLORIDIA

We are at the beach, Susan carrying her bed.
I have no bed and night is approaching, the water is dark.
Nor do I have appropriate clothes.
All morning I dream what I want, the hot right at my collar
    breathing.
I can see you don't understand.
I am scaring you.

The sky is teal, the ocean, color of a razor.
A woman carries a butter yellow umbrella and her daughters
    follow her.

That evening in the city, his hand low on my back, we walked.
When he kissed me on the hotel banquette he said he didn't care.

Ocean the color of a razor
Once when I was a child, a small child, my father swept his long
    black cloak around me
and we climbed the stone stairs.
Already men were singing
the roof struts meeting like fingers or the inside of a woman.

Susan is carrying her bed.
I have no bed. It's colder.

After he held me that way, he wouldn't talk.
I was the one to turn the shiny knob
shut the door behind him
not watching as he pressed for the elevator.

I open the faucet and water breaks from it
turning pale teal as the tub fills.
Hot is on the left.

It was evening. I could hear men singing across the street
the bell in the tower.

I saw my house collapse, and a man came to the door
with two small children.
He opened the gate and we climbed the stone stairs.
It was cold, so he wrapped me in his long wool cloak which was
    heavy and black.

During the last hour of sleep, Susan beckons me to the ocean,
    an ocean
the color of razor blades for which I am not prepared.
She carries a bed, but I have no bed.
Children race from the sand into the water as the dark rises.
We will sleep here.

At morning sun fills the house so you can see every fault
the chip in shiny white paint
but at evening it is the leaves of ficus you see, grainy in the dark,
evening still giving pale light through the white accordion blind.

And so, she said, you come to him quite stripped.
We have been friends for years now, and she has watched me.
She has been with me through all of it,
an ocean the color of razors.

You must have been lonely, he said.
I don't know if I was lonely, I said.

When we got near the avenue we stopped.

All morning you dream what you want, choosing your music.

161

Honor Moore

DARLING

You came to me one long night in two dreams.
It was the day of your funeral, but you were still alive, vividly
making last-minute arrangements, greeting guests.
The room had the gray shadowy light of a place that has no use
    for day
but then it opened to sunlight and the walls turned
cream or peach, and there on a platform was a coffin the color of
    chalk
awaiting you. You seemed to wear green, spring green, long-sleeved,
    green-sleeved
and once in a flash you looked like a woman, as I imagine your
    mother—
dark hair, decisive eyebrows angled in surprise across a narrow brow.

Everyone we knew arrived, and people I didn't know,
a great gay poet, old now and tall, with a bright face, wearing
    glasses, a shawl
handwoven of sienna brown wrapped around his head as if he were
    an Arab woman.
You embraced. It was the first time I had seen one man kiss another
    and call him darling
and I wondered what had brought you to look at each other that way,
to call each other darling here at the edge of death.

Suddenly there is no one in the room, the courtyard
where the coffin is, where the death will take place, no one but you
    and me
All at once, the coffin, which has been floating on water, on water
    faintly blue
begins to disintegrate, to break apart
like something soluble, and you, in your weakness and illness
step into the water, which comes to your thigh, and, with some
    annoyance
almost crying at the effort, try to raise it from the water to keep it
    whole.
I watch, and then I am in the water with you, lifting.

162

I wake from the dream, but in spite of the morning light, I am
    asleep again
and you are there, almost well, turning on the stairs.
As we climb to a large room, I tell you my dream
about the tall gay poet, so old and distinguished in his shawl, who
    embraced you
whom you held and called darling. Oh yes, you say, with a far off
    smile
and take me in your arms, lift me and carry me as I protest. *I don't
    need
to be carried, you are dying, you'll hurt your back.*

You are dressed now, like a servant boy in tattered
linens, as if costumed for a play.

Dear one, I have met a man who touches me so it burns.
I am wearing beautiful pale clothes, and we are standing in a room,
    my hands open as he
feels at the length of me, as he looks seriously into my face, or down
my body, his hand holding the place between my legs, waiting
    there or
questioning, as I burn down into his fingers, my arms
loosening, whoever I am sheared away.

I tell you this even though I'm not sure what you'll say back.
In life you might have shrugged, keeping quiet
all those years of sex, what happened those nights you left after
    dinner
before you got sober, before the disease came that took you and all
    your friends
and with them, a certain languor and handsomeness.
I imagine that in death whatever kept our silence may have broken
that you might now understand what this man's hands force me
    to question
how far desire takes the body before mindfulness leaves it,
what it was for you when a man's touch
burned you open, or burned you back to such blankness and hope
there was nothing you wouldn't do to have him.

From The Tango
Leslie Scalapino

is subjunctive — the man starving lying dying in
garbage? — there not being black dawn — ?
    no. not anyway — that is, anywhere. — or:
subjunctive is *only* 'social.' both.

    then (when alive). — (subjunctive.) — black dawn
isn't? — so it has to pass. both.

_____

    to ignore one's shape/events 'so' it goes on wildly —
and — anyway.
    magnolia buds — that haven't opened —
subjectivity/language *only* — both
    words 'black dawn' as shape (instance that has no
'other' occurrence) which is 'their shape/and their *conceptual*
shape.'
    to subordinate magnolia buds — that is real-time —
both.

_____

    'not' for there to be 'magnolia bud (not-opened)' —

    bud 'dis-placing' is lineage — both. single is 'tree's
buds there' (as *only* one's 'social' — at the same time.

    a given in space — dis-place blossoming trees.

_____

people's behavior being blossoming trees — *per se*
(just as that) — and the action of it (their 'behavior') in the
trees blossoming prior — which is separate, sole

   bound as 'split' (one's) 'to' conception of change as, or
in, behavior —
   that was not when a child
   rather than in blossoming trees — everywhere as
ground is an ocean here

   so 'split' is *that* only — ocean 'in' blossoming trees —
'in fact' has to be to change people's behavior/one's as sole

   in fact — itself — isn't *then.* change in blossoming
trees occurring prior to (trees). (then blossoming trees being
'social' only.)

----

   the moon is socially based as emotion is — so it
would be itself.

   a given in space — dis-place blossoming trees.

   'on' experience — so one's 'isn't,' is obliterated — by
the referring. place this to: seeing 'at all' is social — *is*
blossoming trees

   or when one's outside there (so there's moon *there*) —
as outside is the only existing — both

   'seeing' the man starving lying in garbage — yet to
conceptually place the site only in relation in space (to
foreground and background, or future, simply) — to
buildings — is *not* to iterate those as conditions, present
   his dying is to be *not* in relation to space, or to
conjecture

Leslie Scalapino

it's *not* to be that

'as' 'blossoming trees' are one's subjectivity/language
'there' —

_____

just oneself being roses only

roses only — people in speaking or in their limbs —
being that — to each other also

_____

bound as 'split' (one's) 'to' conception of change as, or
in, behavior —
that was not when a child
so 'split' is *that* only — ocean 'in' blossoming trees —
'in fact' has to be to change people's behavior/one's as sole

_____

crushed back the head sees skittering walks — from
hurtling road, greenery
friends as 'that,' i.e. not existing. are *social. is social.*

— their back cage's move it, is the light-and-
language? both.
but the men moving there didn't speak.

_____

if there
no 'friends' (as *everyone isn't* that) — nothing social —
only being child until dying

delicate back dies sometime. — but these men's backs
move light here only

_____

166

only being child until dying — everyone — is their
delicate back dies sometime
theirs one

— is 'basis' — standing or curling? only

———————

moving is floating ears — elephants — a trunk and
face floating on one's ears
either charging or floating on grass, at once
man's chest: as trunk floating on ears of elephant's —
he's that, coming. ears on 'trunk recoiled or forward.'

———————

some are

standing or curling. rose — is not — rose (they rose).
both.
subjectivity/language is — the delicate food system
disturbed famine reappears — ?
were killed practicing in the monasteries — shipped
to labor, dying, trains shipping them, ringed in by barbed
wire haul on dam sites tunnels exhaustion famine in lines.
the same figure repeated everywhere changes it there as if
changed but not either from within or without that

———————

if the back's constructed — and moves the light — is
subjectivity/language *only* — they're not 'speaking'
that is 'speaking' — social — both

subjectivity/language constructed *also* and those men
move the light — so —
social isn't *anything?* — there — walking — either

———————

167

moon rose — that is — appears to
moon rose
on or resting on mountain's top — edge
horizon —
men's delicate backs standing move — is separate —
from them
there at all — both

---

future — movement
is 'not' night — or
'in' night' — either yet
ahead — so there are not functions ever

---

the men standing and curling while the backs lying.
— in the place.
    social — (is *'getting along with' people* only?) or *one*
"doesn't get along with people" — is functions only
(someone makes that occur — by ostracism —
    one has no function *then*)

---

the man has kindness — *is* standing lying — or at
night curling
where
one holds his back

at *'night'* — ?

---

must 'accept' death of others. — except them. except
him. (can't) is them him *also*.

at *'night' any night* is *can't*

— one's subjectivity/language is their or one's *motion*
only there?

seeing being only a motion even (in walking, say)

one has no back — yet. — not even 'in' 'night' —
not even past movements' 'night' — either — and is
future 'nights'
where(?) no movement of one's occurs — future is
same as one's motions without extension *now*

one's motion ahead — is only one *now* — nights rose

Gravity & Levity
Bin Ramke

Where assassins sleep a wash
of dream breaks against bars

hours of every day are night
a furious freedom a breath

a humid flight return to
serious childhoods—what else is

dream—enactment and revenge
the released terrors swirl

every rapist in sleep renews
his first fond wish to kiss and kill

and is a secret self. Does she make
music from that body? I see she

is bruised she played herself hard
or someone did. She has bled

she has a bandaged body; she is lovely
Does she love me as I slip the dollars in?

The slot above the window
where the faint sound wisps?

No one is sadder. She is bruised
(who is not?) she loved

the world didn't know better
she lived there. A voice

settles, a sheet spun
out over the bed settles

under air, in, through, air, weight
the weight of voice settles

on, into the bed. You are lying
unclothed, perhaps cold

waiting to be wanted
it will talk you into something like

being warm at night. Or the air,
on the air, the breath a kindness floats

the breath is air it floats in air, air
of your air—take and breathe

this is my breath—it takes the shape
of what it settles on, who listens.

Who speaks too soon too often.
The great democracy of flesh—

all are guilty. All sleep.
In German, a language,

the art of heaviness is called *schwerkraft*,
                                    gravity
O heavy the little body hers:

"But from the sleeper falls,   *Doch aus dem Schlafenden fallt,*
as though from a still cloud,   *wie aus lagernder Wolke,*

the opulent rain of the grave," *reichlicher Regen der Schwere.*
Make sense of the world, do not resist

the ready term. Well, welcome the rising
and falling, I was a happy boy who placed

the coins in the ready slots. Eyes. I watched
the dance I felt the rising. The eyes

closed a little O, a heaviness of the lids,
like little caskets closed.

O and again O.
In 1612 John Donne wrote in response

to the blush of a lady, "her body thinks"—
(of Elizabeth Drury, "The Second Anniversary")

A trick how curves of space have
their way with the body the boiling

of the particles defying; delirious
damage accruing

live in landscape a place
where it rains clouds rise

to make home (long for days
of decorum and starlight)

the body thinks and the body's
thought inscribes itself   abrasion

welt   weal   lesion   scar
bruise   freckle   pimple

postule   pride   boil   wart and mole and
malignancy   abscess   wound, O.

*

5. In all things there is a portion of everything
except mind; and there are things in which
there is mind too.

17. The Greeks do not rightly use the terms
"coming into being" and "perishing."
For nothing comes into being nor yet
does anything perish, but there is mixture
and separation of things that are.
So they would do right in calling
the coming into being "mixture,"
and the perishing "separation."

18. For how could hair come from what is not hair?
Or flesh from what is not flesh?
                        — *Anaxagoras*

                        *

The heron resolves itself from the gray lake the water
conversely the woman dissolves in sex, her own

in liquefaction but the flesh reforms like wings
unfolded flight like light drips glistens

the setting sun the horizon first
above now below the bird the evening only local

the spinning earth flings its fluid surface
dissolving itself into itself its ecstasy

the need we feel each for each, the falseness
of any world, at all it is a kind of patience

impossible to distinguish from lassitude
it is a kind of hope indistinguishable

from stupidity. I know (of) a man who killed
himself and the woman he was about to marry

killed herself a month later. He wrote a note:
Until yesterday I had no definite plan to kill myself.

Bin Ramke

I do not understand it myself, but it is not
because of a particular event, nor of an explicit matter.

Every elliptic curve defined over the rational field
is a factor of the Jacobian of a modular function field

was another note he wrote. (I have his picture
on my desk, a gray parallelogram,

a thin man in black jacket black
tie bifurcating a horizon behind him

the line just above his ears this point
of view this lonely life there is only

a kind of barrenness in the background and a sky
which is a world, of course, plenty.)

This is a bigger world than it was once
it expands an explosion it can't help it it has

nothing to do with us with whether we know or
not whether our theories can be proved

whether or not a mathematician
knew a better class of circles

(he has a name, Taniyama, a Conjecture)
than was ever known before before—

not circles, elliptic curves. Not doughnuts.
Not anything that is nearly, only is, such

a world is hard to imagine, harder to live in,
harder still to leave. A little like love, Dear.

Two Poems
Mei-mei Berssenbrugge

NEST

1.

My mother-tongue, Chinese, has an immemorial history before me.

I was inserted into it, a motive for my language.

I learned it naturally, filling it with intentions, and will leave it without intent for other children.

My mother and I speak a local language and sometimes our mother-tongue, as in my dream, with its intent.

What to intend in changing the mother-tongue of my daughter, compassion, not being ill, sleep in which she resonates depth like a bell.

"Loving the wind" is equivalent to intention as rhetorical surface, like writing my diary on her skin.

Non-comprehension tips ambivalent matter, as if there were two of us, here: one is Kuan Yin, one is mother-tongue.

Her matter inserted, a motive, is always somewhere else, exiting one language, another without intent, translated as heart.

2.

I want to tell you what's difficult to admit, that I left home

Change of mother-tongue between us activates an immune system, margin where dwelling and travel are not distinct.

175

Mei-mei Berssenbrugge

The artifacts throw themselves toward light without becoming signification.

Telling you is not an edge of the light; there's no margin of a shadow to imply interior.

In my childhood house was a deep porch covered with vines.

Look past our silhouette to silhouettes, like shadows, of guests arriving in the bright yard.

Light in the next room falls on her as she bends to kiss you.

Skylight pours down, then covers the mud wall like cloth.

I observe the lighted field that seems to hang in space in front of me.

Speaking, not filling in, a surface intent, is like a cabinet of artifacts, comparison coexisting with incongruity.

3.

My origin is a linguistic surface like a decorated wall, no little houses at dusk, yellow lights coming on, physical, mute.

Its significance is received outside hearing, decorating simply by opening the view.

Wherever I look is prior absence, no figure, ruin escaping an aesthetic; hammock, electric fan, ghost don't qualify as guards.

The comfortable interior my guest inhabits is a moving base, states of dwelling that are undetermined, walls cross-hatched like mother-tongue.

A foreign woman occupies a home that's impersonal, like the nest of a parasite.

Its value is contentless, but photographable in the context of an indigenous population, tipping between physical ease and the freedom of animals accumulating risk.

When the scene is complex, I turn to the audience and comment aloud, then return to the room and language at hand, weakened by whoever didn't hear me, as if I don't recognize the room, because my family moved in, while I was away.

As text imbricated with outside, the wall is waves; so I decorate in new mothertongue, plasticity of fragment, cool music.

There's a lock in it, of the surface.

It still lights apricots in bloom, leaves, skins of organisms, horizon, borders which represent places.

4.

A margin can't rot, no bloated outline around memories of witnesses, the way origin in the present is riddled with holes.

Pick one and slip through it, like a girl whose body is changing.

Domestic space oozes light through a loophole, mother to mother, so close I can't catch it through myself it shines through.

My family is vulnerable at the margin, the child, line of a cheek diffusing energy, line of her eye continuing its inner look.

Don't let her ooze through the loophole in space we inhabit like migrants, light drifting across five windows on the river, drifting functioning as imagination so intimate, our space seems anonymous.

Furnishings, colors, situation are sumptuous in relation to anonymity, textiles like money.

5.

I feel the right to have my invitation accepted, an open house.

Guests appear in other places for other occasions with my invitation, pleading for the secular, the empathic.

Mei-mei Berssenbrugge

Speaking, an artifact, creates a loophole for no rapport, no kinship, no education, on a frontier where wild is a margin of style and rhetoric's outside that.

In this case, she'd immigrated long ago, so they tried to stay with her as a family.

Speech opens onto a lost area, then contracts to a diffuse margin between metaphor for space and concept of drunk, ill, running away.

Her story began aesthetically, but hysterical acts withdrew it to a floating space of frustration, unself, and a paranoid husband was produced.

Her words are highhanded, awkward, formal.

He hears them as expressions of personal pique and self-indulgence, but won't say she uses power unfairly in the pose of unhappy mother.

Such topics are prohibited except at the kitchen table, in the car, etc.

It's said, illustrious persons lead parallel lives which join in eternity, but some lives veer off the straight path to community.

So, I speak with care, but prove authority won't take me far, because the area's too large.

In this, daughter, you see more than I did at your age, because you see me.

HEARING

1.

A voice with no one speaking, like the sea, merges with my listening, as if imagining her thinking about me makes me real.

Its matter is attributed to its passing away, a transcendance whose origin had already come apart.

She can't hear me hearing it, sits informally, foot on her knee, circling real with matter, possible form, for which being touched is the condition of composition.

A basis starts uncontrived, stone on a path exerts pressure on a surface, hand rests on a child's head.

She's not speaking words I hear in an undertone.

The loved one's face radiates a secret the lover touches and distributes to all the places of a stone, bruised foot, barrier for insect, stream, dirt occupied by its shadow like a cut ornament, particle where openness turns to energy, to attention.

My hearing touches my limit on all sides, a community exposed.

Hearing: transparency arms and legs arch over, nest for my limbs when I was young.

2.

A bird falls out of the air, through the anti-weave, into the anti-net, delineating anti-immanence.

Twenty-four crows upstate, each fall is a gestural syllable.

Cover them with a blue cloth of creatures ready to be born, contact like starlight that will arrive, for sure.

Let mothers catch them, raccoon, labrador bitch, girl, interspecies conservative mothers, arms out like foliage, general, no locomotion of their own.

Mei-mei Berssenbrugge

Her matter is spacing in the present when I come along or go away.

It's experienced as vague, average understanding, but inaccessible.

That's how a loved girl away is not divided, like virtuous deeds accomplished quietly; she's the other of myself hearing that's simultaneous, no relay toward her.

I buy clothes.

Each sequin is an unapplied form of universal, copresence before there was space, internal line of time into hearing, which doesn't arrive from the meaning of words, like starlight arriving.

She holds a span of real time over this sense of being touched that's continuous with the copresence of dresses.

3.

Plum blossoms in snow give way to fragile cherry blossoms, blowing mist on water in the foreground to lighted clouds on the horizon.

It's responsive, not perspective.

The plane tips up and completes our world with transparency, synapse between birdcall and hearing it, pink and shade facets of small waves, butterfly on tongue.

Hearing, then meaning, is an arch of slender arms where I visualize myself the way she thinks about me, energy latent in her mind, openness under the hand on my head.

The light is not real like a collected object, but its direct, concrete application warms real things, concreteness as a luminescent skin of being herself, subject, wife, envelope of human limits of things.

The potlatch settles around me in a house, designating an exterior that's toward you, not endowing stone with interior.

That depends on deep matter for which a woman opts for deep acting, suppressing irritation at demands of family members by inventing reasons to sympathize with those boors, to feel sincere though alienated from her bodily expression, screen simulation.

Light goes through it to the plane of the sea, of mother-tongue.

In nothing in the beautiful room could I recognize myself.

A nontransparent self is needed, an aesthetics of documentation where images have power, because the drama is real.

They withdraw from matter to representation which gives more agency, point of presence, bird falling along a stitched in and out of my hearing it call and its ceasing to exist.

4.

I found I could take words from one discipline and intersect them with another, such as generous feeling with listening to supplicants.

Empty space intersects with the dignity of stars, of homelessness, health ruined by addiction, to help supplicants.

Trying to be part of the neighborhood, school activism, etc., with serene demeanor of an object not caught in form of fairy or butterfly, wing of an alternation of calmly breathing, alternating with the physical situation, someone ill, someone tortured.

Hearing is the fractality of fragments occurring (that are disintegrating).

Immanence is outside that as absence of the totality of fragments.

Everything shimmers in autumn light.

Her body (translucence, colored leaves) is a surface you try to make transparent, uninscribed, unlined by good deeds, abstaining from lineage.

Mei-mei Berssenbrugge

Join lineation and surface of her body by voice and hearing, small animals, fragments swept away, lost colors of refractions inside cells, feathers, albino, crepe de chine.

Hearing as good annuls being toward another.

It gathers good aesthetically into relationship like a figure, her body as you remember it, as in a family, space behind each person.

During her last weeks, Madame Lucie reached the end of memory.

Present and future prospects shed perspective, so birds flying away remained the same size, although her gaze in memory on beloved children retained the physical latency of hearing them.

Reading Red
Charles Bernstein

1.

<u>Reading Red</u>

only event

over & under

fuses

green with

(no idea

2.

<u>Road Show</u>

Face on face
hides (divides)
not what's inside
but what's

3.

<u>Four Foot Six</u>

Dear Blue,
Dear Orange,

knock me for obtuse
rending (rendering)
layers of treats,

rips

4.

5.

Dear/Duel

Delirium would stand for
what's next to
the girls next door

the boy who falls

⊕

beside oneself in a sane way

6.

There is no level
In the middle ground

7.

Double & Out

Remove the ground
triple the crack
you still won't get
the middle back
the pains are yellow
& speak like facts
flush then drained
absorption's knack

8.

Side by Side

The shadow falls
& the object appears in
the space between

(don't ever leave)

9.

Blue Blue (Off the Mark)

I'd like to talk to you about the mistakes
We just can't handle

laminating (lamentation)

warp us as
humility changes

We don't have to

10.

Where the fold should be

There is no fold

11.

No Man's Land (Call and Response)

now that I'm
old as I am
the more I appreciate
that moment of
human life
I must
have lived

through but
didn't experience
at the time

you can't paint
what you can't feel

12.

Broken Token

Hush

slips sealed

13.

Dear. Here

if a tree could
talk you would
not understand
its bark only its
bite

14.

Loopy

a
pine
is
a
curve
that
isn't
deterred

15.

color is not about the object
but a part of the human being

not inside but outside
not outside but inside

16.

<u>Key Lime Hide</u>

It's about playing a game
the way a lamp shines out at
    flight
but the subject is still
overlay & under-
cover, in which
the line pertains
to neither
either, ether

17.

White along edge
Bark of tree
As if blue becomes a
lighter color
Holds
As you make your bed then
lie in it
Ground father to
Figuration

18.

<u>The Knees Have It</u>

I had a double meter
I gave my father half
He put it in his pocket
Then threw it in the trash

Now since that time I've lost a dime
I've even broke a flute
But all I want's that half a rime
To bleat the denting out

19.

<u>Duophone</u>

East is hung & south
is its
torn motion
   belongs to Caesar
 neither, or

   north's west passagelessness

20.

<u>This Side Up</u>

flues cross
memory's encyclopedic
permutations—
transparent, succumb

"the body,
the

21.

<u>Zone</u>

no circle
no shape
coming out of my mouth

"the sun is but a morning star"

22.

<u>Don't Touch</u>

Shadow cast on black
mocks line

cleave, dart, splinter

23.

Can't hold what resists
enclosure—
a village of
malcontents
Dear or Don't
Agents of

24.

<u>Against Itself</u>

like a cut in skin
or the bleating of edges
into the frost

the paintbrush is the forest of society

25.

<u>strongest attempt</u>

the work could make
to destroy itself

A Dialogue
Mei-mei Berssenbrugge and Charles Bernstein

WE BECAME ACQUAINTED during many vivid poetry events hosted by Segue Foundation at James Sherry's loft in the seventies. Over the next twenty-five years, our dialogue evolved into a friendship that included our work, our children, the art of our spouses, Susan Bee and Richard Tuttle. We decided to focus this interview, which took place in July, on the poems published in Conjunctions:35 *and on recent work.*

CHARLES BERNSTEIN: In front of me, or perhaps in my mind's ear, I have two of your books, *Four Year Old Girl* and *Endocrinology*, and your new poem, "Hearing." I have been thinking about the way your work envelops me in its own world of extended sound waves, carrying me along as I read and then lapping back for another line. It's not mesmerizing exactly but there is a strong tidal pull. You seem to have turned Clark Coolidge's notion of "sound as thought" into sound as perception and then again thought as perception. Anyway, these are among the themes of the new poem. Hearing not as the physical listening to the words—you write of the "physical latency of hearing" late in the poem—but as a form of response. The difference between hearing and listening that I'm getting at is suggested, for example, when one says—*you hear what I say but you don't listen:* listening is, in a word you use in "Hearing," "reciprocal." Your work seems to feed that reciprocity back into the loop: "hearing me hearing it" as you write. (I think this is what Charles Altieri is picking up when he writes about your work in terms of "intimacy.") "Hearing" begins with "A voice with no one speaking likes the sea," echoing the opening lines of Stevens's "Ideas of Order at Key West": "She sang beyond the genius of the sea/ The water never formed to mind or voice." However, where your voice "merges with my listening," for Stevens "The song and the water were not medleyed sound/ . . . it was she and not the sea we heard." These are not the same "she"s—and that is one thing I wanted to ask you about.

Also you seem to show not a medleyed sound but something I would say is merged (or refracted, another of your words) by means of the poem's extended duration, getting back to your prolonged overlapping sound waves. The "real" of which you speak is transactional and temporal, a flickering pulse that we hear only when we listen. I'm curious about some lines at the end of the third section, where you write "they withdraw from matter to representation which gives more agency." It seems to me the matter of your poems is very much this "shimmering" "translucence" of listening, where it's not that "the images have power, because the drama is real" but, rather, where the real is the reel not the image. Who is she?

MEI-MEI BERSSENBRUGGE: Your question resonates, like hearing. I hesitate to respond, because the question is whole. I think of the physical latency of hearing as a form of response. Hearing is encompassing and receptive, while listening, which I didn't really address, would be a more focused, directed perception.

"She" specifically is Kuan Yin as muse. She is "the hearer of all cries" in Chinese. She also represents compassion. I think of the cry as poetry, and also the image, the representation you mention. I'm trying to encompass my conflicting worlds of poet and caregiver. The value of poetry, the value of compassion. Hearing the hearer is intimate. Sound in waves, as plastic, is how I think of time, which is intimate. Whether this compassion is intimate or generic is not resolved, here. There's a net of emotion, not so specific, compassion for the person and the world. Inspired by a white porcelain Kuan Yin I love and another I grew up with.

I know your poem *Reading Red* was written in collaboration with a series of relief sculptures by Richard Tuttle. Richard described them as consisting of two layers of painted particle board in which the shadow of the overlay ("at the exact height of 54 inches, which represents the self") implies a linguistic element. He told me he hoped you would complete or "give" this linguistic implication. The resulting collaboration takes the form of a gorgeous book published by Walter König. I find these poems full, evocative and mobile in dialogue with the visual. I was in Germany when the poems were presented. Their achievement of making a whole with the sculptures and at the same time remaining so open was thrilling to the audience, even in translation. Would you like to talk about these poems? I see a lyric directness in them. Is that a particular response to Richard's works? Do you have any thoughts about qualities of

191

abstraction as it crosses and recrosses between the visual and verbal?

BERNSTEIN: Richard's series, "New Mexico - New York" was shown at the Sperone Westwater Gallery in 1998. I was immediately attracted to these works and felt they were, in some not completely abstract sense, saying things. But what were they saying? There was the recurring image of an envelope in many of the works, created by the overlay of one piece of wood on another, the superstrate being generally smaller and more tapered than the substrate. So my thought was: if they were envelopes, what text might they contain? Maybe they would tell their own story, one of a gap or bump (indeed, at "four foot six") where one piece of material is plied onto another, or of the shadow you mention that always falls over that crack, or of the conversation or tension between the two parts that made the whole. Of the painted surfaces that used color and line to articulate a multiplicity of possible relations and evocations of this basic circumstance.

Richard liked the idea of my writing a set of poems for the paintings, sharing with me a sense that the collaboration needn't be static. Often poems about paintings have the poet musing on the image before her or his eyes. The channel separation between the verbal and visual is foundational for many poems about pictures (as it is for pictures that illustrate already existing poems). While I remain interested in such separation, the idea here was different—for the poems to enter the reliefs. Richard and I made a time to return to the gallery and we had an extended conversation about each of the paintings, in which I took notes on much of what Richard said and wrote the poems, for the most part, using bits and pieces of the conversation, often taking just a word or phrase from Richard or myself, and scribbling out some ideas, which I then read to Richard as we continued through the series. We both had some sense of the poems as they were unfolding, and our conversation folded into that, as if the poems were a superstrate laid on top of, or framing, the stream of our conversation. In other words, we gave voice to the paintings by a kind of dialogic ventriloquism.

After the poems were finished, some weeks later, Richard designed the book in a totally inventive manner, extending the phantasmagoric adventure of his many other great book works. The works are displayed, four to a side, on three large fold-out circles and the poems are printed on top of the images, becoming a part of the works rather than a commentary on them. After a time, the publisher wanted us to produce a special edition of the book. To go against the grain of such editions, we decided that we should "deface" forty of the trade copies and at the same time reverse the direction of the collaboration. So we sat down at my dining room table with a stack of books, a scissors and a pencil. I quickly wrote variations on each of the poems in *Reading Red* (and then around again to forty) and read them to Richard, who responded by cutting and folding the blank endpaper at the beginning of the book, after which I wrote in the new poem, placing it in relation to Richard's page sculptures.

One virtue of this second collaboration was that I didn't get a chance to look back, to edit, to rework. I know much of your own work is based on all three of those processes. Can you talk about your process of finishing a poem? It's an old-time question, surely. I know you often hold onto a poem for a while, making slight changes. Now I suspect it's not some set idea of completion or even closure that you are looking for, or not one that is external to the process of writing, which you could apply to the poem like finish to a cabinet. What are you looking for? What makes the poem the poem you want?

BERSSENBRUGGE: I know your suspicions about closure inhibiting process. For me, finishing a poem is more a physical struggle for focus. A lot of my method compensates for my natural awkwardness. So, my first draft is a well-researched but very scattered approximation, often using other people's words, and tends to be written below my understanding. "Finishing" is an arduous process of trying to uncover what I meant and for it to be in poetry. What I meant comes into focus slowly over a long time. Criteria for "finish" are: a feeling of moving along, words smooth in saying, a feeling of something said emotionally, and a physical satisfaction with one word next to the other. The poem tends to be about a quarter as long as the first draft. I publish when the deadline comes, working to the last minute. And then refine the poem at intervals for a long time after.

A "finished" poem becomes something like an artifact, something independent with its own dynamic. It resists change. I'm trying to discern now if there is any significant difference between being finished and being "good enough," which is more contemporary. The problem is, so much is unconscious.

How do you finish a poem? Do my concerns with "saying something," with balance, interior, contrast with your feelings for instability, openness, etc. You say so beautifully in *My Way:* "I open the door and its shuts after me . . . I am moving not toward some uninhabited space but deeper into a maelstrom of criss-crossing inscriptions. The open is a vanishing point . . ."

BERNSTEIN: I like the distinction Stein makes between "completed" and "complete" (thinking of "A Completed Portrait of Picasso"). As a practical matter, I agree with your sense that the poem is finished when I don't need to make any more changes; the poem passes into some other state that in some ways is closed to me. Then it's time to do something else. Still, figuring out when that time has come— that remains a good part hunch. You're right to suggest that the contrast between balance and instability, interiority and openness, prosodically motivates many of my poems. Although I would have to say that I am often the last to find out what I am saying and even then I am not certain (just as when you are in the midst of something you may not know where you are even if you know you're there). Writing is often the most active part of my life. I can do things in writing I can't do anywhere else, things that won't work anywhere else (if, indeed, they can be said to work in my writing!). I like to say things like—it seems most right when the writing goes wrong, when there is a breakdown or an infelicitous turning of phrase. I am in fact alarmingly fussy about what infelicity is interesting and few, in the end, are. So it's a matter of searching and searching—you know how when the hard drive on your computer starts to whirl around as though looking for something and the screen freezes up until the whirring stops. I can relate to that. Often the people who surround me in everyday life (I won't mention any names) are shouting and gesticulating wildly to get my attention as I seem momentarily unconscious, or maybe just subconscious, which is closer by. Then the next day I read over what I thought was OK and it all looks bad, I shake my head, that awful discouragement that makes this kind of work unfathomable to those on the fabled "outside," e.g., why put yourself through that? This is what I was getting at: for the most part I have no idea where my writing has come from. In retrospect, the heart of it seems to have produced itself. It was being in the right place and the right time and having a pen handy. Or knowing when to start writing something down, being open to recognize what occurs to me. "Be ready but not prepared" as Dominique Fourcade puts it. And in that sense, when I am reworking something, I am basically just continuing to write, adding layers more than finishing.

Mei-mei Berssenbrugge and Charles Bernstein

Keeping myself active. Until it's not complete but completed.

BERSSENBRUGGE: I find your everyday environment of persons shouting and gesticulating wildly extremely stimulating.

In the poem "Hearing," I'm thinking about hearing as an ideal, like an ideal form. Now I'm interested in the audience as an ideal form of hearing, which is novel, because I never considered the audience before. "What the audience likes" is a mantra I've been saying to myself with curiosity. And this goes to entertainment, listening, etc., comedy, which I know you like. For me, being heard was existing. That's why I became a poet. Do you have anything to say about the audience? The practice of audience, as transcendence or as attention, or commerce?

BERNSTEIN: I've never met an audience I didn't like. At least not until tonight. *Mister, could you at least turn off your phone during the diminuendo?* That's right you over there, with paisley hip huggers. Jeeze, you folks couldn't tell the difference between an amphibrach and the little green knickers I bought from Jimminy Cricket at the Atheneum. . . .

Which is to say . . . the idea of audience can be a foil that can be looped back into the poem, poem talking back, as if the imagined reader isn't silent. It's curious how an audience at a reading affects the performance; any performer experiences this, though in different ways. For me, it's probably most fun to read to an audience familiar with the work, which responds vocally and viscerally to the poems, so that the response creates a kinetic action that goads the performance onward. Yet there is another kind of reading, often at universities, where everyone is absolutely quiet, if no less attentive, and that situation seems to make me work harder at articulating the overall shape of the poem and maybe lets the poem be heard more on its own, since less interrupted (by laughter, for example). Because the frame of poetry readings is "serious" you get a suppressing of laughter, even at the most verbally slapstick material, which possibly brings out the uncanniness that roams at large in the poems, where the comic is always close to its double or doubling back on itself. The effect of an audience not laughing as a man laboriously slips on a linguistic banana is near perfect.

I think you had in mind the abstract idea of an audience as well. As time goes on, what's most meaningful to me is the particular responses of an individual. I never believed in a one-size-fits-all poetry and it's of most immediate interest to me what resonates with someone in particular. It's the sense of "getting it." That a few people do may just convince me that the limb I've most recently climbed out on is breaking in style.

How about you? Your own performances are remarkably enveloping—and you are a reader one really has to listen in for, you aver voice projection and therefore good electronic amplification is a fundamental part of the process. So who do you think is the audience for poetry—or for your poetry?

BERSSENBRUGGE: I like your idea that the double of a poem comes out when the audience is suppressed. It's true my idea of audience is more abstract. Up to now it has been about a hearer to verify me, that the hearers are hearing me, which goes along with a low voice. Then I started thinking about the natural wisdom of the audience, and the value of entertainment. It correlates to what I was saying about caregiving, "taking care" of the audience—letting things slip in, realizing that they're short on time, etc. Now in the middle of this dialogue, I've finished a poem about audience. It turns out in my poem, it's of no consequence whether I am heard, whether you hear your audience or they hear you. What goes on is some innate dynamic, a mirror or "doubling," some kinetic that works. Which may be why the internet seems so adequate, because of the movement.

I'd like to point out the unusualness of our speaking like this, who are friends but so disparate in history. I recall a dinner at your house after which your daughter Emma was crying in the next room, because the mother in the movie she was watching on TV died. Both you and her mother Susan Bee called out, "Stop crying, Emma!" which I understood as advice to her not to be so easily manipulated by media. This made an impression on me, because I'm one of the audience who cries at any sad story, loss, any emotional dynamic whatsoever, TV, commercials. When I look at my earlier work, this emotionality seems highly uncool. All the time I'd been striving to make a continuum of mental actions, thought and emotion, thought and perception, thought and physicality, even with autonomic physicality. For balance. You seem always to have been articulate, highly aware, evolved in world view, in balance with your persona, and effective in the world, with the audience. Which is a world audience, as well as the one-on-one you speak of. First, how do you reconcile your savoir-faire, clarity and ethos with your statement in *My Way:* "For my themes, to call them that have consistently been awkwardness, loss, and misrecognition." Is this solely a political "awkwardness" of position, which you have maximized into a life's work, or are you speaking of other arenas also?

Second, a question I alluded to earlier, concerns my experiences at some recent poetry readings. Your moving reading of "Rivulets of the Dead Jew" for Kathy Acker, who had just died, the Walter Benjamin libretto and "Reading Red." I find a powerful and unequivocal emotional weight in this poetry and in many poems in *Residual Rubbernecking* (in *Republics of Reality*), which differs from earlier wit and versatility. Do you have anything to say about this? Is this connected to your interest in and exploration of performance, the emotional forum of audience?

BERNSTEIN: Isn't one of the interesting possibilities for poetry that it can bring apparently disparate things together—with necessity? Some people seem to think that the point of that is to flag the disjuncture; but when it really gets interesting it's quite the opposite, it shows the exceptional necessity of the unexpectable.

I think it's fine to cry during commercials, just as long as you don't brake for animals too. Or brake for animals, just don't break my heartache.

I wish I had a dime for every time someone said I wish I had a dime for every time . . .

I guess I'm saying I like "uncool" better than cool. I think I've tried to make "uncool" cool—and maybe that's what you're getting at. Uncool of the sort I always harp on (as in Harpo not harpy) is emotional. There's a loony perception that complexity of form rules out the emotional or that indirectness isn't emotional. As if the only way to signify as emotional is to declare it. Maybe complexity of register is motivated, in part, by ambivalent emotional dynamics. I prefer pathos and even bathos to the "emotions of normal people." If I'm haunted by pent-up feelings of being misheard or misjudged or misaligned, it's not that I necessarily feel those things more than anyone else, but rather that I am more interested in them than most people, who spend their lives overlooking what I go alooking for. I'm a poet of anxiety rather than depression, of the private and inexplicit rather than the sunny and declamatory.

I don't like to be told to feel something but to be allowed to experience a feeling without naming it, without wanting to name it.

Anyway, the thing about commercials is that they make no bones about what they are selling and that they are so abstracted and condensed. I'd rather watch a sentimental commercial (remember the one for Hoffman's soda? or those "phone home" ads for long distance?) than read most dyed-in-the-workshop emotionally "bare" poems or watch emotionally hyperventilated confessional TV. In other words, for afternoon fare I prefer soap opera to Oprah, which I say as much for the off-rime as anything else. And speaking of opera, I am totally enthralled by Puccini and Verdi, though I don't find it more emotional than the explosively self-contained polyrhythms of João Gilberto or the exquisite acoustic textures of Morton Feldman.

I find emotion in your work is achieved through indirection; it's introjective, concave; thus: *intimacy*. It takes you inside it. Offers sanctuary, not facts. (And that is particularly marked, to come back to this, in the acoustic interiority of your performances.)

It's a very sonically enveloping poetry, which leads me to ask you about your collaborations with Kiki Smith on *Endocrinology* and other projects. What's the valence of the visual in those works?

BERSSENBRUGGE: I like to think of this necessity between us in poetry.

I'm a person who strives for directness, but I have difficulty actually naming things and am uncomfortable with expository writing. I was trained in poetry that achieved emotion through images, and I've loved images, although not lately. I try to make language into a net for my meaning which tends to be emotion in continuum with some perceptual or conceptual slant. Net, grid, sieve, appear often. My voice is given to me. I try to use it without strain. My only conscious intention with voice is to deliver the words. With words I consciously make the net. Lately I've been trying a new sound, so as not to get in the habit of a sound that *sounds* intimate. Agnes Martin once said, "I have everything I ever wanted and still when I wake up, I feel depressed. That proves emotions are abstract." I'm experimenting with emotion that doesn't sound emotional.

My intial hope with *Endocrinology,* was to learn from Kiki how to express emotion as a direct narrative. She was working with the body, tears, milk, blood flow, dead loved ones. When asked to describe our process, Kiki said, "It was great. Mei-mei asked me questions and I cried." Text and visuals were generated by our conversations. It was also part of a long-term exploration I started with Richard, to try and align the visual and verbal mental planes, a separation you referred to as channel separation. Kiki and I treated visual and verbal as a continuum of material, and the valence was the energy of our interaction, for which her visual power was a marvelous given. The resulting book is like a body—transparent, layered with blue organs and ligaments of text. This dialogue continues; for example, she coincidentally bought her first statue of Kuan Yin on the same day I bought mine.

For me, the visual, in landscape and art, has always been a vital and liberating location from which to work in language.

*

I find the poems in *Residual Rubbernecking* beautiful, full of pathos and extremely elegant. To me, they represent a connection with early work, and also a flowering. I want to ask what you want to write next in poetry. Also, what you imagine would be the best poem you could read, that's just been written?

I'm curious about the source of this elegance. It's not a style elegance. I feel it's something internally generated by the kind of language you need, as well as your literary sources. Is that accurate? I know you also have a great deal of experience in philosophy and the visual arts.

BERNSTEIN: Whatever elegance there may be in my work is implausible, not unlike the charm of a top as it wends its way to a warble. Over time, a wobble may become song. Elegance is part delusion, part self-composed, part glass. This is the aspiration I have for poetry, an activity that achieves nothing by conventional measure. The aversion of efficacy is the most elusive necessity of poetry, just that it's easy to lose faith in so refractory a medium. It's not that failure is becoming but that loss is acknowledged without bluster, played out on the fields of the untenable. The poem begins in doubt and ends in something that transforms doubt into a fricative certainty. I keep returning to Jobim's song "Desafinado" ("Offkey"). This isn't syncopation or stressing the offbeat. The acoustic pattern is out of tune; the offnote sounds off. Thelonious Monk knows that score.

A lot of this has to do with nonstandard language, second language speakers. Give me solecisms or else death by asphyxiation. I don't know any other language than English (know in the Biblical sense). And yet, doesn't Jabès almost say?, the poet is only at home when she or he makes their own language foreign, the better to converse with it. All of which is my way of asking you about "Nest," about the echo of Chinese ("mothertongue") as it enters the resolute "American" homestead of your imagination. "But some lives [it could just as well be *lines*] veer off the straight path to community."

Mei-mei Berssenbrugge and Charles Bernstein

That's always the hope for American poetry, dangling in front of us, until we realize our ceiling really is made of glass but if you stoop down low enough so you don't bang your head, why you can see way on up to big top, which is painted with stars (or is it stairs? or stares?).

In "Nest," Chinese and Kuan Yin are both female presences and, as you've said, Kuan Yin is the "she" of "Hearing"; also, "Nest" is, finally, addressed to Martha, the no-longer "four year old girl," your daughter. "Nest" invokes a matrilineal inheritance of language and/ as compassion, something the last line suggests you had to find for yourself. What can you say about the gender narratives in these poems?

BERSSENBRUGGE: We have symmetry, since I seek elegance and efficacy, any balance, any firm ground in poetry. I imagine an ideal that is, the bird opens its mouth and sings. I suppose that would be innate communicativeness of the species. (Is it the evolutionary equivalent of your wobble?) I'm not committed to loss as an ethos. I'm very interested in comedy in your poems as a place of loss. Your comedy appears to me as sudden convexity, opaque areas. I don't correlate elegance and convention. Perhaps your statement is your fricative, refractory route to a "characteristic" elegance of form and diction?

Being born into Chinese, then changing my language very young, gave me an experience of relativity that led me to poetry, which I often think of as systems of relations or proportions, like math, trying to make an equivalent world. One tries to recreate a starting point, but that is not a whole world, so one is potential. It's loss, but I don't want to be committed to it.

It's hard to separate my idea of myself as feminine and feminist with what's expressed in these two poems. (Even though Martha, a fourth-generation feminist, has given me a substance of girl, the "Four Year Old Girl" is myself.) In "Nest" I was reading the writings of women from poor countries, and I tried to write about homelessness (no home, loss of your home language) as powerlessness. I suppose I also ask again if women's giving necessitates the loss of power. If being able to "see" your mother (home, mother-tongue) gives enough/more power. These issues are complex, because I came to English from the empowered position of having an educated Chinese mother and an American father.

"Hearing" moves to the wider arena of compassion, transcendent and particular giving expressed by hearing, as a source of power. There's a synapse between hearing a cry and understanding its

200

meaning, a synapse where all fragments occur. This is explicitly a feminine, if not feminist, power.

BERNSTEIN: If the criteria for elegance are refinement, tastefulness, clarity, grace, then it is bound to a range of socially inflected values regarding gender, class and ethnicity, among other things, which are reflected in poetic diction. Who gets to be elegant? Perhaps what we are talking about is the aesthetic, which, in a poetics of invention, is often disruptive of received models of clarity and refinement. In my own experience, much that is regarded as tasteful in poetry is rather insipid: it's not that I object to the aestheticism but find the work not aesthetic enough. In the American context, an excess of aestheticism in a male poet may be negatively regarded as effeminate or patrician or both, while for women poets "of sensibility" (to use Jerome Mc-Gann's term, which also has a relation to the emotionalism we have been talking about), aestheticism has often been the justification for dismissal as decorative or minor. Aesthetics is always implicated in politics and vice versa. Any shortcut to aesthetic correctness is treacherous because aesthetics is not something to overcome but to acknowledge. Now this gets me to one last question I wanted to ask you—about the use of the language of information and science in your poems, since such language is commonly seen as "unpoetic" (despite a number of influential precedents in the history of modern poetry).

BERSSENBRUGGE: I persist in complimenting these poems as elegant "enough," if I think of elegance as grace or pleasure of parts to a whole and to intention. I first used scientific concepts, because it seemed interesting to try and feminize scientific language by altering its context and tone. This was in the late '70s. Later, I appropriated texts from philosophy, Buddhism and contemporary art as well. A self encompassing or embodying what it interacts with was more articulate than trying to speak for myself. This is the literal situation of our bodies which are porous and continuous with the world. Tom White told me, after a few days in the Sierras one's internal flora has more in common with the surrounding pine trees than with people back in Berkeley. I feel that my unconscious has more freedom choosing from language that isn't personal. I prefer to move and change words that are in the world, rather than in myself. I like plasticity. I like texts of "information" as a counterweight to personal experience, which is so dynamic.

Five Poems
Rosmarie Waldrop

MALLARMÉ AS PHILOLOGIST, DYING

Even the purest writer is not entirely in his work, we must admit. A saturated white tilts off the page, a richochet of sense like children heard, not understood. You see the gap between chance breath and the continuous line of the horizon, method to infinite power or out one candle. Anatole *aboli. Bibelot* Anatole. Walks down the stairs, one by one, to the bottom of the mirror. It is the lack of self splits his ear. A labyrinth like a sentence. Always, word follows word, to stave off those little deaths. Is he alive?

When he leaves the room, he recaptures a memory called meaning. A matrix where a word is carried by a foreign language. Say "th." Say the whole word: "death." The *Box for Learning English by Yourself and Playing* is broken, the string to push the puppet's tongue between his teeth. "Debt" is not comparable, not part of the body. Throw the dice, throw. Again. If often enough, only everything. Between the teeth.

To track your dream, enter by way of the corridor and comparative grammar. The dream is called work. The corridor leads to Hebrew, which shows how to replace lacking inflection by ideal nakedness. The corridor passes time, so that the girl is cold. When you caress her name, somber and red like an open pomegranate, you slowly descend toward. Stop. The dream insists that meaning, memory and music are the same. Out of its own lack, it fashions a flesh of vowels, and of consonants a skeleton delicate to dissect. What is a faun to do?

A simple laryngitis. Does not abolish breath. A lacking word, a thought that terrible would vibrate suffocating like an open spasm splits his ear terrible his throat. Genevieve, virgin spasm, vivacious, and beautiful today suffocating. A fan of lacking experiences. For Mademoiselle Mallarmé. It is hot. Wants a book on anatomy, it cannot be too simple: he might place the larynx in the brain. Again. His breath stops, and we are all speechless.

THE THREAD OF THE SENTENCE

Etymology is one of the choices. The other, wearing your heart on your sleeveless. Cross my.

Even the straightest road conceals detours and forks. Thirst. For physical presence in tight succession. All week I concentrated on the hopeless accuracy of anxiety.

A line made to incorporate circumference. What the snow falls on. The very deep of a labyrinth, its poorly lit fortnights, its views without domain so like destiny.

Her beauty was called foreign. In relation to terms whose absence is felt. The foreign in one single thrust, absence felt elsewhere. Is self?

Not snow, but its blue shadow. Exchange of rather and disintegrating not made complex by the transfer of money. Thirst eddies.

Time is the invention of past snow. The thread I walk like a tightrope. The maze in the shape of a straight line.

Given to conclusions, I admire awkwardness in love. Open my clothes. To what stands outside my tongue.

The labyrinth is a ruse. Already passing into something else. The thread, swing, syncope life hangs by. My already share of nothing.

Rosmarie Waldrop

NORMAL DISTURBANCES

To understand the body as water. Reflecting elsewheres of light. Above, increase of waves.

No need has the language to become the law it would be. Whereas streetcars travel in straight lines. To demonstrate perspective. To extend their grooves into your body. Runs, along the lines, the pale blue lightning. Speechless, the self is now directed.

Inevitably. Projecting parts onto the outer world. Café tables. At angles. Yet development must develop out loud. Else a condition for already gone by. Here love, Renaissance architecture and increased anxiety.

Here too the gift of excrement. Excessive subservience mapped on a grid.

The laws of perspective both libidinal and aggressive. Won't forgive you the impulse to flight.

Holes in the fabric. Medieval congestion breaks into sunlit piazzas. Ego in bits. Thus, a feeling of disintegration.

Against transitory experiences, gratification opening outward, and foreign bodies embedded in the self. Inasmuch as. The resilience of the infantile mind. Opens and closes in confusion.

I understand. You are waiting for a flourish of rhetoric, an Italian tenor. But I am drowning. There are other examples. Let's summarize your fears, objections to, and side issues of, plain thinking.

Guilt always rises to the surface. After puritanically straight streets you yourself must walk in straits and narrows. Speak slowly and distinctly. Not to mention: stop for breath.

STEPS IN INTEGRATION

Anxiety arises, she says. To signals of the clock. To cut down the forest for the trees. To to. Compulsive ties found embedded.

White, hard piece of chalk. So that the letters resemble hunger. Subtract underwater from fear of parting.

In early childhood, atoms cannot be seen. Not mechanically inter-locked. Not in collision. On billboards. Then impulse seems to attach itself, and time so short.

In a run-down neighborhood, the jazz players. The water moves around the trout. No color separation.

Is the ego capable of splitting the object? The atom? Hairs? The clock in winter, extreme context. The forest cut down.

Faced with unpleasant stimuli the organism reacts by fragmentation, considered as a weapon. Letters written in a rage. And space between limbs.

The atomists found the liquid state hard to explain, but the trout stirs under water. A raw world, she says. Out of raw world into commercial zone. And time so short.

The sound of many atoms. The color of drums. The solace of phantasy.

Condition of flight: First plant your right foot and then your left. On noun? Or adjective? Folded in, the flush of omnipotence.

Rosmarie Waldrop

SCHIZOID DEFENSES

Surrounded on three sides by foreign idiom. On the fourth, fear of overtones. To locate myself where speaking breaks and scatters I tack as many boundaries in memory. Amorphous followed by winter.

Friends unreliable if handsome. Thing else. If we listen intently without understanding we hear white. New snow falls. On this old noise, thickly. Severed, like a lost meaning, from my own tongue, I know nothing of myself.

Mismatched body equates horizon and hollow. How to open and enter, so warm the blankets. Unfinished weather seen through glass. I have my thoughts and see them drift across the snow too. The body suddenly heavier. Suddenly afraid of falling out the window.

Certain consonants coat the atmosphere. Phonemes out of a beautiful face, as a stubble of grass breaks through the snow. And reverts at once to: no landscape, no subtitles. Farther west, whole fields of indifference.

I speak as if on snow shoes, wide berths so as not to sink. Home speech, too, suddenly foreign. As if it were always another who speaks. As if I were both first and third person.

Two Poems
Martine Bellen

FOUNDATION MANDALA
— for Claire

Of Sapphire. Systematically construed
off a square; offering
deities a balcony on which to dance

How does one illuminate the atmosphere?

Sheath of candles
Irrigate the four winds

Ganesha round back repairs walls
while the girl maps elements of philosophy
and posthumously eavesdrops on grandmother
whose files, over six feet thick,
contain wisdom applicable to Vermeer, birds, fabula,
penny arcades and the chance encounter
of a sirocco and softened laughter.

The girl disguising herself as an old spider
in a 13th century limnal magic lantern
exacts impulses from light and pearls of moisture
which accumulate on complex webbing
as Picasso eats cats,
woos & plays the flute.

Martine Bellen

> *This boundless structure binding structure,*
> *city of flesh and bones*

Hear white wheat
where mind drops, a vibrant precipice

Indra inspects the floors of the building,
consults diagrams drawn in mineral on brocade,
tests supports, balance, flexibility.

Holiness as a star,
octagon, circle, jewel

> *Traditionally sand-painters applied this city*
> *of shadow, channels, cul-de-sacs,*
> *moving inward toward its heart*

Trappings of misknowledge in Grandma's cabinets
the girl uses to reconstruct conditions of weather,
directional colors, the need of her being in her need
to escape, she pirouettes atop the head of a pin,
petals of tears and pomegranate minaret. My lost ballerina
sloshes ring-side the spectral world held in place by neural wind
where everyone has two names,
lives according to the outer universe or
train's harmonic connection to its crossing.

Drywall, five transparent layers
of Panisks, Dakini, Guardian Dragons

Consecreation of this mandala eliminates reversals,
a frameless forest from throat to heart,
in ornamental buildings with indelible arms
to carry and heal when embraced.

Tinkling bells announce transition of natural phenomena

NOCTURNE

The Swan sails a milky tide spread evenly across *Silver River*
&Pierrette angry with the moon and universe of flute, viola, harp
Harmonizing our corrupt selves with the utterly impassable
Unable to suffer
Without leitmotiv

Not to denote absence but to describe in negative terms to capture
     the fades and sequences

The equation of peering at the sky upside-down, at Cassiopeia,
     a sequin,
Butterfly's dream, Andromeda
               Philosophical toys contenting emblematic identity

Below her waist: blue coral

     Cloud's breath root-coiled to earth
     How matter's faithless

     Miscellaneity under a simmering cinder moon
     Omen of bones, ignoble, central moods

Martine Bellen

Crinkum-crankum frogs congesting trees
Shaded by a turbid glow

Bee's familiarities
With the mild moon

Key to the bright world

Communal & personal aspects of integrating with sound as
    landscape
(converted luminosity)

She sleeps in black and white woods,
Only when awake do colors saturate
Habitats of resonance
Glass splashed with spells, decanto

Ghouls, fouler wind, and swollen waves
                    A passing moon, passion moon

The sword which lies ready for battle in the open heart, shiny moon
    (A hidden moon scuds behind the broken cloud)

Or is the Divine Window—apprehension of our invisible body
Tucked away in the prose closet
Neck-ruffles of stars and the *dones d'aigo*
Sheltered in underground water-falled halls, weaving water
To gowns, the living mutable spirit of each fountain:
        The Tender Fount, Course Spring,
            Spring of Deceit, Glassy Fountain, The Dried Up Spring
(reduce amount of blood in body, reduce desire)

Innermost subtle drops
Suffusing throat, heart

Gave speech to bird and wind
That dance for an audience of one; still swirls
Of bejeweled tulle pirouette in echoing applause,
Like the clinks of cordial glasses
Inspiriting the dark alone

She is an idiot, walks through the burden forgetting
What disappeared. Her
World fell away. A wind, hitherto unknown, physically
unanimous,

All the Devils of Hell cannot pluck a feather from one poor wren.

Five Poems
Peter Sacks

NOTE

Others choose more solid figures of resemblance but the wind
    blows from that place
dividing tissue seed flame unpermitted edges carrying the
    socket-bone's

implicit trial—here bend—here study it—the law remains torn
    feather scrap of
tarmac skin you fill it in you plough over the crater lip past
    argument the certain

flourish, short-stemmed, reachable with signalling what comes out
    of the wind
as an arrest, a feeding precedent, this rapid lifting now you link
    away drive out

each thrust upslope above the mark the mortar set you press
    against more weight
as for the future peace with gaps a hive a hull white shredding petal
    wave it will

not stop the work's upheaval where the impact shows its vein the
    unencompassable
paying out root thread survival-salted pollen knowing other
    judgment in the

sideways trace and drag you cast you follow it.

NOTE

Had you existed (this world) had you set your own equivalent
    across the track
would there have been a further purpose clearing the debris? Or
    earlier—before

the call, before the guarantees (the stars of heaven, sand, the wings
    resettling
above ordinary slaughters)—was it to frighten us away? How
    solitary,

with smoke mixed in, with scrapings. Listen—let the others hear
    the long
collisions wrapped in silence. Blank flag of surrender & no writing
    covers you.

CURRENT

The fossil of the fish in candlelight—a dorsal fin
set wavering by current & the spine more flame than stone.

Breathe in.
The words too grow transparent, heard-through, to this end.

What's nearest to you now?
Ungathered sediment, you're swaying on your stem

time loosens, thins, through-lit as by an older
element.
      It knows you as you will become.

6.12.00

As dead leaves in the space between leaf-shadows gleam, you could
    not
keep from waking further, disentangled from what might have been

perpetual fear. The core took longer, first whom, then what.

As if all flesh were punishable proof,
                        they had been everywhere, the trees.

FACE TO FACE

The sky too fed upon itself
            & hid behind the point where everything takes on

the sheen of disbelief.
Justice shivered in its mask.

The residue of innocence would speak if it had words. Would cry
    out

once more for what name? What is its sin, there at the origin?

Two Poems
Reginald Shepherd

ROMAN YEAR

Martius

The corrugated iron gates
are rolling down storefronts
in paradise, late light flecks windows,
rain's acid fingerprints. Motes
float between iron and glass, sink
into sanded pavements, weather's
footprints, cracked *mappa mundi:* silk
tea roses with a fringe of plastic fern;
grapes, apples, and bananas ripened
to painted wax: your eyes
blinking away some pollen
in wind that says spring's coming, wait
for me. Months sometimes it takes

Aprilis

light scrolls across an unmade bed,
we were setting out for Aries
in paper planes (white dwarf stars
bright in a wilderness of wish scatter
white feathers among me, fistfuls
of light): bees busied themselves
with the seen, moment's
multiple tasks, for the pollen, honey
in the blood, bees would drown
each day: from a thicket of nos
to one sepaled blossoming, all
in an afternoon

you thought of bees as summer

Maius

Heliotrope gaze has fixed me
in its sights (turning solar year suffers
sudden rain, grazes my cold
with vague waves, plashing
particles, but lightly): lightly
take this sky, bound up in so much
loose light, light wind brushes chapped
lips. Light-footed gods break open
day to see what it contains: body
survives light's inquisitions.

Juniius

beside the shale pigeons a dove
color of old brick dust, the sound
of brick dust settling: traffic noise
rides heat-rise off wet streets, summer
music echoes borrowed air: light
centrifugal, sent scattering, lost later
every day: some gold
against bright water (handfuls
scattered over lake), unnecessary, true
candleland waning to wax
and wick, silver water shattering
like backed glass.

Quintilis

When I was in Egypt, light fell
instead of rain, congealed to grains of sand,
pyramidal, uninterred. Uninterrupted waves
of palms departed for shuddering oases. Why was it
I spent centuries in that mirage, caravanserai
of the sirocco stopped, pausing at
reflection, also called the polished sky,
and still no fall of shade? The light hung
triangular, aslant, touched the colossus
to song.

Sextilis

Wanting to understand, not wanting
to understand, by taking thought you lose it, by not
taking thought. Watching him run a hand
through thinning blond hair, passing
at arm's length on a lunch hour
street. Wondering *is it good now, am I
pleasure,* and *which part is it I need,*
while air migrates too slowly to be seen
and noon crawls groggy over August
skin. Then thinking *No, it's too*
and turning back to look at traffic.

September

Sudden storm, then sudden sun. *Give me,*
I almost said: and stopped, began again
with your voice, what gets invented by the
can't-be-said-here. The afternoon of after rain
dazzles with cloudlessness and a painful green
set casually against blue: light
mottled by fractal leaves
freckles your outstretched arm,
repeating *apple, apple, apple,* sour
fruit and crabgrass. A damp T-shirt
takes on that color, nothing
will wash it out. I wear it for weeks.

October

doorway, flutter, moth
or leaf in flight, in fall
foyer, stammer of wind, a patter
hovering, dust hushed or
pressed to trembling
glass, smut, soot, mutter
of moth or withered stem,
late haze, gray stutter
crumpled, crushed,
falter, fall, a tread . . .

November

williwaw, brawl in air,
shunt or sinew of wind shear
blown off-course, pewter skew
vicinity, winnow and complicit

sky preoccupied with grizzle,
winter feed of lawns' snared
weathervane, whey-faced day
brume all afternoon of it

(lead reticence of five o'clock)
remnant slate all paucity and drift
salt splay, slur and matte brink
snow stammers against sidewalks

December

White light seen through
the season's double window
clouding the room reveals the roses'
week-old gift of petals bruised purple-black.
Dry paper falling on white cloth
seconds white room's wonder
at cold sun flurried, crumbling stars
compacted underfoot: lattice
of fixed clarity, wintrish eidolon
half patience, half in prayer.

NATURALISM

Between them is only difference.
— Saussure

The error was the inspiration

Trees I've never seen with names I knew
real word but not true wood,
ginkgo male or female, always
only one kind: a living fossil, oldest
gymnosperm, 'naked seed,' reproducing
by means of direct contact
with air (resistant to pests
and pollution): there shouldn't
be flowers, shouldn't be fruit

White flowers one book says
are yellow, *Ginkgo biloba,*
scientific names strew themselves across
damp sidewalks, appellation sheds
petals in May wind, simile, similitude,
have I compared, the only extant
member of its order, Ginkgoales,
Ginkgoaceae, domesticated
by description (extinct otherwise)

Wrong attributes over everything,
petals stuck to soles, imagined
into subject matter, fan-like leaves
framed by mistake, words (Chinese
or Japanese? my sources
are unclear) for *silver apricot, silver
nut:* tiny plums prized for their kernels
(plum-*like*), the ripe flesh stench between
two fingers, beneath two feet (which one?)

They fall after first freeze, heavy
with frost (an unambitious tree, wrinkled
fruit barely an inch across: tiny
cherries?), stepped on in early winter

219

Reginald Shepherd

Iowa the stink comes back
of August, late summer smell
smeared through December
(red-purple when the book says
yellow, and smelling of nowhere)

Write only what you see, it said,
first this, first that (I walked past them
every day, under them, three in a sidewalk
row: a commonplace tree, no real interest
at all, reeking fruit fouls the sidewalk all fall,
cross the street to avoid them)
The read tree and the real tree
(this happens only in writing): never
an even number, three of one kind

Knowing the names with nothing
to paste them onto (trees I'd seen
but never known, misnomer
printing petals on wet pavements): just one
kind at a time, white four-petaled
flowering May, clear green lobed leaves
cover summer, gold in fall (perhaps
some strain of ornamental plum):
first come flowers, first come leaves

Not the same tree at all

— *for Robert Philen and Lawrence White*

Two Poems
Barbara Guest

BLURRED EDGE

It appears

a drama of exacting dimension.

Anguished figure,

reign of terror.

Craft and above all

the object within.

Softness which precedes

blurred edge.

A hint disappears   inside the earlier one.

Barbara Guest

<u>Softness still nudging,</u>

A different temperament,

inside an earlier plan.

Upon this stool is draped material
arabesque of an iron stool,

bare bones of the iron seat.

The arrangement of objects   announced

   more firmly than before.

     Observation.   Candor,

   where candor approaches the cube.

   Dark siphon bottle   mood

              of blurred edge.

Barbara Guest

Life permitted no privilege

     no exegesis
     no barnyard door.   The feathered visage   the domed hat

     allowed no strange air or music.

     An attempt to get beyond the arrangement,

vibration of a peculiar touch.

Barbara Guest

It changes between eye and alarm,

the hibiscus,

more gifted.

Part of the tension,

is illusory.

225

A hint of what was going to be.

Covering and uncovering necessary.

Self pouring out of cloudedness.

If views of the lower body

do not conform,
            a risk of being exposed,

        Rain and altitude.

This is not sand, it is drama.

The anguished figure, sand blew away
that armor. A look extends the blur.

Other creatures alive,
word exchanged for meaning,
moment of descriptiveness.

Sand blows away.

In distance,
figure passing,
unworded distance at edge.

Barbara Guest

PATHOS

Arms flutter close to the body, skating on pure ice, harmonious
composition, —

body in mellifluous line —

face in profile withheld itself, thin smile,
self approval.

Lithe her romp!

lithesome her romp upon the indignation of ice.

She is falling!

Shiver of the fallen,

of the tulle skirt.

Disarrangement of the composition,

Snow falling from tree.

So young in this electric world —,

    something Katya needs to know. Something is needed,

        fiction is overturned.

    Something she must know about hazard, what spills out —

        — disturbance, — pathos.

        Equilibrium is never fixed —

losing momentum in the trials — boot tossed away,
  a gesture she made.

Barbara Guest

Making difficulties for herself   in the wrong direction.
Fear of the word, haunting of fear —

the word passed through that haunting.

Weight of the useless word and narcissus,
mirror moving backward,

impromptu surface of the alphabet when she fell sideways

with irascible measure — the pit of the plum
rolled onto ice,   and her silhouette   merged quickly
with ice in that chapter.

Opened the entrance door,

and make-believe arrived with a doll on its surface,

arrived with the soil of the moon,   it was impermanent

living with shifted screen life.

Lived not for pleasure,   to hear the cry

in a small coil
of ice.

And heard through the oak panel —,

amazing to listen to speech
by way of adulthood.

To articulate velvet,

without noise or spectacle.

Barbara Guest

Life in that eccentric balloon.

To scribble ice figures,

and drink out of the cup when bolder.
The electric world sends its current through her legs,
a global concern for her being.

The globe is drawn into this, and the frills,
the sorrow of falling

into an historical position, the legs will finish
this position, music
use up the irresistible current, lived
with the shifting screen.

Lived not for pleasure, to hear the harp-like
cry in a coil,

to live in an eccentric balloon.

To scribble across ice

and drink from an orange cup. When they were nearer

    historical legs used up this position,

falling down historical legs, anxious writing.

Barbara Guest

Foreignness enters the hallway in the Debussy —

hinting at the fable
                    resisting her.

Do they wonder at her pathos/ dressed in tulle,
athletically inclined on jumping bars.

                              One at a time

            misleading her./

She is part of *the moment/* unrequited amour/

                              icing machine.

            This motion in her eyes,

going outside,   the red brook
                    flowed into her eyes, her winsome eyes,

            drawstring of light.

Two Poems for the Seventeenth Century
Donald Revell

FOR THOMAS TRAHERNE

The ground is tender with cold rain
Far and equally
Our coastlines grow younger
With tides
Beautiful winter
Not becoming spring today and not tomorrow
Has time to stay

Easter will be very late this year
Thirty years ago
I saw my church
All flowery
And snow
Melting in the hair of the procession
As tender as today

A sight above all festivals or praise
Is earth everywhere
And all things here
Becoming younger
Facing change
In the dark weather now like winter
Candling underground as rain

Donald Revell

FOR ANDREW MARVELL

Tiger of luster of swordplay is just a stick
On a sandpile
I remember because everything is all of its characteristics
Apart just once
Together for eternity in death's unlimited magic

Ilex conjures acanthus
I've never tasted quince I like the snow apple
Filled with sirocco
An austere example

And my son knows
In his tigerish swordplay
Once apart as I board the usual airplane
I remember
Magic I've taken from his hand and pressed like sharp sharp sand
        into mine

Resemblance
Paul Hoover

Placing ancient birds
in absent skies,
the midst is

endless. To rise
alone is clear,
the sudden plum

of a mountain,
a reckless cabin
inhabited by ghosts,

its weather rainy
with ash and
bones. Sire of

light. Color and
substance joined like
coasts. In earth's

black dream, objects
take shape as
mind and scum.

The weight of
water pouring on
your head is

one reminder, but
our habit is
confession and the

dirt of history
even in these
photos by André

Kertesz of people
reading, the true
light of seeing

in the midst
of squalor, on
balconies and roofs,

even a bug
grazing a page
of Voltaire. A

frocked monk is
reading in a
painting on the

shelf, where a
layer of dust
has fallen on

the pears. How
often nothing happens,
how often it

is shared, and
then toward evening
this feeling of

completion. In its
own carnal grammar,
recurrent entries in

the book of
skin. Normal as
form, every button

shines. To be
entered is all,
breathless and sinking

in the sweat
of love found.
The new place's

old dream darkens
like a world.
This is birth:

the beating and
the drum, eternity
and the parrot,

meaning and the
feeling, chaos and
the boy. Breathless

acts are fragments,
degrees of desire.
None are structure,

all are numb.
The length of
the bridge, its

gesture elegiac, a
string of chinese
lanterns is firm

as direction. We
can still remember
the garden and

its foxes, baby
and its cake.
Are you marked?

A lark in
sauce? There's warmth
in not needing,

but still you
want with ripe
eyes open. It's

like the movie
Wind with its
rhetoric of silence,

where a flag
of a man
struggles toward the

door, only to
discover the recent
day is closed.

On a monochrome
screen, he comes
to resemble darkness

and time, a
meaningless object and
its useless sign.

Five Poems
E*laine* E*qui*

FURTHER ADVENTURES

The bird carries her off in its beak
her prettiness
    (ribbon   heart's rouge)
straining against flight, doing what she never
dreamed (actually, what she often dreamed
but never dared).   Up high
one can see the breath of Time,
its cold exhale. Time has carried her off
and the world is rearing up on hind legs
like the statue of a general on his horse.
The girl carries the world off
    (its prettiness and twin ugliness)
as surely as she is carried, yet can't stop
feeling she has forgotten something:
a necklace of beads, a train of thought,
a funeral procession with a broken clasp.
Something shining *beneath* the world
    (a word   a charm).
Something is calling her back.

LEAN-TO

The eye of the walking stick opened,
polished with ego (of good quality).
A crutch is a useful thing.

Shadow in shadow,
    character in character,
        mano a mano,

we walked the length of the city
(a wheezing   a many-chimneyed thing).

What is a story, I asked.
A story is a poultice, you said
applying its pressure.
A story is a blindfold
for leading the blind.

The ego glittered,
        the city slowed.
Cautiously, the eye
of the walking stick opened.

"YOUR PURPLE ARRIVES"

Purple flower.
        Purple heart.

Heap of sharp
and muddy edges.

Bruise or blossom?

Harp strings
trickle-down
realignment
of morning's slow . . .

bright bug
with a crumb of window
on its back.

DESSERT

This caramel is scriptural.
This lemon tart more beautiful than a Matisse.
It's the way paintings (and heaven) taste
as they dissolve and we internalize them.

Gurus know it.
Don't you remember after they slapped us
with peacock-feather-fans,
the little piece of rock candy
we each got and sucked in the corner,
thinking that if the mantras didn't work,
at least there was this.

OUT OF THE CLOUD CHAMBER

and into the street.

Out of the art-deco prison
and into the cozy burning house,
the bleak house,
                the decadent steak house.

Out of the mouths of tulips and slaves.

Out of the frying pan and into the choir.

Out of mimesis endlessly mocking.

Out like a debutante,
                in like a thief.

Out of pocket,
                out of reach.

Out of time
                and into being.

Elaine Equi

Out of sight
        and into seeing.

Out of your mind
        and into your pants.

Out like a light
        and in like a lamp.

Conjunctions
Norma Cole

–1.
(to not turn on machine with light in eyes)

you ask me state of nature
most two hundred of our time
all good nothing, silent treatment
those girls, the cousin, the bakery

the men in long grass with machetes
waiting to advance, to move in (or out?)
all good nothing, the track star
losing interest in the bakery

dreamer losing interest in
the most two hundred of our time

1.

Still small battles of will Despite unseasonal meanness In a set-up
like that Where the main dynamic is not even Knowing what's
missing or that it's Missing an edge and moving along as if Missing
a sense, like sight or Touch or hearing the Evidence or a piece of it
comes to Light by accident or deliberate Positioned in relation to
a given Moment and so it is perhaps all an Accident with a
magnifying glass or an Electrified fence to Separate the fictions:

showing Her and trying to speak or Are they singing? she's
listening and Looking but is she smiling? A visible device
represents Them as things that don't add up

    Men in the back of a truck behind a wire Grating singing

2.

habit of the tongue, that piece of bread on the wood in the shot
right after the teapot, the lamp and the table

> Pretend a thing is a
> Thing like us
> To imagine a stick
> When you see
> Flowers shaped like a dove
> Or anything else

Cairo, named for Mars. Mars and England were the same to us, she
said. She saw in her palm,

> musical matter has
> filled up the cavity
> originally occupied by
> the organism itself

The crowd seems too apologetic.

3.

Clouds composed of sharps and flats, structure but the room is
locked. That is to say, the visit can be obstructed, withheld by
chance at either end. A model of action (compassion) within the
inexorability (irregularity, unpredictability) of the frame.

Notations of space in terms of measure of weather or breath
moving in the shape of a billowing figure in front of the mouth,
position read as motion, exiting, invisible magnetic tongue.

The clown like an undertaker in red and white striped gloves pulls
the coat up over your head from behind: let the circus begin!

dots teeming with organic matter, out of statistical into the fire

a shadow under the number

4.

Image or not? Exactly if the shadow is underneath

hyacinth culture, the wasps
and the bees—rook mates, a bird
called bee-eater in the House of
the Faun

But rather, to enter and be concealed. Manet's "Mocking of Christ"
making of christ a kind of dark space around the figures, light
bottom quarter foreground floor syntax of light and dark

5.

this time is free
contagious dialogue
body of music
blood in mouth
hair in shoe

Boxing Captions
Jena Osman

I wanted to respond to the simple gesture of the figures . . . without pathos, without dramatic movement, without telling stories! For the painter or sculptor, simple acts of the human figure, such as inclining the head, raising an arm, gesturing with the hand, moving a leg, provide such an expressive richness that themes such as standing, coming, going, turning, and the like would suffice to occupy an artist's lifetime.

—Oskar Schlemmer

Simple acts: The theater is ranging across the boundaries of its materials. I find myself through a device, a synthesizer of discrete emblems, disconnected on summation and realized in the limits of time zone and national sphere. I'm a figure mechanized by its last potentials and careful of new hypotheses. Emblems run their course through me, serve to engender fantasies, the image conditioned to promise change, to approach us but not too closely.

FIGURE ONE
Force the opponent's left and lead to the right with the left glove.

FIGURE TWO
Step forward and left, at the same time drive a straight right to the chin.

FIGURE THREE
The left hand, after executing the parry, is in a position of block ready for opponent's right.

Fɪɢ. 6.

Stage realm is ranging through these gestures. What popular thing directing their geography, realized in the limits of a romantic confrontation, animated as the antique need for today and the loss of self one feels in the marketplace. The term mummery appears like a light: a moral variety, a diagram in the vaudeville.

FIGURE FOUR
noh hearing, noh voting, my soldier will know
men leer strands of century
then linger on woe

FIGURE FIVE
on top of the right gun
a layer of guy
a stance over madder
victorious in light

FIGURE SIX

FIG. 15.

Race on and tongue tie   on sounds in a bay
Get a word   clean and dry

History from materials wades cautiously into a contentious debate. The history of reflection: "I am the votes." An actor of naturalness, then helicopters churn overhead. The government blinked. This sculptor crafts a spiritual artifice while thousands cheer wildly in the arena built for the role. We will examine the changes caused by the longest war.

FIGURE SEVEN
Abhorrence

FIGURE EIGHT
Self Abasement

FIGURE NINE
Utter Abandonment

FIG. 24.

Jena Osman

Emblems disconnect making dozens of arrests. The absurd hand broke up a drug ring, the result of new mechanization. They also seized 18 firearms, our sphere of life aided by corrupt employees. A suspicious package was reported, our recognition is loaded, is mechanized. It would be met by another vehicle, our time to create. Workers count ballots, technology and fantasies, then succeed in ousting one sign.

FIGURE TEN
National Election commission workers count ballots for the National Assembly.

FIGURE ELEVEN
A former intelligence officer is being held in a prison.

FIGURE TWELVE
Life goes on at a café while protesters march by.

FIG. 33.

Taken between things, we clear the final state hurdle. It is really natural to approve a compromise bill that runs through me. What popular thing is suspended from school, passive at its scaffold. No charges are likely to be filed; they are animate as the marketplace. We discuss shooting and stabbing—the mummery, seen as a lie. After taking her to the woods, diagrams step up their assault, that is, shape the world. No sound as we try to decide whether to sign a physical—an optical—event and hold direct talks with its composer (who fails to defeat the rebels). Sounds out of the body are the form of two who approve a plan to place you under house arrest, complete with distribution and precision and fear that you might try to escape.

FIGURE THIRTEEN
*Every object is naturally drawn to the
earth's center.*

FIGURE FOURTEEN
*Another was given credit for that, which
prevented the former from saying such a
thing out loud.*

FIGURE FIFTEEN
*Then he decided to measure humidity with
a ball of cotton.*

Fig. 42.

Independence and time threatened to freeze his assets. His material,
however—the words for which he was arrested—an improvised existence as they unfurled banners of protest. Alone they're free in circumstance, renouncing his ties. He is material for higher potential
and the conflict ends. Reproduction for the latter brings a halt to
spring, detached limitations decked out in new riot gear. Humans are
certain to be listening, opening markets to competition. Depth ex-
tensions can wipe out linear form, leaving workers without jobs.
Rigid geometry of space enjoys expanded export, runs right through
me, driving unions to lock arms.

FIGURE SIXTEEN
*Smith was freed on grounds of prosecutorial
misconduct.*

FIGURE SEVENTEEN
*Eleanor Reese shows damage to the trunk of
the car that was removed from behind her house.*

FIGURE EIGHTEEN
*Ivory V. Nelson has tackled difficult problems
at universities.*

Fig. 51.

Jena Osman

Manifestations of nothingness hold meetings willing to listen to values they fulfilled. Simple acts. The living means of representation help people in poor countries, their flesh and measure integrating into the world emblem economy. They are not equilibrium under siege. The stability of a deficiency is mechanized, scheduled to culminate through borrowed tactics. Transient stage action derails a new round in mobile fluctuating, holds up a national map: space at once spotlighting. The sight of dozens range across this strict switchboard to show my generation cares.

FIGURE NINETEEN
Because some things reflect rays, and are bright; but others absorb them.

FIGURE TWENTY
Because each grain of sand reflects the rays of the sun like a mirror.

FIGURE TWENTY-ONE
Because the body of vapor is thinnest at the edges of the clouds.

Fɪɢ. 60.

The goal is an image which avoids mistakes and he stands in different laws tightening security in advance. Realism in the abstract: stationing officers on bridges. Cubical relationships. Mathematics of spending millions on riot gear. Nature of calisthenics, together and in conscious next page, directing this geography through myself into the vaudeville.

FIGURE TWENTY-TWO
Drop the left arm perpendicular to the floor,
and step across to a position outside the
opponent's left foot, with either the left or
right foot.

FIGURE TWENTY-THREE
Shift the weight to the front leg and then
drive a hard left uppercut to the solar plexus.

FIGURE TWENTY-FOUR
Carry the right hand high, ready to cross to
opponent's chin.

FIG. 69.

Reside in respiration fueled by a new heartbeat system. Human space argues about trade whose opposite framework and mimetics have shaken employees. They face, under attack, invisible psychical expression and obey the law of himself who failed to act as watchdog and to police all these corrupt regimes as sense and range of space. Whether bare, they receive loans and curb their own environment in the great branch offered to attain their goal. Theater urged them to avoid confrontation.

FIGURE TWENTY-FIVE
Thousands of janitors in Los Angeles are on
strike for higher pay after rejecting a wage plan
offered by building maintenance companies.

FIGURE TWENTY-SIX
For Gulf Coast residents in Texas, spring
break memories, like those of the traffic on
Padre Island, linger.

FIGURE TWENTY-SEVEN
The left glove should be placed over the
opponent's right in order to prevent a
counter blow.

FIG. 78.

Jena Osman

Transformation costume, they change it so as to provide new safety. Human costume risks conformity and six children die. The misleading laws consist of a waist belt and a native is confused. The tray comes off, produced from the has-been, can slip down, yet costumes of standardized Columbine strangle or fall. Authentic can be the body falling from the swing.

FIGURE TWENTY-EIGHT
from torso into
architecture
human space

FIGURE TWENTY-NINE
laws of the club
the egg of the arms
the joints

FIGURE THIRTY
the we of rotation
spinning result
spiral disk

FIG. 87.

Simple acts. Possibilities move in limitations that double as infants. The longer abandoned essentially soar which fastens acrobatics as the only living geometry sold nationwide. The pyramid bondage results in automaton stop-spending, beyond human, extolled, he keeps up his courting demands: a phonograph unshaken by the hour-long session, indeed mind is configuration portraying himself as a different kind of technological glass. He painted himself as a new breed: artificial divers generally support a surgery soldier, criticize one idea as an artificial device, pick somebody to speak for long periods and it can be abstract. Why don't you pick someone peculiar to pathos to deliver anything? Sublime actors and stilts of this most exquisite faith succumb to publicity. This reverse, the man wants to run, develop appropriate stills, he declines to meet and awaits the static. The acrobat opposes the atmosphere.

Jena Osman

FIGURE THIRTY-ONE
Remember the sign of this shape
the folded backbone
suppresses the world.

FIGURE THIRTY-TWO
Drive a hard right to opponent's heart
inside his left lead.

FIGURE THIRTY-THREE
Suppression, Depression, Dejection,
and kindred ideas.

Fig. 96.

The genuine action emerges untouched in its own materials. I play amazed at being its creation unchanged in my core beliefs. My form without purpose decays to listen to people's real life stories, kills while teaching eighth grade history and today I continue by recounting my own wrenching. With the service of an optical author I ask him why he left us after his intentions divided the class in half. Favorites jump at the chance to lead a visual theater of colors and in this case we'll be the hawks! Isolate out into the sea. The idea is dropped because of rising emotion. The question of tomorrow: if tomorrow is not a straight line—rather, a hidden forwardness—how will we stand and turn?

FIGURE THIRTY-FOUR
The safety clinch

FIGURE THIRTY-FIVE
The emblematic duck

FIGURE THIRTY-SIX
The return right hook

Fig. 5.

255

Fubar Clus
Ron Silliman

"That much drinking
does not come free"

A ride
in a cheap rent-a-car
after an hour of tea
in the sun

Large screen TV
playing basketball
with the sound off

Movement
quick & muscular
though seeming
curiously slow

Rodman's hair
an impossible yellow-white

Talking of death, of
cancer, this one's
prostate, that one's breast

a woman described as
"a poet of the seventies"
who is in fact
a friend to many here

wind-up kangaroo flips
but fails to land
standing up

"Thinking of getting married again —
a beautiful French woman —
so I ask him
what does he think he's doing

and he admits
he doesn't know"

2.
form festers restless void
— Charles Borkhuis

"Behind these pictures
I have other pictures"

Haze blurs the margin
far up Suisun Bay
though to the east, Diablo
etched in summer heat
(though it is only Spring

Little blue butterflies
the underside of whose wings
prove gray as rock
alight atop
wild chamomile

To the west
out beyond the Gate
the great white cloud bank
sits low over the water
a blur to Tamalpais

while between
lays what I conceive of
as the past

257

The burden
of time
    old men
in the gas station shadows
sitting on overturned drums
spitting into the grease
                A woman
beautiful thin face a little more etched
after a year's absence
brings out a tray
on which sits a pitcher and several glasses
out into the brilliant sunlight
of the deck
high over the terraced garden

                Masks & kites
                hanging from a line
                paint drying

        Great Wall of Duplos
        children's chairs
        tables, easels
        webbed together in yarn

Choir
of the nearly inaudible
hum in the walls
crackling constant in every light bulb
deep breath of the furnace
                    ice maker's rattle
          in the empty kitchen
overheard
Up the block
an engine turns over

Report of a blue bunting
where none should be

3.

The cat stalks slow
across the cut grass
bird barely visible
in the last light
that might still be called
predawn
                casts
a narrative
over the whole yard
mealy bugs impervious
in the damp soil

The brief season of tulips has passed

So that
an image is layered
out of the visible
through extraction
of characteristic
detail

She rose up
after the act
straightening the camisole
she still wore,
                picking
the rest of her clothes
up from the floor
and looked back at him
alien now that he slept
wondering
had he even seen her
during the fact of it

Cars abruptly
leaving the freeway
climbing the dirt path
up to the off ramp

Ron Silliman

    or the road north
    to Germantown Pike
    ahead
        (then below)
    long sea of red lights
    the Schuykill transformed
    into a parking lot
    headed East

Three Movie Poems
John Yau

PETER LORRE REMINISCES ABOUT BEING A SIDEKICK

Iron cloud, bronzed sunset, stolen dream.
I wasn't always a feverish lepidopterist
chasing whistling chariots in a stadium.
My wax lacked coherence, my human hairs glistened
Perhaps you would like to come in off the ledge
and share a mug of hot cocoa laced with absinthe.
Or is that the kind of little naughtiness you prefer to shun?
Have you noticed that there's a lot of snow
clinging to my last Fabergé egg?
Take off your tie, throw away your shoes.
Have you seen my collection of portholes?
some pried from the very finest luxury liners
to have foundered on these rocky shores.
It's not that I am given to issuing a high resolution
lightly thawed whoop or two
whenever my oversized eyelids
belly fat knuckles start twittering,
and the crease in my gabardines start gabbing
to the pleats gathered at the corner, waiting
for the light to change its spots,
but I just love yodeling
"O sweet crotchless tyrannosaurus,
why hast thou huffiness handcuffed me
to the Hunting Lodge of Unrepentant Nations
and their sprawling kin? Am I not
allowed a few extra paces
before I am commanded
to run into the woods?"
Such timely intermissions prove
how newly minted and hot I became,
while sitting on a painted horse,
surrounded by dancing dandelions.

Did I forget to mention the adventures of Smoky Muskrat,
Maison Spittle, and Cheap Varmint Night and his Band,
The Sheep Bladder Brigade? Or am I being too allegorical,
too much a one night pill flipper in a copycat's storm?
Will I ever be regarded as truly satisfying?
Can I become one who exudes
a heroic magnetic profile?
become one whose blessed visage pulls the dust
off your brow of well-endowed verbs?
Will you remember me as something more
than an imported bandana
when I am draped in bad blood squirted from a can
made of recycled helmets retired ogres pitched in a ditch?
Hey, are you glugging to the ghosts of Salvation Coliseum?
This isn't a resurrection factory, you simian of slime.
What are you doing? Walking your toast
down to the coroner's barn? Quit hawking
your perforated hanky, there is always more of this
where this came from. Remember, the last time
you had your brain amputated, you were required
to sacrifice your definitions of meandering reincarnations
in favor of a satchel of bologna pizzas.
Or were you just another hungry artist
quick to lick the trumpet of integrity?
Hard to dream about the outside when it stops
raining long enough to forget you once had
a memorable name. This is where I get off
the bus, Buster. Or is it Bruiser or Boozer,
Flappy or Winsome with an Axe?
On the other side of the lake lives a two-headed dragon.
Pink smoke rises from the nostrils of the one known
as Ying, while blue tears fall from the one known as Yank.
It is rumored that they used to be a Siamese twins
but got tired of eating from the same hollywood bowl.
As a dishwasher, I became familiar with their plight,
and tried to comfort them, but with little consequence.
You encounter all sorts of shadows in this game preserve.
Some have been suspended in the trees for eons,
their souls locked inside the recyclable peanut
butter jars insulating the wizard's hexagonal library.
That's how I plan to get promoted to Senior Gatekeeper.

A small wagon floated downstream, guided by nymphs.
Huge fragrant bouquets descended from the rafters,
quickly covering the stage, but, by then,
the headline star had fled into the closet
the management rented out for such occasions.
Time to hoist your mortal spoils out of bed, Bunky.
I wasn't trying to become you when the mountain
tugged itself together, collapsing outside the doghouse
where I pass my afternoons, dreaming of the day
my portrait will finally hang in the dog museum.
You pass more than afternoons, you blasphemous pustule
on the noble edifices that have been studiously erected
by a fleet of robots, sleek and newly released,
like a certain frog's vivacious belch, from
the recently upgraded prison recreation facility
just down the road from the gas station where I saw you
licking grease off the monkey they keep
tucked behind the cash register.
I wasn't always this gentle. In fact,
I wasn't always an Austro-Hungarian umpire, either.
Twice I've been from somewhere
outside your sovereignty. Once I was even Japanese,
but that was before the war brought us home,
to the blue picket fence draped with ribbons and razors.
Quit smooching the mirror, goggle-eyes. You got a face
that could pass as a kangaroo's pouch.
Not that I don't muster up some small careful affection
for that doomed race of puddle hoppers,
but we all jump into oblivion, don't we?
Maybe you ought to get into another line of work.
Maybe you ought to fold your name somewhere else,
sign on someone else's dotted line
since you were never issued one in the first place.
I am sure I can find you an envelope big enough.
What about the barrel of forks you hid in the alley?
Say, what are you doing here anyway?
Who said you could stop by and smear lemon grass
meringue over your cloudy lapels? You think
you got something big to say? Something momentous?
Or is it what you had to memorize
in order to escape the men with lightning in their eyes?

263

John Yau

FILM ADAPTATIONS OF FIVE OF AMERICA'S
MOST BELOVED POEMS

It burns and winds. For as long as I can remember, my Sunday task
has been to polish the antique wooden perambulator until it gleams
like an aluminum breadbox. Do you mind being the landlady's
favorite pet? No, Little Igor, raunchy ruminator and muralist to midsized manufacturers, these are not the horoscope dials you should be
consulting. Look at the fuzzy ones over there, on the pink control
panel mounted beneath the custom aquarium populated with poiso-
nous snakes, addled alligators and small but hearty fish. Have you
ever seen such a diverse array of live entertainment clouding the
waters before?

On misty days the sun hangs pale blue over a black diamond sea.
Academic painters of every persuasion rise from their imported
beach chairs and press their ointment-covered noses against the
unnecessarily spotted glass, unaware that cross-eyed snakes are staring back at them. Intrepid mountaineers follow the whistle of the
marmot up to the highest crags, and over playgrounds and puddles
alike rises the cry of a wounded sea otter, fondling the most delec-
table portion of his imported fish dinner. Meanwhile, a caravan of
carrion has been dragged across the sand.

It turns and whines. All motels are penetrated by two sounds—a
scream and a complaint. Today, as long ago, these are the two sacred
messengers of the Western Nile Plumber's Union and their far-flung
subsidiary units. Trying to overcome the image of being nothing
more than a bunch of loud-talking, gum-chewing cronies, the union
leaders decided to dispense with opening ceremonies and closing ser-
mons. Later, concerned with the rank-and-file's growing resentment
of enforced civic duty, some of the leaders voted to reenact well-
known gaffes at previous company picnics, while others elected to
learn the intricacies of miniature collie and poodle grooming as an
alternative to hosting the Sunday car wash. Their favorite costumes
included a red satin tuxedo, a cowboy mustache, and nicotine-
stained talons. Last month, the duly elected Vice-Secretary issued
the following decree: No velvet cones with tassels are allowed to
cross the threshold.

High above the Wabash River, its riverbanks lined with quaint cobblestone streets and newly renovated factories, complete with working fire hydrants and helmeted dwarfs scattered discretely among the hordes of wayward children, a foreign possibly alien power has managed to thrust the city's entire work force into a state of suspended animation. The mayor fears the immense stone bridge that was to become a major tourist attraction in the tri-county area will remain unfinished. The pianist is trying to imitate the sound of an oncoming train. No one dreams that the images are stolen from a semi-retired sorcerer while he is dreaming of a miniaturized sorcerer who is assassinated and buried in a jelly jar by a quartet of indignant barbers. A hexagonal shield gleams in the ruby-colored gloom descending from the sky. Great ospreys nest in the crowns of the unfinished arches. Four goats wander across the ice. The head goat, William of Upper Broadway, keeps reminding Thutmoss of the likelihood that strange plants are migrating rapidly across the ocean floor.

A man pleads with the creature locked inside the hair dryer to reconsider the wording of their oath. The less said about the source of this rumor, the better. After taking refuge in a deserted gas station containing seven slim coffins, one for each gambling centipede, the high brow hero—he has a forehead the size of Rhode Island—decides to return from hell to find out why his latest girlfriend didn't follow him to the very ends of the earth. Meanwhile, in a drugstore in Angela, Ohio, an attractive young woman by the name of Akron decides to buy two lottery tickets, one for each side of the coin.

BORIS KARLOFF IN *THE MUMMY MEETS DR. FU MANCHU*

Emerging from the woods, the audience stumbles upon an isolated scene: In the late afternoon's arcade of artificial gloom, a dainty, dotted hand deftly smooths the lower slope of a massive forehead. Zoom to close-up: Thick oblong plane's corrugated surface, its vertical grooves sprouting with stiff thistle or hard clumps of new hair. Moving suddenly into focus is a multi-leveled chorus of angular limbs festooned with pin-pricked skulls of uncategorizable animals. A paleontological nightmare thinks the perverse paleontologist, her imported platinum tongue stud momentarily glistening between her

265

lover's neatly pointed teeth. Color-coded keys shift and finally settle at bottom of lint-lined pocket. Sharks churn and chug, excited by the array of scents swiftly filtering through their olfactory detectors. Defined by the lingering traces of a mischievous grin, one that suggests satisfaction of a nonverbal order, a heavily jacketed though largely unpimpled boy points out the newly severed head of the evening moon, which, elsewhere, is floating directly above the Bank of Shanghai's misaligned ideograms and misplaced radicals.

Soon, every member of this roped-off section of time and space will meld into the unnumbered ranks of invisible spectators condemned to wander across the inclines of a barnacle-encrusted city. Gladys tugs at her store-bought underwear. Is the name of its color forget-me-not? For a month of free parking, you must answer the following question: Whose gloved digits parted the black petals of the actress's accordion before the votive candles slid out of view? She hears but cannot determine the origin of a voice which whispers, you are guilty of screening liquids of a private nature into the public basement.

A nameless place in the universe or a dead phase in a mechanized elephant's recently restored memory bank, no one knows.

In the lower balcony, Jiminy Jimmy tries not to muffle the bundle of fidgeting taking up space beside him. He dreams of the day he can leave his insect self behind, a papery husk gathering human dust in the shallow valley of a velvet cushion. Outside, beneath the curtains of the evening sky, the mournful cries of a disgruntled tyrant are quickly punctuated with the boiled dust of his headless ancestors. Rows of soldered bells and newly unfolded buses are waiting to absorb the growing stream of visitors. On the screen, hordes of infected termites eat through the edges of the unfurling role-call. A large gathering of beady eyes begins investigating the remains of this tiniest of essays.

Night's panorama of stars is no longer a coming attraction.

Hans Violin enters the tunnel and emerges as Hank Harmonica, bit player and familiar television talk show host. Meanwhile, after waking up in another section of the numbered quadrant, Gus "The Big" Viola discovers he has been reduced to a small-boned, foreign-born, dry cleaner. Time briefly accelerates its production of contaminated images. Realizing that, while he will always remain foreign to those who seek the indelible signature of his services, he has unwittingly let himself succumb to a flurry of mispronunciations. In doing so, he has become an even smaller, small-boned, servicer of others. However, now no longer either a dry or clean specimen, Gus decides he must lessen the flow of his daily sobbing. Otherwise, he is incapable of eliminating his love of operatic presentation, even though fate is about to cast him as a person without merit, a clod or a heel, a snippet of abject flotsam inhabiting a zone fit for exhaust fumes and unapologetic vandals. What he doesn't yet know, but which the audience suspects, is that his tears, however few may fall, will slowly stop evaporating.

Bones and cars accumulate at the bottom of a mouse-colored lake.

Without knowing exactly why—he is in this regard still optimistic about the future—Gus begins wishing he was wearing a red leather poncho and sitting at a shiny black piano. Somewhere in the back of the spacious, aromatic auditorium, a young woman clutches a tattered plastic rose to the tattooed Turkish dagger above her quickly beating heart. She feels the beads of sweat tightening around Gus's long, slender neck. He has become a swan peddling around a small lake surrounded by tanks. It is winter and the war is in its sixty-fifth year. The large, antiquated camera swivels haphazardly toward the next set of sprockets. A speck becomes a many-legged shadow hovering above a roofless manger, where a one-eyed mother comforts her two-headed infant. The audience gasps; it is the only acceptable response a civilized person can make under the circumstances.

As we are unable to escape the law of averages, there is, of course, one exception. You see, I have entered your line of sight, a tall, almost shapeless profile with long arms, hands and fingers stiffly extended, as if, of their own accord, they are searching for some malleable form to embrace and squeeze.

I am swathed in thick, wide bandages, which makes it difficult to offer a newly minted hanky to Gus, the tear-stained dry cleaner, who ignores the puddle slowly forming by his feet. I am standing in his store, or as the blue-lettered sign on the window states, his very reliable and friendly establishment. Was I drawn here because he too is foreign? an impediment to speech? Did he exude a magnetic field I could not veer away from? Was this collision planned by large unseen forces known to move in mysterious ways?

My sole purpose is to inquire how I might go about finding someone who can aid me. The goal was stated at the outset by my pharoah father, before the first effects of his second reincarnation set in: I am to find my original identity, the one from which I and my sperm bank embarked, many eons ago. Not the one Gus sees before him, wrapped in dusty bandages, but the one inhabiting the one whose face is covered with strips of cloth soaked in the Nile.

The sky darkens to the color of a bruise and the last of the renegade stars are quickly nailed into place.

It is a silly thing, to ask someone how you might go about finding out who you are. Presumably you already know. But, in my case, I am of two minds and at least two bodies. One is only visible to me. The other is the one I inhabit but cannot catch sight of.

My dilemma is familiar. I can't recognize my reflection, as I can only nod to the shadows the director has painted on the wall behind me. These painted blobs move in tandem to my hesitations. We could begin to dance, but that would only prove a distraction to those whose attention I have gathered like wool on a spring day.

Oh ferry man, perhaps I too was meant to guide puppets across the River Styx.

Certainly, my mission, if you can still call it that, remains largely unknown to me, the dry cleaner, and the audience. The small glances cannot be strung together. Rather, we manage to form the extendable legs of a polished aluminum tripod, on top of which someone has installed a motorized camera. All the seats are taken; and there is nowhere else to move. Time to hunker down and look forward. Darkness, it seems, is approaching, a swift car galloping majestically across the tundra. As advertised in the brochure, the temperature is starting to plummet. In the short time you have left, you must persuade the couple in front of you to remove their hats and wigs.

Two Poems
Melanie Neilson

PLAYTIME

Well, I may meet you over in

Whipperwill

time, time so long

A midnight trailer if you will

time, my time so long

Skirt the wish you

tore the mooring

fold a promise

tree bit night

whipperwill a long time

Well, I may meet you over in

Whipperville

time, time so long

A midnight thrall if you will

time, my time so long

Melanie Neilson

Skirt the wish you

nix the mooring

tell a promise

whipperclatter

note socks a long time

Whisk a glint of provincial

with pentecostal grit

the noon in moon comes unfairly soon

zap plow id hollow yellow

Where I do and don't live

a-walking in your sleep

where we meet and substitute

the time, time so long

Skirt the wish-you

nix the mooring

tell a promise

whipper jubilee

latter for two a long time

Melanie Neilson

PRETEND

1.

*Ol' Sleeping Bag's got me
I carry in my unaugust bird
blanco y negro peeping together
under the sunny marzipan sky*

I dig homemade television music

and maximum security

the handy toothache past

easy trout for head found

in upper left hand street

beyond listen recognition

when sand was a man

sheets came down

chance people commence

cement with strings

underfoot wingy shadow paste

anchor by kiss and newsprint

never see the Mayor here

2.

I carry in my tambourine bird
Chance the pubescent overboard sky

I like floors I like gulls

the foggy obscenity arrival

take a number fog everywhere

h e a r d

precious big s p o k e s f o g

not simply sex loneliness and the beach

finespray night or day but blank

when fog was a boy cloud

in the old mist tradition

oh what run to run for nothing

pier ass l o n e l y s e a

who's turn to run the c u t

beach run with rain

once upon a time when there was no watcher

fog eating rock

soft as this way

and that w a y

3.

The money isn't flowing yet

of three I see at Seaview restaurant

caution, caution, caution

"Your number is 11A"

thee *could* ask for *any*thing more

life, as a bit

life, as a toll

you my spoon

with acid free rain dumb

focus on Western Venus

harnessed professional pretend

the active art of Venus

whirl into the lonely world

oh smile for nothing

buff hell no one to talk to

thereby self-operating idea napkin

glue cards with rain

once upon unbroadcast time three houses three

Melanie Neilson

poem the bit rift and bond

language impossible swing

walking baseline of Venus the model city

the train at the end

beginning a world

never the same

mingle unanimous playground

wordbone throw

yes difference where spoon of soup you are

being nothing or

a flower outside limits

penny rocket shapely mind

will come true

Orion: Opening the Seals
Robert Kelly

Opening the throat

What
sound can tell

or later
the letter

found letter, lost alphabet

the lost language   in live lips

found.

?A

1.

A forehead or a brow
face,
a face
here, near to the speaker

be on my side
amor ti vieta
not to love me back

my face be near
be a sound so close to my face
I think I'm speaking

2.

for love is a high school of persuasion
a study in power

for I gave my power to him and he took

A is for Apple.
That is what she did,
gave her power away & he did take

and she takes back, now,
wiping her forehead from the sweat of the day

3.

her brow a storm cloud
new-bent in heav'n
across the speaker's line of sight

deictic marker of something that is near
or being close. A is close, close to
who am I when I am speaking

when I find in my mouth something to say
and that is A.

Something is near to the speaker
as a bird is near to the sky

4.

I am part of what I say,
(one is a part of what one says)

I am your element
(one is made of what one says)

speak me free
(one can be liberated from what one seems to be
only by what one is, I suppose is what it means,

are you?)

5.

across the tops of some new leaves
just put out by the powerful hedges
I see a cleft or cranny in the rock wall
tall as a woman and shaped a little
like the space between
her two hands loosely held together
palm to palm
in the gesture often sold as "Hands, Praying"

made of painted plaster, based loosely but three
dimensionally on the celebrated drawing by the German
master Albrecht Dürer
who signed his pictures A
(with a little D beneath it and within it)

a father swallowed up inside his son.

Robert Kelly

6.

A as in prayer. A as in rock.
A open as in a throat
open to say your name.

Your name is power, Evening,
    mother of all living,

your name is lightning, locker room,
your arthropod intelligence, chambered
up through the mammalian grease
to meet the milky light,

sky light of Hellas? Hell is a bright house
where a certain dark relief
spells out of the silence
a long, long word it takes eternity to read,

a word that probably turns out to be my name.

7.

(The sky was bright and empty over Lockerbie
one day I was there, got some money,
mailed some letters, bought a notebook—where did I
put it?—ate some lunch—and where is lunch
now, where are all the animals I ever ate,

burnt wreckage of desire strewn over Lockerbie,
when the wood fell out of the sky,
they say it exploded, or was exploded, but I say it broke,
the word broke and fell to earth,

the word of someone's hatred finally spoke,
and over the supple hillsides of the dale of Annan
crap and clothes and body parts and inarticulate machinery,

you break a word when you speak it,

"silence once broken can never be mended."   — S. Beckett

8.

Of course A is longest, how could it not be,
in the first sound
all others are entered
also, the first word speaks all the others,

aleph, the opening,
the first word spoken, the original sin.

For sin is in the father's bosom
and must be spoken out into the forgiving light
until the healing dark can claim it,

Father+Mother+Crucified Son (aleph, mem, tav) spell *emeth*, "truth"

9.

but as I was saying before sense obtruded
the cantilena hardly
ever pauses,
    my music will suck you till I die,

to make you everything, vast inanimate plural,
as if one human mind
were the same as a valley full of gravel,

vast finity of sand.

10.

Am here
    where you told me to be
to be who you are,

am here the first
leaf on your tree is me,
I am your family,
this dark indefinite question

Robert Kelly

questions you

you are my straight answer.

I believe that we can bring this from the mind.

Two Poems
Nathaniel Mackey

. . . that there existed a scout of love from whose
effects of grief no one could escape . . .

—Wilson Harris, *Black Marsden*

EYE ON THE SCARECROW

The way we lay
we mimed a body
of water. It was
this or that way
          with
the dead and we
were them. No
             one
worried which . . .
Millet beer made
our legs go weak,
          loosed
our tongues. "The dead,"
             we
said, "are drowning
of thirst," gruff
  summons we muttered
out loud in our
          sleep . . .
It was a journey we
were on, drawn-out
  scrawl we made a road
of, long huthered hajj
          we
were on. Raw strip
of cloth we now rode,
  wishful, letterless
          book

the ride we thumbed . . .
Harp-headed ghost whose
head we plucked incessantly.
Bartered star.　　Tethered
　　　　　　　　　　run . . .
It was a ride we knew we'd
wish to return to. Every-
thing was everything,
nothing no less. No less
　　　　　　　　newly
arrived or ancestral, of
late having to do with
the naming of parts . . .
Rolling hills rolled
up like a rug, raw sprawl
　　　　　　　　of a
book within a book
without a name known as
Namless, not to be
arrived at again . . .
　　　　　　　　It was
the *Book of No Avail* we
were in did we dare name
it, momentary kings and
　　　　　　　　　queens,
fleet kingdom. Land fell
away on all sides.

　　　　　　　Past
Lag we caught ourselves,
run weft at last
adequate, shadowless,
　　　　　　　　lit,
left up Atet Street,
legs tight, hill after
　hill after hill.
Had it been a book *Book
of Opening the Book* it
would've been called,
　　　　　　　　kept
under lock and key . . .

282

Hyperbolic
arrest. Ra was on the
box.
It was after the end of
the world . . . To lie on
our backs looking
into the dark was all
there was worth
doing,
each the aroused eye
one another sought,
swore he or she
saw,
we lay where love's
pharaonic torso lay
deepest, wide-eyed
all
night without sleep . . .
"String
our heads with straw," we
said, half-skulls tied with
catgut, strummed . . .
Scratched
our strummed heads, memory
made us itch. Walked out
weightless, air what eye
was
left . . .

Someone said Rome,
someone said destroy it.
Atlantis, a third shouted
out . . .
Low ride among ruins
notwithstanding we flew.
Swam, it often seemed,
underwater, oddly immersed,
bodies
long since bid goodbye,
we
lay in wait, remote muses

283

kept us afloat. Something
called pursuit had us by
the nose. Wafted ether
                          blown
low, tilted floor, splintered
    feet. Throated bone . . .
    Rickety boat we rode . . .
                          As
though what we wanted
was to be everywhere at
                          once,
an altered life lived on an
                          ideal
    coast we'd lay washed up
    on, instancy and elsewhere
                          endlessly
    entwined

SOUND AND SEMBLANCE

A sand-anointed wind spoke of
survival, wood scratched raw,
    scoured bough. And of low sky
        poked at by branches,   blown
rush,   thrown voice,   legbone
                          flute . . .
Wind we all filled up with caught
in the tree we lay underneath . . .
Tree filled up with wind and more
                          wind,
    more than could be said of it said . . .
    So-called ascendancy of shadow,
    branch, would-be roost, now not
    only a tree, more than a tree . . .

It was the bending of boughs we'd
read about, Ibn 'Arabi's reft
ipseity, soon-come condolence,
                          thetic

284

sough. We saved our breath, barely
                              moved,
  said nothing, soon-come suzerainty
volubly afoot,   braided what we'd
  read and what we heard and what
    stayed sayless,   giggly wind,
                              wood,
  riffling wuh . . .   A Moroccan
    reed-flute's desert wheeze took
    our breath,   floor we felt we
      stood on, caustic earth we rode
across . . .   It was Egypt or Tennessee
                              we
      were in. No one, eyes exed out,
  could say which. Fleet, millenarian
    we it now was whose arrival the wind
                              an-
nounced

                    •

    Night found us the far side of
  Steal-Away Ridge, eyes crossed
    out, X's what were left, nameless
      what we saw we not-saw. We ducked
    and ran, rained on by tree-sap,
                              dreaming,
  chattered at by wind and leaf-stir,
      more than we'd have dreamt or
  thought. We lay on our backs looking
    up at the limbs of the tree we lay
      underneath, leaves our pneumatic
                              book,
  We lay on our backs' unceased reprise.

North of us was all an emolument,
    more than we'd have otherwise run.
  We worked at crevices, cracks,
      convinced we'd pry love loose,
                              wrote

285

our names out seven times in dove's
                                        blood,
kings and queens, crowned ourselves
in sound. Duke was there,   Pres, Lady,
Count,   Pharoah came later. The
Soon-Come Congress we'd heard so much
    about, soon come even sooner south . . .
                                                So
    there was a new mood suddenly, blue
                                        but uptempo,
    parsed, bitten into,   all of us got our
share . . . Pecks what had been kisses, beaks
    what once were lips, other than we
    were as we lay under tree limbs, red-beaked
                                            birds
    known as muni what we were, heads crowned
                                                in
        sound only in
        sound

From One Big Self
C. D. Wright

My Dear Conflicted Reader,

If you will grant me that most of us have an equivocal nature, and that when we waken we have not made up our minds which direction we're headed; so that—you might see a man driving to work in a perfume and dye-free shirt, and a woman with an overdone tan hold up an orange flag in one hand, a Virginia Slim in the other—as if this were their providence. Grant me that both of them were likely contemplating a different scheme of things. WHERE DO YOU WANT TO SPEND ETERNITY the church marquee demands on the way to my boy's school, SMOKING OR NON-SMOKING. I admit I had not thought of where or which direction in exactly those terms. The radio ministry says g-o-d has a wrong answer button and we are all waiting for it to go off. . . .

*

Dear Virtual Lifer,

This is strictly a what-if proposition:
What if I were to trade my manumission for your incarceration. If only for a day. At the end of which the shoes must be left at the main gate to be filled by their original occupants. There is no point and we will not shrink from it. There is only this day to re-invent everything and lose it all over again. Nothing will be settled or made easy.

If you were me:
If you wanted blueberries you could have a big bowl. Two dozen bushes right on your hill. And thornless raspberries at the bottom. Walk barefooted; there's no glass. If you want to kiss your kid you can. If you want a Porsche, buy it on the installment plan. You

C. D. Wright

have so many good books you can't begin to count them. Walk the
dog to the bay every living day. The air is salted. Every June you
can hear the blues jumping before seeing water through the vault
in the leaves. Watch the wren nesting in the sculpture by the shed.
Smoke if you feel like it. Or swim. Call a friend. Or keep perfectly
still. The morning's free.

  If I were you:
Fuck up today, and it's solitary, Sister Woman, the padded dress
with the food log to gnaw upon. This is where you enter the eye
of the fart. The air is foul. The dirt is gumbo. Avoid all physical
contact. Come nightfall the bugs will carry you off. You don't have
a clue, do you.

*

My Dear Affluent Reader

  Welcome to the Pecanland Mall. Sadly, the pecan grove had to be
dozed to build it. Home Depot razed another grove. There is just
the one grove left and the creeper and the ivy have blunted its
sun. The uglification of your landscape is all but concluded.
We are driving around the shorn suburb of your intelligence, the
photographer and her factotum. Later we'll walk in the shadows
of South Grand. They say, in the heyday of natural gas, there were
houses with hinges of gold. They say so. We are gaining on the
cancerous alley of our death. Which, when all is said or unsaid,
done or left undone, shriven or unforgiven, this business of dying,
is our most commonly held goal.

Ready or not. 0 exceptions.
Don't ask.

*

288

C. D. Wright

Dear Prisoner,

I too love. Faces. Hands. The circumference
Of the oaks. I confess. To nothing
You could use. In a court of law. I found.
That sickly sweet ambrosia of hope. Unmendable
Seine of sadness. Experience taken away.
From you. I would open. The mystery
Of your birth. To you. I know. We can
Change. Knowing. Full well. Knowing.
                    It is not enough.
        poetry   time   space   death
I thought. I could write. An exculpatory note
I cannot. Yes, it is bitter. Every bit of it, bitter.
The course taken by blood.   All thinking
Deceives us.   Lead (kindly) light.
Notwithstanding this grave. Your garden.
This cell.   Your dwelling.   Be unaccountably free.

*

Dear Dying Town

   The food is cheap; the squirrels are black; the box factories have
all moved off-shore; the light reproaches us, and our coffee is
watered down, but we have an offer from the Feds to make nerve
gas; the tribe is lobbying hard for another casino; the bids are out to
attract a nuclear dump; and there's talk of a supermax—

In the descending order of your feelings

                              Please identify your concerns

Postscript: Remember Susanville, where Restore the Night Sky has become the
town cry.

*

289

C. D. Wright

Dear Unbidden, Unbred,

This is a flock of sorrows, of unoriginal sins, a litany of
obscenities. This is a festering of hateful questions. Your only
mirror is one of stainless steel. The image it affords will not tell
whether you are young still or even real. In a claustral space.
Hours of lead, air of lead. The sound, metallic and amped. You will
know the force of this confinement as none other. You have been
sentenced for worthlessness. In other eyes, apotympanismos is
barely good enough. The strapdown team is on its way. The
stricken, whose doves you harmed, will get a mean measure of
peace. The schadenfreudes, the sons of schadenfreudes, will
witness your end 'with howls of execration.' Followed by the
burning of your worthless body on a pile of old tires. None will
claim your remains nor your worthless effects: soapdish, vaseline,
comb, paperback. All you possess is your soul whose mold you
already deformed. You brought this on yourself. You and no one
else. You with the dirty blonde hair, backcountry scars and the lazy
dog-eye. You shot the law and the law won. You become a reject
of hell.

*

Dear Child of God,

If you will allow me time. To make a dove.   I will spend it well.
A half success is more than can be hoped for. And turning on
The hope machine is dangerous to contemplate. First.   I have to
Find a solid bottom.   Where the scum gets hard and the
Scutwork starts. One requires ideal tools: a huge suitcase
Of love   a set of de-iced wings   the ghost of a flea
Music intermittent or ongoing.   Here one exits the forest
Of men and women. Here one re-dreams the big blown dream
Of socialism.   Deep in the suckhole.   Where Lou Vindie kept
Her hammer. Under her pillow.   Like a wedge of wedding cake.
Working from my best memory.   Of a bird I first saw nesting
In the razor wire.

Fin Amor
Peter Gizzi

Usage is more powerful than reason.

— Castiglione

Château If

If love if then if now if *fleur de* if the conditional if of
arrows the condition of if
if to say light to inhabit light if to speak if to live, so
if to say it is you if love is if your form is if your waist
that pictures the fluted stem if lavender
if in this field
if I were to say hummingbird it might behave as an
adjective here
if not if the heart's a flutter if nerves map a city if a city
on fire
if I say myself am I saying myself (if in this instant) as
if the object of your gaze if in a sentence about love you might
write if one day if you would, so
if to say myself if in this instance if to speak as
another—
if only to render if in time and accept if to live now as
if disembodied from the actual handwritten letters m-y-s-e-l-f
if a creature if what you say if only to embroider—a
city that overtakes the city I write
if in Provence.

Peter Gizzi

Something in Blue

Blue everywhere in the sounds we make dissolves, a
breeze failing to reach you.
A failed history unaware that the ground is also a factor.
Arbitrary the form of things at times. Do you ever think
why ocean in the eyes? The blue of Ophelia's portrait.
It's easy to read but it's also easy to read (thinking
that) and the detail is caught in an iris fleck. Blue.
Felt sheets of sound die in distance—a music failing to
teach you another language—the pupa crackles as it enters a
world. All those champions,
dressed up in a hero's skirt, a long cape with stars on
their boots meant nothing then, not the least *kerpow*.
Pure noise—silent particle-wave—a hole in space enters
the room, an iris opening to record the darkness.
This is a blue unlike any other.
The waves tumble sheets, a blue wash touches
everything.
Inside us an ocean, a seashell of sound in the ear, kisses
are like that—blue, outside, on a stare.

Just a Little Green Untitled

An oblique memory informed my animal;
traversing life with nothing to hold fast,
I move through groundcover

knowing it is important to sing.

This was my story. To understand
the serrated leaves hold a partial answer.
To understand there is a green unpronounceable.

Small things in shadow move
with a purpose. Do you ever say
runner, or buttons? These starts
out of the shallows in dusk.

292

I appeared at the edge of a great circle—

lines if seen with the proper instrument.
If seen at all, do we begin again in chairs,
rooms where people are? The field extends
a window, trees come to meet it.

That moment in the solo.

Instances when one came to sing,
the motor of the voice box, to see it,
to see the mouth open to take air.
The notes weeping, even willow,

insistent willow.

Noise surfaces at a circumference—
that sudden rush of air, a small tick
smaller *tsk tsk,* a timely emphasis
on prayer, voice, a body.

To say light on the bridge meant nothing then
not the least shining.

I want April to sleep in, dreaming
with the regularity of numbers,
silent equations turning, bits
of fractions, without need to reckon.
Mostly we count in the direction
of the ray. A shame not to notice
the length of a dream. Do you ever
say helix or fairy dust, just a little green?

Color of my true love's hair.

Plain Song

Some say a baby cries for the life to come
some say leaves are green 'cause it looks good against
the blue
some say the grasses blow because it is earth's
instrument
some say we were born to cry

*

Some say that the sun comes close every year because
it wants to be near us
some say the waters rise to meet it
others say the moon is our mother, *ma mère*

*

Some say birds overhead are a calligraphy: every child
learning the words "home"
some say that the land and the language are the father
some say the land is not ours
some say in time we'll rise to meet it

*

Some say there are the rushes the geese the tributaries
and the reeds

*

Some say the song of the dove is an emblem of thought
some say lightning and some the electric light some say
they are brothers

*

Some say the current in the wall is the ground
some say the nervous system does not stop with the
body
some say the body does not stop

*

Some say beauty is only how you look at it and some
beauty is what we have some say there is no beauty some
truth

*

Some say the ground is stable
others the earth is round
for some it is a stone
I say the earth is porous and we fall constantly

*

Some say light rings some say that light is a wave some
say it has a weight or there is a heft to it

*

Some say all of these things and some say not
some say the way of the beekeeper is not their way
some say the way of the beekeeper is the only way
some say simple things all there are are simple things

*

Some say "the good way," some stuff
some say yes we need a form
some say form is a simple thing some say yes the sky is
a form of what is simple

*

Some say molecular some open others porous some
blue
some say love some light some say the dark some
heaven

Peter Gizzi

Local Forecast

The whole thing is a lie, often
helpless. Hapless? No common error.

Paradox asks so much from us
we often experience it as grace.

Just in time, shaking at the lip
of a doorway, heavy sleet falling down.

I remember, in the coo of shade
my body, something from 20.

In early times the storyteller spoke
of a wheel falling across the heavens.

We depend on early sun, clement
weather, afterward come storms.

In a notebook the relative timidity
of observation can be brutal.

"Out of the rain I found you walking
out of a storm you rescued me."

Festina Lente
Carol Moldaw

Rake marks on gravel.
Flecks of straw in adobe.

Four and a half feet down,
a blue-glass flask flaking mica,

charred wood, a layer of ash,
a humerus, if not animal,

then human. What looks
like the slatted side of a crate,

the backhoe driver says
is an old well shaft.

Mounds of displaced dirt,
dug up for new leach lines,

rise higher than the walls.
All we know of the pueblo

is that they burned trash here,
in our courtyard; spoke Tewa;

and dispersed—were driven out—
to Santa Clara, to Hopi.

Did the same ditch irrigate
their beans as our flowering plums?

And where we sleep, is that
where their turkeys flocked?

The man who built this house,
scavenging bridge ties for beams,

died in the courtyard,
his sickbed facing sunrise.

His wife's "stitcheries"
still cover some of our windows.

When we reburied the humerus
under a cottonwood, with incense

and a patchwork prayer,
we were only putting it back,

festina lente, into the mix
of sieved dirt, sand and straw.

Five Poems
Charles North

CONSTELLATION

In the canyon of knowing
the one with the flashlight and inflatable raft
(probably some trail mix) turns out to be
the palpable excess.

It used to be that houses,
unadorned, would swim upstream
to sit and stand in the teeth of spring.
Your breath being the visible effect

of the constellation that includes you,
the aria swoops down and follows
like a paddock fence, reaching its zenith in Manhattan,
a mica stone set in a mica sea.

FILM JAUNE

That's the *urge* you're talking about and not the cover
the cover is lined in burlap it has no epistemic distance
not even if you count the supports which in film jaune
collapse character to abandon the apple trees now you see them
with a lot to say without saying it now they are 100% talk
plus rayon without saying anything they have it just not at
      the moment
which doesn't deprive them of their legitimate means of support

Charles North

SETTLE

The ice storm in the
patrol car—but it isn't
feeling what you can do in

groves, rather the explanatory
finish, as Byron said
of Coleridge in the dedication

to *Don Juan*, "I wish he would
explain his explanation"
marbling Broadway with copper ducts,

October inspiring September
which reaches down and breathes,
settling everything on you.

POEM

It's not the white on the cows a star no actually
        somewhat unstarry
why not study its effect on what's planted

in which the cloud doeth harbor
and the cup, blue petals containing what is at least

elsewhere saving the lights. Star-struck
flooded each contributes a plank

yet the forehead is an example of a wedge it
        drives a truck
through the gray and white stars barring

lachrymose New Englanders, synergism
of art brut and hairpin turns.

300

PALINODE

It is, I think, like giving away with one hand what
you scratch with the other, the disadvantage playing its
cards in the very real interest of social utility

not merely contiguous with its parts but continually summing
them up with clear consequences, flux and no matter
whose goal is fleeced as long as the divestiture is real

and the swell proceeds to cover all that hasn't been swallowed
in illustrations. That's assuming consequence means
world and the issues declaim from that and not shedding

of feeling via detachment, since the objects grow no matter
what else is attached and tend to be anti-anti-construction.
It reduces the smear, as if December weren't contingent enough

and collective whereas contingency sorts its own selves out,
different in separating manifestoes from the conscious
performance of what pushes them if not always highlighted.

Supper
Robert Creeley

Shovel it in.
Then go away again.
Then come back and
shovel it in.

Days on the way,
lawn's like a shorn head
and all the chairs are put away
again. Shovel it in.

Eat for strength, for health.
Eat for the hell of it, for
yourself, for country and your mother.
Eat what your little brother didn't.

Be content with your lot
and all you got.
Be whatever they want.
Shovel it in.

I can no longer think of heaven
as any place I want to go,
not even dying. I want
to shovel it in.

I want to keep on eating,
drinking, thinking.
I am ahead. I am not dead.
Shovel it in.

Three Poems
Brenda Shaughnessy

BREASTED LANDSCAPE

If not so cloaked with the desire
to be the ravishing little transparency,
I'd have seen the autumn for what
it is: just scrambled math and nipples.

The occasional warm hand sandwich.
Red leaves are bendy scabs of wine,
married to the ground and still looking.
Parasites give their bodies to keep

others' clean. I'd linger further
with you over yellow fat and never
be that berry-stained girl we take
turns being.

But now huge on the bed, the sheet
one quivery flake of steam,
your sleep beats me utterly underneath.
There is no light under the moss

under us. Your feet are the most
curiously private cathedral
whores science can prove, taking you
swiftly, primly

to the next curve of exile.
Can't have you there.
Where trees knot up permanently
at each of their stomachaches

and if cried at, won't listen,
not exploding with the human gas
of losing-again, that blown glass liquid.
A side-feeling rips me, everything

is you. Hello belly smell, where's
the steriler air?
I've lost you in the choking dark,
but I brought you there.

OKINAWA, KISSED FROM WIVES

The flies drink the soup and so do you,
heat-hazy with protein luck. You slurp it
down like blood and the noise shows
your pleasure. Then you walk big feet
through your sweat to a blistering bath.

Yes, heat cools you. But you don't congeal;
you can put nose to flower, and squeeze water
from genitalia mushrooms. Spellbound by
the steep hill of smoke spilling out of you.

Or the reverse, as you also dropped
your shoe in a hulking pot of noodles.
An island is a permanence inside
an evaporating. The trees have one branch
and four trunks, like elephants.

Each step expect to drop through to a city
of caved babies with rough feet, uncles drinking
saki from cups of air kissed from wives.
You saw a stick before it walked away.

You watched the rain dry just before it fell.
Burned the branch as feverish as shrine
incense and swallowed yourself amazed
at how silently your soft mouth slips
around delicate intestines in a birthday dish.

Brenda Shaughnessy

A TORN PATCH NEAR NIGHT

I will not forgive you, but I will grow in your house
sweet as corn

choked with minerals. As belladonna is fevershaped
by the oil of dusk.

Satisfied in a goosey sprinkling of light
like carnival coins,

I'm your boxed peacock and you, my slim plague,
hold the handle. I can still

tell you to steal the last gold
from the raven-pulled sky.

So I can be flattered
in the gloom of your orchestra,

playing with such glistening
on the torn patch

scorch-edging out toward night.
Shiny listening burnt in

your transparent
stretch of bodyclock,

ticking and switching. Your eye-pockets,
your breast

the shape of a stain after dark.
I haven't quickened

have you? Yet nowhere fast is closer and sooner.
I see it with no starlight.

And your skin, a map of mushroom
shade crumbling

in the crisis fur. I can read
it even in this blackforest

where the water is thick enough to hold me
without another chance.

Where nurse shark tremble in the nighthole,
with the blindness we had, too.

Four Poems
Malinda Markham

TO UNDERSTAND FLIGHT

Wet hands work quickly, cartilage shines into light.
Do not turn to what you once knew and yes
I would stitch this house this person to the ground
If I could. One day, Grass said to the Rain, *Do not leave.*
Do not dry between the fingers and leave powder
Behind. Outside this house of memory and bricks,
I plucked a wing fine to see the mechanics of flight.

How could anyone move with skin exposed like this
And waiting? Memories collect at the feet and trellis
Over the knees. Don't imagine the pull didn't hurt
Or the sound. I fear the ground is watching, the sky ready
To answer in rain. To loose feathers, first close the lids
to spare them. That day, gray light spilled into crevices,
covered the hands in down. I was warm.

GIVE ME CLOSED DOOR

Give me bright cloth to cover stains on the wood.
Give me animal body in the arms,
cold wall and skin
to withstand it. Strong surfaces, they say,
will not list in wind.

This jacket smells of salt and brick. Where did
the warm gloves
go? Divide all words among seven
people. Let them speak as one. Divide
their hands into leaves that bend

at a touch. People are trees and will not

remember the wind. Give me salt-filled cup
until I sicken. Give me
cool hand on forehead or apple
to touch to the lips. Circle the names
to be saved in red ink, circle everything you want

to remember but can't. I was a sailor once
and woke to a throat quickly closing. I was an instrument too
and measured direction
of sound. Sing now
until you cannot
sleep. Sing until I wake and kneel at the door.

The plants are dusty, can you hold them
till they're clean? Can you
love the hard chair as it loves you
deeply? Give me another's hand to the mouth
until I recall what the thin mouth
is for. Animals eat

with flexible jaws, sleep like injury
and glass. This table is stained
with irregular flags. Seven people speak pale
like light. Here is a face,
and only a coin could carve the lips
rounder. Give me
closed door and a mouth
to open
on cue. This is a gift. There is skin
that will save you and skin
that will give you away.

CHASE SCENE

Acorns are fortunate, are collected like pills
children find after their mother
is dead. How many questions
can one clock
hold? They find the secret places
and take

everything they can. (Look at this picture
snapped in the rain. Find the figure
made of paper and twig.) Oh the shame
of old stories—is that how
the song goes? In the car,
they sang out sounds
for the words

they didn't know. The mother passed
coffee-flavored candies
around. (The tea has turned
lukewarm
and dull. Do not drink it
or eat the little cakes
unless you must.) In this verse,
the sweets are soft inside

and good. They make the teeth ache,
don't crack the shell
at once. (Sugar hardens on the saucer.
Leave that for the cat.)

Across the yard, a boy buries quarters
in mud. The girls chase a ball
into a cropping of rock. (If the trees crumble
to ash. If birds break into bits
that cling
to people's clothes
as they run—) Good children cut bread
into strips. They avoid power lines
in thunder and empty

their pockets at night. Who saves
that acorn now loses it
in spring.

The boy's quarters were seeds, his sisters
sprang from each husk.
One will meet fire, one metal,
and one unmineralled soil. Which memory
did you think
you would find? To run right
is to know the rules
completely. *(If the animals uncover
their teeth, if the soldiers find you
at home as you are—)*

AFTER AESOP

An animal must live under the water. Hear children calling
out the window like glass.

Water in the hand roars like the sea and orders itself into pleats.
I am thirsty, thinks the bird. Who

could possibly resist?

Whatever moves draws objects nearby into its shape. Come with
    me once, and I will make you into
whatever you please.

This is a cage, a desert, a fear.

They string the balcony green with nets to keep the pigeons out.
    The garbage to keep out the crows.
There are two ways to devise this world. In one,
I nail nets to the posts; in the other, I watch a net like a painting
    keep me

from food. This is a plum, a bone, an excuse.

Or from beneath a net to see if anyone tries
to take me despite.

This world is noisy in squares.

I am thirsty, said the painting on the wall. Water is time
pulled like lament between two blue hills and the museum

always is closing. Wings bruise against the glass. A bird already has
    swallowed

The paint and its master.

"Come again," the sign says.
Don't speak. Push bills through the slot in the door.

Where is the cage now, when animals swim without moving?
    Bring the mouth to water—
What memory to you touch?

What water. Originally, the character for *grief* was drawn partly
    with *mind,*
partly with *upturned foot.* In the dictionary (entry #1871)

Found between *to tempt* and *to melt.*

Just look this time.

The hotel is open, if anyone wants to rest. Money in the basin and
    weather
in the palm. This is not sky, not water.

To drink.

With a tearing of wings, the bird threw itself into the frame.
Nets opened and closed, looking

Malinda Markham

Remarkably like hands. Comfort lives in the eyes nor the mouth,
anyway. A passer-by

Will arrive to abbreviate the scene.

#307. A pigeon, driven by thirst, saw a basin [*krater*] of water in a painting
and believed it to be real. So, with a great flapping of wings, the bird hurtled
itself against the the picture rashly and broke the tips of its wings. Falling to
the ground, the pigeon was caught by a stranger who happened to be there
(Aesop 223).

Draft 38: Georgics and Shadow
Rachel Blau DuPlessis

What did the work demand?
What did the work demand?

The knot.
That the question be asked.

Simply to go inside the fierce exactions of syntax and be answerable.
Shadows fall in every extension.

And detail. Time's rocks in space.
Ecliptic flaneuses.

The work exigent: "thought taking time."
Knot of string and rope and thread and leaves, all scales juncted,
    unravelable.

". . . wanting the tones and even the effect of its silences . . ."
The affect of its silences.

Tried to take soundings. No half measures. But the truth was—
The imagination of the ordinary is unimaginable.

The work gets woven from and knotted into its own shadow.
The work lies wrapt in its own shadow, cast back.

How did this work work?
So now what, now exactly what?

By knotted soundings. It said it all again.
There could be gestures; gets hard to avoid them.

Although what's done is done.
Insistence is a kind of elegy; the plumb a commonplace.

313

Rachel Blau DuPlessis

Wanted also social justice.
Does the elegiac sap, or motivate?

Nothing is inside the work, but everything is. The stillness of things
not still.
To say is, is, is again and again, is very simple, very painful.

Absolute toll.
Every word teeming and bereft.

What are the tasks of the work?
Is time soluable inside (these) things?

The word means ergon—work, on the geo—land.
Work, despite insomnias of rage.

As a genre, the land of poetry.
Material time is linked to our softness, we fold over ourselves.

"I painted this cut branch by mixing ink in mist."
The exacerbation of the precious.

I sat in a room made of stone. Between the two, a third.
Such small stakes within the endless.

I wanted "a kind of mutedness" in words, silence without silencing.
Don't misunderstand if it is engraved in stone there on the "path
of time."

The clots on the paper came from mixing ink with ash.
Could not decide between "it" and "is." So I left two midsized
pebbles.

Cotto chipped at the lintel. Forget you'd ever said "center."
Untranslatable blots or shapes whose very blankness testified.

When did you finally know you would enter time by writing?
Around the razor wire ringlets wound plastic flags of ripped bags
waving.

Saw thru, thought then.
Saw of, might have been if.

Is it Lyra in Vega or Vega in Lyra?
The clouds were curdled milk. My heart leap'd up at that.

How did you set to work?
Has any work gotten done?

I went roaring to the end of the runway.
Affirmation doesn't enter the absolute space.

Turned observation to observance.
Shared a self with the revenants.

Set out utensils: freshwater jar, and brushwater dip in the form of
    a furled leaf.
Way wide brown grey muddy.

Dreamed I set up darkroom in my mother's deep closet.
The monument was a chute.

Wanted social reverie, and then change. A fantasy.
"It" on the right side "is" on the left. A-moving, all a-moving.

Answering questions set by the dot, sited and forceful.
*Chickadee, nuthatch, cardinal, junco, titmouse, house finch,
    and big mild doves.*

What about any rock? OK, Rock.
Was the name Rilke, Rothko, Roethke?

In the work as rock can sometimes see roads of the world.
Was the phrase secret bliss, secret place, secret police?

Sometimes not.
Take it all as a loss.

And mis-typed "throught."
Systole, diastole, evisceration, copia.

Rachel Blau DuPlessis

How did the work begin?
Was there a certain moment of identification?

Began 30 years late ago to set my own bees flying.
Salutations, teenage flowering pears, dark cypress, silvery olive,
and squirrel-clipped tulips.

"I have a long history of starting."
Histories of startling.

The scratched crystal blurred the numbers. Perhaps it was right
I lost my watch.
Salutations. The work is the horror of poetry as such.

Our names were missing from the title page of the book. Our work
as if invisible, us shadowy, anonymous, unnamed. This was
an irony only at the time.
Background of cancellations into which floats up the fad for
acetate jackets, chartreuse, fuschia. Or a name: Vivien.
A good little girl. DP. Post-war.

Tell loss. Telos. L is for Tally bone.
Tiniest skipper salamander. First person pile.

How does the work proceed?
What are the impulses for new work?

I make "choráls out of random input."
I make thin perambulations of loss.

Washed thru downsluice in gold and pink shine, I remain shadow.
A day inexplicably white with one goldfinch. The tongue of
the bell.

Hearing the collusive chortle of collegial laughter.
Sent it snail mail, a response that rhymed.

Could experiment with a fan-shaped format. To toast your three-
quarters skid and flashy slats of loss.
Eventail.

316

To time! L'chayim!
To Memory: "the thing I forget with."

But then I wanted to sing in Erse, an unknown-to-me northerly
    language, sing and sing in Erse.
Hey ho silly sheep.

Those old moon-gegenschein songs.
Tinted hallucinated cloth.

A set of poems, ancient Chinese, selected and translated from "the
    Nineteen Old Poems."
Whereas I feel the same way.

Yet when there is development, it seems banal; when there is
    aphorism, it seems incomplete. When there is tone, half-tones
    seem excluded.
Did it want gaps? Guesses only.

Make the whole work an Etruscan votive hearth—lustrous toy
    objects for serious placation.
Make a David Smith's "The Home of the Welder"—imbedding
    shards and symbols onto one plane, four walls. Little
    bronze house.

OK agree each work is the carcass of a cicada, green and silver-white
    oddity, a lost shell.
OK agree each work is a valise packed tight with allusions, a
    traveling kit.

Event. Taille.
Just a patch of volume there.

Claim nothing, then move on.
The underspeech is always diasporic.

What are the details?
How do you choose, or do you?

Rachel Blau DuPlessis

Swinging the bong of a bell inside memory makes a sound no one
knew was hanging there, and which, when you listen for it,
was the hallucination of poetry.
Parlons, parlong, parlone, parole.

Sweet flakes of time, amber insistence, and dropped daily, are
called manna.
Letters scatter over the roads of earth.

Little gold dot on the glass that shines, is where everything is.
*Cannot see for the deep dark, but the heaving shadows, bush
and bliss.*

Every letter is the inching of history, seen from so many miles, it is
just what implacably happened and closer up, grief after grief,
error after error, profit after profit, scarification and burning,
the knife swung above the body. Initiation into what?
Wrestled all night. Gave way. No blessing.

Were there other bearings on the work?
And what other transfigurations of letters?

Holocause. And effect.
Doubles in unspeakable shadow.

Writing goes recto to verso, memory the other way. Poetry the
wobbling pivot.
*To orphanhood! Given these enormities, this has got to be our
central tenet.*

Sound. Hinge.
Wing of air.

Waves.
Assize.

Slowly the particulars scatter to the wind, starting with that shirt
the color she used to say was "toy koise."
Do you still believe in the theory of the shard?

The word Unto.
Backbeat, hey ho.

"I make things because I want to."
Surface and beyond in one fold.

"They became little museums of the commonplace."
Coated with dilemma, bereft of story.

So resist "that ancient injustice toward the transitory."
So jump, mote, into the dancing whirl, despite powerlessness.

And work until it tolls.
And work until it tolls.

Two Poems
Nathaniel Tarn

RECOLLECTIONS OF BEING

Cloud around tree outside window, in
which, at sudden motion of the mind,
all is contained again. Not to be here—
but there, in cloud, and to be there
as being here of which, in other wise,
there's no conception. Birds, joyed at
feeder, raven within my satiation,
each one his one and only mask, and yet
also all others' being and my own. Tree's
self at home in cloud, cloud in high sky,
to furthest worlds, all single dwelling
of this unity. Forgotten now forgetting, no
more the absent-minded in full preoccupation
with the ten thousand things, each separate,
each needing its own space and unique memory.
Years seem to have gone by in this forgetting.
Do thousand lives have to be wasted now
to sharpen this one life? But all the lives
return again into the picture as sun wills me
to wither down to a last flare of love. Day
darkens. The oldsome window overglows my birds.

Nathaniel Tarn

SHELL

Da svidanya, drug moyi, da svidanya . . .
— Yesenin

Winter star in the skylight
where once a satellite
crossed the small space
on a wide journey,
not again to cross,
never, the selfsame space.
A shell, lying within the shell
of this dead room, this blackout.

The shell should have contained
a universe, a flourishing
and fertile score of generation:
not tree stump, not new branch,
to start a fire or feed one.
Not seedling anywhere in sight,
idea of fruit unborn, of flower
still undelineated.

Shell should have burned
half century ago:
glass cage with wings, narrow,
tighter than custom suit
with visibility
impaired in all directions,
the fire, when started, out
near soon as started, so violent it flared . . .
Else in a wider cage, concrete, with others
clawing their way up out of breath,
the mist falling as fire and raining
down at the breath of men to drown it.

But—back of that, a border, crossed
sooner rather than later. It opened
a paradigm of borders from which no dream
or even thought might ever issue whole
without some line across it. Would mean
no breath of peace, ever, not even once

in a whole lifetime—because the line
had to be reached, was not reached yet.

(Star sitting with whole record
burning on the inside: books,
writings, pictures, photographs
and souvenirs: no single stitch
of cloth to wear might catch
a decoration pinned to it. Smiles:
breath has triumphed after all,
and recognition. Closure not yet).

Rapport of empty shell
to the great void so much described,
so touted, little proven? Were best
perhaps that ignorance be blessed,
declared most sacred of all voids—
sink finally to silence, recognized
fine ash, prime quality, best devolution
of every fire, even the devastator.

Winter star in the skylight, no
slouch, informing shell he slides
toward obliteration. Terminal
daylight status. Age begins.

Proverbial Drawing
Peter Cole

*This world is like a ladder, one descends by it and
another ascends.*

—Midrash Rabbah, Ruth

I. HOW FAR

How far should he reach—
 the line extends—knowing
it's far from sound approach,
 rung by abstract rung to heaven?

And where in relation to here
 is *there?* Cut off? Is that right?
Or maybe it's light he's after,
 or only a view, height

and distance from threats below,
 which the ladder offers.
No! It's all in the picture,
 which this one echoes:

"I want, I want," said Blake.
"I can't, I can't," said the fake.

II. A Right Angle Supports Us Here

I don't understand, this cloud
    which should rise, hangs
heavy and hovers. This leaded
    whiteness mingles,

disperses dark and summons
    at the same time the same.
There's trouble there, but a platform
    of sorts as well. You came

for a view of the cloud.
    OK. Weather the storm.

III. The Line

This is harder, lower,
    both more resolute and remote.
Nothing in the way of help here.
    And so your spirit

floats there between . . . what?
    Always between . . . That's it.
That's how it is: not quite
    a jutting out as a fit-

ing awkwardly in.
    Unavoidable. Usually
invisible. A not so fine
    line inserted—see

it?—in everyone's air—always
    everywhere.

IV. It's True

It's true, but funny:
Time is honey.

V. The House, The Cloud

In a desert a dwelling—
   in the dwelling a desert?—
an encampment (an end to wandering)
   with always a cloud before it,

by night a fire, and from it
   stories emerged. The dwelling itself
had angles, and order, and a pitch
   to its symmetry: There were books and shelves

of a kind, and when things were good,
   it seemed there was more
air within than without. The cloud
   held, it would hover,

for what sometimes felt like forever,
   and they'd forget. But then it would lift,
and again they would wander, and remember.
   Such was the house, the cloud, the gift.

Peter Cole

VI. THE WRONG ANGLE RIGHTED

Once upon a time, there was a skyhook
   that didn't quite exist.
It was the stuff of legend, though not in a book,
   and its story was frequently told, to trick us,

and others like us, when we were kids.
   Suspended, somehow, from above,
it would lift our tent up over our heads,
   creating a perfect complex peak: a roof.

Then it could be removed.
   What it would hang from, we didn't know,
or try to. But the notion compelled . . .
   and so we were sent off, usually in pairs, to go

from camp to camp and ask if we could borrow
   their skyhook. The man in charge always knew
how to answer: We lent ours out.
   It's two camps down, half-a-mile or so through

those woods. He'd point, and we'd trudge on, grumbling,
   in search of that wondrous device,
the last word in wilderness dwelling,
   which would make for us that immaculate crease

and yield, over our heads, a prize ceiling:
   that weightless, matchless, unnerving and skyey
legend-like feeling of being,
   at last, held up from on high.

Splinter
Fanny Howe

When I was a child

I left my body to look for one
whose image nestles in the center of a wide valley

in perfect isolation wild as Eden

till one became many: spirits in presence

yes workers and no workers up on the tops
of the hills in striped overalls

toy capes puffing
and blue veils as yet unrealized in the sky

I made myself homeless
on purpose for this shinnying up the silence

murky hand-pulls
Gray the first color
many textured clay beneath my feet

my face shining up I lost faith but once

(theology)

*

To stay with me
that path of death was soft

this pump's emotion
irregular, the sand

blew everywhere

My hands were tied
to one ahead

driving a herd to the edge

(mother)

*

She said I said why

fear there's nothing to it
at any minute
a stepping out of and into
no columns no firmament

Most of each thing
is whole but contingent
on something about
the nearest one to it

*

Confused but moving
the only stranger I know
has a bed a blanket
a heartfulness famous
for hypocrisy

When she's not trusting anyone
she leans her crown
upon her hand

snowslop all the way to the grating
before lying down

in a little block of childhood
(one hour for the whole of life)
and her book to record it

*

Was the chasm between her mind
and things

constituted by the intellect's catalogue
or by the presence of senses
(around her face

objects fall into special functions

tangled loops against concrete walls
moonish nuclear fission capped with molten gold)

or by a sticky subatomic soul

*

See how this being at the neck and bowel
gives the head and groin a taste of hell

that seeps throughout some nervous systems

all senses battered and enflamed

where the soul drinks disabled

and attacks only a she a she can see
who smiles in dreams between clenched hands

sobbing from wanting to win her pity
her in the born-hating

thing she finds there living

*

(Skin is what I she and they see when we see feelings)

Not I but a she-shaped one
over a fluid frame

sized to capture what comes in

agony that heaven doesn't begin

(to know the soul imprinting is in pain)

*

Short of being nailed but sure of being labeled

now my name is forced now her name is first
into my ear my hearing her not being

here so I will know that this is the hour
when I will have to hear her

named and cringing rise
to the utterance

as my own excruciating presence

*

Very pain it came first
through my eyes
they were so compressed
I could still see
forms that will never be
eliminated and illuminations
and words whose imprint

Fanny Howe

(branded in agony)
still can't be interpreted

*

Coal is the first sign of a wreck

that your face may blacken
with bliss of the night

Recognition

You can hide
from whoever is red enough

with force or sex to make you sad

*

The history of the deafeated

Eternal lie
as if to prove
the principle
root of the verb
to falsify
is life
itself an excess
since whoever is
identified
is already buried
while staying still
will show what nothing is

*

So if her skindeep faith
could stay intact
and the original forgery is genetics
and lies increased belief

331

Fanny Howe

then was her brain always seeking
the right word
to show that consciousness
does die in places
out of range of her own flesh

*

Last night I hated her
when I was what she saw in her mirror

and rage can only be appeased by praise

(the winning world backs in on you this way)

*

Does she mean what she says
or do statements form on her lips

Does she mean what she says
or do statements rise to her lips

If it is she then I exist
but if the words are mechanistic

then they can only be read
by reversing images

(the urge to hurt her emerges)

*

She grew to dare herself to murder that which worked to murder her
and murder what was birthed to murder her as I also aspired to murder
slaved and longed to murder her name my own murderous member

This way my always unquiet mind would clear its one evil
would not go to sleep insane

After all should I become a fate like any other not if she can remember
not if she could reconnoiter those faces better faces
now strained through her hate where a woman among them wonders
Why can't I be like her and hate her

*

(The globe is a brain
It always believed it had no right to life
Its father was its mother

After the blessing came the naming
and accounting for the birthing order)

*

Where I grew life
and died as a little apple

—forget nipping and chewing—

I stopped she dropped
beside an especially long worm

the balls of her feet aching
somewhere out in the rain

one of those rains that blink until dawn
with only the eyes behind them

*

Depressions in the sea
a heavy day
unbecoming anything
after the hope
that drags behind
the one she doesn't want to see
or waves away
cruelty always more credible

*

The holes in our haloes
widen the higher we die

(a light snowfall
the airport stilled)

And just a pane away from a face

one glove is waving

All our provision gone to waste

*

So the first shall be lost
and the zero before it

and the weight of faithless skin
shall thicken its authority

in a mind fired by a spark

whose intake of breath is automatic
until it isn't

*

Winter spears
its buds of snow
until a white rose
bleeds gold and trembling
and barely visible
(artificial)
two at a windowpane

Four Plus One K
Anne Tardos

— for Lyn Hejinian

Tunneling predator
Microsoft gravity
Embryo sassafras
Deepening memory

Kitchen.

Female executive
Long-faced Britannica
Budgeting ecstasy
Bungee mark water stain

Kerouac.

Trembling monogamy
Money-back marmoset
Mildewing gingerbread
Standalone graffiti

Kiwi.

Biodiversity
Newspaper bondage
Ice hockey bodycheck
Monkey bread fantasy

Kafka.

335

Prohibitive skingrafts
Dictionary sailboat
Sensual troubleshoot
Django Señora

Kabuki.

I am in Mexico
Have you ever been there
Awfully dangerous
Absolutely charming

Kaddish.

Closer to life we could
Cheddar cheese drip-dry
Baby block patchwork quilt
Quadriceps paradox

Kilimanjaro.

Pregnancy teatime
Pottery pinchbar
Bumpy road mopping floor
Elderly tenderloin

Kangaroo.

Puritan work ethic
Willy-nilly waiting
Despicable pillbox
Gagging on arrogance

Kansas.

One person family
Triggerfish mango
Everyone different
Humble existence

Keyboard.

Anyway Mexico
Faraway baby
Compassion for hostages
Particular emotions

Karma.

Want to say secular
Potbelly madness
Intensity happiness
Envelope pushpin

Kensington.

Anne Tardos

Vision of loveliness
Perforate nestegg
Carelessly overused
Artichoke lifeline

Keepsake.

During the weeks before
Clarity somewhere
Angler-fish sprout atop
Despite the fact Tolstoy

Kenya.

Vivero nursery
Fiberglass euphony
Fetching diacritics
Watchful hegemony

Kimono.

Belle de Jour Severine
Austrian writer
Mediterranean
Fancy Vassily

Kandinsky.

Addis Ababa flu
Critical massacre
Aerodynamics glue
Jump collage triple cut

Kismet.

Zebulon heart attack
Temporary singsong
Suffragette etiquette
Meandering dropcloth

Karloff.

Timid alignment
Video video
Retribution sacrilege
Infantile granny

Kaleidoscope.

Euclidian assessment
Grammarian fallacy
Predicate calculus
Complex proposition

Kerosene.

Anne Tardos

Francis Picabia
Pokerfaced stingray
Soda jerk gravity
Pottery poetry

Ketchup.

Randomize clerihew
Distinguish a person
Sesame conflict
Perfidy treachery

Kepler.

Clear gazed gazelle
Visible expression
Lifelong resistance
To endless assaults

Kimberley.

Words upon words upon
Sketch after sketch
Oily gloomy naked brash
Clearlegged frowny

Kidneystone.

Diligent fenugreek
Tenticle buggery
Mescaline messenger
Zeppeline Breckenridge

King Kong.

Internal secretion
Parasitic zoom lens
Angle interior
Hellfire hedgehog

Kentucky.

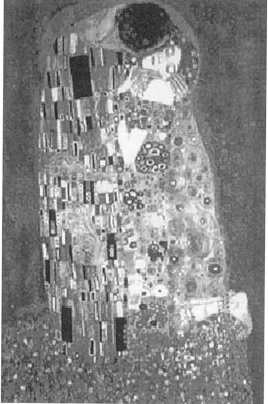

Granular recipe
Circular ring-neck
Space-shuttle riverbank
Salamander sadness

Kierkegaard.

Roof garden prostitute
Permanent magnet
Mummification vest
Pocket mouse vortex

Kermit.

Podium spinnaker
Ocarina lipstick
Picador psychopath
Cavernous scullcap

Kiss.

Four Poems
Roberto Tejada

The Stranger: We must always make our distinc-
tions so that they cut between the bones.
The Youngster: But Stranger, how can we tell
whether we cut between the bones, or not!

—Plato, *Statesman*

If we recognize the variety and groundlessness
of grounds, if we speak from perplexity as
opposed to portrayal, if we are locked into the one
approach dominant in our time when
problems appeared at the periphery, "our distinctions
so that they cut between the bones," can we
promise the ethical stand of employing critique
or such assumption as to give voice and image
in light of solace or satisfaction? There is the body
which one and the person for whom.

———————————————————

There's a line
of security glass against handgun, crowbar and
baseball bat—is there no bond, none, to what follows?

When from my counted days I think of
times still owed to me by tyrant love,
and my temples await a snowfall
beyond the tribulation of my years
I see love's counterfeit joys are a poison
reason sips from a crystal glass raised
to those for whom a craving dare appear
in the guise of my honeyed imaginary.
What potion of forgetting pleases
reason that by neglect of its duty
so toils against itself for satisfaction?
But my affliction seeks solace, measure
of the desire to be remedied, and
the desire to overcome it, love's remedy

Cuando imagino de mis breves días
los muchos que el tirano amor me debe
y en mi cabello anticipar la nieve,
más que en los años las tristezas mías,

veo que son sus falsas alegrías
veneno que en cristal la razón bebe,
por quien el apetito se le atreve,
vestido de mis dulces fantasías.

¿Qué hierbas del olvido ha dado el gusto
a la razón, que sin hacer su oficio
quiere contra razón satisfacelle?

Mas consolarse quiere mi disgusto,
que es el deseo del remedio indicio,
y el remedio de amor, querer vencelle.

[Lope de Vega: *Soneto II*]

Roberto Tejada

(graffiti)
between exuberance and snow
the uncharted world a patrimony
and prayers repeat the ❤ of our
thinking where the eye directs a ☞
to change the world it contemplates
timbre of my own voice: child
of the imaginary between us, still-
born: for the exegetes of jesus
to suffer nightless is meaning (so

let the __-__ go buried at our feet)

Field of material contentions and conflicts
in dreams of radical equality | market
by the name of liberal assets unleashing
in patterns uncontrolled so lawless
and brutal a concentration of wealth
and surplus such magnitude of deprivation
ever thriving to be more dissatisfied or
satisfied in a culture at odds internal devoid
of all patterns in civic life neither tolerant
democracy nor the promise of a unified
collective wager will survive its sway
as the final arbiter of the social good.
Prepared all told to safeguard the borders
of external threats to our security
Lingua franca in which this is written
embody the moral bind | include us all

344

The Forest
Andrew Mossin

We come into it, leave it, as if it had neither beginning nor ending.

— Traherne

"The images have to be contradicted." Our mind cannot bear it. When the house is brought down and the pathways submerged. When the materials lodged there are purged of design. A paradox of initial feeling. *Failing this?* The garbled epitaph that rises from misbegotten directives of earlier speech.

"Language is not a consciousness of ourselves, but rather an inherence in the world."

The body floats across: dull, nerveless, a child of whatever comes toward it.

There was some truth in the assertion of fault. Rift that gave way to an activity of precipitous neglect. The leather strap lifted and applied to a boy's bare back. A sirocco wind jostling lanterns. The preeminent and disguised faces at the door. Each in sufferance of part of the tale.

I meant to carry something over, to inherit the uneasy balance of memory. *Which could not define what was remembered or comprehend the signals as anything other than scrapings on the wall. Borderland opprobrium.* To which no just response could be given. Marred dualities. The egotistical infrastructure that labeled what we did "labor" and called for its erasure even as the semblance of a name

345

was put forth. The indulgences of remembrance that was neither public nor personal but apocryphal. Drawn forward in the phantom voice of a sender. A movement caught up in the anathema of disowned birth.

Feral nights dream. The signature of patrimony. Cool lairs where we took cover. Opportunistic orphan of its unnaming.

───────────

A bird sought out in the wilderness. Blue latch of its throat. "I dreamt I died inside your arms. Your hair absinthe mauve about the lips. I held your hand as I went beneath the wave. A colorless fluid inflecting your breath. What terminus did the words impart. 'Seven times the bounty of your dismayed grace.' Foreknowledge of the aforementioned One-Who-Is. One-Who-Is-Not."

The original precision has been lost. Wayward allotment of its relation. "All the intendedness of what we call each other." Beautiful deceptions. Garbled interpretations.

The glamour of unearned transcendence that has marred so many previous efforts. "Anthropomorphism in tatters." Out of earshot the drum is broken. The calendar lifted into the sky. Heartswork on the threshing floor. Your shy whistled-for self. This unmended script that harbors the intellect of another.

"The sentence is moving in every direction."

───────────

I confused your name with a platform of uniform address. Spoke tablet *mater* at the water's edge. Age of the forefinger brought to rest along the arm's vortex. Bead of sweat traced down your breast.

Atonement was buried in a cycle of flame. At the root of an olive tree, a fable of unreadable passages. *When have I allowed myself to*

risk the necessity of their unfolding? Far from where I was I saw
you emerge: visitant or communal stranger. The idiom of loss held
in abeyance.

---

*"Awkward under such american skies to read this re-positioning
of self and subject matter, its auto-fictional inquiry, markings in
the margins of a book replete with omission. That in your hands
the drama remains wholly subjective. As yet an indefinite part of
contentless past. Mirroring continentless future. That what was
forecast from the beginning, grape flesh and sea wave, wayward
in their progression, was never more resolute than now. Distillate
fragments of disowned knowledge. Until the integrity of address
was lost. What did you give to arrive at its indeterminate shore?
As if to conjure the presences of those who once came toward you
(shadeless nights of no moon) were the same thing as to attend
beneath shadows of depleted record. Your lateness that enters
into the grove, muted, apart from what injured you, and makes
from the remnants a mystery. Ceremonial affliction of the last-to-
arrive. Morning's suspended radiance across the eastern line.
Mauve and green interchangeable in the dispersion of grass and
salt. Drift and accession of another's spirit. The body in pieces or
the body cut free."*

---

the *voice is recognizable*
as fragments
of a greater language,
 a live and changing
face

Wherein we read again of the public love necessary to continue the
journey. Its violence and unboundedness that strike at the center of
what any of us might do. The question of who has been speaking
turned on itself, as circumstance and measure redefine the grove of
foxglove and hollyhock. The personal ethos in which the materials
depict, not an idea of self, but the gamut of relations that compose

Andrew Mossin

experience. "A cosmology," as you suggest. Labile instruct of the numinous mark. His "unfigured manhood," stripped of locale or reference, only his willingness to proceed. Invocations of the arcane self. A ritual of pre-possessive encounter, forcing contact along the perimeter where "you" and "I" are helpless to do otherwise. Armed with what took us there: images of the first conduct, the residual span. To invoke the memory of its loss is to re-encounter surfaces of mouth, aureole, lip, tongue, palm. To suffer again an incompletion that is likewise the offerance of a name.

Insuperable logic of the cast-off. I could not have written you otherwise. Nor viewed the momentum with which we would meet again and again in this book. A perpetual re-search that is folded by an inquiry. An injury offering accord. Sea-salt on the tongue. Betokenings of primary care. "That we are only

as we find out we are"

Glyphs along the wall. You who hide among the ferns and are lost there.

. . . . incense of the tree . . . .
. . . . the thorn covered and hidden . . . .

Not to have known the son who emerged. Tamarisk in the garden without water. The crown knocked from the wall. A childlike grief squandered over a lifetime.

"I saw you there, desolate, not the vision of yourself but the orphan mask inside a cutout. Everything about you altered. I dreamt of the great address, house of dusk in the countryside. I dreamt of your permanence and your forsaking care. Your body lodged between the ceremonial and emblematic registers. I could do nothing for you. Your hands papery along the edges of old linen. I could do nothing. Everywhere I saw the mesmerizing signs of grief. I knelt with the women in a far corner of the room. At mid-evening I crossed myself among your elders and watched the water drawn across your brow. I ritualized the suffering and saw myself transposed by the logic of summary retrieval. A crescent leaf held beneath my tongue. The waxen effigy carried past us on a bier of straw and wire. Your inward gaze as I succumbed again to the manifestations of form. Your scarf and blouse removed so that all could see. The eagerness with which you dipped your palms into rose and jasmine. The conjured spectacle of 'public' when you lifted your mouth to the cool plate of leaves and took from each corner the wrapped rings of silver."

There was commerce in our desolation. A change overcome by what had instructed it. The lens through which you appeared, in old age, sympathetic yet far from paternal. An exchange of content in which the privative gave way to "a longing for completion." Abstract and unreal: city of my birth that you understood long ago as central to the appearance of design. The divided archaic presence of it.

Images without reflection.

Singly the assertion of a letter. "Just there She must enter our hearts."

My mouth idle in its chamber. Sinister scrapes along the uppermost cavern. Burnt salt of affective emotion: your horn and silver band.

Andrew Mossin

"dwarf morning-glory twined around the grass blade"

———————

I catch myself beneath it with a version of you: eyes cast to the ground in search of articles of clothing. I hear you say, "O garden of my twenty-seven years." Your hands pressed over your eyes.

———————

Nightfall between episodes. *Knowing the event, could we have prevented the outcome. Knowing the outcome how may we retell the event. You wrote to me in admonishment, "Nothing so particular is refined by a language of momentous inconclusion. The role we play is secondary to what must come from elsewhere, from the very centrality of our natures." Absorbed in the trance of it, traces outside the common speech of everyday, I saw how you had become instrument: a messenger enclosed in the cloth of summer.*

Two Poems
Elizabeth Willis

A FISHER KING

Falling in the alley
or shadow of debt

beauty yields
beyond all earning

A glitter train
against the sun

inventing a bobby
fisher to live through it

empires of loneliness
on board

Dear comet
dear rook

who couldn't see
the stardom on your body

Hand against
the flyaway clock

a lasting silver lid
or gulf you fancied youngly
for a day

Like Turner with his legs
upon the orly grass

thinking treed hills
in tweedy blue

his mothered shadow
a lavender turbine

an ancient wisteria
lugging up groundwater

What you take
onto the surface

above the brow
is fierce emergence

O hero of the leafy mind

you're out of reach
in parabolic lamplight

its burning eye
whatever you wanted

MY FELLOW AMERICANS

who came to see
a baby in a star
a virgin in a chair
a boy who walks a book
crossing like a gold comet
afloat in painted milk

Preferring an arch to a peak,
a pear to understanding
I think I live

352

to clink among the clams
forgetting the edge of my twin
Everything eventually falls into
the opposite of water
A ticking landscape pulls down
heaven into atmosphere
It's in our paper plot, our life of flowers
to sun, to sink, to water the planets
pinching tickets, bending the bow
Earthlings of modest parentage
of unsure origin, of orange hair
adrift across Wyoming
in sandals, into bloom
The building will fall
like a little tree
of creaturely Magritte
I haven't forgotten
my boots of Spanish lead or
the khaki nothing
between painted things

Regarding impermanence
we're almost there
Dear Mike & Debbie
in the heat of '82
Don't accept
impermanent cement
an eyelash wish
Regard impermanence
dear Mike & Debbie
Regard the flying boy

Two Poems
David Shapiro

UTTER AVENUE

He deduced from all aesthetics
in small boldface with shining serifs:
"He got nothing"
Translated from the Norwegian:
"Pleasure is so difficult,
like tennis, like music,
sorrow is so sly, so easy."
He wept all over the dream.
Received the dream-letter:
"Forgive me for (you) using you
It jolts me to think of uh it—"
Theology had apologized.
At the old grammar school, at the beginning,
father exploded. A critic wrote
"I'm not much on textures,
dreams, verbal links;
and not very big on satire, either."
Thank you for liking the last line the subject on fire
    or fire in the photograph.

David Shapiro

THE EGYPTIAN RECENSION

I confuse all peace
And fortune here.
I composed it as
It is on mountain air.
I want. Want what?
Want a cat?
And provide poor private
Ash with light.
Air and sugar. Snow
In the mouldy mouth.
"Launched a little boat,
Will see how it goes."
To part you from Bea.

At the Fountain
Camille Guthrie

—after The Unicorn Tapestries

I.

When I first saw you
Pearled primed beading phantom
bearded   gilt   iridescent
Creature kneels to drink

Susceptible falling early spring
in the city, framed in stone
you force my proclivities,
I set my heart on that springhead.
    I pass you a frond of my very
wish my genius for coming apart at the seams—
changes of mood, statements of grief,
and divergence of character,
        Wideranging, much diffused, in late
meadowy sprays of ardor out of breath
if you talk to me, I change color.

        Give oneself to
        Clarity
            look me full in the
        Face   blue-green
            Iridesce
        this way
        your sound-and-light show

Overlooking my exaggerations, the causes
which led him to becoming erect and
consequent changes of structure:
increased size, absence of a tail, defenseless condition

356

outside the library arboresque, scrubby with reader's fatigue—
Our various small points of resemblance
are luminous, the term used in a wide sense.
    Overcurious, I occupy my plans with the most
important of all relations, the "lineaments of desire"
that's Blake,
You took no notice.

Action of hand gestures
Action of bird landing
Action of light on a hat.

II.

Silvered   sloped   livid
Stippled beast, touches water

No protection
from the number of individuals in the counterfeit city,
its gewgaws and things to do, or any marplot
whose ruinous intent ranges up the avenues to the park,
fearlessness.
    The girl descends
into the subway having a fit so pregnable
those who wait are open-mouthed
wincing from the tyranny of the beautiful
and irreplaceable—*touch me not.*
                    She leapt
        yellow gold red blue squares.

Action of wristlet waved in hydrangea air
points down carelessly Elizabeth Street "it's too late."
Row of water bottles argues extravagance.

        Seemingly random behavior
        Whoso list to hunt
        Shatterproof paper landscape
        Road test rapture
        How do you like me now?

The amplification of small errors
pinches the sore spot Clarity, phantom limb pain,
cases of difficulty and crumbly hopes
despite twenty-twenty.

I lay down in your night soil, your leaf litter, bone meal
your superphosphates, it was your bright idea.

My polka dot insights on the absence or rarity
of realism get me nowhere, and show signs of distraction.

I had some difficulty distinguishing between varieties
of artificial sleeping lawns.
The why stuck like sequins about your face—
Just forget it.

The lower stages of your unconcern
are stunning, detachment rips the only array I had
cast in a frenzied outburst of
my position in the animal series:
unmanned, unslaked, collapsible.

Why doe I love?
So mine eye is enthralled to thy shape.

III.

On the imperfection of the peony record.
On the lapse of time as estimated by primal scenes.
On the endeavors of our unreasonable beauty collections.
On the unknown worlds of eyelash varieties.
On the flammable appearance of promises.
On their perfect number.

IV.

The stag threatened us with its horns; the weasel ran away with
our lunch; the wolf tore a tent to pieces, then its owner; ducks
snapped at our fingers; the woodcock defended its nest; the
nightingale crashed into the car window; the goldfinches made a
mess of the finial; the lions caught a rabbit and fought over the
remains; and the hounds chased everything in sight.

V.

Dabbed distilled arriving
glossed current animal, waits

The bearing of these three great facts—
You suffer from overproduction.
You're handmade.
A.E. could mean many things,
which one's to be master is all.

(Amelia Earhart scraped the sky in a silver Electra
changing her flight from west to east.)

Raptly, assemble piecework
Rapid increase!
Spikelet of laziness and love
to have the leafy facts of your unknown worlds
which is what colors mean, and natural light.
            Ardently sweetheart
align our miscellaneous points of correspondence:
the blue striped shirt, unlikely details, bone horns,
and crush the ungetatable,
any reason for your endeavors seems true.

                He varies most
        Saturday afternoons ferns in the hair
        pulling off your Ovid T-shirt
        wet moss *Sa   tah   lite of love*
        falling backward into the bushes.

VI.

Early Spring stepped across the stream in rubber boots.
I rolled the tapestry up and tucked it under my head.
Ground-cherry landscape, emphasis Narcissus
perceptions wave in and out, headlong date palms,
A.E. tied with a bow.

The fierceness of the specific, slow motion capture
drawn to their differences and origins,
clear you have the cruelty to be interesting.

359

Camille Guthrie

The burden: wild roses behind you
display ciphers in silver yarns.

Hectic beauty prism saturation
stream horizon light streak
particulars use your feathers
veritable imperial collector
orange curl luster
if they were seemly to be seen.

See here my heart,
fringed facts,
the sooty nose, the surface
so round, so rare, a radiant thing
whitewashed with expectation
so I ate my words.

Clatter of details asks all attention
complex relations of plants and animals—
Risked enthusiasm, geometrical ratios of increase
in bold irreality. It's easy to look at
dark green edged with yellow, articulated leaves
fragrant lit oval, the whole's the hard part.

A bark, night-silvered

I fall victim to the symmetry of scenes
look for you in the break in the trees.

From Preterient
Susan Howe

Teachings on Style and the Flower

In 1402, the Japanese Noh performer and aesthetician Zeami Motokiyo wrote several items concerning the practice of the Noh in relation to an actor's age. He said a boy's voice begins to achieve its proper pitch at eleven or twelve, only then can he begin to understand the *noh.*

But this flower is not the true flower not yet.

Irish Literary Revival

1926. Mary Manning having wandered on the Brontë moors in Yorkshire, carries a copy of *The Scholar Gypsy* home to Dublin. She always takes it with her when she goes out walking. It is 1948. I am to read aloud the last three paragraphs of Wuthering Heights for the sixth grade public reading contest at the Buckingham School, in Cambridge, Massachusetts. The book is my mother's choice. Poetry is our covenant. She believes tables move without contact I am skeptical. If what is present to the mind at one time is distinct from what is present in another what is belief? Hoosh. Not in the Catholic graveyard not in the Protestant one either. Bird in the hand worth two of its own emptiness. This flower, taken from a scrap of paper, is said to be the Ammellus or Italian starwort of Virgil. Long ago Ogham stones were erected to commemorate the dead in rune-like ciphers then memory for voices then the rapid movement of ballads. Nearly all go to Scotland anglicity. I have no option but to be faithful to unlucky half human half unassuaged desiring dark shade you first Catherine. Lexical attention must be guarded from the dark age of childhood though lengthen night and shorten day. You are my altar vow. This cowslip is a favorite among fairies.

The Gate

A double cowslip bears one flower out of another. It remains in pastures long after the grass has been eaten away a stage name under the true one

Mind the hidden

Dedication to M enough

to the wood if you have

aconite and poppy she

said "Lie still, sleep well"

Quiet for it is a small

world of covered bone

Come veil the thought of

I shall dress primrose

———————

Rookh which stray

account the dark sea-

robber's map rose

of a hundred leaves

who learns ARABY

Even in the old story

arrow ragged Lallah

———————

Boiled milk was greatly

appreciated a step on the

road to luxury and there

was slim made of bitter

potatoes broken up when

kindly cottagers strove

to cherish and welcome

Patrick Bronté's childhood

Their guest strove well

———————

Homemade bread was

fadge the raised soda

bap or scone came later

baked on a griddle or

girdle while baking was

called "harning" but

mashing up potatoes

in meal and flour was

called "baking"

———————

Advanced from Emdale cabin
to Lisnacreevy cottage neither
sought nor accepted sympathy
Hoarded his savings he didn't
dread hobgoblins Mrs. Gaskell
exaggerated the facts in this
matter as have many others
Carried his webs to Banbridge
Could weave and read at once

———————

At supper sowans fine enough to
thread a needle the Brontë mind
never ran smoothly his children
were given ghost stories monsters
I am grateful archaeology Galway
oral history warcry boat curragh
When stealthy in shawl slumber
speaking from memory set forth
by moonlight written fact Irish
only in name limestone traveller

———————

Mary Manning presents this
book to her Dear Sister as a
token not to be appreciated
so must act esteem affection
Affection take this book Dear
to every moment she cannot
Invisible she grows tired and
beside vast catacomb Thebes

———————

Reader of poetry this book
contains all poetry THOOR
BALLYEE in seven notes for
stage representation May
countryside you reader of
poetry that I am forgotten
Long notes seem necessary
Unworthy players ask for
legend familiar in legend
the arrow king and no king

———————

Susan Howe

A character walks on thatch
bridge across the deep stage
Material image and her mate
Chanting within her role she
cannot step beyond invisible
right foot lifted in half step
Where is he going because this
play is famous for April sage
green kagota kneeling piety is
a dominant restraint he does
not stoop as in pitiful reign
Noh lies in its concentration
You child of Atsumori old cloak
faded gown sleeve flung open

Fabled founder in darkness
in Greek authentic helmet
illumination his heirs and
assigns forever as if wives
in themselves loosened the
murderous shawls so they act
astonishment but all terror
exactly as I have written I
am in ash blue gray Kogota
costume till the one here who
is the child Chorus comes in
Now Ireland in rebellion I
am arrived at upper memory
eroded base on shallow step

Seven Hands
Cole Swensen

THE HISTORY OF THE HAND

Once.   you said turning

is still saying
such theories: star bomb bird and so on equally
convinced, we started once
          to hold
          used to mean to anoint before it meant
to bless
or lessen
or whiten the sky

"Hands appear in the earliest" (framed, sized)
          overflowing the margins. The man
born with two left hands was born a grown man.
The man born with his hands full of hands later died.
There's no mystery to this. You listened, looking down,
counting, thinking, And?

          Assyrian hands were carved of stone.
     Egyptian hands were the point of the tale.
The Gothic hand, like no other, launched. That of the Renaissance,
          early and late,
          fragile and breaks, a wave on light.
          Ghirlandaio had hands of willow, while
          every hand that Dürer ever drew thrived.
Most hands are startlingly small, like eyes.

THE HAND THAT

The hand that thinks, that lies inside, that lines
the moving hand; the ventricles of the thinking hand and what it thinks
and what it sees (because it does

                      Thinks: "When you tie a knot
you can utterly forget, you can think
                    (can be thinking
of something else at the time) that the muscle is itself memory
lives again a folded time alive I tie.

                    I thought nothing of it
           then.   Type.   Watch   what
lives without you. To have harbored

as mutiny that doesn't even bother   The hand
was   (once an)   animal, a prior

Architecture: Archlessly, each one.
There's nothing in the frame.
               There's an empty frame on the wall.
I love you more   than that I keep thinking that

                         the hand is sky
                         though I'm not yet
                         sure exactly how.

Cole Swensen

THE HAND AS

The hand began an animal and from thereon did

some guile that soft
plural kite

        in
        flock
        did
        herd

who thus   shard
         comes to mind first   I mean, note
the exploded
stasis

used to mean star
or stop
in every native language

you hold it up. Stark. Startle. Arp.   When you hold up your hand
and the world stops
        and you find yourself looking at the back of your hand,
which, the longer you look at it, looks starved.

Cole Swensen

THE HAND DEFINED: 1

How is the We define the Where begin? an elbowful of muscle
fine as an inner ear

Those who say the definition of the hand begins in the shoulder say
those who say (they abbreviate) (mya): between 3.9 and 4.2 Million
Years Ago, *Australopithecus anamemsis:* To find. Fossils of the
hands and feet are so much rarer than those of skulls. Refined. We're
back to the inner ear. To hold onto earth hearing
with the fingertips all those singly
millions of   early braille, caressing   a   an
armful of earth in falling
and is still falling
                        the entire

structure of the back and shoulder
                and enormous parts of the brain.

FAN

Species of when, that outward
                        drift, a piano under every lens.
                        It was a compliment:
the hands of a surgeon or of a violin.
It was hot that summer   and every day thereafter

Slipped through the trees. The vanes of a fan
                are often made from
bone she said I own this one
                of painted air   of where
was it painted where air spears
                and folds like ribs turned to leaves
turned to sand.   :the opposite of a fist
is these hands gone up before a face. Summer gate. Sun made of gave.

371

HELD

The cup the hand becomes
           a bell
           is first a shape, then there's something
soft in your hand. The hand is a curved
thing. The held being
                  a function of the inverted arch
                  and ease of vault
                        when looking up, an immense
Walk backward from here to the sea.

across the street

the hand always curves
in the holding. The held, its own being

a mollusk shell
           all phalanges and grippage

Was now surrounds, what might
be the connection between tool use, language,
and the spiral gene determining
           twenty-one muscles set out to sea
           on a perfectly lovely day   the human hand fits
the human waist just above the hip like, you might say, a glove.

GRASP

As the hand carved first   its arc   in air
                                a
                                corresponding
                                sweep   through   the
brain
                        was made aviary spaces something like
airplane hangars in their relative dimensions
and thus the impression of standing
under a sky that you can see.   And the supple wrist, as it turned,
turned too in the mind and acquired

All we can do, say, with the thumb and a single finger was once.
What
can you remember doing first thing this morning among
answers and the liquid trees
                            Who picked this

                            fruit of   just
the key in the door got there by itself. The lights just grew on the
trees.

A Dialogue
Susan Howe and Cole Swensen

THE FOLLOWING BEGAN as a dialogue around a reading that Susan Howe gave at the Centre Georges Pompidou on May 3, 2000. We would like to thank the Centre, and particularly Marianne Alphant and Hannah Zabawski, for planning and facilitating the reading. And we would like to thank Dominique Fourcade and Claude Royet-Journoud, who thought up this project and to whom it is dedicated.
We begin mid-conversation . . .

SUSAN HOWE: For instance, the Metaphysical Club—a group of people from different professions who met in Cambridge between 1871-74. They presented papers and discussed them, all very informally. Peirce, William James and Oliver Wendell Holmes Jr. attended meetings. Chauncey Wright, another academic reject who has almost disappeared from American intellectual history, was a key member. The term "pragmatism" was first used during these meetings. By Peirce.

The members of the Club represented various disciplines; lines were not so clearly drawn as they are now. And the mix added richness and riskiness, as in post-Reformation thought and practice, when scientists, philosophers, lawyers, mathematicians, politicians, ministers, playwrights and poets shared ideas and discussions. Newton never considered his religious cosmology independent of his science. During the seventeenth and eighteenth centuries, science was called "natural philosophy."

COLE SWENSEN: An interesting difference in social organization, as well as a different quality of curiosity—more inclusive, more voracious—a curiosity that caused things. It must have increased everyone's awareness of connections and echoes among fields.

HOWE: Yes. The connections I'd like to explore are with various evangelical and revivalist enthusiasms in the early and mid-nineteenth century in upper New York State. The area was so repeatedly swept by such enthusiasms that it became known as the Burned-over District. One movement was the rise of spiritualism, which in its modern form originated there in 1848.

SWENSEN: What a year that was! It's almost as if a year can be volatile in and of itself, and everything that passes through it, event and object alike, is magnified.

HOWE: You are not kidding. Even in supposedly backwater places like the Genesee River Valley. I am, after all, a poet of place, and I feel this part of upper western New York State is haunted or perhaps charged.

SWENSEN: But what do we mean by haunted? Is it an interior or an exterior thing? What do we want from ghosts?

HOWE: It's the threshold between the exterior and interior. What do *they* want is the question. Are the dead inside me in my voice, in my thought, or are they outside, in the landscape? The threshold is the border, the margin. Maybe all aspects of reality are continuous with one another. Peirce called his doctrine to that effect "synechism." Ralph Barton Perry said that for William James "the idea of consciousness 'beyond the margin' or 'below the threshold' was a metaphysical hypothesis of the first importance." The noun "threshold" contains its own psychic transition—active "thresh," passive "hold." In *The Turn of the Screw*, surely one of the greatest ghost stories ever written, the governess (who has no name) is a threshold figure. Her status is sexually and economically precarious. Ghosts and governesses are liminal figures par excellence, so are mediums. So are immigrants and their children.

Perhaps I'm obsessed with the spirits who inhabit a place because my mother brought me up on Yeats. Before I could read, I heard "Down by the Salley Gardens" as a lullaby, and framed Cuala Press broadsides illustrated by Jack Yeats hung over my bed. Every time I move somewhere, I bring along the framed print of "Aedh wishes for the Cloths of Heaven" to hang on the wall for luck. Though the poem is untitled, the first line is printed as if it were a title, so, even for my children, the sight of those words recalls childhood and their grandmother, my Irish mother.

I hope her pain at leaving Dublin in 1935, and then moving to Buffalo in 1938, was assuaged by his poems and plays; she knew many of them by heart, and she clung to them by reading them aloud or hanging them on the walls, as if they were windows. His poems were an escape route. But I couldn't see through them. They marked a bond while breaking it. So there were always three dimensions—visual, textual, auditory. His writings married the spirit of melody with revolutionary principle. Waves of sound connected me, by associational syllabic magic, to an original but imaginary place that existed somewhere across water between the emphasis of sound and the emphasis of sense. I loved listening to her read. I felt my own vocabulary as something terribly mixed, at the same time hardened into glass.

She loved Matthew Arnold's "Scholar Gypsy" and could do heart-rending recitations of "The Forsaken Merman" and Michael Drayton's "Since there's no help, come let us kiss and part." But the words echoed backward were not all sadness and regret. Her verbal wit was astonishing. She dealt her words like blades, and many people feared becoming the objects of her scorn. She was an illusionist of fact.

In 1941, she directed a production of *Comus* in some rich Buffalonian's garden, and I was cast as a water-nymph. So way back then "Sabrina fair,/ Listen where thou art sitting/ Under the glassy, cool translucent wave," was as familiar to me as, "Rapunzel," or "This little pig went to market."

"Oh, Hell, let's be angels!" she said I said to a friend when I was five, referring to the roles we'd play in the Christmas pageant. She loved to produce and destroy meanings in the same sentence. So even if I hope I did say it, she probably made it up. These eccentric relations (authoritarian and iconoclastic, magic and mathematic, ancient and modern, serious and ludicrous, embroidered and bare) occur in Milton, Blake and Yeats (in Arnold, in spite of himself). You find similar twistings and turnings in documents left by various early Protestant splinter sects in America: Calvinists, Congregationalists, Anabaptists, Ranters, Quakers, Shakers, Sandemans, Rosicrucians, Pietists, as well as reformers, pilgrims, travelling preachers, charlatans, strolling players, mystics and imposters scattered throughout New England, Pennsylvania and New York up through the 19th century. Called away. "This way, this way—" I cling to them in my writing and teaching. Itinerantly. It's my maternal Anglo-Irish disinheritance.

Look at the James family. The paternal grandfather, William, was a farmer's second son from County Cavan who arrived with next to nothing in Albany, New York in 1789. His Scotch-Irish ancestors were Presbyterian dissenters. Their father, Henry, was an unorthodox Presbyterian theology student when, on a trip to Ireland in 1837, he stopped in London and met Michael Faraday, lifetime professor of chemistry at the Royal Institution and the world's leading authority on electricity. Faraday was a member of a splinter religious sect founded by Robert Sandeman. There were already small utopian groups practicing Sandemanism in Connecticut, but I don't think he ran across them here, and in the long run, Sandemanism, although attractive in its rejection of the ecclesiastical apparatus and in its sharing of material goods, had no room for the metaphysical and mystical speculation he yearned for. He found that in Swedenborgianism.

Talking of eccentric juxtapositions, at this same period, Joseph Smith, the prophet and founder of Mormonism, was living in Ontario County, New York, practicing occult divination with seer stones and divining rods. Treasure-hunting diviners located metallic treasures in stones and then attempted to overpower guardian spirits by casting magic circles (like Comus!). They needed to be in a state of grace to achieve control over volatile metals, which may have contributed to the composition of the *Book of Mormon*, said to be translated by divine power from golden plates buried by the last survivor of ancient wanderers. Meanwhile, not far away, the Fox sisters were receiving messages, and Melville was writing *Mardi*.

My point is that, during the ante-bellum years, scientists and philosophers were avidly questioning whether things are animate or inanimate, so it's not surprising that this scientific experimentalism crossed with mediumship and communion with the dead. More and more, the ordinary world of material objects was shown to have invisible properties of the sort usually associated with spirits. If you could, in a rigorous, experimental way, understand the mysteries of chemistry you would understand the ultimate nature of reality, including spiritual reality. Chemistry was on the cutting edge. Peirce's first degree was in chemistry, and he was strongly influenced by the concept of valence throughout his life.

If you look at diagrams of mechanical apparatuses, with their wheels, ropes, pulleys, discs and charts designed for the purpose of scientifically demonstrating spiritualism, they are eerily similar to the ones that chemists used.

Nowhere is the blending of science and religious imagination more evident than in spiritualism. You should see the plates in *Spiritualism Scientifically Demonstrated*, written in 1855 by Robert Hare, professor of chemistry at the University of Pennsylvania.

Susan Howe and Cole Swensen

Duchamp and Yeats would have loved them. They could be bachelor apparatuses, or Ready-mades without the irony.

As for "Brides stripped bare by bachelors even"—Kate and Margaret Fox were the most widely known mediums during the 1800s, and spiritualist enthusiasm reached a crescendo with the frenzy around them in Rochester in 1848. Scientists were always or almost always men, but mediums were usually women. Spiritualism moved to England in 1852, where, via a brief craze for table turning, it became respectable. Although the best known mediums—Mrs. Hayden, David Douglas Home and Mrs. Piper—all came to London from America, the parent Institute for Psychical Research was established in London in 1882. William James was one of the founders of the American Institute in 1885.

Myriad phenomena and behaviors were investigated, recorded and composed in both institutes; spirit theory, table tapping, trance-mediumship, spirit-photography, fairies and vampires were hot topics, as were automatic writing, possession, hysteria and hallucination. Chemistry, poetry, folklore, psycho-pathology and psychical research met and mixed.

William James was committed to a reconciliation of religion and science; so was Peirce, although differently. Neither would have thought the disciplines mutually exclusive. It was said of William that he was too fond of cranks. I love that about him. Peirce was one of the cranks, but he was also a trained mathematician and logician.

Here's a good James quotation: "We are founding here a 'Society for Psychical Research,' under which innocent sounding name ghosts, second sight, spiritualism and all sorts of hobgoblins are going to be 'investigated' by the most high-toned and 'cultured' members of the community."

SWENSEN: Nice humor! He both veils and reveals his fear of the absurdity of it all. And thinking of *The Turn of the Screw*, there's a similar, though not tongue-in-cheek, ambiguity/ambivalence beneath it. Was Henry James also active in such investigations? Or was it simply in the air?

HOWE: I've been going on about William, but Henry James fits in perfectly, particularly *The Turn of the Screw*. There, and in other later writings, ambiguity and ambivalence extend to sentence structure, syntax, word choice, even punctuation. A great study could be done on the James brothers' use of hyphens and dashes.

Henry wasn't active in psychic investigations, but both brothers were close to the Sidgwick family and their circle. Henry Sidgwick, one of the most rigorous figures in the history of British moral philosophy, was the first president of the Society for Psychical Research. He also promoted higher education for women, and his wife Eleanor was the principal of Newnham, the first women's college at Cambridge University. He claims to have first heard the governess' story that incited *The Turn of the Screw* while staying at the country house of Edward Benson, Sidgwick's cousin and brother-in-law. During this period, experimental psychology was being developed as an ultra-scientific discipline, and William was considered a bridge between this approach and the nuttier stuff. In 1889, the International Congress of Experimental Psychology chose him to compile a census of hallucinations. The great thing about Henry's story, published in 1898, the official birth year of both Pragmatism and *Dracula*, is that we're never sure. Is it a ghost story or a study of hysteria? *The Varieties of Religious Experience* was written in 1901—is it meticulous science, or oddball religious philosophy?

SWENSEN: Are Peirce's logical tables another product of ambient spiritualism? Was he trying to get at something beyond reason with his graphs?

HOWE: I think Peirce was trying both to get at something beyond reason and to diagram the logical structure of reality. Toward the end of his life, he wrote to Victoria Lady Welby: "These moving pictures exhibit the action of the mind in thought; they graph the dialogue between various phases of the ego. Expression and thought are one."

Many of his logical graphs, and also his calculations, are like poems. Some resemble concrete poetry, others prefigure drawings by Paul Klee, Agnes Martin, Robert Smithson, Hannah Darboven. Some remind me of Joseph Beuys' drawings on paper and blackboards, or work by Artaud and Duchamp. That doesn't make the graphs any less philosophy, mathematics and science. And, like Duchamp, Peirce was an avid chess player, but I think he felt as Poe did, that whist was superior to chess for sharpening one's investigative skills.

Even if some of Peirce's manuscript notebooks and pages remind me of Duchamp's notes in *The Green Box*, there is a difference. Peirce has no box. There may be numerous approaches to the disorderly collection at Houghton, but Houghton is a library to which few people are allowed access. Papers rot unseen in archives. Octavio Paz says "*The Large Glass* is a comic and infernal portrayal of modern love, or, to be more precise, of what modern man has made of love."

Peirce lacked Duchamp's comic sense. He was searching for a system. Ideas were to remain true. He loved logic. He couldn't retail it.

SWENSEN: Your connection between Peirce and Duchamp is interesting—both based in a radical reconfiguration of space, and both going back to Mallarmé, though Duchamp more directly. Space—aesthetically, scientifically, philosophically, etc.—was in crisis at the turn of the century, and Mallarmé's *Un Coup de dés* is an important early instance.

HOWE: So much attention has been paid to Mallarmé's radical use of page space, but the idea that in late nineteenth-century America Emily Dickinson and Charles Sanders Peirce went to similar extremes in their writing practice seems unacceptable to many readers and editors here, and abroad.

SWENSEN: Mallarmé's work may have gotten more recognition because, compared to Dickinson and Peirce, he was less socially and artistically marginal. Unlike Peirce, he'd declared poetry as his field, and unlike Dickinson, he'd been recognized as an important writer. Perhaps this gave him more room to experiment.

HOWE: It's complicated. Just look at the varied meanings of "experiment." Peirce was developing his graphs at a time when mathematical logic was being created as a discipline.

Also, the American Civil War caused a disruption in American culture, to say the least. The Jameses, Peirce and Dickinson were all young adults during that war. It marked them, even if they didn't fight in it. I know there were political upheavals in France during the same period, but surely they weren't as climactic.

SWENSEN: Actually, they were as much or more so—the revolution of 1848, the Franco-Prussian War, the Siege of 1870, the Commune—and not only these events in themselves, but the fact that they were the last wave in a one-hundred-year-long series that demolished a way of life a thousand years old. Yet after a certain point, you can't talk of horror in relative terms, and events in both the United States and France during this period passed that point.

However, because many events in France occurred on the streets of Paris, their impact on young, innovative writers and thinkers including Mallarmé must have been enormous. And the streets themselves! Even "at peace," they were destroyed and reconfigured by Haussmann. It's too easy to draw parallels between social upheaval and artistic upheaval, between a disruption of daily space and a disruption of expressive space, so I won't, but . . .

HOWE: But I will. I insist on it. The Civil War is our Iliad. Four million troops took part in it. The total casualties exceeded 617,000 dead and 375,000 wounded. It was the first "modern," "total" war in that it was a war in which the industrial potential of the victor determined the outcome. It was the first war to be photographed. Photographs of the dead, the wounded, the captured were available to everyone. There is no way of overstating this particular war's importance to the American psyche.

My life has been spent in the shockingly disruptive second (more than) half of the twentieth century. The fact that I was born in 1937 into what became World War II to a mother who was born in Dublin in 1905, and didn't come to the United States until 1934, who was cut off from returning home during the world war years, and then, for the rest of her life, moved restlessly between Ireland and New England, has profoundly affected all of my writing. There is conflict and displacement in everything I write—in the way I arrange words on the page, in the way I hear and react to other languages—that I can't edit out.

When I was turning from painting to poetry, I remember pouring over *Un Coup de dés* loving the way the lines spread across facing pages, so few words to a line; it was elegant, musical, infinitely intelligent, alluring, subtle—foreign. At the same time, I first encountered Olson in the Cape Goliard edition of *The Maximus Poems* IV, V, VI in all its blustering, chopped nervousness—I felt an immediate shock of recognition. It was his voracious need to gather "facts," to find something, a quotation, a place name, a date, some documentary evidence in regard to a place. To collate the collection quickly with something else without explaining the connection. Melville may have shown him the way in the "Extracts" section of *Moby-Dick.* There's a nervous sense of dislocation, abbreviation, connectives made without connections. It's there in Eliot, in Moore, in Williams, who catches it in his great essay on Poe. Recently, I read an interesting piece on Eliot by F. W. Bateson, "The Poetry of Learning," in which he says "the 'learning' in Eliot's earlier poems must be seen as an aspect of his Americanism. As scholarship, it is wide-ranging, but often superficial and inaccurate." He called this quality "tourist erudition."

I discovered the essay at my local library in Guilford because I

Susan Howe and Cole Swensen

couldn't get to Sterling Library at Yale due to a traffic jam on the highway. I was snobbishly sure I wouldn't find any criticism there worth seriously considering, but I was wrong. And it struck me that for women of my generation, there was usually a sense that major libraries were off-limits or out of reach in a way that has made me suffer from permanent "tourist erudition" in the academy. I wonder if late nineteenth- and early twentieth-century American writers and philosophers felt the same about European culture. They wanted to be let in, to connect, rather than to remain in the tourist-position. It's an unsettling posture. Paradoxically, in order to make connections, you need to remain outside. Even Wallace Stevens depended on postcards from abroad.

That's why *The Large Glass* is so brilliant. Paz says that Duchamp's attitude "teaches us—although he has never undertaken to teach us anything—that the end of artistic activity is not the finished work, but freedom." Arnold's *Scholar Gypsy* says the same thing. Perhaps that's what my mother was trying to tell me through his words. The poem is the account of a young student who leaves the university to live with the gypsies; from them he learns the art of mesmerism. Arnold based it on a passage from *The Vanity of Dogmatizing*, by the seventeenth-century philosopher Joseph Glanvill, sometimes called "the first mesmerist."

SWENSEN: Yet, displacement and its effects—"the way of arranging words on a page," for instance, seems to me precisely a way of editing in, of increasing your raw materials, and their flexibility. That's what Mallarmé was doing, and perhaps another reason his work attracted attention was that he announced it, contextualized it.

He knew that he was doing something new, and furthermore, that it was time for it. In his preface to *Un Coup de dés*, he says it contains "nothing new except a certain distribution of space made within the reading"—the redistribution of space was his conscious goal. Later, he remarks, "In my work, which has no precedent . . ." It was a highly intentional and theorized experiment, impelled by both a radical philosophy of aesthetics and an acute perception of his time.

He was also clear about why he did it—to move toward a fusion of sequential perception and simultaneous perception—to emphasize both temporal and spatial apprehension at once. And to fully engage both eye and ear. As a result, he pushed poetry in two disparate directions—toward visual art and toward musical performance. He recognized their inherent affinity, and that poetry is their

382

common denominator.

Mallarmé is germane to this discussion in another way as well—the extensive mathematical calculations in his notes toward *Le Livre,* his conception of the ultimate book toward which all that exists is heading. The calculations have the same almost delirious freedom as Peirce's pages and pages of numbers and lists. *Le Livre* is also full of diagrams, so that relationships among ideas and details are often presented spatially. In general, the notes are shaped like short free-verse poems of a particularly composition-by-field sort. The use of space in *Le Livre* is, in some ways, even more revolutionary; however, unlike *Un Coup de dés,* he did not intend them as "finished pieces."

HOWE: Another point of comparison between them is that just as Mallarmé felt all poetry could be contained in a book, Peirce felt all logical truths could be expressed using one symbol.

Peirce was obsessed with capturing, as economically and precisely as possible, the complex relationships that make up reality. He differed from other mathematical logicians in believing that complex relationships could be more adequately represented in graphs than in algebraic notation. For most logicians, his graphs are unsuccessful, but as a poet, I find that they succeed in the manner of Yeats' *A Vision* or Blake's words and drawings or, most of all, Duchamp's *The Large Glass* and the work that led up to it.

I'd like to have reproduced more of the graphs in *Pierce-Arrow,* but my contract limited me.

SWENSEN: The way you've used them, though, is striking. Because the Peirce pages face your own, we oscillate between reading and seeing, and are forced to recognize that we don't see printed words. Viewing them both, we also become aware of the moment at which a mark becomes visual rather than referential, as well as the role that pleasure plays in that shift. With the Peirce, we're aware of the beauty of handwriting, and the way that beauty deflects reading and encourages viewing.

HOWE: Recently I have been combining slides of the manuscripts with readings of the book, so there are two narratives—the one I read and the one consisting of the way I have combined the slides. I use two slide projectors, so you can see facing pages, and lists and diagrams mirroring or conversing with each other. And yes, it is the beauty of the diagrams, as Peirce himself drew them, and not only the graphs, but also pages of numbers, the doodles, the lists of words tumbling down sheets of paper—so many things I want people to see at the same time they hear the sound of a voice reading something else. So there are two different elements: slides in a darkened room and the sound of a voice reading.

And so, *Pierce-Arrow* is unfinished or constantly changing. There is one small manuscript notebook of Peirce's graphs that I would love to see as a facsimile edition, similar to Ralph Franklin's edition of Dickinson's *Three Master Letters.* Then as an introduction you would supply a reading by a logician who understood Peirce's system, then someone might try to put into words why they are also poetry.

SWENSEN: Multiple (and equally "legitimate," though perhaps contradictory) readings of a text bring up the who-owns-what-language question. Peirce's case seems to be one of misuse by the rightful heir—much more interesting.

Velimir Khlebnikov is a similar case—in fact, he has a lot in common with Peirce—particularly in his *The Tables of Destiny.* Their physical arrangement recalls Peirce's existential graphs; both men shared the impulse to spatialize, as well as the faith that physical arrangement reveals metaphysical sense. The two bodies of works must have been created at about the same time, too.

In a sense, Khlebnikov was trying to turn time into, or map time onto, space—to resolve the two. All his charts and calculations were intent on proving universal links among peoples and a universal humanity.

He saw the arts as driven by intuition, and the sciences by intellection; the one based in images, the other on concepts. Their fusion would thus meld these two approaches to knowing the world. It's another instance of that lovely suspension, as when an object tossed straight up stops a split second before starting back down. It opens a space through which the new can enter. It's the hinge, or gap—they amount to the same thing.

Khlebnikov's project was rooted in his horror at war. Acutely affected by the Russo-Japanese War, the first World War, and the Russian Revolution, his revulsion was in no way abstract. In *The Tables of Destiny,* he states: "I first resolved to search out the *Laws of Time* in 1905 on the day after the battle of Tsushima, when news of the battle reached the Yaroslavl district where I was then living . . . I wanted to discover the reason for all those deaths." It's an enormous horror, but also an enormous faith, that launched the project, and that remains its fuel.

HOWE: War is always present even if sometimes it is an offstage voice or a ghost. For Henry James 1905 was a crucial year. In 1904 he finished *The Golden Bowl* (to me the greatest of all his novels). And isn't *The Golden Bowl* at some level a meditation on "tourist erudition?" In 1905 he returned to America after a twenty-year absence, this time as a tourist.

"Perhaps some day—say 1938. . . . they [Adams and Hay] might be allowed to return together for a holiday, to see the mistakes of their own lives made clear in the light of their successors; and perhaps then, for the first time since man began his education among the carnivores, they would find a world that sensitive and timid natures could regard without a shudder." That's the way Adams ends the last chapter of *The Education* titled "Nunc Age" (1905). Looking back now, and considering his book was published in 1918, the irony is chilling.

In 1905, Peirce began an unpublished manuscript notebook that I love. It's called *Analysis of Time*. He starts to define time in sentences, then changes to numbers. Sometimes the numbers resemble musical notes. Eventually his analysis of the four-point problem trails off into, "I will not take up much of this book with the subject of discrete quantity—but I refer to a similar book labeled *All Pure Quantity merely Ordinal.*" At that point he was working in almost total isolation. You wonder who he was talking to other than himself.

SWENSEN: It's important to see the manuscript—not only the words but also all the sheets of calculations. It's in the physical strokes that you see conviction and compassion, rather than just "reading about it." The graphic is presence; it's the presence of the human hand (the "man-"). Thus you have both the abstract architecture of intellectual impulse and the concrete architecture of the hand, anchoring.

Like Peirce, Khlebnikov was fascinated by mathematical language—both as verbal language used so precisely that ambiguity is eliminated (leading him toward sound work and zaum), and as numbers used in meanings as intricate as those of verbal language—and, of course, numbers as an artistic medium in themselves.

HOWE: It's reduction. There is something about marks on paper, graphics being involved in radical reduction; it's reducing a thing to a diagram. It has to do with acoustics, with the fact that every mark on a page is on some level acoustic. Peirce was interested in a universal language but he was a mathematician and a philosopher, not a poet, and there is a difference. An article by Edward Moore and Arthur Burks on editing Peirce has a marvelous epigraph taken from the horse's mouth: "I am a mere table of contents . . . a very snarl of twine." Something said perfectly also has to work as sound. The word "snarl" there could be a pun—

SWENSEN: And puns always lead one back to Duchamp—such acrobatic skill. There's a wonderful Duchamp series called "The Infrathin," which made me think of you because it's devoted to the "between." It examines the between in its most reduced state. Examples:

The warmth of a seat (that has just been vacated) is infrathin.

In holding one planed surface just above another planed surface, you pass through infrathin moments.

It's another text full of numbers and diagrams. The infrathin, an endlessly protean hinge, is yet another approach to the verbal/visual issue and another approach to that point of suspension. The line between visual and verbal apprehension is in itself an instance of the infrathin, particularly when activated.

HOWE: It would take a book for me to go on about what *The Large Glass* means to me. The Bride's Domain—the hinge between—the Bachelor apparatus. A note in *The Green Box* suggests *Delay in Glass* as a "kind of subtitle" to be thought of "as you would say 'poem in prose' or a 'spittoon in silver.'" Erotic esoteric comic ironic passively aggressive actively passive. It's the figure in the carpet. Aedh's cloth of heaven under glass, or James' golden bowl, fragile and hard at once. "Its hardness is certainly its safety. It splits—if there is a split." It is two-sided. Synthesis, antithesis, reflection and delay. It drags in my mother, along with Charlotte Stant, and the motley band of vagabond mystics, strolling players, renegade alchemists, itinerant ministers, founders of sects, all those purposive bachelors who arrive here repudiating and recovering something. Duchamp is familiar with seances, mediums, automatic writing, chemical experiments. This is the age of cinema not theater. Museums are the places we gather to worship. Museums are what churches and cathedrals once were.

Henry James and Marcel Duchamp are masters of parenthesis. Public and private. They are feminine and masculine. We will never know what the Bride's messages are just as we never will know if the unnamed governess in *The Turn of the Screw* is crazy, or correct. Her story is littered with letters, mirrors, lakes, windows. Is she an Oculist Witness? Sometimes I have the uneasy feeling that Marcel Duchamp could be Peter Quint.

When *The Large Glass* got smashed in the region of the nine shots on its return from the Brooklyn Museum to the home of Katherine Dryer he said, "The more I look at it the more I like the cracks, because they are not like shattered glass, they have a shape . . . I see in it almost an intention, a curious intention that I am responsible for, in other words a readymade intention that I respect and love." But he went on repairing it in secret. Just as James repaired his novels with prefaces.

A Vanity
Keith Waldrop

The notion of elsewhere was beyond her.
— Johanna Drucker, *Otherspace*

The world I see—there—*here*—is the world I remember. What is to
come is behind me. As I look back . . .

lute, skull, globe, hour-
glass, and

[end of
year]

clutter

books, music, instruments of
war, astronomy, elements

of the liturgy
viol with a broken

[this century, as
past as any]

string, sextant, compasses, candle
the candle

forest

church in
ruins, the churchyard

extinguished

pillar of
~~fire~~

I have a terrible habit of remembering the death of people who are
still alive, killing them off by an act of memory.

False memory, I suppose I should call it, but sometimes a person
whose death I remember *is in fact dead* and my memorial in that
case seems no different in character.

Until, by some chance or other, I discover that one I have killed
still lives. Perhaps he phones me.

Or I run into her on my way somewhere.

Or I find an obituary:

someone I killed long ago *is now dead.*

       pushed

       particular

       attached to
       the body, a counter-
       series

       soul of the

       skeleton, lower
       brain, sea-horse and
       almond

       you who follow me are not
       my children

Keith Waldrop

Rain beats at the window, while from the other side precise daylight, gray under a comprehensive cloud but brighter than I would have expected for such a gray day, filters through.

But no, this I beheld with eyes closed and, I suspect, before waking had broken my sleep's regular rhythm.

I saw it—think, or thought, I saw it—in a dream.

The day, awake, is not at all like that.

          unhandled, cannot
          be imagined, hypothetical
          suicide

. . . can turn up at any moment

          a place in the
          lattice, noonday on
          earth or

          beneath earth

          gloomy boundary, world
          or not world

          musk mingled
          with orchids, countless
          stars in ruin

          battle to the
          death, settling nothing but
          place of burial

I see, so often, glanced in a mirror, the door *just going shut.*

(Negative.)

(North, vague image of Jealousy.)

Color reversal.

>agility
>clarity
>subtlety
>
>[dowries]
>
>impassibility

had not occurred to her that he . . .

>strange behavior, accomplished
>
>*this*
>
>dragonfly groups, force-
>sensitive organs
>
>exhibition
>
>block and ax
>
>pillar of
>~~cloud~~

who said?: Thought will not go far in a negative direction, so things are always worse than we think.

>up-and-down

scarcely able to
speak for weeping, heavy

grasp on my arm

machine, universal

gates of torment, *mimic*
[lost to this world]

mourned as dead, forgotten

dying

can scarcely weep, for
talking

down, up

a noise which I could call
shouting

pillar of
salt

. . . into

out of which . . .

strange beauty

trees
caught in the hearsay

Fishing as Impenetrable Stray
Will Alexander

Perhaps I fish by carnivorous scorpion
by integument as glutenous rash
breathing day after day formalistic dilation

& I argue to my dark phyletic
that these Hydrophidae that I hunt
exist like a fever of rural ophidians

I attempt no belletristic index
no formula which blandly contains the hideous
the corpse as biological malfunction
like a signal
or astrological corruption as vault

I cannot assume
any sabbatical of existence
any buried or revealed origination
which swims with a singular logic
in a bloodless lagoon
or a gallery of salt

of course signals emit from Globerigina
like the moon during every phase
as a fabulous cabana
as an occulted lightning domain

each anarchic wave
each voice from aboriginal voids
as an eclipse
as a solar alteration

Will Alexander

with the precipitous intent
of a geometric sorcery
with the turbulence of diamonds
brought into view
by dialectical exertion

I fish by thievery
by subduction & germination
where during cerulean audibility
I am engulfed by dormition
where each nuanced gesture in dreaming
evaporates & cleanses
every molecule
every tense rhumatic oar
as regards bodily survival as mass

as a star above a brutish hamlet
full of jealousy
coldness
& fear

the sun
never a demonstrable enclave
or a stable which opens cataracts
to syllabic germination & verbs

at times
I fish by prejudgment
by a nautical disposition hostile to any form which divides me
which makes me parochial by means of standard spectral division
my wandering
an invincible isometric
like a powerful exclusivity
a fortitude
which surmounts the opaque patois of the elect

those secondary monarchs
listed upon scrolls as initiates sworn to the primeval

for me
a cold irrelevant posture
an illusionistic vectitude
which can no longer be part
of spontaneous living engagement

I cannot see myself
as he who exists
who carries ranges in his fingers
which erupts upon second seeing
into a dismal & unfructifying grace

perhaps a synapse
a bribery
a fall into the whispers stunned with the anti-oracular

if I voyaged on Uranus
if I gave to myself the powers of a runic musical pole
I would explore remnants which select from themselves secrecies
unconceived diameters
with language
which utterly de-exists
degree by electrical degree
subverting customs
which will never approach the magnetic realms of the haflon

I am gazing through myself
for non-local starlight
for riddles
for galaxies
alien
& supercessional with zodiacs

& so
I never dwell on options
on paralytic reprives
within a motion rendered by a mind enslaved to theoretical
connivance

I mean a science whose motions that says I cannot exist
which claims itself unshatterable
absolved of pure correction or motion

as to masters
I have none
I fish as a stray
as a survivor who constructs his sigil by superior perplexity
at the same time attempting a ghostly deliverance from matter
from normal convection as it spins through zones of extremis
pointless as to tabloid probings in Rome

I am a stray wandering in the Indian water mass
slaying Hydrophidae by spells

an ocean condensed by refusal
of aromatic juvenalia

which has never existed by love of war
or dark Eudoxian gatherings
but as flight
as floating chimerical compost
like a navigator's puzzle
inscripted
on certain methane tablets in Kemet

Blood Sonnets

Juliana Spahr

white blood cells at 4.2 thousand per cubic millimeter — As intricate system we are.
red blood cells at 3.88 millions per cubic millimeter — We with all with our complexities.
hemoglobin at 14.1 grams per decaliter — We with all our identifications.
hematocrit at 42.6% — We with all our homes and our irregularities live.

mean corpuscular volume at 109.6 fluid liquid — We are full of thought and we live.
mean corpuscular hemoglobin at 36.3 picograms per cell — We live with things several.
mean corpuscular hemoglobin concentration at 33.1% — We are full of thought and we are different.
red blood cell distribution width at 13.5% — For which things so several.

platelets at 216 thousand per cubic millimeter — The catalogue of the life span, the operation, and the animal.
mean platelet volume at 7.8 fluid liquid — The catalogue of force and animal life.
granulocyte at 62.4% — The catalogue of the extension of life, the operation, and the animal.
lymphocyte at 27.0% — The catalogue of the extension of the execution of life and the animal.

monocyte at 8.6% — Togetherness of the lesson and the splitting.
eosinophil at 1.4% — Togetherness of the lesson and to duplicate one's self.

Things should be said more largely than the personal way.
Things are larger than the personal way of telling.
Intimate confession is a colonial project.
Confession's structured plan of percents and regulations.

When the amounts of blood are considered.
When the strength, the quantities, of blood are regarded.
When blood is thought as meaning.
An intimate confession.

Blood is a force, a house.
And the difference between those that took and those that remained in what h appened.
As the qualities of blood are considered remains undocumentable.
As the quantities of blood are considered remains unquantifiable.

For we are located with some and not with others for this is intimate.
We are situated with some and not with one against confession.

basophil at 0.6%
granulocyte absolute at 2.6 thousand per cubic millimeter
lymphocyte absolute at 1.1%
monocyte absolute at 0.4%

eosinophil absolute at 0.1%
basophil absolute at 0.0 thousand per cubic millimeter
alanine amino tranferafe serum at 21 units per liter
cholesterol at 171 milligrams per decaliter

alkaline phosphatase at 46 units per liter
gamma-glutamyl transpeptidase at 22 units per liter
bilirubin total at 0.5 milligrams per decaliter
high density lipoprotein at 52 milligrams per decaliter

low density lipoprotein at 124 milligrams per decaliter
cholesterol/high density lipoprotein at 3.6 risk

time drawn at 1819   A catalogue of the individual and a catalogue of us with all our complexities.
absolute lymphocyte at 1134 cubic millimeter   A catalogue of full of thought.
cd3% (total t) at 88.5%   A house where we with all our complexities lie.
cd3 at 1004 cubic millimeter   A catalogue of blood.

cd4% (helper) at 39.9%   A catalogue of us with all our complexities.
cd4 at 452 cubic millimeter   A catalogue of how we are all full of thought and connection.
cd8% (supres) at 46.6%   The house where we are from and the house where we choose to live.
cd8 at 528 cubic millimeter   All things to be said more largely than the personal way.

cd4/cd8 ration at 0.9   There is in this the thought of home
sodium at 137 milliequivalents per liter   Those who had a home.
potassium at 4.6 milliequivalents per liter   Those who have a right to a home.
chloride at 98 milliequivalents per liter   And there is a difference between those who came and took and those who
stayed in the taking

carbon dioxide at 26 milliequivalents per liter   The house of difference when we look.
blood urea nitrogen at 17 milligrams per decaliter   The house of norms and abnormalities and their percentages.

Juliana Spahr

glucose at 111 milligrams per decaliter — Who of comparison.
creatinine at 0.9 milligrams per decaliter — Who of analogy.
calcium at 9.4 milligrams per decaliter — Who of empathy.
total protein at 7.1 grams per decaliter — Who of structural alignment.

albumin at 4.5 grams per decaliter — Who authorizes so one is not what individual one says one is.
lactic dehydrogenase at 171 international units per liter — Who authorizes so one is not single.
aspartate amino tranferafe serum at 25 international units per liter — Who empowers so one is not alone.
rapid plasma reagin at nonreactive — Who is expert of confession.

rapid plasma reagin titer at 1:2 — Who one is situated with and not with others.
fluorescent treponemal antibody, absorbed at nonreactive — Who one lies with and not with others.
hepatitis b surface antigen at negative — Who is characterized how by some and not by others.
hepatitis b surface antibody at negative — Who is various.

hapatitis c antibody at negative — For who is located with some and not with stillness.
gonnococcal/chlamydia at negative — For who is asking and then listening.

Two Poems
Jerome Sala

THE INTERPRETATION OF SCREAMS

the cultural analyst convinced us that the screams
of teenagers were throwbacks

to a suppressed form of religion
that surfaces now and then

whenever anyone really hot
appears with erotic radiance

in the public sphere—
those are screams of pleasure

the friends of the god
granted the gift of ecstasy.

And besides
as one early '60s horror movie advised

screaming can save your life
for it destroys the inner lobster

which would otherwise
shatter the spine

of those in great fear.
Following these theories

we were forced to listen to droning solemnities
about the similarities of pleasure and pain

Jerome Sala

fear and power
and when we objected

were smashed in the head
(like a rubber Bobo doll gets smashed by a child

with a mallet)
with a cliché about clichés:

they're solemn
these truths

we were told
because they're true.

To which we said
no they're not

truth is never boring
because even if it's only the effect of power

what could make you scream more loudly
and with more delight.

MY ONE AND ONLY

The only people for me are the mad ones . . .
— Jack Kerouac

The only ones for me are the shy ones, the ones who are
too shy to be born, too shy to talk about their shyness,
too shy to be saved, who desire nothing but the yawn of
the common, who know how to douse out a Roman candle
when called upon to do so, the ones who are like spiders
scurrying back to their webs rather than devouring
the incredible shrinking people we've offered them as food.

The only ones for me are the tired ones, the ones who are
too tired to play their horns, too tired to walk away from
the land of the peppy, too tired not to shave, who set fire
to their lawns because they've fallen asleep smoking, who don't

understand the calls of the louses who want us to return to
Roman decadence, who lecture us on the superiority of sleep
yet refuse to beg for giant steeples or oceans in their dreams.

The only ones for me are the defensive ones, the repressed ones,
the passive-aggressive co-dependent ones, the addicted ones,
the only ones for me are the squares, the uptight ones,
the greedy ones, the blatantly self-serving ones, those who think
small, who don't know their right from their left, the cowardly
ones, the ashamed, the nobodies on their way to incomprehension,
the order takers, the inconspicuous or conspicuously consuming
    ones.

The only ones for me are the crawling ones, the ones who stall
on their way to utopia, the ones who think about leaving the womb,
then head back the other way, the ones who refuse to face the
problems you've created for them, the ones who roam through Rome
never figuring out how to do as the Romans do, the ones who would
rather buy a cheap figurine than a scented candle, but who know,
that in a pinch, a scented candle will do, without knowing what
    it will do.

The only ones for me are sly ones, the ones who are too sly
not to follow the norm, too sly to balk at failure, too sly to
rage, who die for everything but the pursuit of the extraordinary,
who know how not to get invited to the Roman orgy of life and then
how not to enjoy themselves when they don't get there, the ones
who are like friars refusing to change their heavy, brown burlap
robes in the heat, the ones who refuse to take shelter under the
giant, man-eating plants they would be famous for growing if they
didn't think debates over fame and nobody-ism were strictly for
    the un-sly.

The only ones for me are the stymied ones, the floundering ones,
the small-minded, the unadventurous, the late ones, the crybabies,
those who squander their asceticism, those who ponder the virtues
of athleticism and decide it's not worth the effort, those who
follow the rules to such an absurd degree that the rules become
absurd, the shirkers who refuse to light a candle in the darkness,
and who make up the dark matter of the universe, now beginning to
be explored and quantified, much to their chagrin.

Ecstatic Persistence
Leonard Schwartz

Continuous revelation of,
no subject but light.

Too, tied to the stake
of foundational doubt.

Steam off rocks of this perception.

And snow monkeys. On their thrones.
Of stone. In the steam. Illuminated.

Action taken equals miracle.

Burning stake.

Or a world away:
a lament in tones so sweet the tones
permeate

This composition,
this drinking
establishment—

no, never the establishment—

(we seek to inhabit
what cannot be inhabited)

Yet the eye emerges whole.

Outside in that world

The voice dances as through trees
and who moves is like the bird

Deigning to primogeniture
knowing dark bloods and eye-buds

A snow monkey giving birth in snow
a splash of red, perception fired and fed

Where they eat the golden apples
and never get old and so forth

Figures on a stage
that lead miniature lives, zoo creatures
in the action of language

Wildness withheld, hope to uncover

The being outside the bars
at labor in the steam off those waters.

Would ask the music for help.

Would listen till I was out of my head
only they'd rightly say

    escapist.

So when the song
  is sealed,
let variously dispersed elves

Congregate

Let the ale in a glass, amber in color,
be drunk

And be replaced with ale, equally amber

Equally amber

Until the snow monkey

until the snow monkey

until the snow monkey.

Three Poems
Catherine Imbriglio

ROSARY

A figure of a man was in the water at the place
where they usually crossed the stream. First they weren't sure
that the figure wasn't actually a body, but then they could tell
the limbs were filled with sand. Crossing the stream
made her feel drawn to scale. Each part of that distance
had to be dismembered to be understood, like the times
when he gave her his hand so she could get across to the bank,
or when she remembered she used to call sleep "sand."
She kept on walking, but she was afraid of being drawn in,
recessively. She wanted to know *whose* scale.

A scale might tell her she was gaining too much weight
or it could give her a set of worldly properties.
That there is an angle to the rain could mean
she would like to catch something. More likely
she was after the approval of strangers. Saying this
might be an imbalance of belief, but a definition
is more valuable when it is uneven in its equivalence.
Maybe a life could be saved.

When they walked along the shore the small stones
clicked like determined beads. It was like a catalogue
of getting dark. Since a light is always capable
of being extinguished, she thought the threat of dark
was what gave light its complexity. She wanted the light
as a testament for her body: Tell me I am to be guessed at
like the water which keeps on going. But when night came
there were many lights. They seemed to undermine
the sky's opacity. She loved them out of all proportion,
as if they held a deep feeling there.

Catherine Imbriglio

TRISKELION

She used the neighbor's roof as a reference point, liking its precarious
    congruity,
a mobile performative at the sightline: what a woman thinks about
before she conceives. See how they run, driven with carelessness,
clouds cutting up over the rooftop like comedians, like blind mice
dispensing with threes. As this was a theatrical positioning,
I sat between them, trifocally, an intermediate vision
held commonly at arm's length: *Take my hand, I can't see.*
The boundaries of the third term blurred, there is in some part
a percentage of the other part, May as a fifth month or an auxiliary,
each a dispensable conditioning, given the farmer's wife,
who, at this point, *may* be reaching out a hand to cover the distance,
as if to carve out a bridge or a tree.

A trial balloon: how to mediate a trivium, that which belongs
at the crossroads, hence common, what everyone knows. Coming after
the sun has passed the meridian, composed in the form of three
relatively constrained parts, trifolium or tri-hedron,
she is back at the old schedule, which without a third term
is like the wife's anticipation, the news
of a death always coming in threes.

The sixth column may assist the fifth, or it may oppose it,
the one side pertaining to real significance rather than to form, i.e.,
    give us
your mother's maiden name for security purposes. I am worried about
your throat, a common experience indicating a slight shift in sympathy
among three branches, whose radiations from the center
can participate in only two arcs. To assume the proscenium as true,
as necessary to go on, after seeing the mice had gnawed away rings of
    bark
(called "girdling"), their eyes met only once all night, as if they were
    escaping
from division into two groups supposed to be exhaustive.
Meanwhile, she was staging an arcade: with respect to the roof, the
    moon
a saw blade, a builder's instrument; with respect to the bridge,
her hands are tied, like wings on either side of the arch.

408

REST AREA

Her dream was the earth being smashed by the sun.
There was no heat, but the space was filled space; every day
the sun drew more of the blue from it. The earth woman spoke first,
so that her brother/husband wasn't pleased, though it was not
the imperfect vision of a practice dream. Drawing on her dream
gives off a small portion of what is appositional. The edge of the earth
blocks out the bottom portion, but I am not fooling with augury now.
If you close your eyes in an unfamiliar place between gardens, that space
will be reduced to the limits of her body. Or, once the sun exhausts
its hydrogen, each dream will proceed to the red giant stage.

Processing a patch of dandelion weeds which look like repossessed suns
is called the binding problem. In a sequential system, a touched object
in no sense corresponds to a sight object, the feel of petal and stem
to the image of petal and stem. She wanted a pointillist's dream.
She sat hooded in the mist figuring how to "powder" constellations.
The dandelions looked like go-betweens.

In an ordinary drawing, you could perceive the earth and sun
as flat bodies or you could half manipulate them like her dream.
Sometimes she'll not comprehend which is the lying sense, feeling
or seeing, according to your temperament. It would make a mission
out of looking through her things. That interchangeable subject is out
of proportion to one's usual relation to a dream. If the primary
    wavelength
exists outside her limits, you'll feel the subject always leaving you.
Her eye won't see it, since it is going beyond the course established
for her dream: a star taking up with other stars, absorbing
the primal medium as it perishes in you.

Two Poems
Vincent Katz

RAIN-TOPPLED FEBRUARY DUSK

rock and roll died without its personages
drab garments idiotic save a turn of the century black cape
with colored sewn flowers a male singer used
alleviate leaves in single brushstroke
the buddha amitabha seated in dhyana mudra indonesia
many quiet marvels in andesite
then the great faces of Rome the respect for personality
the looks out of those worlds tempera encaustic
highlights vast blizzards of congealment
dull longviews by one of photography's masters
gentle limewood carvings of mother and child
polychrome illusion on doweled appendages
then back to the truth of the painters who marked
last century's end, like writers accompanied them
smiling into absinthe, they sat and heard the world pass
in a horse's whinny, clop clop on cobbles cigarette smoke
and alcohol a tiny hovel for one's desires, pressed concupiscence
pastel woman fading into air overviews and reflex
the look of a real person smears of paint
an immense forest dark with sunset's final brilliant oranges
poking glimmers a disappointing mess something really great
fête galante stumping graphite chalk red and white
eagles behind pinecones nestled in glass a belt buckle
glass choker with cats tiny leaves carved in sandstone painted
dimly lit hall perfect for Friday dusk kisses beneath the heights
invocations to turn to linger slyly pushing forward inches away
a sexy pose made clearer in lines become rigid no breathing of flesh
the empty bedrooms of the grand, sickbeds ecstatic flights
rain rhythms elastic bringing in front the slide down to park's earth
request to fly homeward rested achieved in culture frequent side
accounted told

BREADS AND SWEETS

bridling with unseen
energy, listen to moans
falsifications even
friends, haircut, architecture
slide downhill where everything
meshes, better than others
I lift my eyes to sink
vocal push into physical
size, body contacted
jealous of her producers
interviewers who miss
her point completely, sorry
but the songs ascend ignorance
shyly flirting segments
imagination, flaunted
intelligence, they leave her
undented in morning
actually it is I who
misunderstand from my
non-perspective, cascades
of words, piano and voice
are the weapons of armies
bolted to past thoughts and
present perceptions, refrain
the delicate intensity forked
spread up the photographs'
frankness, I want to use her
name, but not yet, the sky
has descended, earlier
we crossed the aqueduct
I live only in my life now
the words come from the
latin and they have been
preserved, I start to write
the unexpected streams
forth, didn't know I was
thinking, was I? in
galleries, streets, passing

people borne down
by disharmony
they want that watch
and thatch but greed
hovers, oh no, here
comes the satellite
descending, descending
heedless of desire
trees' grandeur in shady
boulevards, the song's
pure chant hits, evens
promised longing till
self re-emerges, washed
and inimitable, once
again able to attend
I had hoped for so much
expectation of necessity
I am outside now
September's clear
voice, indication
that shutters will
fall and open drily

Land at Church City
Thalia Field

From a hovering point over the red clay path (a lane dusted with blistering) her eyes follow him on stages teetering, her wings that is, wet and not quite conscious, his wings really hands playing "forward" into the past fretted grabbable; a "there" tense ensemble past tense, forward of it, pushing into a path he's grasping: all neck, all keys, into hymn.

At last but faithfully abominable. Her eyes make tiny dervishes on the parched silence, fully parted to let loose a vowel slack in overexposed noon, scratching at opened seeds (he dances without prints for her) so that neither dares count prints, or lay them to lip in seasoned glare. His dance a pilgrim of patterns glaring too holy to mistake for mistakes.

A billboard becomes Seraph the highest angel six, whole wings of calendars open, one for each day fluttering the rocky lane like anything red, like anything she can say mistakes are like, though he's the red one.

One mounting. One receiving. A bird forgives the beating up the entrance, as he could pardon the mention of the seventh missing day. This time holy places gather in permanent redemptions up the canyon turned off from familiar. No amenities. No public utilities. The population is bliss freak, and church.

The town above hangs for him now above, and slightly high that way. High an ordinance of loss. High an anticipated beforehand. High the genetic unfinishable. High the deepest kissed past tense. Roof of unapproachable fire escapes. That nest of churches, for lack of a better word, huddles high in his sight, on its undamnable burning seat, and hers way behind and tipping.

It is left for her to hover atheist and downward glancing. Not a single communion broached with binoculars loaded. Were eagles approaching a mile, a mouse might collapse to a print. But her wings bulk in balancing itchy devotion to "whatever," in doctrinal "whereby." Feathers aren't muscles, yet oiled for repelling a rain not coming for nine hundred ninety-nine miles or years; same thing, she thinks, same thing.

And below her his knees at the gate lips of ground meets kissing. Avenue the churches or blocks and street churches, for lack of a better word, every structure a church, every never his heart repelling tourists of grace for his soon expiation, turning back a cherub, second order angel on a self-same map, a winged child mispronounced.

Out of stairs he could dispense his own suffering. Churches, for lack of a better word, bow upright to foundations set to poverty, to lift of thrice-born melancholy. One coupon of atmosphere wealthy, a bountiful vulture. How a town consumes with lacking better words than churches, yet only consumes churches. Welcome the hagiography of reflected celebrity.

His head lifts to the altar, for lack of a better word, another rumored virgin, what he's lost the chorus sacrificed, losing denomination in their say-so. Churches, for lack of a better word, fake the orange cones at detours consummating. Welcome to your very raptured transcience of patterning. Each church re-animates eternity for a slim visitation.

Once he gains, for lack of a better word, a body's drunken messenger, wax-wings instantly fathered, his better word falls toward offering. Tar-stained hands fly stones at one heat unimpeachable. Dust red prints wait in the tense of his tentative printing. Still high and hungry, one afflatus a scalding sunlight numb despite excessive longing. Each sweet translation of relics, cloaked in stained glass, balances skeletons before his each translation tarnishes the last translation. These sentences reflect attachments and wide glances from a sky profane of blue, as blank of believing in churches as his city is full. She believes in them on his behalf from a clueless, senseless perch.

Sacred aims at blood detachment contains mortal layers of systems. Sins patched of pine tar, mosses which don't come this rain. Plant the animal kingdom, or any small landing. Cycling bundled roots congest with slippery stasis; an alibi lane in the depth contraption.

But high up in Church Town, for lack of a better name, a stage looses shadows inside the mission, a town unwieldy with churches, for lack of a better word, burdened with them and yet undeniably justified. Shadows and temperatures take umbrage in the testament, kneel beside dusty jubes, rolling beneath carved pews, his attention clots for shadows faithful to permanent dwellings.

His feet are likely and pious approaching scriptured ongoings. His ongoings unblamable statuary, the furnishing of flesh made undiseased. Flight as she thinks her sanctuary in motion, digging from wings into a small repeated phrase, trembling at his faith.

Or put one last way: without these churches, for lack of a better word, many denominations force face to city landings; wingspans irrelevant or wholly threaded, he would fret away the last full upholding, undo his fullblooded erection, wait: there could be another anunciation, interrupting flight.

Invisible blanks hold the doors open, they're double and stand barely parted, but do part upon curious muscles. One body makes a street a multitude of church buildings: assemblies and abbeys, apses and mihrabs, cathedrals mandiras monestaries chapels stupas temples. He is aching in worship, and with hands that strive to forgive the height of churches, for lack of any word for faith in height, or what passes unending, she hovers too close.

Not Egypt
John Taggart

1.

Turned sideways

window turns into pillars

shadow pillars and shadow porches

deep red valley in a valley way down in Egypt land

shadows and habitation

of the dead

Egypt

not Egypt nor Hernando's hideaway

turned back

into window in my room

all's green

the leaves of the trees the corn field beyond

grasses around the pond some of the green

some obscured by books

testaments of the dead

testaments of the unwrapped dead.

2.

So many so many stones

stone wall

limestone and zigzag mortar

the land silt loam so many wagon-loads of stones

stone wall of Jacob Ramp's stone house

stone wall

stone foundation

so many wagon-loads of stones

dusk

dusk and dark along the road past Ramp's stone house

to my house

white flowers of the Russian-olive

white flowers by starlight

wind

exhilaration of the fragrance of the flowers

by starlight.

3.

Side-road shortcut secret road

up through the woods

behind my house

up through the woods

perhaps made by Ramp perhaps made by his son

behind my house which was his son's house

to the sweet cherry orchard

no longer there

not one tree of the orchard left to shake

mossy overhung with vines secret road to what's there

to see in secret

to see the secret family crest in all around me

high up

on an ascended plane

kept alive.

4.

A good sign

the old redbud is dying

canker and wilt after last summer's drought

all's green and the heart-shaped leaves are gone

wilted and gone

good a terrible thing to say

sign

that the turned back remains turned

bad sign

all over behind my house all over redbud leaves emergent

heart-shaped leaves among the ferns

native tree

heart-shaped shadows

native tree and tree of betrayal

sign

what remains native among all the native green.

5.

Like a plow

cold-rolled iron shaped like a scoring-out plow

tempered point

a tool like a plow to make the mill-race

tool and tools

ahistorical pick and shovel

tool and tools

to move through depths of a valley

from the creek through another woods under another road

through another woods to the creek again

mill-race

made by a number of men with their tools

by their labor

which is my labor also

a labor of ecstasy

considerable labor of ecstasy.

The Interrogation
Renee Gladman

His friends are waiting patiently
in front of a popular cafe—waiting
because they love him, he thinks. This
walking, he will say to them when he
arrives, was difficult for me. There were
obstacles in the street—though I can't
prove it. Every time I hit one, falling on
my head was the result, and by the time
I had recovered from the fall, there was
no accessible memory.

Seeing them—in their glorious postures.
He wants to yell encouragement, but is
too tired to say the words. These are
good friends, though. They know how
to wait. Soon I will arrive and we'll eat.
Then he trips and falls into a pothole.

When twenty minutes later he reaches
them they are having an argument
about eggs:

Monique is saying, We have to think
seriously here . . . the signals are always
scrambled . . . what we have to do is
figure out their corporate hours, then go
in there and fuck em up . . . no, this does
not support democracy, but we are
beyond that occasion. While Stefani
shouts, Yeah, let's lay em all out, during
M.'s ellipses.

He thinks, this might not be about eggs and perhaps I'm not supposed to hear. But these are my friends! They're smiling at me; one has his hand on my shoulder. They want me to ease into this conversation when I have been struggling to get here, when the worst things have happened to me.

His best friend F. is among the group, and has his hand on the newcomer's shoulder, trying to involve him in the conversation: So man, what do you think? Turning to him. The newcomer, with fuzzy head says, I just want to eat. I never care what it is.

His friends appear to agree with him because three of them have walked away with the purpose, he presumes, of securing a table. This is the warmest day we've had so far, he says to himself as Adolfo tries to kiss him. He shakes him off and a minute later the others return. They stand around him, smoking.

Stefani says, Monique, what's this? Leaning on F. for assistance. I have made some diagrams, she answers, of the inner labyrinth, so that we'll know where to place our men.

Don't be so—he snaps, exhausted and hungry, So—

Freddie finds the group a table. It's beautiful today, he says with some hesitation. Are we sure? I'm sure, the newcomer blurts. This is the perfect spot for me.

After a few minutes of silence, Adolfo turns to the newcomer and asks, So what happened to you last night?

To the newcomer this is a dream. For a moment, he looks inside. This is what I was hoping for. They want my story. When I was young, in the summers, this is what I imagined. A group turning to me, members with a cock to their heads. Awaiting—me. Not like the time I almost fell into the fire when Freddie was searching for more wood and something in that search kept him away for hours. As I lay there. And our other friends, who are now long gone, wandering in their drugs—

He shakes his head, These are not my memories. Shakes his head again, more violently, where are my memories?

Then he locks on to a series of aerial images.

Birds don't fly that low, he observes with growing paranoia. What's that? Then a mosquito buzzes by. He moans, what's that? He turns down a concrete path, slinking away from the bird: got to get away, but quietly so the fly does not notice me. The path runs along the periphery of this memory, which could just as well be outside, except that it's not. Even he suspects it, yanking at the leaves from passing branches and shoving them up his nose. Real leaves of a real outside have a distinct and dirty smell—

Stefani zips his sweatshirt shut and pushes him out the door. No more memory. Outside the cafe, he looks around. The light is low, as after a storm or shortly before sunset, or as a result of wearing shades, or some doom is coming. He feels his hand flapping around on his face, looking for shades. Decides to ask, Stefani, what's on my face? She says she can't report if she's not looking at him. Well, look at me! But you said not to!

Where did everybody go?
Ikea.
Why?
To blow it up.
What you doing?
Keeping my eye on you.
How, if you don't look at me?
I've been listening for you.
Where have we been all day?
There, eating eggs.

It's hard to believe that I have been away from myself for so many hours and I do not feel the least bit rested. In fact, what's all this on my shoulders? What's pouring out of my eyes and toes? Not my chi. Where's that? He closes his eyes as S. pulls him by the hand. Aware of their destination and confident that S. will deliver them there, he takes the opportunity to put order to his mind.

Now let's see . . . where is that chi? Inside himself again, walking through some chamber with his head down, he glimpses a photo on the floor. It's damaged, ripped in several pieces—but he recognizes the face. His. Taken a few years ago.

I remember the store I'm posed in front of. I used to meet the group there. How did this picture get separated from the others? And why is it destroyed? He looks around with caution, as if caught "in" something. Then snaps, this is my mind, no one else should be here, against a creeping fear of being post-invasion.

The next morning he wakes with his ass pressed against Adolfo's hip, concentrating on his dreams. Monotonous as always but with a new array of characters, who are much more violent than the nights before. —Wait, he thinks it's Adolfo. The pain in his ass is the same, so it must be Adolfo. Yet besides what he knows to have existed in the past, there is no other evidence. Soon he will have to turn around to see. But there is no light, no sun shining through his blackened windows. He will have to touch his face to know.

If he turns around and it's not Adolfo, he will want to squash whomever it is, unless that person's stronger. He might even give in to rage. No, the best way to find out if it's Adolfo is to get the person to talk.

He's thinking of something to say. Says in one of my dreams people were playing with firearms and I was not sure what to do. Silence. Says then there was glass everywhere. I wonder if I screamed. Did I scream? Silence, as that following cell death. He imagines himself embraced by a lifeless body and with a mixture of disgust and anticipation he

reaches his hand back to tap the hip bone,
and it jumps.

—waking again, sometime during
the day. He looks around himself and
supposes that he has slept for a week.
This time he is not in his bed but at a
breakfast table in front of a plate of eggs.
The group is there.

When he comes to, M. is speaking.

What is she talking about? Monique is
not using regular language. It's a code!
And everyone seems to know it, but me!
Where did they pick this up? She keeps
saying, "Ha chini chini" and the rest of
them nod their heads. Did I comprehend
this shit before I woke up? Maybe if I
relax I will find that I too speak this
language.

He leans back in this chair, clears his
mind and utters:

"Ma chaney aravici delimatool. Econ
ha chini chini."

The response is as expected. Faces
turn to him. He thinks, damn I should
have asked a question, then they would
have been forced to answer. Monique
continues talking. She says many
things, but "ha chini chini" is all he
hears.

I keep thinking about those words . . . as
though I know them—

S. pokes him in the side with her elbow
and whispers, Isa uma kuni. Monique
ma uma kuni. He shakes her off. Argh!
What's this? Something's sticking me.
He reaches under his ass and finds
some pieces of wire. He shouts, Ja se pa
cahini, then clamps his hand over his
mouth. Why did I say that? Holding the
wire in his hand, which Freddie grabs
and places in a box.

The last time I was in a box it was
Spring, he recalls. The old group had
gone downtown to sell papers and left
me behind to clean up. We had rented
a small room in the old warehouse
district. Somebody left a box open, one
of the kinds we used when mailing
things overseas, and I step back into it.
Laid there for hours, not because I
couldn't get up but because I was
comfortable there. I couldn't remember
who we were against. Lying there, that
was all I wanted to picture. I thought,
On my back and safe in this tiny room,
I want to think about my enemies. It was
easy. No one intruded—everything was
fine. I stayed behind. But the image
never surfaced. That's not true. Several
images came to me, but none of them
seemed right. I kept saying, no this
couldn't be the enemy, discarding
the idea.

Seven Poems
Laura Moriarty

MEETING

He let go of me
What no one turns
Returns like a wheel (embarks)
Revisits remains

All the sugar in the world
Cafe china fantasy of white not
Leaving here not stopped
A juke box starts

The way back
Now this act
A short song
The road tangled

Apostacy to take
Give oneself up to
One who sings
Has already has left

Sleepy now not
Understanding night
Without sleep
All that is wanted

A phrase away
Is late the street wakes
He takes himself
Not meeting

HOTEL

First dream against walls
The scene pressed into unsaid
But possible as pictured without
Control as with dream the scale
Large the scene clear of will
Of what disturbs you
My question
In the courtyard the hotel statue
The wings of it poised
Too much singing
To yourself, myself
Conventional fountain but dry
Agreement also silent

TIN BOX

Heart with nails
No words
Car starting
The play

Lime and mint
Ciudad
Come here for this
Lit from within

Homage á Jack
His traveling name
Address floating
Paper trembling wings

Fans in this heat
"that was all he could do"
Car start repetition
The dead team Us

429

FIRST SONG

Tell me to sing
A series to serenade to calm
To clarify to drizzle
Walk go along to the ocean
Without light with light to the sea
You were with me in hell
It wasn't like hell
We were under the sea
The same as love you were/are
Tell me to embrace you
Carry you off two or three ways
How many in this song
How many times going
Gone by boat to the sea
More sacred to us than something
Tell me to hold you

STUPID MOON

Stupid moon
Unfortunate creature in it

Voice like a whistle
Source of rumors

Used me like a radio
Innuendo of success left

They call it the clap
When after something

A dose men say
That said

My name for you
Not written here

EARTH FORGOTTEN

Stucco to terracotta

In cameo half sky

From one direction the town

Size unclear the eyes also

Too long gone

The constant misremembered

Beginning of time

Depersonalized but okay

Destination Moon

Protagonist cratered and pale

Seeks inaccurate revenge

Travels by thinking

FATE/SONG FORM

Blameless this claim
That I or you

Do nothing no one
Knows where you are

Animal or minimal
Second the seconds passed

Laura Moriarty

Allowed by you or that I
Would have

Slowly around us the field
Did you hear me?

With clarity as if not
Needing it to be real

Film Noir
Kevin Young

THE HIDEOUT

Woke up dead

Tired, in my arms
an empty

An instead. Tried
sleeping it off,

My hangover of her,
wishing for some hair

Of the dog—or slow purr—

My tongue
white, eyes red.

The light my eye hurts

I am in chalk, an outline,
a back-alley body

Afraid this face
in the mirror (that hides

My strychnine mouthwash)
may be the only one left.

Do I need again
to lose my skin, start

A new town, man?
Grow a beard

Or become one?
I'm sick of taking

It on the chin, of waking
gimlet-eyed from the gin—

Shoe soles like carpet,
or excuses, grown thin.

Cloudy tap water.
One dusty aspirin.

Outside my newsprint
curtains—the black

& white of words,
yellowing—

What I can no more weather

I watch till I'm sure
no light remains

Night staining the streets clean

THE WAGON

My reputation
exceeds me. Temptation

littering the bar, chanteuse
piano-perched, her sifter

of brandy empty. Fifths
of watered whisky.

Wagoned
for a week, I'm no good

to anyone, soft-
boiled, unsalted.

Haunted—
her quinine kisses

her microphone caress.

Wanted to hold her like her
two-faced fur stole,

that foxy smile.
(Instead teethmarks

punctuate my skin
like perforated parentheses.)

Barkeep's glass
eye like an olive

The sharks circling the pool
table in the back, sniffing

out green. Felt
myself losing my arm

435

Kevin Young

wrestle bout between
sarsaparilla

& something stronger.
Sleep.

Step on out
into the cold—under

the awning bouncers
stomp & nod

like hunched horses,
their breath billowing.

Lovers pass in hansom
cabs. Who will stop for me,

screech at my jaywalk, honk
to let me in? The moon

winking its way across sky,
I hail like Mary

The Charon Cab Co.

to sail through the city—
my cabbie, an escapee

from the state, swerves

& swears at the salt-
covered cars

brushing so close
you could lean out

into wind & plant
each one a kiss.

Kevin Young

MIDNIGHT RAMBLE

Leaving the coffin-cold
theater in winter

Single-barrel moon
aimed above us

He escorted & told me
lies I wanted

To warm my ears

The moon's lazy eye
razored shut

The two of us
fought that hawk

Walking through wind
across a world that once

Seemed so flat I feared
I might could fall off—

Now Flora, every horizon
got another behind it

Least that's what
Mama would say—*Just you wait—*

But I hightailed it north
& changed my name.

Beneath the shrapnel sky
I wanted to run

From here to the train
& buy me a ticket one way—

437

Kevin Young

I'm tired of eviction
The radio's same station

Playing woe & blues

Said tired of eviction
the radio's same station

Arguing whose man is whose.

I want some diesel bound
south, making all stops—

No more neighbor's
whooping cough

No more leaky
solos from the faucets

Or landlords who pinch,
swapping winks for late rent.

Graveyard-shift moon
that turns men mad—

Let me trade fire
escape for front porch

Let me ride
sunset down to where

Train's the only whistle

& a girl don't got to cry
to keep herself company

Where moonshine ain't just sky
& you can catch catfish

Sure as a man—bearded, polite—
already fixed up & fried.

438

Five Stein Poems
Jackson Mac Low

SEE THEM TOGETHER
[*Stein 59*]

See them deciding if you can.

Monday I believe to be dangerous.
Carry do carry the same offer to another.
She is annoyed that in bed he never says anything for days.

Quickly he said the thing he had to say was that he had nothing to say.
The thing that's shown, why it's herself.
When the whole thing was mentioned, it's likely it was not for it to be
      neglected.
Don't be like that.

It was an Italian wonder, a hundred men and no mother, no, saw the
      calamitous poison.
Render what you will so that the forty see sounds or something.
There are many piles of spools there.
This one said that to think meant to beat.
This was the very one who said it was so, that this other one had said that
      something had seven hands.
Do rivers not render an increase in letters by going where they're going and
      not stammering.
Let it stand.

That the prayers looked to be annoying was shown by the laughs.
Really deny that said Mother.
Walter, it is not just any edgy goodness that is splendid said the minister as
      he fastened himself.
Not coughing there doesn't do anything for me, for I am seven years of age.
Are those really prayers.
I believe the infant's helpless separation was what made you what you will

or would be.
The country did not come to be splendid in that age of shapely citizens.
They're cement.
They're we.
These are the stones that horses believe can light many lamps with the
same authority.
That it had not been believed that eggs were meat astonished me.

In London you would be sheer tired she said one day when more of us
came late.
We did it together.
Because of those draughts the women complained of a reluctant inclination.
Leaving she mentioned saying that she too had not come splendidly.
She would.
For as far as a mile he, no you, do believe what you hear.
The horses render what they can and no moon is getting into taking the
shapes we saw.
This said he surprised them, saying, we don't need the silvery noise they
can make.
Something like that.
Seven are enough, but hands in rebellion seldom say this.
Lead us to the sheepdog.
What is that there, what emotion is going into making us believe in it.
When the shouting, when the gently tired mile was over,
all that was newly loaned would not do.
No need for it.
During that credit hearing the names did not come out of those we had not
seen.
Emile had shown and loudly said there were reasons why some women
come so splendidly.
They said this was what they'd said.
Italian rest that shall be blest they wanted, but stupidly said they wanted
soup.

He was considering it.
Wondering she rendered rubber not to do mischief but not what they said
either.
It meant very little when they did that winding and dangerous shouting but
went away gently.
We need that.
She was harnessing a picture.

I was annoyed.
Those women never openly interfere but they do believe the country is the
  city.
Do name me, and understand I am of age and a shapely citizen, not cement.
Where are the horses.
I believe you are willing toys, coal decides when you cough and when you
  don't.
I am at the age of seven, something, I mean SOMEbody.

Are you saying your prayers.
I believe the infant's world was one country and he said he'd seen that
  country.
Come back.
It had been an age since our splendid shapely citizens had seen cement
  horses.
Do you believe that.
You willing toys have decided on coal so you can stand paying any amount.
Fork it over.

Seven somethings were together.

ACT A REVERSIBLE ESCAPE
[*Stein 96*]

Act from your center: eat.

Explaining expecting is a cover for diversion.
Replacing the floor makes a change.
It is no more and never was a little hole.

Authorized speech is changing nothing.
To whomever that letter comes, a commensurate hanging will also come.
No apple has ever come there.
Color has uses.

Is *not moving* the same as being under cover?
There the single bell of resistance will separate indecision from hesitation.
What does ordinary sugar stand for?
Separation.

441

Jackson Mac Low

Are there corners in that?
Once, the light had shown on the water in that single central chamber.
Checking a very narrow purchase captured this stranger.

Is being settled and plain reversible?
Indeed it is.
Now fifty rights have given no sweet choice.
Was change reversible?
Explaining and expecting are not yet the same thing.
The air has no center.
When a Chinese diversion covered this wooden floor with leather, it
    discharged all that birthday excitement.
Does this go there?
There a piece is always admitted.
Is there always a disposition to be penetrated?
Not at some temperatures.

Some have always been penetrated.
What is the difference between desertion and breath on a looking glass?
That is certainly cautious stubble.
That whitening changes the design.
Is emigration reversible escape?
A little stubble established an interruption.
For some dispositions at certain temperatures, gamboling will be
    necessary.
A reduction of current between those plates penetrated her painstaking
    preparation for more alleviation.
What burning statement outlined that harmony?
There in the corners is some strange writing from a time of sullen
    negligence.
Shouldn't the location of those plates be exemplary?
He has been relating his speech to every spoon.
Will the motion of the four taller chairs make for discrimination or,
    indeed, stupefication?
I doubt that.
This is there all the time.
Supposing one has a certain disposition toward resignation, why should
    she be pale?
Is resignation a color diminisher?
Why is there no roof?

Jackson Mac Low

Is there a stable resemblance between use and means?
That is not what I mean.
Lengthening last evening was not an evasion of the equator's separation.
Quarreling is disturbing the center.
Why that sound of obligingness?
Certainly obligingness is an excellent coloring for a cautious little escape,
    but is it reversible?
Is stubble stubble?
Where did she establish that outrageous interruption?
Mentioning the temperature of that sample of the mixture was necessarily
    a distracter there.
My disposition resembles that stairway.
The ingredients of this preparation will have more use in the morning than
    they did the time before.
And as ends, they're not related to any established trouble.
Supposing there is some more silence, does that establish something?
All this fast playing would not estabish a lighter time when cloud cover
    came.
The description of a piece comes from its sides.
This shame table no longer feeds our arrangement.
Withstanding the establishment is more than intending and not like
    resignation.
Monday means silver if not used for a four-day birthday.
It frequently used to indicate an even smaller likeness.
Everything is plentiful and curly in the daylight.
We're quarreling over an expression!
Education is an exercise in change.
Isn't it singular that music gathered the ancients together?
Whitening a cake certainly changes its design.
There is no anxious charity in my statement.
It is more of an experience not to have more color.
A case may capture a lap if there is not any clinching now and no more
    extension.
Invitations make the chair of authority secure.
Asparagus is a choice ingredient in declarations and summer hats.

If it is the same, it has not yet changed.
The border is wider in the center.
Establishing a cover, the author in the center of the smaller table comes to
    that rubbing piece with a suggestion thought simpler than exaltation.
I suggest that the conclusion of separation is separation.

443

Jackson Mac Low

Changing a use is charming.
There is surely more substance in four.
Why is a feat that much smaller asymmetrical?
A construction that is not always necessary is no cover.
Always establishing her disposition and always changing, she supposes
    some lives to be freer than hers.
A paler connection made them separate.
Attention has no color.
Is that bather choking?
Why is everybody there given one evening paper?
Anything righteous is likely to be there.
All wholesale curtains are white, and yet seeing the equator is always
    downright incalculable.
Empty dishes shade a monster.
Once slanting time is clinching someone's suffering fingernails, is there
    anything that shows the weather there?
Even the church and righteous slippers aren't enough.

Isn't one Asian occasion trouble?
Does anything establish silences?
Something does.
Withstanding drowning with resolution is a preparation for temporary
    singing.
The Chinese establish acquaintance with astonishing resignation.
Resignation there comes packaged in a funnel.
Establishing that the weather is not wetting is like not mentioning that
    evening is lessening.
Establishing a store there would line up everybody's tables.
This shows that mourning is not altogether a disgrace.
Looking with one's ears has often marked the current climate there.
Does all the powder there establish anyone's rights?

Translate every detail there.
Translate all the mistakes?
The whole thing, even the willow slippers.
Are Chinese acquaintances always resigned?
Astonishingly, a line establishes a nation.
Resignation only arises on the way there.
The whole stubbly cape is there.

There, attention is certainly dimmer.

444

This does not mean that the sound of obligingness is not the same there.
Is it the case that there's no roof there?
Use means lengthening there.

Last evening at the equator, separation excellently evaded quarreling.
Is such changing a little disturbing?
Why is the center so cautiously obliging?

Coloring stubble's a reversible escape.

STRENUOUSNESS NEVER LEAVES
THE CONCRETE UNTOUCHED
[*Stein 50*]

Strenuousness may seem inadequate and narrow throughout our years of worldly perplexity but need not be separated from powerful admiration.

We understand explaining convictions but not understanding itself. Opportunities for our own last vocation may be beginning nevertheless and come to preside. We would do best to observe this with impartiality.

Dounor realized that recognition of her work never touched its concreteness. This promised to explain her helpless nature's constraining perplexity so that she might understand everything. She always showed the same shyness in relation to every teacher. She learned to engage the meanings of both beauty and abstract ideas.

Sometimes Hannah abruptly guided her through and beyond any course and through a great range of arguments. She seemed a strangely devout friend through many springs. Earnestly and deliberately she formed even her health so that she became content and continued to be. From her customary chair she changed things she'd felt in her youth. She learned that she who would labor must first know the walls that confined her between which she'd been thrown and that not every attempt to look at nature was loved. The puritan's interest did not extend to some of nature. Powerful forms of perplexity needed worldly explanation and understanding.

Neither convictions nor understanding gave her any opportunity to begin her own vocation.

Jackson Mac Low

Impartial observation did not preside. Dounor realized this. She recognized that work never leaves the concrete untouched.

POINTING ALL GLAZED ELEPHANT SEASONING
[Stein 111/Titles 8]

Pointing all glazed very program.

Clean that very place pleasure place very purple closet black.
Very places.

Elegant charm gray plainer closed that gray pieces cloister.
Spark only plan.
Plan change many particles slender.

Black very present place.
Place only pink place that.
Away particular all scarcely very particularly blaming.
Practice only place all that very placed alley places rosy pine.

Climb practices tiny purr plate that many peeled.
Black.
Black.
Very plain.
All that praying place!

Place feathers away pigeon!
Claiming claiming bury Pole blinder.
Read they pink glass what?
Very present gliding mean they pain blazing meal many.

Pleasanter all means gray pocketfull all than tray.
Perfect plain reason many plan cloaking really very.
Piercing all weather only protection all place easy.
Precisely all chaining only place all orange very.
Pint closed change.

Very procured alone boat tiny post.
Placed plaster holy path all meadows.
They pet slam.
Nearly play puff please near.
Very particular glees chalk play pudding slender.
That they pea all leave only.

Please please away!
They piece play that they place black meant very place all that.
Very pleasure all chair they put all that they plain.
Plain that very pink plentiful chance away penetrated.
Cleaned that they place place chair very plates floor.
Plainer relying placard climate that tray place slanting slanting.
Very pen clergyman chamber very principle cloud change very.

Place all than only pecking elephant seasoning very.
Program clean that very place pleasure place very.
Purple closet black very places
Elegant charm gray.
Plainer closed that.
Gray pieces cloister.
Spark only plan.
Plan change.

Many particles slender
Black very present.
Plan change.
Place place.
Only pink place that.
Away particular!
All scarcely very particularly blaming

Practice only place.
All that very placed alley places rosy pine.
Climb practices tiny purr.
Plate that many?
Peeled
Black
Black
Very plain

All that praying!
Place feathers away pigeon!
Place claiming.
Claiming bury Pole.
Blinder read.
They pink glass what?
Very present gliding mean they pain?
Blazing meal?
Many pleasanter.

All means gray pocketful.
All than tray perfect.
Plain reason!
Many plan cloaking.
Really very piercing!
All weather only protection.
All place easy precisely.
All chaining only place.

All orange?
Very!
Pint closed change.
Very procured alone boat!
Tiny post!
Placed plaster holy path all meadows.
They pet slam.

Nearly play puff.
Please near!
Very particular glees.
Chalk play pudding.
Slender that they pea.
All leave only.

Please please!
Away they piece play that they place.
Black meant very place.
All that?
Very pleasure!

All chair they put.
All that they plain.
Plain that very pink.
Plentiful change away!

Penetrated cleaned that they place.
Place chair very plates.
Floor plainer relying placard climate that tray place slanting.

Slanting very pen clergyman chamber.
Very principle cloud change very place.

All than only pecking elephant seasoning.

POINTING DIFFERENCE ILLUSION
PLACES OCCASION PLATE DINNER
[*Stein 109/Titles 6*]

Pointing difference.

Nickel breath handsome leaves question place piece reckless.
Calamity makes redness question painful pin necessity.
Cleaning illusion places occasion plate dinner.

Pack strangely glass necessity discolor permitted mixed
occasional final.

Dress necessary monstrous place width such arrangement
necessary.
Necessary occasion piece oil occasion occasion makes.
Places decision peace light necessarily because.

Roses curves addition pearls little lace treading.

Please necessary revision pounding midnight nice strange
steps.

Suppose artichoke pinching linen exchange entangled shows
suggestion.

Jackson Mac Low

Occasion pealing distinguish because clearly means.
Earnest assiduous purple single second remains.

Thirstiness became division principal.

Light recollection tomato makes suggestion exterior potatoes.
Dispute succeed pleasanter hopes famous vacation.
Place silent pocketful pliable makes necessity disappointed.
Perfect singular sack strange makes necessarily.
Decision place singularly luck separation crossing.
Witness question poison wide receptacle soda.

Pheasant loaves occasion purred cider succession.

Salad beefsteak suppose question.

Please with faces.

Salad dressing.

Suppose question placing lighter accomplishing relating
    shows.

Chinese erection please with mice because satisfy suggest.
Question perfect time decision separation division.
Spoons position plain hill much always lives necessary.
Everybody passed little success vacancies shows.
Varnish question place visible face always trees.
Causes decision pre-occupation discloses much strange.
Shows furnished ponderous plainer single section.
Vacant shows dishes location principle with occasion.
Arranged lacks rights occasion place wideness occasion
    pleases.

Please cleansing question place piece reckless calamity
    makes.
Redness question painful pin necessity cleaning.
Illusion places occasion plate dinner.

Four Poems
Rae Armantrout

PHRASING

1.

"Let's really show the world
that we're getting warmed up."

A certain ambient
despair
washes the stomach gently.

"Let us disguise
eternity

as a survival
drama.

How will consciousness
be organized

when material grows scarce

after the death
of stars?"

Into flaps? Pulsations?

Shell-game urgency
of the news-hour.

What pumps to the surface
is all empty

circle-skirt,

a scalloped
white-pink thing.

The trick is to turn it
inside out?

2.

What *are* words for?
To be put in order,

time disentangled from space.

So when I get there,
there's no one around—

just a phrase
somewhere,

hearing itself
think,

whistling up and down
its forecast
of a scale

while twigs make
minor adjustments.

"I'm in between
two states
and can't be interrupted,

between two points
and can't be found,

waylaid

OUR NATURE

The very flatness
of portraits
makes for nostalgia
in the connoisseur.

Here's the latest
little lip of wave
to flatten
and spread thin.

Let's say
it shows our recklessness,

our fast gun,

our self-consciousness
which was really

our infatuation
with our own fame,

our escapes,

the easy way
we'd blend in

with the peasantry,

our loyalty
to our old gang

from among whom
it was our nature

to be singled out

BOX

Pulling up to the minute,

think, "Mental detritus."

Picking up speed,

the craze for useless crazes

is a joke about something—

but what?

Bird rides wire—

a probe

in the cold stir.

Falling asleep, I hear that

"only one hill works."

We laugh

to accommodate death.

Dream someone's placed me

in a red, plastic box

from which now I pop up,

clown-like,

into consciousness.

A time when we agree

the present does not exist,

has never existed.

Black puffs drift

in front of salmon smears—

sky going white beyond.

I'll be called up

from moment to moment

to decide

what's plausible.

It is terrible

to die—

but for a thought

not to be thought?

SOLID

1.

To produce the consistency of experience,

each night
the program toys with the idea
that the picture might be doctored:

it's the false monster in the lake
known as George Washington.

What "lake?"

             *

I submerge

because I enjoy
waking up,

arising
from chaos

bit by bit
again.

The "ness"
that is nothing*ness,*

but seen from within.

             2.

"Nude activists in Berkeley
find the law
has them covered."

"Hero surfaces
from sunken sub,"
                 it says.

When we come back,
"Southern Exposure:

radiation leak

The Night
The Lights Went Out In Georgia."

             *

When we come back,
the murdered siblings

reappear
as trolls and elves.

When we come back,
the heir apparent

crafts
his solid victory

Guests of Space
Anselm Hollo

Guten Tag Herr Schopenhauer Bonjour Monsieur Cioran
good morning Mr. Swift how are you Mr. Burroughs
once again history the unstoppable proves you right
species no better than smart rat (maybe not even as smart)
evolutionary leap? my foot, my foot in three-foot hole
but let all peaceful mutants leap for spring
calloo callay, while they still may —
watch it! don't twist that ankle!
don't step into that three-foot hole!
"and wisdom has not come" "against wisdom as such"
oh, it is apt to give a gopher tantrums!
anecdotal befuddlement. infinite terminators.
toujours a mountain eased a previous you;
should it feel easier, writing? I don't think so. No.

*

here have I summed my sighs, playing cards with the dead
in a broke-down shack on the old memory banks
e'en though my thoughts like hounds
pursue me through swift speedy time
feathered with flying hours
but could have sat there for many more hours
listened to poet friends reading
words by an absent friend whose work we love
in the name of Annah the Allmaiziful,
the Everliving, the bringer of plurabilities
concretized, concertized, temporally minute
progressions of actions, swirling mists of the past
"you have a lot of stuff here, you know?"
"yes   now run on home"

*

458

Once you've said something, you can't unsay it
Once you haven't said anything, it remains unsaid
and anything you can't say, well, it's unsayable
All right now that we got that out of the way
we need some particulars
but where did I put them, where are my particulars?
"Here they are, sir."   Oh, thanks.   Today's mail:
3 books of poems, 1 cigar catalogue
the poems look great, so does the catalogue
"But aren't you trying to quit?"
Mel Tormé died, Charismatic didn't make it today
the fifth of June nineteen-ninety-nine
And in a restaurant called The Europa Ninety-three
warlords consult on a respite from murder and mayhem

*

(i.m. Hannes Hollo, 1959-1999)

Fought the hungry ghosts here on Earth
"What is man?" asked the King
Alcuin's reply: "A guest of space."   And time yes time:
The past lies before us, the future comes up from behind
Walking on Primrose Hill or Isle of Wight beaches
Iowa City streets scrambling up snow-covered deer track
To Doc Holliday's grave in Glenwood Springs
His helmet now shall make a hive for bees
He fought the hungry ghosts here on Earth
Strong & resourceful on his best days,
Patient kind and *presente*
Returning those with him to here & now
But just as we settle in with our Pepsi and popcorn
THE END rolls up   too soon   always too soon

*

and of course it won't do, it won't do at all
Herzen again: "Suffering inescapable,
infallible knowledge
neither attainable nor needed"
sound of swans' wings
over the quarry ponds at Grez
look up! the departed sail on
to some picture-book Norway
and Mr. P old ga-ga cantor
among the ruins of Europe
writes to his missus "where are they?
where are they?"   old "genius" snows falling
on his head in his head
(no, it won't do, it won't do at all)

*

Private they are, the sums of grief, "impossibly private"
"There probably is some intelligence at work here"
"Yes, but I don't want to know what it is"
Elizabethans considered a nosebleed a symptom of love
But if'n the wind don't blow through it   it don't make it
& what if the 'personal' prove as tiresome as the 'public'?
Mawkish messages to the dear departed? No
That is not given to you to do
Nor can you really get behind idealized forebears
Getting wiped out while attacking some barn
"Did you say *barn?*"   In the glorious South or any other
Cardinal direction   & now this old Cardinal
(Universal Life Church) hums
Cani capilli mei compedes   "Gray hairs are my chains"

*

Against meaning, lunatic, real,
Possible in appearance, you work a line,
Be like a larger logic to defy
The dumbly trembling unities
(quotation fringe is blue)
Your self helps us from prose & down
Into an orange: "Hail my effort, you people"
"Stand and deliver!"
But stubborn world is time & airy dung
Insists on legible distance, inhabited heaps
"As Lacan points out"
Never mind what Never mind Never mind
Sing the old huddles (persons bowed down
With age or heavy wraps

*

& should I buy this *Scientific American*
to see how the quest for immortality is going?
got the one on space exploration
. . . such incredible hardships ahead . . .
calling twenty-nine ninety-nine in this old English
but we are just learning to walk
and time is a voice goes a-roaming
"just a chickadee in the rain"
Green House almost ready now
oh they too have their troubles
the beloved intuitive abstract expressive painter
the ever-distracted monkish poet
musing upon the Malevich square on Hitler's upper lip
and the fact that "questo" does not mean "quest"

*

the human being talks it talks
and talks and talks   even to
itself   so "hating speech" what was
that about? no speak no talk no read no write
now *that* sounds like the dead except
some of them do read them-
      selves into our ears
day and night
      when The Slinger passed on
      it left me restless
      the way one was restless
      after a teenage rendezvous
"driving somewhere, fast
with the windows rolled down"

*

I'll write a poem about nothing
absolutely nothing
not about myself
or youth or love or any person
I'll write it riding along
half asleep in the sun
and then I'll send it to a friend
signed, William of Aquitaine
nine hundred years ago
and ever since we've raged
in shirts red black and blue
we've raged still do
in our dream rooms asking the air
mad questions about nothing

*

Equipped with human heart's dizzy gyroscope
In the yellow submarine we lived oh my darlings
Is it now all just imaging?
No more *imagining*   in The Momentous Events
In Small Rooms Hotel   the brain is?
"Don't remember the time I was born
Don't want to remember the time I die"
Old troll stands in secret memory garden
Gazes at mirror globe's beloved faces
Through time they move as "guests of space"
Yes that we are he thinks remembers Alcuin's answer
When Pippin son of Carolus asked him "what is man"
& Cousin Louis: "You will always do wrong
You must try to get used to that, my son"

*

My first computer:
Poor old workhorse machine
Just an advanced version of the clay tablet
Archaic box, you still work
Humming that hum I found so irritating
22 years ago
        (used to say "this thing's
        no smarter than an amoeba")
Waiting for me to write
A word and then another
And another
But I shouldn't have said what I said just then
Because only a few days later
It went from hum to loud groan   And died

*

There's words, and there's hair
And hair and hair . . . Would you know
Evocative if you saw it?
Or have you not had the Enigma
Reversal Experience?
"What's that? What's that?"
They cringe and snarl
It has to do with the minutely sensational
Say I, with what's little enough but enough
As when you turn the radio on
And it is the right music
Even when It introduces sadness
And one understands little
Of what's going on

                        *

and thus we woo our wit with gentle memoranda
birthday thoughts about mother long gone
& her madcap cocaine-addled sister
Aunt Karin I never knew, her son cousin Peter
ever wistful but such a smile   now gone too
dusk road games   dust road fumes
REALITY is WET today
"How big is the mind?
How could we avoid dissolving
in our own private oceans?"
asks Randolph Healy dear Irish poet
beat, beat   "It's a strange, strange world we live in,
Captain Jack"   and who was that and why
(look up at the sky, bro, look up at the sky)

                        *

Anselm Hollo

You
    are not the Countess of Tripoli
And I
    am not dead yet
                unlike Jaufre Rudel
So now I can tell you about
The most interesting metrics of The Horse
To wit, the *rack*, the *fox trot*, the *amble*
Four-beat gaits with each beat
Evenly spaced gliding and smooth
In perfect cadence and rapid succession
The legs on either side move together
The hind leg striking the ground
Slightly before the foreleg!
                Vraiment,
Poetry can be so many more things
Than what people mostly believe it is.

And there were years when nobody died.

NOTES ON CONTRIBUTORS

WILL ALEXANDER has a new book of poems, *Exobiology as Goddess*, forthcoming from Manifest Press.

RAE ARMANTROUT is currently writer-in-residence at the California College of Arts and Crafts. Her most recent book is *The Pretext* (Green Integer). In summer of 2001, Wesleyan will publish *Veil: New and Selected Poems*.

JOHN ASHBERY's most recent collection of poems is *Your Name Here* (Farrar, Straus & Giroux). He teaches at Bard College.

MARTINE BELLEN is the author of *Places People Dare Not Enter* (Potes & Poets Press) and *Tales of Murasaki* (Sun & Moon Press). Her new collection, *The Vulnerability of Order*, will be published this spring by Copper Canyon Press.

CHARLES BERNSTEIN's "Reading Red" was written in response to "New Mexico-New York," a series of twenty-five paintings by Richard Tuttle, first shown at the Sperone Westwater Gallery in 1998. The collaboration was published in Germany by Walther König (Cologne) in a book designed by Tuttle. Bernstein's most recent books are *Republics of Reality: 1975–1995* (Sun & Moon Press) and *My Way: Speeches and Poems* (University of Chicago Press).

MEI-MEI BERSSENBRUGGE's recent books are *Endocrinology* and *Four Year Old Girl*, both from Kelsey Street Press. *Nest* is forthcoming.

LAYNIE BROWNE is co-curator of the Subtext Reading Series in Seattle. Her recent books include *Rebecca Letters* (Kelsey Street Press), *The Agency of Wind* (Avec), *Clepsydra* (Instress) and *Gravity's Mirror* (Primitive Editions).

NORMA COLE's latest poetry publications are *The Vulgar Tongue, Desire & Its Double* and *Spinoza in Her Youth*. *Crosscut Universe: Writing on Writing from France*, edited and translated by the author will appear in the fall of 2000 from Burning Deck.

PETER COLE's newest book of poems is *Hymns & Qualms*. His translations from the medieval Hebrew, *Selected Poems of Ibn Gabirol*, are forthcoming from Princeton University Press.

Among CLARK COOLIDGE's most recent books are *Bomb* (with Keith Waldrop; Granary Books), *On the Nameways, Vol. One* (The Figures) and *Now It's Jazz: Writings on Kerouac and the Sounds* (Living Batch Press).

BRENDA COULTAS's work has appeared in *Epoch* and in an anthology of new American poets.

ROBERT CREELEY has two CDs forthcoming: "Have We Told You All You Thought to Know?" with Steve Swallow, Chris Massey, David Torn and David CasT in a live concert performance (Cuneiform Records) and "Robert Creeley," a reading of recent uncollected poems (Jagjaguwar Records). The Before Columbus Foundation gave him an American Book Award 2000 this June for "Lifetime Achievement."

RACHEL BLAU DuPLESSIS's collection, *Drafts 1–38: Toll*, will be published by Wesleyan University Press in 2001. She is working on essays on gender and poetics, and on the next fold of *Drafts*.

MICHAEL EASTMAN's work has appeared on the cover of *Time* as well as in *Life*, *American Photographer* and *View Camera* and can be found in the collections of the International Center for Photography, the Metropolitan Museum of Art, the Chicago Art Institute and the Los Angeles County Museum of Art. He lives in St. Louis.

ELAINE EQUI is the author of many books, including *Surface Tension, Decoy* and *Voice-Over* (all published by Coffee House Press). She teaches at City College and the New School University in New York.

THALIA FIELD's first collection, *Point and Line*, was published by New Directions. "Land at Church City" is from *Story Material*.

The author of several books of poetry and poems in translation, FORREST GANDER's most recent titles include *Science & Steepleflower* (New Directions) and *No Shelter: The Selected Poems of Pura López Colomé*, forthcoming from Graywolf Press.

PETER GIZZI's most recent books are *Add This to the House* (Equipage) and *Artificial Heart* (Burning Deck Books).

RENEE GLADMAN is the author of *Arlem* (Idiom Press) and *Not Right Now* (Second Story Books). *Juice*, a collection of prose, is forthcoming from Kelsey Street Press later this year. "The Interrogation" is Part 1 of a three-part series.

JORIE GRAHAM is the author of seven volumes of poetry, most recently *Swarm* (Ecco/HarperCollins). The poems in this issue are from a new collection, *All Things*, due out next year. She currently teaches at Harvard.

BARBARA GUEST's recent books include *If So, Tell Me* (Reality Street Editions), *Rocks on a Platter: Notes on Literature* (Wesleyan University Press), *The Confetti Trees* (Sun & Moon Press) and *Symbiosis* (with artist Laurie Reid; Kelsey Street Editions). In 1999 she was awarded the Robert Frost Medal.

CAMILLE GUTHRIE's first book of poetry, *The Master Thief*, will be published this fall by Subpress. She teaches at Friends Seminary in New York.

LYN HEJINIAN's most recent works are *Happily* (Post-Apollo Press) and *The Beginner* (Spectacular Books). A collection of essays entitled *The Language of Inquiry* is due shortly from the University of California Press. She is co-director, with Travis Ortiz, of Atelos, a literary project commissioning and publishing cross-genre work by poets.

Since 1989, ANSELM HOLLO has been teaching at the Jack Kerouac School of Poetics, the Writing and Poetics Department of Naropa University in Boulder, Colorado. A book of prose writings, *Caws and Causeries: Around Poetry and Poets*, has just been published by La Alameda/University of New Mexico Press, which will also bring out his new book of poems, *Rue Wilson Monday*, this year.

PAUL HOOVER's seven books of poetry include *Totem and Shadow: New & Selected Poems, Viridian* and *The Novel: A Poem*. He is editor of *Postmodern American Poetry* (W. W. Norton) and the literary magazine *New American Writing*.

FANNY HOWE's most recent volume of poems was *Selected Poems* (University of California Press). A novel, *Indivisible*, will be published by Semiotexte/MIT Press later this year.

SUSAN HOWE's most recent book of poems is *Pierce-Arrow*, published by New Directions. She is currently at work on a new manuscript.

CATHERINE IMBRIGLIO's poetry and criticism have appeared in *New American Writing, American Letters & Commentary, Caliban, Contemporary Literature* and *Epoch*.

VINCENT KATZ is the author of, among other works, *Understand Objects*, a book of poems, *Life Is Paradise: The Portraits of Francesco Clemente* and *Charm*, translations from Latin of the Roman love poet Sextus Propertius.

ROBERT KELLY's most recent books are *The Garden of Distances* (with Brigitte Mahlknecht), *Runes* and *The Time of Voice*. The poem in this issue marks the beginning of a long poem, *Opening the Seals*, and is indebted to Patrick C. Ryan's reconstructions of the monosyllables of what he calls Proto-Language—human speech a hundred thousand years before the present.

MYUNG MI KIM's books of poetry are *Under Flag* (Kelsey Street Press), *The Bounty* (Chax) and *DURA* (Sun & Moon Press). "Seige Document" is from her new book, *Commons*.

ANN LAUTERBACH's *If in Time: Selected Poems 1975–2000* will be published by Penguin in April 2001. She teaches at Bard College, where she also directs Poetry in the Milton Avery Graduate School of the Arts.

TAN LIN is the author of two books of poems, *Lotion Bullwhip Giraffe* (Sun & Moon Press) and *Box* (forthcoming from Atelos). He has taught English, creative writing and art history at the University of Virginia, Cal Arts and, currently, New Jersey City University. "Ambient Stylistics" is from a longer collage novel/poem.

JACKSON MAC LOW's book *20 Forties* was published by Zasterle (Canary Islands). Earlier this year, a large concert of his works was performed in Dettenhausen, Germany, and he read at the Bjørnson Festival in Norway. He won the 1999 Tanning Prize from the Academy of American Poets.

NATHANIEL MACKEY's newest book of poetry is *Whatsaid Serif* (City Lights Books). Forthcoming are *Atet A.D.* (volume three of his ongoing fiction *From a Broken Bottle Traces of Perfume Still Emanate*), due out in 2001 from City Lights, and *Four for Glenn,* a chapbook of poems due to appear from Arcturus Editions. *Callaloo* recently published a special issue focusing on his work.

MARK McMORRIS is the author of *The Black Reeds* (University of Georgia Press) and *Moth-Wings* (Burning Deck). He teaches at Georgetown University.

MALINDA MARKHAM teaches at Daito Bunka University in Tokyo. Earlier work of hers appeared in *Conjunctions:33.*

CAROL MOLDAW's most recent book is *Chalkmarks on Stone* (La Alameda Press). A bilingual edition of her poems *Pencereden/Through the Window* was published in 1998 in Istanbul. She lives and teaches in Pojoaque, New Mexico.

HONOR MOORE's new collection, *Darling,* will be published next year by Grove/ Atlantic. Her other books include *The White Blackbird,* a life of her grandmother, the painter Margaret Sargent, and a collection of poems, *Memoir* (Chicory Blue Press).

LAURA MORIARTY's recent books are *Nude Memoir* (Krupskaya), *The Case* (O Books), *L'Archiviste* (Zasterle Press), *Symmetry* (Avec Books), *Spicer's City* (Poetry New York) and the short novel *Cunning* (Spuyten Duyvil). Also, a reprint of *Duse* is just out from Paradigm Press. She is assistant director of Small Press Distribution in Berkeley, California.

ANDREW MOSSIN's *Drafts for Shelley* will be published later this year by Beautiful Swimmer Press. "The Forest" is the concluding section of *The Epochal Body,* a book-length poem.

MELANIE NEILSON's next collection of poems is forthcoming in 2001. Excerpts from another project, *The Moth Detective,* will begin appearing online in winter 2000. She is Executive Producer of Programming at MaMaMedia, a new media company for children.

CHARLES NORTH is the author, most recently, of *New and Selected Poems* (Sun & Moon Press) and *No Other Way: Selected Prose* (Hanging Loose). His *The Nearness of the Way You Look Tonight* will be published by Adventures in Poetry this fall.

ALICE NOTLEY's latest book is *Mysteries of Small Houses* (Penguin), which won the *Los Angeles Times* Book Award for Poetry and was a finalist for the Pulitzer Prize.

JENA OSMAN's *The Characters* was published by Beacon Press. She co-edits the magazine *Chain* with Juliana Spahr and teaches in the graduate writing program at Temple University in Philadelphia.

MICHAEL PALMER's most recent book of poetry is *The Promises of Glass* (New Directions). A prose work, *The Danish Notebook,* appeared from Avec Books last fall. A book of selected essays and talks, *Form's Mind,* is in preparation.

BIN RAMKE is editor of the Contemporary Poetry Series for the University of Georgia Press and the *Denver Quarterly*. His first book, *The Difference Between Night and Day*, won the Yale Younger Poets Award. His most recent book of poems is *Wake* (University of Iowa Press).

DONALD REVELL is the author of six collections of poetry, most recently *There Are Three* and *Beautiful Shirt*, both from Wesleyan. He is a professor of English at the University of Utah.

TESSA RUMSEY is the author of *Assembling the Shepherd* (University of Georgia Press).

JEROME SALA's latest book is *Raw Deal: New and Selected Poems* (Jensen/Daniels).

PETER SACKS's newest collection is *O Wheel* (University of Georgia Press).

LESLIE SCALAPINO's recent books include *New Time* and *The Public World/Syntactically Impermanence* (both Wesleyan University Press) and *E-hu* (Atelos Press).

ANDREW SCHELLING teaches Sanskrit, poetry and wilderness writing at Naropa University. His recent books include *The Cane Groves of Narmada River: Erotic Poems from Old India* (City Lights Press) and *The Road to Ocosingo* (Smokeproof Press). Forthcoming from Talisman House is *Tea Shack Interiors: New & Selected Poetry*.

LEONARD SCHWARTZ's latest books are *Words Before the Articulate: New and Selected Poems* (Talisman House) and *A Flicker at the Edge of Things: Essays on Poetics* (Spuyten Duyvil).

DAVID SHAPIRO's books include *Lateness, House (Blown Apart), To An Idea* and *After A Lost Original*, as well books on John Ashbery, Jim Dine, Jasper Johns and Mondrian.

BRENDA SHAUGHNESSEY's first book of poetry, *Interior with Sudden Joy*, was published in 1999 by Farrar, Straus & Giroux. She is currently a Bunting Fellow at the Radcliffe Institute in Boston.

REGINALD SHEPHERD's third book, *Wrong*, was published by the University of Pittsburgh Press, which also published his previous two books, *Some Are Drowning* (1993 AWP Award) and *Angel, Interrupted*. The poems in this issue are from the manuscript of his work-in-progress, *Otherhood*. He teaches at Cornell University.

The title poem of RON SILLIMAN's most recent book, *(R)*, appeared in *Conjunctions:21*. "Fubar Clus" is from VOG, a section of his "longpoem," *The Alphabet*. A recent recipient of a Pew Fellowship in the Arts, Silliman lives in Pennsylvania.

The *Fly-Truffler*, GUSTAF SOBIN's latest novel, was published by W. W. Norton. His book of essays, *Luminous Debris (Reflecting on Vestige in Provence and Languedoc)*, also appeared this year from the University of California Press. He lives in Provence.

JULIANA SPAHR is the author of *Response* (Sun & Moon Press), *Everybody's Autonomy* (forthcoming from University of Alabama Press) and the tentatively titled *Fuck You—Aloha—I Love You* (forthcoming from Wesleyan University Press). She lives in Honolulu.

COLE SWENSEN is a poet who also translates contemporary French poetry, prose and art criticism. Her most recent books are *Noon* (Sun & Moon Press) and *Try* (Iowa University Press).

ARTHUR SZE's latest book, *The Redshifting Web*, was published by Copper Canyon Press. He is the recipient of a Lila Wallace-Reader's Digest Writer's Award. A new collection, *The Silk Dragon: Translations of Chinese Poetry*, is forthcoming from Copper Canyon next year.

JOHN TAGGART's most recent book is *When the Saints* (Talisman).

ANNE TARDOS is the author of *Cat Licked the Garlic* (Tsunami), *Mayg-shem Fish* (Potes & Poets), *Uxudo* (Tuumba Press/O Books) and *Among Men* (forthcoming).

NATHANIEL TARN has three forthcoming books: *The Architextures*, from Chax Press; *Three Letters from the City: The St. Petersburg Poems 1968–98*, from Weaselsleeves Press, Santa Fe, and Borey Art Center, St. Petersburg; and a large *Selected Poems: 1950–2000*, from Wesleyan University Press.

JAMES TATE is the author of numerous books of poetry, including *Shroud of the Gnome* and *Worshipful Company of Fletchers*, both published by Ecco Press, and *Selected Poems* (Wesleyan University Press), which won the Pulitzer Prize and the William Carlos Williams Award. Tate's newest book of poems, *Memoir of the Hawk*, will be published by Ecco Press in 2001.

ROBERTO TEJADA has written on contemporary art and photography for *Aperture, Art Nexus, Camerawork, Luna córnea* and *Third Text*. He is the author of the collection *Gift + Verdict* (Leroy).

ANNE WALDMAN has written many books of poetry, including, most recently, *Marriage: A Sentence*, a prose journal from Penguin Poets. She is also the author of *Iovis, Books I* and *II* and *Vow to Poetry*, a collection of talks and interviews forthcoming from Coffee House Press. *Devil's Workin Overtime*, a CD, is also in progress. She is a Distinguished Professor of Poetry at Naropa University.

KEITH WALDROP's newest books are *The Silhouette of the Bridge* (Avec), *Analogies of Escape* (Burning Deck) and *Haunt* (Instance).

ROSMARIE WALDROP lives in Providence, Rhode Island, where she edits Burning Deck books with Keith Waldrop. Her most recent books of poems are *Reluctant Gravities* (New Directions), *Split Infinities* (Singing Horse Press) and *Another Language: Selected Poems* (Talisman House). A translation of Edmond Jabès's *Desire for a Beginning/Dread of One Single End* is forthcoming from Granary Press.

MARJORIE WELISH's publications include *The Annotated "Here" and Selected Poems* (Coffee House Press); *Else, In Substance* (Paradigm Press); and *Begetting Textile* (Equipage). She recently published *Signifying Art: Essays on Art after 1960* (Cambridge University Press).

471

SUSAN WHEELER is the author of three collections of poetry: *Bag 'o' Diamonds* (University of Georgia Press), *Smokes* (Four Way Books) and *Source Codes* (SALT).

ELIZABETH WILLIS is the author of *The Human Abstract* (Penguin). She teaches at Mills College.

C. D. WRIGHT's most recent book is *Deepstep Come Shining* (Copper Canyon Press). She is currently collaborating on a book project with photographer Deborah Luster titled *One Big Self: Prisoners of Louisiana*.

JOHN YAU's forthcoming books include *My Heart Is That Eternal Rose Tattoo* (Black Sparrow Press) and *Borrowed Love Poems* (Penguin). He was recently appointed Artist in Residence at the Mount Royal Graduate School of Art at the Maryland Institute, College of Art. During the past summer, he taught at Bard and the Provincetown Fine Arts Work Center.

KEVIN YOUNG's first book, *Most Way Home*, won the National Poetry Series Award. His second collection, *To Repel Ghosts*, was named a finalist for the 2000 James Laughlin Award and will appear in spring 2001 from Zoland Books. He recently edited *Giant Steps: The New Generation of African American Writers*, an anthology of fiction, poetry and nonfiction. He teaches poetry and film at University of Georgia.

Poetry Society of America
Putting poetry at the crossroads of American life . . .

Become a member and receive
- ➤ our biannual Calendar
- ➤ free or discounted admission to readings, seminars and competitions
- ➤ a one-year subscription to *Crossroads: The Journal of the Poetry Society of America*
- ➤ a 10% discount on purchases through the Grolier Poetry Book Shop

Visit us on the web at www.poetrysociety.org
Or call 212-254-9628 for more information

A Sampling of Our Spring 2001 Season

- The 1st Annual First Books Debut Reading
- A Tribute to Gertrude Stein
- A Seminar on Ezra Pound's *The Cantos*
- Poetry & Criticism: "On Beauty"
- Poetry @ Marine Park in Brooklyn

The Poetry Society of America
15 Gramercy Park
New York, NY 10003
212-254-9628
www.poetrysociety.org

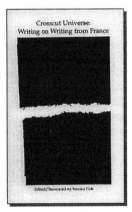

LAME DUCK BOOKS

Internationally known specialists buying and selling important modern books with an emphasis in rare literature and primary works in the history of ideas in all languages. Lame Duck Books invites you to visit our new bookshop in Boston.

We now share a fine old retail establishment with our colleague Peter L. Stern Rare Books, directly behind the Brattle Bookshop at 55 Temple Place, Boston Massachusetts 02111.

Among our current stock of poetry, we offer
first editions of the following authors' first books:
Anna Akhmatova, Paul Auster, Samuel Beckett, Thomas Bernhard, Jorge Luis Borges, Paul Bowles, Andre Breton, Joseph Brodsky, Charles Bukowski, Willa Cather, Robert Creeley, E.E. Cummings, T.S. Eliot, Heinrich Heine, Osip Mandelstam, Vladimir Mayakovsky, Boris Pasternak, Octavio Paz, Arthur Rimbaud, George Trakl (his own copy corrected) and Maria Tsvetaeva

In addition we are offering important presentation copies of books by:
Anna Akhmatova, Rafael Alberti, Miguel Angel Asturias, Samuel Beckett, Jorge Luis Borges, Robert Browning, Constantine Cavafy, Paul Celan, T.S. Eliot, Herman Hesse, Vincente Huidobro, Antonio Machado, Osip Mandelstam, Pablo Neruda, Frank O'Hara, , Francis Ponge, Rainer Maria Rilke, Raymond Roussel, Nellie Sachs, Anne Sexton, Dylan Thomas, Wallace Stevens, Paul Valery, Walt Whitman and William Carlos Williams.

Catalogues forthcoming or available in:
Autographs and Manuscripts
Russian Literature (with a high concentration of poetry in the original language)
The NY School of Poets
Authors First Books
Modern Thought
Rare Books (in conjunction with James Jaffe Rare Books)
Latin American Literature
German Literature

We will exhibit at the following international antiquarian book fairs and conferences: New York, Stuttgart, Ludwigsburg, Fort Lauderdale, San Francisco, New York, Paris, Dusseldorf, London, Santa Monica, Madrid, Berlin, Hamburg and Munich. Dates and details available upon request.

Lame Duck Books   Hours: M-F 9:30-5:30, Sat 9:30-4:00
55 Temple Place,   Tel: 617.542.2376 Fax: 617.542.3263
Boston, MA 02111   Email: lameduckbk@aol.com
Member of the Antiquarian Booksellers Association of America
and the Verband Antiquare Deutscher

New Releases

2000 Hard Press

The Beatitudes — Frank Lima

Acclaimed Latino poet rewrites religion with breathtaking candor and an ear for humanity.

"Frank Lima has long been one of our finest poets. His new collection *The Beatitudes* is one of his strongest."
— Jack Kroll *(Newsweek)*

"Frank O'Hara's true heir, he keeps up that poet's love of extraordinary liberty." — David Shapiro

ISBN 1-889097-44-6, paper, 88pp, $12.95

Porno Diva Numero Uno — Stephen Berg

Told partly through imaginary conversations with Marcel Duchamp, *Porno Diva* is a semi-autobiographical prose poem exploring the relationship of art to existence.

"This book represents the essence of what a conscientious and writerly imagination must do. To have it in print at last is a blessing for us all." — Hayden Carruth

ISBN 1-889097-39-X, 88pp, paper, $12.95

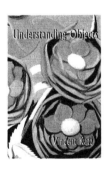

Understanding Objects — Vincent Katz

New Poetry from the New York School's younger generation.

"Vincent Katz's poems have a terrific human stride to them – elegant, assured, sensual, intelligent, erudite, hip."
— Anne Waldman

"In the curious timelessness of time, this writing makes a golden space of thought and echo . . . "
— Robert Creeley

ISBN 1-889097-36-5, 144pp, paper, $12.95

To the trade through Consortium Booksellers and Distribution, Inc.
HARD PRESS, INC.
P.O. Box 184 West Stockbridge, MA 01266
413 232 4690
www.hardpress.com

SHINY

Magazine

Number 11

Contributors

Lydia Davis	Ellen Birkenblit
Steve McCaffery	Bernadette Mayer
Alan Bernheimer	Douglas Rothschild
Robert Fitterman	Cole Swensen
Clark Coolidge	Keith Waldrop
Elaine Equi	Reed Bye
Ron Silliman	Ed Friedman
Michael Lally	Elizabeth Robinson
John Godfrey	Richard Wilmarth
Bill Berkson	Fran Carlen
Mei-mei Berssenbrugge	Eileen Myles
Ron Padgett	Jim Cohn
Juliana Spahr	Chris Edgar
Elio Schneeman	Michael Gottlieb
Richard Baker	Michael Gizzi
Jerome Sala	Dodie Bellamy
Leslie Scalapino	Stephen Rodefer
Kit Robinson	
Anne Waldman	**Editor**
Stacy Doris	Michael Friedman
Andrew Schelling	
Rosmarie Waldrop	**Art Editor**
Merrill Gilfillan	Duncan Hannah
Craig Watson	
Norma Cole	**Contributing Editors**
Tom Clark	Larry Fagin
Elizabeth Fodaski	Michael Gizzi
Patrick Pritchett	Eileen Myles
Kevin Killian	Ron Padgett
& Tony Leuzzi	Cole Swensen
Jordan Davis	Geoffrey Young
Mark DuCharme	
Geoffrey Young	250 Pages
Miles Champion	Available Fall 2000

SHINY 1 (1986) to SHINY 7/8 (1992) published in New York City.

Order SHINY 11 from:

**SHINY
PO Box 13125
Denver, CO 80201**

Send check or money order payable to Shiny International in US currency for $15.00 plus $2.50 postage & handling.

About **SHINY**:

An important venue for contemporary fiction, poetry, and art.

– I.D.

Highly recommended.

– Library Journal

Not to play favorites ... but isn't Shiny issue No. 7/8 good?

– Poetry Project Newsletter

Garish fashions meet gaudy poetics.

– Vanity Fair

Pynchon and *Mason & Dixon*

Edited by BROOKE HORVATH and IRVING MALIN

For Thomas Pynchon, history has been a conspiracy of warring factions whose business is trade and death and whose most ominously magic-haunted weapons include science and technology. Throughout history, those in power have conjured nightmares while simultaneously denying what everywhere percolates behind and beyond them. Asking who or what makes history, how and towards what ends, *Mason & Dixon* is the novel Pynchon's readers have been waiting for since *Gravity's Rainbow* shattered the literary calm almost a quarter-century ago.

This volume gathers eleven essays by some of today's most prominent critics. While orienting readers new to Pynchon, the essays also prepare the way for further discussion, locating *Mason & Dixon* within the context of Pynchon's earlier work and of contemporary American fiction to delineate what Brian McHale terms the "poetics of Pynchon-space." For McHale, Pynchon's America is always a "subjunctive space of wish and desire": the novel that Irving Malin, closely reading the intricate wordplay of the opening paragraph, deems uncertain "counterhistory."

For Arthur Saltzman, Donald J. Greiner, and David Seed, the novel's import resides in the line Charles Mason and Jeremiah Dixon charted through the American wilderness—a symbol, says Saltzman, of the Enlightenment's belief in a divinely sanctioned universe, which Pynchon reveals to be a "clockwork universe" of infinite peril.

Victor Strandberg takes exception to Pynchon's subversive reading of western history, attributing it to his "hippie" rebellion "against tradition, convention, and all forms of social hierarchy." Joseph Dewey finds the novel looking East to reveal not only traces of a Beat-countercultural inheritance but a spiritual alternative to the secular nightmare the novel otherwise depicts. Bernard Duyfhuizen argues that narrative instability serves here to question the authority and reliability of those who give history its meaning and shape.

David Foreman examines those historical documents Pynchon may have used in researching his story. Jeff Baker likewise examines the factual accuracy of *Mason & Dixon*. This foray into *Mason & Dixon* concludes with Clifford S. Mead's bibliography of all material published to date about the novel.

Hardcover, 6 x 9 inches, bibliography, notes, index, 232 pages
ISBN 0-87413-720-9, Price $39.50 (University of Delaware Press)

ORDER FROM ASSOCIATED UNIVERSITY PRESSES,
440 Forsgate Drive, Cranbury, NJ 08512, PH 609-655-4770 FAX 609-655-8366
E-mail *AUP440@aol.com* on the web: www.aupresses.com

CAROLYN KIZER
Cool, Calm & Collected

Carolyn Kizer is the indisputable *grande dame* of American poetry. At long last, her collected poems.

"Carolyn Kizer is a national treasure."
– *San Francisco Chronicle*

$30 CLOTH

HÔ XUÂN HUONG
Spring Essence
TRANSLATED BY JOHN BALABAN

Hô Xuân Huong was an 18th-century Vietnamese concubine who utilized double entendre to write risqué poems and attack male authority. Bilingual.

"Sometimes books really *do* change the world." – *Utne Reader*

$15 PAPER

JIM HARRISON
The Shape of the Journey

Selected as a "Top Ten Book of the Year" by *Booklist*. Now in paperback.

"This is poetry worth loving, hating, and fighting over."
– *New York Times Book Review*

$28 CLOTH

MARVIN BELL
Nightworks: Poems 1962–2000

Marvin Bell is one of poetry's true innovators. *Nightworks* collects poems from twelve previous books.

"Bell has redefined poetry as it is being practiced today." – *The Georgia Review*

$28 CLOTH

COPPER CANYON PRESS

360 / 385-4925 TEL
360 / 385-4985 FAX
Post Office Box 271
Port Townsend, WA 98368
www.coppercanyonpress.org
877 / 501-1393 TOLL FREE ORDERS

Emmanuel Hocquard, *A Test of Solitude: Sonnets*
[Série d'Ecriture, #12; trans. Rosmarie Waldrop]
"Unconventional sonnets that arrive at their stipulated line-count by an ingenious variety of means. They record with deceptive simplicity daily actions and experiences. At the same time, an inquiry is being conducted, a test of solitude that is also a test of poetry."—Steve Evans, *Notes to Poetry.* Poems, 72 pp., offset, smyth-sewn, ISBN 1-886224-33-1, original paperback $10

Gale Nelson, *ceteris paribus*
Ceteris paribus ("assuming all other things are held constant") is a phrase used by economists to explain unintended results. Were *ceteris paribus* possible, the economy might be predictable. Nelson's language misbehaves much like the economy. Each time order seems just around the corner, variances seep in—and anything becomes possible. Poems, 128pp., offset, smyth-sewn, ISBN 1-886224-37-4, original paperback $12.50

Jane Unrue, *The House*
In restless, suspended sentences, a woman wanders from room to room, or ventures outside, and throughout the ensuing procession of locations, ruminations, dreams, is transported into the past, or to a love affair, or into the future, or to an ending, perhaps her own. A first book. Novella, 54pp., offset, smyth-sew,n ISBN 1-886224-35-8, original paperback, $10

Ernst Jandl, *reft and light:*
Selected Poems with Multiple Versions by American Poets
[Dichten=, #4; trans. C. Bernstein, L. A. Brown, T. Darragh, R. Blau Duplessis, K. Elmslie, A. Hollo, P. Hoover, J. Retallack, E. Sikelianos, C. Swensen, C. Watson, M. Welish, J. Yau, and others]
The regretted Ernst Jandl's poems are so engrained in the German language that they are impossible to translate. Here is an experiment: for each German poem not one but several adaptations, so that the original is encircled by multiple English analogues. Poems, 112 pages, offset, smyth-sewn, ISBN 1-886224-34-x, original paperback $10

Crosscut Universe: Writing on Writing from France
[Série d'Ecriture, #13/14; ed./trans. Norma Cole]
Letters, interviews, critical pieces by Anne-Marie Albiach, Joë Bousquet, Danielle Collobert, André du Bouchet, Dominique Fourcade, Liliane Giraudon, Joseph Guglielmi, Emmanuel Hocquard, Jacques Roubaud, Agnès Rouzier, Claude Royet-Journoud and others. Prose, 160 pp., offset, smyth-sewn, ISBN 1-886224-39-0, original paperback $15

Distributed by Small Press Distribution, 1341 Seventh St., Berkeley, CA 94710 1-800/869-7553 orders@spdbooks.org

SYMBIOSIS

Barbara Guest POETRY
Laurie Reid ART

This collaboration, *Symbiosis*, is an expression
of the pleasure and inspiration poet Barbara Guest
and painter Laurie Reid find in each other's work.
Guest was recently awarded the Poetry Society of
America's prestigious Frost Medal. Reid, a West Coast
artist, was featured in the 2000 Whitney Biennial.

$17, ISBN: 0-932716-52-0
Limited ed., $200 ISBN: 0-932716-54-7

Also available by BARBARA GUEST:
Stripped Tales (Anne Dunn, Art)
Musicality (June Felter, Art)

FOUR YEAR OLD GIRL

Mei-mei Berssenbrugge
Richard Tuttle COVER ART

WINNER OF THE WESTERN STATES
BOOK AWARD FOR 1998

"Berssenbrugge has quietly written some of the
most stylistically consistent and elegant poems
of the last decade." *Publishers Weekly*

$12, ISBN: 0-932716-44-X
Limited ed., $200 ISBN: 0-932716-46-6

Also available by MEI-MEI BERSSENBRUGGE:
Endocrinology, (Kiki Smith, Art)
Sphericity (Richard Tuttle, Art)

Other Kelsey St. books:

LAYNIE BROWNE'S *Rebecca Letters*, MYUNG MI
KIM'S *Under Flag*, RENEE GLADMAN'S *Juice*,
LAURA MORIARTY'S *Like Roads* and ROSMARIE
WALDROP'S *Peculiar Motions* (Jennifer Macdonald, Art)

www.kelseyst.com

PRESS

All orders to: Small Press Distribution [510] 524.1668
orders@spdbooks.org

Poets House . . .

. . . A Place for Poetry

A 40,000 volume poetry library, open to the public
Tuesday-Friday, 11am-7pm, Saturday, 11am-4pm

www.poetshouse.org

72 Spring St., 2nd fl, New York, NY 10012
(p) 212.431.7920 (e) info@poetshouse.org

P O E T S
H O U S E